"WE BOTH WILL TAKE THE LADY HOME."

"You will do no such thing," said Consuela, her little chin setting. "Whatever you say, I am not going to be packed off home to worry myself into a decline while you rush out and get yourself slain!"

Jack Vespa's heart warmed at her declaration. "You are very dear, but you must see that Manderville and I can't drag you about all over France, with not the whisper of a chaperone. Your reputation would be forfeit."

"Look about you," she commanded. "Where are the crowds? Where are the leaders of the *ton*? Who will know I am here? Rennes is not very far away, and certainly you will go in some sort of disguise. I shall be your sister—or your affianced, or the Lady Consuela of Ottavio, whom you escort to the duchess . . ."

"My little love, it will not serve. I have no coach, and may have to ride a donkey or go on foot. To be always responsible for your precious self would be a constant worry. You must go home so I can know you'll be safe."

Consuela began to sob. Why did everyone treat her like a silly child?

Books by Patricia Veryan

THE RIDDLE OF THE LOST LOVER

Patricia Veryan

ZEBRA BOOKS
Kensington Publishing Corp.

http://www.zebrabooks.com

ZEBRA BOOKS are published by

Kensington Publishing Corp.
850 Third Avenue
New York, NY 10022

First Zebra Printing: January, 2000
10 9 8 7 6 5 4 3 2 1

Printed in the United States of America

For Florence Feiler,
my agent and my friend

Prologue

St. Jean de Luz, France
Winter, 1813

Outside the building that was now Field Marshal Lord Wellington's headquarters the grey afternoon was made greyer by the unrelenting rain. Inside, Colonel the Honourable Hastings Adair waited uneasily in the passageway and jerked to attention as a door opened. A tall officer came out and nodded to him "Go on in, Hasty. He's alone."

Adair half-whispered, "How's his temper?"

Colonel John Colborne grinned. "He's melting down his barometer!"

Groaning softly, Adair knocked as he opened the door.

The great soldier sat turned away from a littered table, and was rapping on the top of the tubular barometer that accompanied him on his Peninsular campaigns. He muttered something about not knowing why he bothered with "the stupid thing." A keen stare was directed over his shoulder and he added, "Well, sit down, Adair. You're wet. Damnable weather. But we're more comfortable here than we were in Lesaca. Food's better, as well. I suppose London's not bright and sunny, eh?"

"Cold and foggy, my lord. I wonder if I might take off my coat?"

His lordship turned the chair back to his table. "Do your best," he said dryly and, indicating another chair, added, "Throw it over there. I presume you've brought me something?"

"Yes, sir." Adair scrambled out of his coat, slung it aside and pulled several letters from an oilskin-covered bag. "From the Prime Minister; Sir Henry Wellesley; and Lady Wellington."

The Field Marshal stared at the letters as though he could see through the sealed paper then pushed them aside. "Very good. Now let me have your report. As fast as possible, if you please. I've left orders we're not to be interrupted but I can't give you much more than ten minutes. What the devil was Sir Kendrick Vespa about in Dorsetshire?"

Adair's brain raced, trying to reduce a twenty-page written report to a brief verbal account. "You knew that his heir, Lieutenant Sherborne Vespa, fell at the Third Siege of Badajoz, sir?"

"Since his brother John is—was on my staff, I'd be a dunce not to know it, wouldn't I?"

Adair reddened, and sidestepped the rhetorical question. "The thing is that an estate called Alabaster Royal, which would have gone to Sherborne from his maternal grandparents, thus passed to John, who was later severely wounded at the Battle of Vitoria, and sent home." He glimpsed the pit yawning at his feet and added desperately, "As you also know, my lord."

"I do not want to hear what I *know*, Colonel. Let us commence with what I *do not* know! This Alabaster Royal is a Dorsetshire estate that was of interest to Whitehall?"

"Yes, my lord. Sir Kendrick Vespa had approached several gentlemen in Government with a view to locating the proposed subsidiary arsenal on the property."

The dark stare pierced him. The voice was a rasp of anger. "One trusts that is not common knowledge! If word leaks out that we're even thinking of a secondary arsenal the newspapers will scream that invasion is imminent and we expect Woolwich Arsenal will be captured!"

"No, no! It has been handled as Very Secret, I assure you."

"Yet Kendrick Vespa learned of it!"

"He is—was, a diplomatist, sir. At all events, there is an old quarry on the Alabaster Royal estate. No longer in operation, but it is located close to the village and at one time provided employment for—"

"Why and when was it abandoned?"

"It was closed down several decades ago. An underground river flooded some of the lower tunnels from time to time when there were heavy rains."

"Sounds like a stupid location for an arsenal, but they'd have picked a site away from this quarry, I fancy? Certainly, government surveyors would inspect the ground."

"Yes, my lord. However, Sir Kendrick Vespa discovered that thé tunnels are far more extensive than was generally known, and in places descend to several levels. If this became known, he would lose the sale, and he stood to gain a pretty penny from leases and rights-of-way, and such, so—"

"But I understood you to say that the estate had passed to his surviving son, John Vespa?"

"It had, my lord, and that presented a large problem for Sir Kendrick. From what I've gathered, Sherborne, his heir, was easily influenced. When he was killed and John inherited, Sir Kendrick knew he had a different tiger by the tail."

A twinkle came into the eyes of the Field Marshal and the harsh lines of his face softened. He said, "Aye. Jack Vespa's a stubborn rascal. But—good Lord, man! The family is far from purse-pinched. I've visited their Mayfair house, which is very nice, and I believe they've a fine property on the River at Richmond. The loss of one small estate is scarce likely to throw them into debtors' prison! Why all the desperate doings?"

Adair tightened his lips, then said reluctantly, "I'm sure the Field Marshal is aware that Sir Kendrick Vespa was a remarkably handsome man, much admired by the Fair Sex?"

"Aha." The famous bray of laughter rang out. "Set up another mistress, did he? I wonder he could keep count!" He coughed and said severely, "A fellow has to know where to draw the line, Adair. Remember that! Too much dallying with the ladies has been the ruination of many a fine career!"

Well aware that Wellington had a reputation of his own along those lines, Adair managed to keep his face solemn. "Sir Kendrick had several—er, *affaires de coeur,* my lord. One of the more recent being with the young lady who—er, was to have wed Sherborne."

"The devil you say! That must have set the gabble-mongers by the ears!"

"Yes. But it appears, sir, that there was yet another—and secret—entanglement. This with a beautiful lady from India. Sir Kendrick was deeply enamoured. He planned to divorce his wife and marry his latest love. As you may guess, such a union would have been condemned both in her country and in Britain, especially in view of the scandal involving his late son's lady. Sir Kendrick was determined, and apparently did not feel bound by moral or legal considerations. He devised a plan to sidestep both. To succeed he had to raise a great deal of money, but his London property is entailed, and to have sold the Richmond house and liquidated his other assets would have taken time, besides causing more scandal and most probably a family uproar. He was not prepared to wait, so he planned to sell the Alabaster Royal estate to the Government at a much inflated price, no doubt. With the proceeds from the sale he meant to build a palace on a small island he had bought and dwell there with his lady."

For once rendered speechless, Wellington stared at him.

"So," went on Adair hurriedly, "he had the main quarry tunnel sealed off in such a way that it looked as if no work had ever been done beyond that point. It was then that his younger son, John, was sent home, and to Sir Kendrick's considerable annoyance, decided to live down at his Dorsetshire manor."

"A deuced good thing, by God! John Vespa was one of the finest fellows I've had on my staff. I'm only sorry he was so badly mangled at Vitoria. He's not the man to stand still for any hanky-panky." Wellington said shrewdly, "Though I was of the impression he idolized his father—true?"

"Quite true, sir. Sir Kendrick tried very hard to steer John away from Alabaster Royal. Nothing worked. I'm told John's decision may have been prompted by grief. He and his brother had been very close, and the family residences likely held too many memories."

Curious, Wellington asked, "Do you cry friends with Captain John Vespa?"

"Er—not precisely, my lord." His colour a little heightened, Adair said, "We both admire the same lady, in fact."

"Aha. Go on. So John persisted in moving down to this Alabaster Royal, did he?"

"Yes, sir. And just as his father had feared, started to poke around."

"Of course he did! Bright lad, young Johnny! So his sire had to abandon his plans, eh?" Wellington took up the Prime Minister's letter. "He must have been addled to think he could pull it off. Once the surveyors looked over the place it would have been ruled out, at all events."

"They did look it over, my lord. And it was judged perfectly sound and eminently well-suited to—"

"What?" His heavy eyebrows bristling, the Field Marshal slammed the letter down again. "Were they daft, or what?"

"As I understand it, my lord, there was a—er, sizable exchange of funds. . . ."

"Bribery?" Outraged, as always, by any hint of misbehavior in government, Wellington's roar made Adair jump. "Now *confound* the makebait! Well, he'd never have convinced everyone. John must have known the true state of affairs, and the scheme would surely have been discovered."

"It was, my lord. It chanced that Preston Jones lived nearby."

Lord Wellington frowned. "Preston Jones . . . I know the name, but—I have it! The artist. Very clever chap. Lady Wellington is a great admirer. But—wait— Died, did he not? Fell, or something of that sort?"

"Allegedly—yes. Mr. Jones was fascinated by the manor house at Alabaster Royal. It's a quaint old place. Jones took to wandering about the estate, sketching. Sir Kendrick and a couple of neighbours who were partners in his schemes objected to Mr. Jones' trespassing. Violently."

"Are you saying Preston Jones did *not* fall accidentally? You surely don't hold Sir Kendrick Vespa responsible?"

"We know Mr. Jones discovered that the ground on the estate is undermined. If he had also discovered there were plans to build a large arsenal on such land and fill it with weapons and high explosive—"

"Which would be to invite disaster," growled Wellington.

"Just so, my lord. Especially since there is a good-sized village adjacent to the quarry. We believe Mr. Jones hadn't dared voice his suspicions until he was sure. The very day he had his proof he was seen, apparently under the influence of drink, being supported by two strangers. Next morning, he was found at the bottom of the quarry."

"Was he, by God! So Kendrick Vespa didn't draw the line at murder!"

"At several murders, unfortunately, my lord."

"It's past belief that a well-bred gentleman as widely admired as he could have sunk so low! Where was young John? Was he as gulled as everyone else? I cannot think he'd have been party to such treachery."

"He wasn't, sir. There were several attempts on his life, in fact, when he started to investigate. He thought he had identi-

fied the conspirators. He didn't discover until it was too late
that the man at the top was his own father."

"Poor fellow." The Field Marshal shook his head sombrely.
"What a devilish fix to be in! Poor fellow. Still, he did what he
had to do. No one could fault him."

"Your pardon, sir?"

"No need to wrap it in clean linen, Colonel. It has been
spread about that Sir Kendrick Vespa was swept away by an
underground flood when he and his son surprised some ruffians in the quarry. I can see as far through a brick wall as the
next man." Taking up the letter once more, Wellington said,
"We must make very sure the tale dies here, is all."

Colonel Adair paused, then said reluctantly, "I'm afraid—it
er, doesn't, though, my lord."

The stern lips tightened. "Why did I guess you were going
to say that?" Tossing down the letter, Wellington leaned back
in his chair. "Very well. Don't hide your teeth."

"As I piece it together, sir, things came to a head in the
quarry. John went down there to test his suspicions, and his
father offered his aid. The other plotters arrived and John
learned the whole ugly business, and that the mastermind was
his own father. Or—the gentleman he thought was his father."

The dark head jerked up. "He—*thought* . . . ?"

Adair nodded. "Sir Kendrick, it seems, had for four and
twenty years accepted another man's child as his own. He was
never faithful to his wife, as all London knows. Apparently, Lady
Faith Vespa was so wounded when he set up a mistress only a
year after their marriage that she gathered a court of her own."
He shrugged expressively.

"And John Vespa was a child of her—indiscretion?" Grinning
broadly, his lordship drove a hand against the table. "I'll be
damned! Now that I think on it, John's colouring is fair, and
Sherborne was as dark as Sir Kendrick. Come now, Adair. Do
you say the man didn't *know* he'd been cuckolded?"

"Oh, he knew all right, and was enraged. But his pride
wouldn't let him admit it publicly. He's not the first, sir, to
accept a bastard as his own to protect the family name."

"No, by Jove. And he concealed it well, appearing to be the
proud father. The boy gave him plenty of cause for pride, of
course. When did John find out the truth of his parentage?"

"In the tunnel. Sir Kendrick showed his true colours and

told John very explicitly how he had loathed and despised him all these years."

"By heaven but that was a wretched thing to do! The poor lad must have been shattered. Small wonder he retaliated!"

"He was not responsible for Sir Kendrick's death. Another man claimed that privilege after John had been shot down."

Wellington shook his head broodingly. "What a tragedy! Greed, and a woman—a deadly combination. I'm glad my fine aide survived. How is he, Adair?"

"Going along remarkably well, sir. Under the circumstances. And full of determination. They all are."

"Determination about what? Who?"

"His friends. Lieutenants Paige Manderville and Tobias Broderick. They were all sent home after Vitoria, and they're united in trying to help him in his quest."

"Good Lord above!" roared the Field Marshal. *"Will* you have done with all this roundaboutation! *What*—quest?"

"To find his real father, my lord. John had hoped to be married, you see, but cannot approach the lady without a name—or without at least knowing his parentage. He refuses to use the Vespa title or to accept the fortune or the properties. The only thing that keeps him from revealing the whole ugly story is his loyalty to his mother."

"He had *best* not reveal the whole!" Wellington sprang up and began to pace about the room. "We don't need a scandal like that breaking over our heads while we've Bonaparte to deal with! The men in government who took Kendrick Vespa's bribes will be punished. But quietly, mind! And there must be not a *whisper* of our plans for a secondary arsenal!" He halted, head bowed and brows fixed in a frown. "By Jupiter, but I'd like to give young Vespa a hand. Does anyone know who was Lady Faith's side-door lover?"

"Yes, my lord. It explains to an extent why Sir Kendrick harboured such a hatred for John. Lady Faith gave her husband back his own—and more. She chose his most bitter enemy for her lover. And John grew up to resemble the man. Most people assumed that the boy took after the Wansdykes, his mother's family. But you may be sure Sir Kendrick was all too aware of the truth, and reminded of it each time he looked at John."

"Well? Well? Never back and fill! Who was the fellow?"

Adair leaned to take up the letter from the Prime Minister. "Perhaps you should read this, sir."

With a snarl of irritation, Wellington broke the seal. His eyes ran rapidly down the page. When he looked up, he was pale. "I cannot *credit* it! Of all the men in the world . . . !"

Adair watched him gravely through a brief silence.

Wellington folded the letter again and stared at it blankly. "I've a real sympathy for John Vespa," he muttered, as if to himself. "He's a fine young fellow and was a splendid officer." He looked up from under his brows and said with grim intensity, "A deuced ugly mess you bring me, Colonel."

Apprehensive, Adair said, "Yes. I apologize, sir."

The great soldier grunted and dealt the barometer a sharp rap.

Adair's apprehensions were justified.

"You shall have to tidy it up," said Field Marshal Lord Wellington.

One

"Disgusting!" Jerking aside the heavy draperies that shielded her drawing-room windows, Mrs. Fortram scowled down into the rainy darkness and said in her elderly and irritable voice, "Here's *another* of 'em rattling up the street to shatter our quiet! Look at 'em, Hubert! Confounded idiots! There ought to be a law against routs and balls and musicales and falderals being carried on in this peaceful and refined neighbourhood!"

"Mmm," said her son, savouring another sip of his port.

For all her apparent frailty, Gertrude Fortram was not easily diverted from a Cause. Choosing to forget the many occasions on which her own parties and balls had disrupted the neighbourhood peace, she went on fiercely, "Cluttering up the streets at all hours of the night! Keeping honest folk from their rest! You'd think people could find better ways to amuse themselves than to put on clothes that belong more to midsummer than a cold wintry night, and drive halfway across Town to answer the summons of Esther Wolff, as if she were one of the almighty *ton* leaders! Which she is not, and so I've told her!"

Receiving only a sympathetic grunt in reply, the old lady continued, "It's not as if we were at the height of the Season. I'd thought London thin of company, in point of fact, but— Heavens! If ever I saw such a crush! Much good those special constables do! Lud, only look at how the carriages are obliged to wait in line! One might suppose Wellington himself was among the guests!"

Mr. Fortram settled his portly self more comfortably in his deep chair, stretched his slippered feet closer to the warm hearth, and turned the page of *The Times*. "In that case I would have accepted the invitation, Mama," he murmured, drowsily content. "I can only be glad that—"

He glanced up, startled, as his words were cut off by a shriek. "That wretched *cat!*" shrilled his mother. "The fur will fly now!"

His curiosity aroused at last, Hubert puffed and huffed, extricated himself from the chair and crossed to the window. "Who? Oh, Gad! The Hersh dragon! I thought she was in Bath."

"As she should be at this time of year. And— Look there! Lucinda Carden, and on Ted Ridgley's arm! Who's next? Ah, that horrid Phineas Bodwin escorting . . . I cannot recognize her, but she looks a trollop, which surprises me not at all."

"Gathering of the gabble-mongers," sneered Hubert. "I wonder whom they mean to flay tonight."

"Sir Kendrick Vespa, of course!"

Shocked, he protested, "Jupiter, ma'am! They can't flay poor Sir Kendrick. Dead, y'know."

"No, I don't know! Nobody knows for sure. And his son's not gone into mourning, I heard."

"What, is Jack Vespa in Town, again? Gad, but that was a fast recover. Last word I had was that he was at death's door."

Mrs. Fortram turned her attention from the window and eyed her son with rare interest. "Well, he's not there now, and I'm glad of it, for I like the boy. What else have you heard? The gabsters who usually know everything are suddenly like so many stuffed owls. Why all the secrecy?"

"Be dashed if I know. Paige Manderville was in White's yesterday, and all he'd say was that Jack and Sir Kendrick surprised some rogues hiding in an old quarry on Jack's Dorsetshire property, and—"

"And that Captain Jack was shot down and his father pushed into some sort of underground flood. Outrageous! Despicable! Dastardly! But that was weeks ago, and despite all the flurry at Bow Street and Whitehall, with Runners and Special Constables and dragoons galloping about hither and yon, what have they accomplished? Have the culprits been arrested? No! What mischief were they about down in that old quarry? No one knows—or will admit to knowing! Why is Bow Street mum, and the newspapers scarce mention the business? That's what *I'd* like to know!"

"As would we all, ma'am. It's a regular mystery, especially when you consider that Sir Kendrick Vespa is—was a distinguished diplomatist."

"True." Mrs. Fortram restored her attention to the window. "The thing is, they haven't found his body yet. Might never find it. Which will leave his surviving son properly in the suds, eh?"

"Mmm." Putting up his quizzing glass, Mr. Fortram admired the points of a fine chestnut team now pulling up before the great house across the street, and murmured absently, "I wonder if his poor mama knows of her bereavement."

"Poor mama, indeed! All Faith Vespa ever did was whine about Sir Kendrick's neglect of her. I doubt she'll grieve him, though she's missing a splendid opportunity to moan and wail and weep crocodile tears all over Town. I don't see how she could know of her widowhood, at all events. The silly widgeon ran off to some relations in South America, didn't she?"

Hubert pursed his lips and returned to his chair. "So they say. I for one cannot blame her. All that scandal about her husband's lightskirts. Terrible embarrassment for the lady."

"Well, running away added grist to the gossip mills, which she'd know had she a particle of sense. Kendrick Vespa was too handsome, and that's always a danger. But had Lady Faith handled him properly . . . instead of which I'm of the opinion her complainings fairly drove the man to infidelity."

Again reaching for *The Times,* Hubert murmured, "Now we don't know that for sure, Mama. And the Vespas, after all, rank among our most ancient and respected Houses."

"The more reason for Sir Kendrick to have guarded his name against scandal! It's downright shocking that a fine old family could be thriving one day, and destroyed the next. That's what comes of— *Look!* Only look! The *Ottavio* woman! I haven't seen her for— Doesn't she live in Dorsetshire? I'll warrant *she* knows what went on down at Alabaster Regis—or whatever it's called."

Joining his parent once more, Hubert put up his quizzing glass. "You're right, by Jove! I remember the little lady. French, ain't she? A duchess or some such thing."

"Italian. She claims to be the duchess of Ottavio, but her husband died just before inheriting the title, and she is no more a duchess than am I! Whatever can have brought her back into Town, I wonder? Well, that bears off the palm! Lord, are you lumping back into your chair again? Come, Hubert!

Up! Up! Rouse your lazy self! No use looking so hardly done
by. The whole town's talking and with the gathering of gabblers
across the way there's not a doubt in the world but that Sir
Kendrick's escapades with the Stokely hussy will be the prime
topic. I don't mean to miss it, and so I warn you! Change your
dress. I'll be ready in half an hour!"

"But—Mama," wailed Hubert. "You said you didn't want to
go out tonight. It's raining! And besides, you declined the invitation."

"Well now I'm accepting! Half an hour, Hubert! Stir your
stumps!"

Mr. Gaylord Wolff had instructed his architect to design a
ballroom in the Grecian style, and the results of that talented
gentleman's efforts were much admired in London Town. Despite the cold air outside and the abundance of marble inside,
the impressive room was crowded and very warm, and when a
quadrille ended many of the guests made their way to the cooler
dining and reception rooms where an elegant supper was
spread on long tables. Laden trays were borne off to adjacent
ante-rooms whose smaller tables, chairs and sofas filled rapidly.
The air hummed with polite chatter, aristocratic faces were vari-
ously sad or titillated, and on every tongue it seemed was the
one name—Vespa.

Seldom had the *ton* enjoyed a more delicious scandal. Sir
Kendrick Vespa had long been known to have a mistress in
keeping, in addition to other ladies believed to have enjoyed
his protection from time to time. What had not been known
was that the much admired gentleman had lately enjoyed a
secret *affaire de coeur* with Mrs. Esmeralda Stokely. The widow
was lovely, but she was young enough to be his daughter, and,
worse, had been on the brink of marrying his eldest son prior
to the young soldier's tragic death in battle.

Mrs. Fortram and Hubert, having made their way to the supper rooms, gathered plates of delicacies and drifted unobtru-
sively from one group to another, their eagerly stretched ears
gathering a choice harvest of gossip.

". . . and not to speak ill of the dead, my dear Lady Vera,
but to think that *lovely* man could have been so *devious!*"

". . . poor Mrs. Omberleigh. She was never good *ton,* of
course, but my heart bleeds for her."

"What did she expect? The Omberleigh was his mistress for ten years at least, and few gentlemen keep a fancy piece for that long. *My* sympathies are with . . ."

". . . *poor* Lady Vespa! She knew about the Omberleigh woman, of course, but to then discover the *others!* My dear! And now . . ."

". . . is it truth that The Stokely was betrothed to his own *son?* If *ever* I heard of so shocking . . ."

". . . and that he was involved with the Widow Stokely even while poor Sherborne was *still alive!* Can you credit . . ."

Having at this point reached an especially fruitful source, Mrs. Fortram drew Hubert to a halt close to one of the sofas set about the fringes of the dining room.

Mrs. Anne Hersh, seated beside her friend Lady Grey, arranged her sharp features into what she supposed to be a look of piety and said with a sigh as deep as it was insincere, "Now Captain John Vespa is the one *I* sympathize with. First his brother, and now his father gone, and his mama flaunting off to the other side of the world!"

Not to be outdone, Lady Grey moaned softly. "How *alone* he must feel, poor boy. And there is no bride in the offing, as I recall."

"If there were, *you* would surely know of it! You always are so well-informed!"

Lady Grey smiled patronizingly. "Thank you, my love. One does not care to *gossip*, you understand. But when one is well acquainted—well, how can one refrain from . . . hearing things?"

"Exactly! So now, *do* tell me, *whatever* do you think of this latest ghastly *on-dit?*"

Her ladyship, who had been in the midlands visiting her mama-in-law, knew of no 'latest ghastly *on-dit*' and tried in vain to hide her chagrin.

Gertrude Fortram was also chagrined, for she could not quite catch the whispered confidence when Mrs. Hersh spread the good word.

Accustomed as she was to London's gossip mills, Lady Grey uttered a shocked squeal and dropped her fan. *"Another* one?"

"And a foreigner, no less! The hints are that she is very beautiful, in an exotic uncivilized sort of way. At least, that's what—" Mrs. Hersh stopped speaking, and turned around.

Mrs. Fortram returned Anne Hersh's haughty stare with an

unrepentant display of brown teeth, then tugged imperatively on Hubert's arm and they resumed their enlightening stroll.

The orchestra was striking up for a country dance and the guests started to drift towards the ballroom.

"What now, ma'am?" asked Hubert, as intrigued by what they had gleaned as was his mother.

"Over there," hissed Mrs. Fortram. "Manderville. If anyone knows who was Kendrick Vespa's 'other one,' that impudent young rascal does. Come on!"

"If he does know, he won't tell you," warned Hubert. "He's one of Jack Vespa's best friends."

"Then we won't ask him, you flat," snarled his doting parent. "Come—*on!*"

"It was the most horrid party I ever attended!" Miss Consuela Carlotta Angelica Jones twitched her cloak tighter about her small and shapely self and snuggled against the squabs of the carriage. "I wonder the musicians even bothered to play; the only reason people came was to gabble and gossip and giggle about the Vespas!" She was a little flushed, her blue eyes reflected her irritation and she pushed back a straying curl impatiently.

Seated opposite her, Paige Manderville reflected that although she could not be judged a beauty, Miss Consuela Jones was very pretty. Her disposition was sunny, her heart warm and her loyalties deep and unwavering. If she was also unconventionally frank, inclined to act on impulse (sometimes disastrously), and had a quick-flaring temper, those were qualities he found charming, so that he envied Jack Vespa, who was in love with her, and to whom she was devoted. He said an amused, "You look like an irritated little pouter pigeon, m'dear. I'll own it's as well Jack was not present this evening, but considering the party was so 'horrid,' you did not want for dance partners. Indeed, had Jack and your gallant Colonel both been present, they'd have had small chance of writing their names on your dance card."

Even in the dim light thrown by the carriage lamps it was clear that those who named Manderville one of London's most handsome bachelors were justified, but Miss Jones viewed his dark good looks without rapture. "If by my 'gallant Colonel' you refer to Hastings Adair," she snapped, "you give me too much credit, Paige!"

"Since Toby and I are both lowly lieutenants and Jack a mere captain, whom else should I—"

"Jack is not *merely* a captain, but was one of Lord Wellington's personal aides, which makes him very special indeed! Furthermore, how could he possibly attend a ball when he is—or is supposed to be—in mourning for his—his father. Horrid, wicked creature that he was!"

The diminutive Francesca, self-styled 'duchess of Ottavio,' who was the third occupant of the luxurious coach, yawned, and demanded, "Well—and well? What have you expect, my meadowlark? Jack was shot, so people they sympathize. But now, he is recovered, and does he go into blacks? He does not! Does he use the title that is now legally his? No! Will he stay in the Vespa mansion in Town? No! Has he once set his feet into his great house at Richmond? No again!"

"You *know* why Jack refuses to use the title and the Vespa properties," said Consuela defensively.

"Oh, *si. I* know. *You* know. Lieutenant Paige and Tobias Broderick, they know. But does the *ton* know?"

Manderville inserted quietly, "Can't very well tell 'em, can he, ma'am? Not without disgracing his mama."

"So what does your *ton?*" demanded the old lady. "It seethe. It revel! It is *contissimo!* Rumour, she spread her feathers and fly like—like the tempest about this old town! I will speak of the silliness that *I* was hearing at this very silly ball. One—that Sir Kendrick Vespa is not killed in that quarry at all, but has run off to some secret paradise with his beautiful Indian lady. Two—that Lady Faith Vespa did not go out to South America to visit her cousins, but that Sir Kendrick strangled her. And, three—she is buried somewhere—"

"In the quarry at Alabaster Royal, no doubt," put in Manderville derisively. "Which is what Jack and Sir Kendrick were occupied with down there when they were attacked. Burying the poor lady."

"Exactly so."

Consuela gave a squeak of rage. "No! Surely, *Nonna,* they did not say such things!"

"I heard much the same sort of slanderous nonsense," drawled Manderville. "Only in even more lurid detail. Is it so much worse than the truth?"

Consuela frowned broodingly at the window. "They don't know the truth. So they make up things!"

"They've learned enough to discover that Sir Kendrick Vespa, the pattern-card of a British diplomatist, was at the least a womanizing rascal. He has betrayed the Code. They won't soon forgive him."

"Me," flared Consuela fiercely, "I shall *never* forgive him! For what he did to my beloved Papa, and to Jack, who loved him, he should have been taken and hanged by the neck till he was thoroughly dead! Dead without question! Nor need you pretend you did not despise him as much as I."

"True," admitted Manderville. "I'd enjoy to have called out the bas—er, to have had the gentleman in the sights of my pistol."

Lady Francesca said, "All of this it tells us nothing in the matters, saving that no one of us has learned anything of what our Captain Jack hopes to discover. I myself have try many careful ways. I did the giggle and gabble with the most spiteful of the *ton* cats, and could learn nothing of the *affaires* of Lady Faith Vespa. That woman with the long nose, Gertrude Fortram, has learn that we are the neighbours to Captain Jack's Dorset lands, so she come and smile and coil around me like a dried-up serpent, as if I am not awareness that she have much despise for me. And why must you laugh so much, Lieutenant Paige? Have I perhaps lie in my tooth?"

"Certainly not," said Manderville unsteadily. "But your expressions, dear ma'am, are so delicious. Do tell us if this—this 'dried up serpent' of a lady was of any help at all."

Mollified, Lady Francesca said that Mrs. Fortram had been of no use save to confide that in her younger days Lady Faith Vespa was believed to have had 'some interesting liaisons.' She sighed. "Which we already have know. But the naming of these 'liaisons' gentlemen I cannot come at."

Manderville chuckled. "Phineas Bodwin managed to imply that he'd been Lady Faith's lover at one time."

"Pah!" said Consuela. "That one—he would say anything to be interesting! Oh, but it is all so discouraging! We try and try, and learn nothing. I had so hoped we might have some news to cheer Jack!"

Lady Francesca squeezed her hand comfortingly. "So had we all, my little one. And we will do this, I know it."

"The problem is," said Manderville, "it's a—um, delicate

matter. Begging your pardon, ladies, but one can't very well go smack up to a likely prospect and say, 'How de do? We've just found out that Jack Vespa is a bastard. Might you be the fellow who really fathered him?' "

Consuela's giggle was drowned by Lady Francesca's squeal and her outraged declaration that Lieutenant Paige's language was 'vulgar in the extreme!' She paused, and added, "But he speaks truth. I have the fearing we must tread on the eggs and it will be difficult."

"But not impossible," said Manderville. "And Jack's not downhearted. Only this morning he told Toby and me that he has every confidence he'll come at the truth. And with all of us to help—how can we fail?"

Consuela pounced forward and to his huge delight and her grandmother's pseudo-indignation, kissed him on the cheek. "You are a dear and good friend, Lieutenant Beau Manderville! Thank you for that! So—what do we do next?"

"All I have to do," he said with a grin, "is think up more ways to win such lovely approval. No, seriously, Jack's likely with his great-uncle this very minute. The old boy should know all about his mama's—er, peccadilloes."

Consuela said, "If he does find out something, Paige, you *will* come to Claridges and tell us the very first thing in the morning, please?"

"If I do, will I get another kiss?"

"You are of an impudence," scolded Lady Francesca without heat. "But—*si*. You will win a kiss. From me, you rogue!"

He laughed. "Then I cannot fail!"

"Of course I knew your mother well. She was my niece, wasn't she? Watched the pretty creature from the moment she left the schoolroom. One of the most sought-after young damsels in all of London Town, she was."

Sir Reginald Wansdyke refilled the two wine glasses and tried not to betray his impatience. He had always been noted more for his brusque and vigorous ways than for tact. His thick hair was grey now, but at five and sixty his complexion was bronzed, his back straight, and his shoulders as broad and unbowed as many a man twenty years his junior. He'd had a difficult day at the Exchange, a tiresome confrontation with his youngest granddaughter and the totally ineligible young rascal she wanted to wed, and a pleasant sojourn at his club had been spoiled by the arrival of Monsieur Imre Monteil. He'd never liked the Swiss, but not because of the man's jet black hair and eyes and 'pasty-white skin,' as Lady Wansdyke described it. In his opinion appearances seldom counted for much. But Monteil was known to have made his fortune in munitions, and his obvious gloating over this drawn-out war with France was repellent, especially in view of the appalling casualties. He himself had lost Sherborne, one of his favourite grand-nephews, to the terrible third siege of Badajoz; and John had been so badly mangled at Vitoria that they might count themselves fortunate he had survived.

The reminder softened Sir Reginald's irritation that the young man had insisted upon awaiting his return instead of postponing his call until tomorrow. He went back to the leather chair in the panelled and pleasantly cluttered room that was his study and looked speculatively across the hearth at his grand-nephew.

John Wansdyke Vespa had inherited neither the impressive height nor the dramatically dark colouring that had so distinguished his father and brother. Indeed, he'd been quite cast into the shade by the handsome Sherborne. Of the brothers, John had been the athlete, and Sherry the dashing Town Beau. No more athletics for John, sad to say. Still, he looked better than when he'd first been brought home after the Battle of Vitoria, and no one could say he was plain. His hair might be an undistinguished light brown, but it had a tendency to curl that Lady Wansdyke said was very attractive. And if the eyes, which she declared to be 'tawny' rather than hazel, lacked the sparkling jet that had made Sherborne's eyes so striking, they were clear and steady and could be warmed charmingly by a lurking smile. His features lacked the delicate carving that blessed most of the Vespas, but the mouth was firm and the chin strong. The scar down his left temple was less noticeable already, and his limp not as obvious. All in all, a fine-looking young fellow, thought Sir Reginald. And he'd certainly distinguished himself on the Peninsula.

Still, it was odd that having called at such an hour he seemed to want to discuss not the recent tragedy that had robbed him of his sire, but the early life of his mother. It was puzzling also that John, who had worshipped Sir Kendrick, had not yet gone into blacks. Very likely, Sir Reginald told himself, it was all too much for the poor lad. Perhaps he was trying to work his way around to speaking of the tragedy. Whatever the case, he was entitled to be handled gently. It was in a compassionate tone, therefore, that he said, "I presume you've notified my niece of your father's—er, death. Have you heard from her since she sailed?"

Jack Vespa had been quite aware of and faintly amused by his great-uncle's intense scrutiny, and could guess what had gone through the mind of this honest and upright gentleman. He knew that there had been no love lost between the Vespa and Wansdyke branches of the family, but he was also aware of Sir Reginald Wansdyke's fierce pride, and he replied cautiously, "I wish I had, sir. There are business affairs to be settled, and other matters on which I have a most urgent need to consult with her."

'So that's it,' thought Sir Reginald. Slightly disappointed, he said, "If it's a matter of your inheritance, I can likely advise you."

"I have a generous inheritance from Grandfather Wansdyke, sir. And Alabaster Royal."

'That dismal hole!' thought Sir Reginald. "True. But in view of—er, everything, I expect you won't want to continue living down there. You've the Richmond property, and the London house is entailed. Certainly the title will come to you, once—er, that is to say, after— In due time."

Vespa nerved himself and took the plunge. "Then you think I've a right to them, sir?"

Sir Reginald gave him a sharp look. "Why the deuce would you not have a right to them? John—I know this quarry business must have been a frightful experience, and I'd not distress you by referring to it, but—are you of the opinion that your father is still alive?"

"I don't know. That's why I asked about my mother. I'm a grown man, sir, and not blind. I'm aware my parents' marriage was not happy."

"Hmm," grunted Sir Reginald, uneasily. "I think it is not for me to comment on such matters. You must talk to your mama, though I'd have thought this was scarce the time to rake over old coals."

"Nor can I do so, since my mother is now in South America."

Lady Faith's flight from the gossip mill was a sore topic with her conservatively minded uncle, and he growled, "Worst thing she could have done! Kendrick had his faults, no denying, but running away don't solve anything." He caught himself up and said testily, "The thing to do, my boy, is to put it all behind you. Your health is much improved already. You can stay peacefully in that lovely house on the river till your mama comes home again, and if you're in need of the 'ready' meanwhile, I'm very sure your father's man of business—Skelton, or some such name as I recall—can oblige you."

"Felton, sir. But—"

"No 'buts,' dear lad. If there's any difficulty along those lines, you just let me know, and we'll come at the root of it."

"Well, there *is* a problem, Uncle. It concerns something Sir Kendrick told me just before—" Vespa paused, one hand clenching. "Before the tunnel—business. It has to do with the early days of their marriage and a friend of my mother's."

"Hmm. I didn't know all Faith's friends, of course. Still don't. Rather a silly lot of females, if you was to ask me."

"This was a gentleman, sir."

"A *gentleman?*" Sir Reginald's smile faded. "Now what the devil could your mother's friends, be they male or female, have to do with your drawing against your inheritance?"

"A great deal, sir. In fact, according to Sir Kendrick, any Vespa inheritance is not—mine."

Sir Reginald's face turned very red. Staring at his grand-nephew he demanded hoarsely, "What a'God's name are you babbling at, boy? Your father was mighty high-in-the-instep, but—"

"Was he, sir? That's what I'm trying to find out, you see. Did you know him?"

"What the *deuce* . . . ? Of *course* I knew him!" Sir Reginald stood and faced the younger man in consternation. "My poor fellow! You're ill! It's that head wound you took at Vitoria, I don't doubt. You shall overnight here. Tomorrow, I'll refresh your memory about your father. You may ask whatever you wish, and—"

Standing also, Vespa said gently, "I have only one question, Uncle Reginald. Who *is* my father?"

. Sir Reginald drew a deep breath and fought his temper. "Now—now, John, I can see you are not yourself. But this is all very . . . improper. If someone has been filling your head with rubbish, I wish you will name the lamebrain."

"Do you know, Uncle, I wish with all my heart that I could

believe it was rubbish. Unhappily, I have no choice but to think he told me the absolute truth."

"Who—who did?" gulped Sir Reginald.

"Sir Kendrick Vespa."

"What? Your—your own *father?"*

Vespa gave a wry shrug. "Evidently not. Sir Kendrick said that years ago, when my mother discovered he had set up a mistress, she took a lover to spite him. And that I'm the—the result of her . . . *affaire."*

His face purpling, Sir Reginald snorted, "If *ever*— If *ever* I heard of such disgraceful twaddle! I can't *credit* it that—that even Kendrick Vespa would—would have *deliberately* said such a wicked thing! Be so good as to tell me, nephew—*when* did he kindly impart all this claptrap?"

"While we were down in the tunnel at the old quarry, sir."

"Indeed. This would have been before you were shot, then."

"Yes, sir. Just before he shot me."

Sir Reginald dropped his glass.

"You may believe I am upset!" Pacing to and fro at the foot of his wife's bed, Sir Reginald flung one arm in the air to emphasize his vexation and declared untruthfully, "I'm sorry if I woke you, m'dear. Your candles were still burning, so I thought—"

"Yes. I was reading." Lady Paula drew her bed-jacket closer about her ample figure and sat higher against the pillows. "John is adept at concealing his feelings, but I sensed he was troubled, so I waited up for you."

Sir Reginald gave an explosive snort. "Troubled, you say? He ain't *troubled,* my lady! What he is—he's *daft!* Ripe for Bedlam! I vow if he weren't family, I'd have called in the Runners and had him taken away under strong restraint!"

"Good gracious! Now, my love, I trust you have considered that John is bound to be distressed at this time, and we should— Oh, *pray* do not stamp up and down, you'll wake the house. Have a glass of wine. It will settle your nerves."

Muttering ferociously, Sir Reginald did not argue with this sensible suggestion, but filled a glass from the decanter that was always left on the sideboard for him. He sat on the dressing-table bench and sipped the port, only to spring up again and say explosively, "When I *think* what a fine fellow he was before he went off to Spain! And now—whatever wits the poor lad has left are so full of maggots—"

"Yes, yes, Reginald, but you're spilling your wine. Sit here on the bed, dear, and try to compose yourself." Her spouse obeying with marked reluctance, she asked gently, "Whatever has John done to so discompose you?"

"Gone stark, raving mad," growled her husband, not mincing words. "Have I not said it? The first looby in the family! *Egad!* I tell you, my lady, if that boy goes about London Town spreading the balderdash he hurled in my face tonight, our name will be—will be so tarnished we're like to never make a recover!"

This declaration alarmed Lady Paula. She said uneasily, "If it is balderdash, dear sir, how shall it tarnish us?"

Sir Reginald ran a hand through his already wildly dishevelled grey locks and groaned. "It's all so damned ridiculous. But with the rumours that are abroad . . ." His thick eyebrows bristled. He snarled, "Confound it! I always *knew* Kendrick Vespa was a potentially dirty dish!"

"Aha," said his patient lady. "So poor Sir Kendrick is at the root of the problem. I wonder why that does not surprise me. Now, my love, I beg you to tell me. From the beginning."

Her life's companion snorted and fumed, but in rather erratic fashion did as she asked. He was interrupted several times by her shocked gasps, and by the time he finished she had become very pale. When she did not comment, he demanded, "Did ever you hear so much fustian? Nobody will believe the stupid tale!"

His wife said nothing.

Sir Reginald watched her from the corners of his eyes. "You surely do not, Paula?"

By now very frightened, she evaded in a trembling voice, "Sir Kendrick was involved in some wicked plot connected with Alabaster Royal, and Jack found out about it?"

"That's what the boy claims, yes."

"Did he give you any information about the plot?"

"Your grand-nephew was not at liberty, he said, to go into details. Convenient, eh?"

"Did he imply then—that the authorities are handling the matter?"

"He mentioned—Dammitall! He says he's under—under orders!"

"The—*Horse Guards?* Oh, my heavens!"

"And—don't fly into the boughs—Wellington!"

Lady Paula appropriated her husband's glass and took a healthy swallow. She spluttered and coughed, but managed to say breathlessly, "I want you to be . . . honest with me, Reginald. If there is . . . any chance of this dreadful business being . . . *published* . . . in the newspapers . . . I must be prepared."

"Have I not said that it's all so much poppycock? Only consider, my lady. Was there ever a more proud and haughty creature than Kendrick Vespa? Can you suppose a fellow so puffed up in his own conceit would have accepted another man's by-blow as his own all these years? Fed and clothed and educated—"

"It is *exactly* what Kendrick would have done," moaned Lady Paula. "Especially if he knew who the man was. You know as well as I that there are many fine families among the *ton* with children born 'on the wrong side of the blanket,' as they say, yet who are acknowledged as legitimate purely to avoid scandal."

Sir Reginald glared at her and said without much force, "It's all fustian I tell you! The boy's ill. Mentally deranged from his wounds, and should be clapped up. For Lord's sake do not let that imagination of yours start running wild!"

Gripping her hands tightly, Lady Paula took a quivering breath, and as if he had not spoken, murmured, "What a vicious thing for Kendrick to have done! Much worse than having shot down the boy who loved him so. But I suppose it was quite logical for him to have hated John all these years." She smiled wanly into her husband's dark scowl, and nodded. "Oh, yes, I believe it, my dear. It all falls into place, do you see? Why Kendrick was so seldom at home. Why Faith was so neglected. And now, of course, I see the resemblance, so that I can only marvel I didn't comprehend long ago . . . John was so very unlike either Kendrick or Sherry."

"What *stuff!*" roared Sir Reginald, springing to his feet. "John takes after *our* side of the family! The fine Saxon side of his heritage! Whereas Kendrick gave his Norman characteristics to Sherborne! I might have known that, womanlike, you'd fasten onto such a melodramatic explanation! Well, *I* don't believe it! Not a word!" He began to pace up and down once more, carrying his glass and growling to himself, while Lady Paula stared into space and thought her thoughts and was silent. Checking abruptly, he demanded, "Who was it, then? Since you think you know."

She looked at him steadily. "Don't you remember? When Sherry was two years old and Kendrick was flirting with so many of the beauties of the day, and Faith began to form her own court? Think back, Reginald! She was very lovely then, and of all the men who adored her, who was the one Kendrick most hated? The man Faith *should* have wed, you used to say. The man she *would* have chosen for her lover. The perfect way to thoroughly humiliate her husband and give him back his own."

"My . . . dear . . . God!" Sir Reginald's eyes had become very wide. He collapsed onto the side of the bed as if his legs had melted under him. "I wonder Kendrick did not strangle her!"

His wife nodded. "You see the resemblance now."

"Yes. Jupiter! How could we all have been so blind?"

There was a brief silence, broken when Sir Reginald started and exclaimed, "Deuce take it, Paula! We're in a fine bumble-broth! John wants to marry Francesca Ottavio's granddaughter. Kendrick was instrumental in the murder of the girl's father, and the old lady knows the whole story. The *whole* story!"

"Oh, how dreadful! Then John must be equally unacceptable to her as Kendrick's heir, or as a man with no name. Lady Francesca will never permit the marriage. Indeed, I'm surprised he'd approach the girl, under the circumstances."

"He can't fix his interest, of course. But he thinks she cares for him, and he is determined to at least discover his real father's identity. Can't blame the poor lad, but . . . I hope you'll not be so unwise as to, er . . ."

"As to tell him?" Lady Paula sighed and shook her head sadly. "If I had a grain of compassion, I would. But—no, dear. If he's to learn that home truth, it must be from his mama; not from his great aunt."

Sir Reginald gave a sigh of relief. "Faith's off flibbertigibbeting around South America. I doubt she'll ever come back. And if she does, she'll never tell him. The very thought of more scandal would keep her silly mouth shut! I only pray that whatever roguery Kendrick was about don't become public knowledge."

"I wonder whatever it could have been? How dreadful to have real *wickedness* in our family! If the Horse Guards and Lord

Wellington are involved . . ." Tearful, Lady Paula reached out both hands. "Oh, Reginald, I could not *bear* to be shunned by Society!"

"Now then, m'dear," he soothed, holding her hands firmly. "No need to make a Cheltenham tragedy of the business! We may never know the true facts, and if John does say aught of it, folks will surely set it down to the poor lad's cracked brain-box. If there was some really shocking dealing, the authorities may be as anxious as we are to sweep it all under the rug. Whatever the case *we* must keep silent, Paula. Our niece *did* marry a Vespa, so our honour is involved. For the sake of the family name you *must* keep your tongue between your teeth and admit *nothing*—to *anyone!* You promise?"

Sir Reginald's lady nodded and on a smothered sob gave her promise.

Two

It had stopped raining when Captain Vespa left Wansdyke House. The night air was very cold and bracing and a half-moon imparted a soft radiance as it broke through shredding clouds. It was not far to his club, and although the Battle of Vitoria had left him with a marked limp, he chafed against inaction. Thanks to his more recent brush with death there had been little chance for exercise these past few weeks and he stepped out briskly, waving on the jervey who slowed his hackney coach and peered at him hopefully.

Lady Francesca did not keep very late hours, but it was doubtful that she would leave the ball before midnight. With luck, Manderville would escort the ladies back to Claridges and then join him at the Madrigal Club. With more luck, between them they'd have learned *something* of his mother's erstwhile admirers.

Few people were about on this rainy late evening, but when he turned onto St. James's he had to jump back to avoid being run down by a coach racing around the corner, the coachman very obviously the worse for drink. He shouted a protest and was answered by a flourished whip and a muddled response seemingly having to do with Christmas. Muttering indignantly, he walked on, his thoughts turning to the un-happy interview with his great-uncle. Lord, but Sir Reginald had been furious. For a while it had seemed likely that the poor old fellow would suffer an apoplexy. He should have anticipated such a reaction, but he'd counted on the fact that neither Sir Reginald, nor Great-Aunt Paula had been fond of his—of Sir Kendrick. He'd sometimes suspected, in fact, that they thoroughly disliked him. Obviously, he had underestimated their dread of scandal. He smiled a twisted smile. What a multitude of sins was hidden behind the fear of sullying a Family Name. Sir Reginald had all but threatened to have him put away if he dared pursue his enquiries. His jaw tightened. He was fond of the old gentleman and had no wish to upset him. Nor had he the slightest intention of giving up his search.

His introspection was broken as a link boy came running to offer to light his way. Between the moonlight, the occasional flicker of an oil street lamp and the flambeaux that still blazed outside some great houses, he had no need for the lad's services and sent him off with a groat clutched in one grubby fist, and a jubilant outpouring of wishes that 'milor' be blessed with health and good luck ever'n ever.

Amused, Vespa thought that his health was certainly much improved, and as to good luck—he had plenty of that, for there were loyal friends eager to help in his quest: his former comrades in arms, Toby Broderick and Paige Manderville; his Dorsetshire neighbours, the Italian 'Duchess of Ottavio,' and most importantly, her half-English granddaughter, little Consuela Carlotta Angelica Jones, the lady who gave meaning to his life and without whose vibrant presence there would be no life.

If all went well and he discovered that his real sire had been an honourable gentleman . . . Surely Mama would have chosen no less? But even if that were so, he must face the fact that he was illegitimate. The awareness still shocked him, and the hand on his cane clenched tight. All his life he'd believed himself to be the scion of a fine old family. He'd been proud of his name and lineage and especially proud of the brilliant diplomatist he'd thought was his father. He would have been enraged had anyone dared suggest that Sir Kendrick Vespa was a conscienceless villain who had suffered no qualm of conscience in destroying those who stood in the way of his schemes. At least three innocents had paid the supreme penalty for being in the wrong place at the wrong time. And when he himself had unwittingly interfered in Sir Kendrick's plans—

He closed his eyes briefly, fighting the grief that persisted against all logic, and was such a fierce pain. It was over. When

Sir Kendrick had been swept away by the flood that had raced
through the quarry at Alabaster Royal, his schemes had died
with him. Consuela and Manderville and Toby Broderick, and
even Lady Francesca, had each tried in their own way to help
him surmount the tragedy. They each had said with great
kindness that there was a time to put the past behind; to
refuse to think about it; to firmly dismiss it from his mind.
Excellent and well-meant advice. The trouble was, it was easier
said than done.

He shuddered, chilled by more than the icy wind as he
crossed Piccadilly. He was greeted by two friendly but un-
known young exquisites who, between hiccups, invited him to
join them in the chorus of "She Was Only a Fishmonger's
Daughter." Short of engaging in fisticuffs, his attempts to escape proved unavailing. His nature was not quarrelsome and
it was clear that, however intoxicated, they meant no harm.
Bowing to the inevitable he obliged, but stressed that he could
not stay for encores. In the event, he was not asked for an
encore. His new acquaintances were, in fact, quite ungrateful,
and he left them, ignoring their hilarity over his vocal efforts.
Grandmama Wansdyke, he thought indignantly, had always enjoyed to hear him sing. Toby Broderick had once been so
uncouth as to comment that the lady must have been tone-
deaf, but—

From the alley beside him came sounds of desperate con-
flict. The moonlight did not penetrate far between the tall
buildings, but his eyes were keen. Three against one. Thieves,
no doubt. "Hey!" he shouted, and gripping his cane firmly,
limped into the fray.

It was short but sharp. Almost at once he realized that here
were no ordinary footpads. There were no shouts; no curses.
The three, armed with short cudgels, fought in a silent cooperation that spoke of experience. He had fully expected
that with his arrival and his shouts for the Watch, the rogues
would run for it. They did not. Their victim groaned and
sagged to his knees. One sturdy bully bent over the fallen
man, the other two plunged at Vespa. He countered a flashing
cudgel with his cane, then swung it in a sideways swipe across
the third man's ribs that evened the odds. A ham-like fist
whipped at his face, and he ducked then brought his famous
right into violent collision with a craggy jaw. His ears rang to

the resultant howl of anguish. The first bully turned from their victim and joined the fight. Vespa flung himself to the side, but only partially avoided the cudgel that blurred at his eyes.

Through an instant of blinding pain he heard someone yell, "Here's the . . . Watch! Stand, you miserable . . . varmints!" The voice was unsteady but vaguely familiar.

He was being assisted to his feet, and he gasped breathlessly, "Are they gone?"

"Thanks to you, Captain, sir, they are. Oh, dear. I lied to the . . . poor clods. Our reinforcements ain't the Watch after all."

Vespa wiped blood from his eyebrow and saw two gentlemen weaving towards them, clinging to each other while peering at him blearily.

"Be damned," said one of the new arrivals thickly. "It's the—hic—poor chap who—who can't—hic—sing."

"Sho 'tis, dear boy," confirmed his friend. "Can—can fight, though. Jolly—jolly goo' show, shir. 'F I shay sho m'shelf."

"And you've my thanks, gentlemen," said Vespa. "You were—a good substitute for the Watch."

"Even if they can't see straight," murmured the man at his side. "Come on, Vespa. It's starting to drizzle again."

Vespa looked at him sharply. "I thought it was you! What the deuce are you doing here, and out of uniform?"

Colonel the Honourable Hastings Adair drew him away. "Not now. Those louts may return with more of their kind. Come!"

They hobbled on together, investigating their various hurts, and followed by the strains of the shockingly ribald third verse of "She Was Only a Fishmonger's Daughter."

"Going the wrong way," pointed out Vespa, halting. "I'm bound for the Madrigal."

Adair held a grisly handkerchief to his nose and from behind it urged him on. "I'm not. Now that I've found you. I thank you for your help, though."

Standing firm, Vespa scanned the colonel in the light of a flambeaux and noted glumly that, despite a darkening bruise across one cheekbone, a bloody nose, and a graze beside his mouth, and although civilian dress lacked the dash of his military scarlet, the dark-haired young officer was all too well-qualified a suitor for Consuela's hand. "Sold out, have you?" he enquired sardonically.

"You know better." Investigating, Adair muttered, "Gad, but I believe those varmints have loosed one of my teeth. Well, never mind that. For Lord's sake, will you move? I can't lounge about under this light."

They left the flambeaux behind. Lowering his voice, Vespa said, "I thought you'd gone back to France. Did Wellington send you to sniff around?"

"In a manner of speaking."

"You said you'd tell him the full story of what happened at Alabaster Royal."

"So I did. He was most concerned. He spoke highly of you and sent you this letter. . . ." Adair groped in his pockets. "Be damned! Those dirty bastards made off with it!"

Vespa would have prized the letter. "It was kind of the General to write his condolences."

"Field Marshal now, don't forget! And he wrote more than condolences. He wants something of you."

There was a note in the colonel's voice that triggered warning flags in Vespa's mind. He said warily, "For instance?"

"Stop poking your nose into—past history."

"Devil take it!" Vespa halted again. "I've a perfect right to make enquiries about personal matters. Wouldn't you, were you in my shoes?"

Adair hesitated, then said evasively, "You're stirring up more than you know, Captain."

"What difference does it make? The whole story will come out sooner or later. You can't stifle that kind of—of—"

"Treachery? I'm sorry, but there's really no kinder word, is there? And it *must* be stifled! There'll be no more of it in the newspapers, I promise you. Now why look so astounded? Forgive, but your late father—"

"Which one?"

Adair swore under his breath, then hailed a slow-moving hackney coach. The jervey grinned in triumph, and Vespa saw that it was the same coach he had refused earlier. Adair called an order to "Just drive," adding a curt, "Get in."

"Why?"

"Because it's freezing and we can talk in here without getting soaked. Don't be so blasted stubborn. I'll remind you that I outrank you, Captain!"

Vespa bit back an unflattering comment and climbed reluctantly into the coach.

"I'll remind *you*, sir," he said, when Adair had lowered himself painfully onto the seat beside him, "that I am not at the moment on active service."

"Really? And do you feel that entitles you to undermine the security of this nation? Or do you consider your personal affairs more important than King and Country?" Adair gripped Vespa's arm, and looking into his startled face, said in a kinder tone, "Through no fault of your own you've had a wretched year, and I'll own that had you not taken a hand just now, I'd be in a very sticky mess at this moment. I know you must wish me at Jericho, on more counts than one. Please believe that I don't like this. But I've no choice."

Frowning, Vespa settled back against the lumpy cushions and waited.

The Colonel said softly, "Sir Kendrick Vespa almost succeeded in selling the Alabaster Royal estates to the Government as the site of a proposed secondary Arsenal. He was perfectly aware that large sections of the property were undermined by extensive tunnelling, and that it would be dangerous to locate an arsenal on such unstable ground, so—"

"Thank you, Colonel, sir," interrupted Vespa, pale with anger. "Did you really feel it necessary to rub my nose in my family disgrace? I promise you, I'm sufficiently aware of it!"

"Damn your eyes! We know you almost lost your life when you refused to do as he wished. No—don't say it! You don't want my sympathy. But what *I* want—what *his lordship* wants—is that you look farther than your personal tragedy. Despite his cunning and his ruthless disregard of human life, none of it would have been possible had Sir Kendrick not first purchased the—ah—cooperation of several highly placed gentlemen at Whitehall."

Vespa gave a disgusted snort. "What you mean is that rich and powerful men took bribes to look the other way! Good Lord above! Do you say that Wellington wants me to also 'look the other way?' "

"He wants you to consider that we are in a state of war, *Captain*. At least half the people of this island believe a French

invasion to be imminent. Many men behind the scenes of
power struggle desperately to prevent a panic. Were it to become public knowledge that so respected a diplomatist as your
late father was corrupt; that some of our leading citizens exchanged their integrity for gold—"

"It would seem to me," said Vespa hotly, "that the public
has a right to know the truth about great men who abuse
power! They *should* be exposed and held up to shame and to
punishment!"

"The punishment will come, I assure you. But the shame
would spread to some very famous families. Including your
own."

After a short silence, Vespa muttered, "I don't know what
is—my own, sir."

"You're splitting hairs. I know you're in the deuce of a fix.
But you've your mother to consider still, and her side of your
family. Speaking of which—how does Sir Reginald Wansdyke
view the matter?"

"I just left him, as you evidently are aware. He chose to
take the attitude that my mind is permanently impaired, and
that I should be locked away."

"Natural enough." A pause, then Adair murmured, "He is
not alone in such sentiments."

With a shocked gasp, Vespa jerked around to face him. "By
the lord Harry, I do believe you're threatening me!"

"Call it a friendly warning. His lordship asks your cooperation is all. Just during the present national emergency."

It was too bland; too gently appealing. Vespa leaned back
and said thoughtfully, "His lordship sent you home only to
give me a 'friendly warning'? And you found it necessary to
leave off your uniform—in time of war—for such a purpose?"

"I have several commissions for Lord Wellington," said
Adair with wooden calm.

"Yet interrupted them to ensure that I was behaving myself?
I was—that is to say Broderick and Manderville and I were—
warned to keep our tongues between our teeth in the matter
of the Arsenal, which we have done."

"Very good." The colonel inspected his handkerchief in the
glow from the coach lamps. "Ah, my nose has stopped bleeding at last and—"

"The devil with your nose! Why should my search for my

true identity cause the Field Marshal, or the Horse Guards, to be alarmed?"

"I'd think it obvious that your enquiries must provoke curiosity, to say the least."

"Not so! For my mother's sake I've been discreet."

"Yet your search has been noted."

"By whom? Whitehall?"

"And others."

"Rubbish!" Leaning forward, Vespa said intensely, "Do you know what I think, Colonel, sir? Those louts who attacked you just now were not run-of-the-mill street *banditti.* They were professionals. The fellow who brought you down had plenty of opportunity to put an end to you, but did not. They wanted you alive because they want information from you! And if you expect me to believe that one jot of it had to do with my search for my real father—"

Adair exclaimed, "Where the *devil* are we? Hey! Jervey! What are you about?"

The coach lurched to a halt. In a flash, Adair had wrenched the door open and sprung out.

Following, Vespa found that the hackney had stopped on a gloomy narrow street. He was able to distinguish that the coachman had vanished. A shocked cry rang out, and against the dim light from a dirty window he caught a glimpse of Adair, who appeared to have taken wing. Astonished, Vespa crouched, prepared for battle, his cane fast-gripped. The lighted window was blotted out. He had a brief impression that a giant loomed before him. The chances being slim that this giant was friendly, he did not pause to enquire, but with both hands and all his strength thrust his cane at the creature. It was as if he had attacked solid rock. A guttural roar deafened him. He was swept up in a crushing grip and hurled aside. With the instinctive reaction of the athlete he landed rolling. Short of breath, he crawled to his knees and tried to see who—or what—had attacked them.

A mighty hand jerked him up, then released him abruptly as a voice with a slight foreign accent snarled, "Not him, fool! The other!"

"Halt, or I fire!" Adair's voice.

Vespa hoped the colonel could see more than he could, and crouched lower.

A pistol shot shattered the quiet of the night.

Somebody screamed.

There sounded again that inhuman, guttural growl. "Honourable master light lantern? Cannot find—"

And then hooves were coming fast, rattles clattered, and a distant bobbing glow proclaimed the approach of law and order.

The foreign voice rang out. "It is the Watch! *Sacré nom de nom!* How did the imbeciles come so fast up with us? I cannot be seen in this!"

"Master go. I find—"

"Idiot! Come!"

"I bring Barto? Colonel man shoot straight. Barto dead I think."

"Then leave him."

By the brightening glow of the lantern, Vespa saw two men running toward a darkened carriage; one tall and thin, the other shorter, but massively built with long arms that bulged the sleeves of his coat. The carriage door slammed, the coachman whipped up his team. Sixteen iron-shod hooves struck sparks from the cobblestones, and Vespa had to leap for his life.

Adair came staggering up and helped him to his feet. "What the devil was . . . that?" he gasped in a shaken voice. "Did you see?"

"Not clearly, but enough to know I hope never to see it again!"

Two members of the Watch ran up, their lantern swung high. Vespa caught a glimpse of a red waistcoat and thought a surprised, *'Bow Street?'* He said thankfully, "You came just in time! I—"

"You best be movin' along, sir." A pair of narrowed eyes scanned him from under a low-crowned hat. "This ain't no neighbourhood for a gent like you to go for a joy ride."

"Joy ride! I'll have you know—"

" 'Alf a minute, sir." The Bow Street Runner bent above a still shape. "This one's stuck 'is spoon in the wall." He turned to Adair. "I reckernizes you, Mr. Brownley, and I'll take that pistol, if y'please. Up to yer tricks agin, but I gotcha this time, ain't I! In the King's name I arrest you on a charge of murder. Let's 'ave the bracelets 'ere, North."

Seething with indignation, Vespa demanded, "Are you quite daft? *We* are the victims, you idiot! That coach you saw driving off holds the ruffians you want!"

"A *proper* idjut I'd be to believe that one, sir," leered the Runner. "I 'opes I knows when I got me man! 'Ere's our coach at last. We'll be orf, North. And let's 'ave no trouble from you, Brownley—*h'if* you don't wanta bump on the tibby!"

Adair murmured something in a despondent tone.

Vespa sprang forward and wrenched the Runner's hold from the colonel's arm. "You're out of your senses! I tell you we were murderously attacked, and you most *assuredly* have the wrong man! This gentleman's name is not Brownley! He's—"

"It's good of you to try, friend," interrupted Adair. "But it's no use. They got me proper." His very blue eyes met Vespa's levelly, and said a clear if silent, 'Keep out of this!'

A moment later, having mounted the box on the abandoned hackney coach, Vespa took up the reins and sent the tired horse plodding after the Watchman's carriage.

The office at the Horse Guards was not large and in the subdued light of this cold winter morning the presence of five gentlemen caused it to appear crowded. Although nobody spoke there was a distinct air of tension in the room. The youthful major seated at the desk appeared to be fascinated by the quill pen he turned in restless fingers; the rosy-cheeked and robust captain who stood leaning back against the front of the desk folded his arms and stared wistfully at a coat he coveted shamelessly; and the three young men who sat facing the desk exchanged incredulous glances. For several seconds the silence was broken only by the pattering of raindrops against the window.

Lieutenant Tobias Broderick's blond curly hair and cherubic blue eyes made him appear younger than his twenty-four years and masked a brilliant mind. He now said with considerable indignation, "In view of Captain Vespa's extraordinary military record, and the fact that he was chosen by Lord Wellington to be on his personal staff, I find it astonishing that you should question his word, Major Blaine."

"You are mistaken, Lieutenant." Major Blaine lifted a pair

of cold brown eyes to engage Broderick's angry stare. "I do not question Sir John's account of what he believes to have transpired last evening, but—"

Vespa interrupted, "Your pardon, sir, but my name is *Captain* John Vespa! I do not use the title." Clearly taken aback, the major blinked at him and he took advantage of the pause to add briskly, "Also, I am perfectly *sure* of what happened last evening. As I told you just now, a high-ranking army officer was attacked on the street and later arrested, completely without justification, by an officious clod who called himself a Bow Street Runner! It was clearly a case of mistaken identity. I would respectfully suggest that you get in touch with Bow Street at once and arrange for Colonel Adair's release."

"As should have been done last night, when Captain Vespa came here and reported the incident," murmured Paige Manderville, adjusting the cuff of his coat.

The large captain continued to gaze at that superbly tailored coat as he remarked, "And would have been done, Lieutenant, had we been able to verify Sir—er, Captain Vespa's—er, assertions, but—"

"Assertions?" said Vespa angrily. "Now see here, Rickaby, if you've been brought into the business to claim that my mind is still disordered from the knock I took at Vitoria, I'll have you know I am fully recovered!"

"And have recently taken another knock on the head, by the look of it." The military surgeon tore his eyes from Manderville's coat and moved to examine the cut over Vespa's eye. "When did this happen?"

"Last evening. While Hastings Adair and I were fighting off the thieves who attacked him. This cut is proof of what I've told you, so do not waste more time in trying to convince me that none of it happened!"

Major Blaine said gently, "But, my dear fellow, we have no intention of doing such a thing. We've already been in touch with the Bow Street Magistrate and have a full report of the occurrence."

"Then why did you imply that you doubted my story?"

"Only one aspect of the affair," qualified Dr. Rickaby. "You were apparently confused as to the identity of the man you went to help. Logical you would be, all things considered."

Through gritted teeth Vespa declared, "I was *not* confused!

Nor concussed! *Nor* hallucinating! Adair had a nosebleed after the fight. We called up a hackney coach. He said he'd been looking for me, and we talked for a few minutes about a—a personal matter. If you say I was talking to myself, you're quite off the road!"

Major Blaine put in mildly, "I've no least idea of to whom you were talking, but I know damned well it wasn't the man you've named. Colonel Hastings Adair is at this very moment in France with Field Marshal Lord Wellington's forces."

"The devil!" exclaimed Broderick.

"Is he now," drawled Manderville cynically.

Vespa's jaw tightened. "I don't know why you would make such a claim, sir, or why Adair was rushed off to jail for some trumped-up reason. He's not a close personal friend. But he's a good man, and I'd try to help him out of a fix, even if I didn't have my own sanity to defend. Good day to you, gentlemen." He stood, his friends standing with him.

"Where do you think you're going?" asked Blaine, amused.

"To find Colonel the Honourable Hastings Adair," said Vespa, starting to the door. "When I bring him here, you may wish to make me your apologies."

The surgeon glanced at Blaine and volunteered with a sigh, "Very well. I can tell you where to find him."

Vespa turned back eagerly.

"He took a bayonet through the thigh during the Battle of the Nivelle," said Rickaby. "We've settled him into one of our charming field hospitals in Pamplona. I visited him there just before I started for home three days ago."

Blaine said reasonably, "So you see, Captain, poor Hasty Adair is quite unable to walk, much less to have left France and battled ruffians on a London street last night."

"Were I you, my boy," advised Rickaby. "I'd go down to that nice Richmond house of yours and enjoy a warm and cozy winter and forget all this unpleasantness."

It was really remarkable, thought Vespa, that so many people were eager to put him out of the way. He looked from one kindly smile to the other and shook his head in reluctant admiration. "I'll say this for you," he said, "you're jolly good at it!" He followed his friends and closed the door quietly.

After a glum minute, "Damn!" said Major Blaine, slamming his quill pen onto the desk disastrously.

Captain Rickaby sighed. "Stubborn fella, I'm afraid, Ed."

"So I was warned."

"It comes in handy sometimes. After Vitoria, for instance. He should've died. Wouldn't. He's a dashed good man."

"They all are. Broderick and Manderville can be dealt with. One way or another. But—Vespa . . ." the Major scowled. "His lordship's hand is over him. To an extent."

Rickaby murmured, "D'you know, Ed, if it was up to me, I'd tell him."

"Well, it ain't up to you," snapped Blaine, glaring at him. "And it ain't up to me. And how the hell could I tell him what I don't know myself?"

"You don't? Jupiter! I thought surely a man in your position— Then—who does know?"

"I don't know that, either. I only know it's not to be talked of, or whispered, or even, God save us all, thought about! So this conversation must not be mentioned outside these walls."

"Lord, man! I'm your cousin! You surely know I'm to be trusted?"

"Of course I do, you great clunch. Secrecy! It's a double-edged sword at best. The inevitable result of all these cautions and prohibitions is that everyone's wondering what the devil they're not to talk, or whisper, or think about!" Blaine scraped back his chair and went to stand at the window and glower at the rain. "It must be curst big, Rick, whatever it is. Did you notice there's been not one word in the newspapers about that fiasco last night?"

"Early yet, old boy. Besides, London's unhappily replete with robberies. Not surprising if one goes unnoticed."

"Is it not?" Blaine gave a snort of derision. "Yet another murderous attack on a popular young war hero who appears to have become a magnet for violence. Do you really suppose the newspapers would not begin to ask why? Or that they would ignore such a story?"

"Humph. Well, perhaps they—"

"Besides which, Jack Vespa's sire provided the grist for a scandalous rumour mill. And to add to all this, another slippery customer has oozed onto the scene. A rogue we've been after for years, and never managed to so much as detain for questioning!"

Rickaby frowned. "I didn't hear about that. Only Vespa's report that there was a second attack."

"Just so. A second attack involving a tall man with a foreign accent and a giant for a servant who tossed Adair about like—"

"Oh—egad," gasped the surgeon. "You're never thinking it was—"

"Imre Monteil. The very shady Swiss munitions maker. And his monstrous Chinese henchman."

"Be dashed," muttered Rickaby. "If only half the tales one hears about that pair are truth . . ."

"I'll tell you one thing, coz," said Blaine after a brooding pause. "If Imre Monteil has a finger in the pie, it's a rich pie! A very rich pie indeed!"

Three

"I suppose I need not ask if the rain it still drips?" Lady Francesca lifted her eyes from the *Morning Post* to direct a mournful glance at Consuela who knelt in the window-seat, gazing down into the busy street. Her granddaughter confirming her supposition in a rather abstracted fashion, my lady sighed. "A wretched climate has this small island."

"Then only think how fortunate we are," said Consuela, "to be comfortable in this lovely hotel instead of outside in the cold and wet."

Refusing to feel fortunate, my lady sighed again. "How I miss my sunny Italy. Can you wonder that I yearn to take you back where you belongings?"

"And where would that be, Grandmama? In the middle of the English Channel, perhaps? The Italian side of me facing to the south, and the British side to the north?"

"Do not be flippant, *signorina!* Your blood is of a royal Italian House and is warm, and your temper it blows hot, in the Latin manner! As for your British side—"

Consuela turned and smiled at her. "My British side loves this funny old island, dearest. As it loved my adored and so very talented English Papa. And you know perfectly well that I mean to wed an English gentleman, so—"

"An English gentleman who does not even know his real name," snorted Lady Francesca. "No, do not send me dagger glances, miss! I know you are fond of Captain Jack Vespa, but—"

"Much more than fond, Grandmama! He is the bravest, kindest, most truly honourable gentleman I—"

"You will not interrupt, if you please," interrupted my lady, rattling the newspaper at her granddaughter. "For him to try and his interest fix with you, this it is not proper."

For some days Consuela had sensed that her diminutive grandmother was pondering something, and guessing what that something was, she knew this would be a serious talk. She left the window-seat, therefore, and came with her light dancing step to sink onto the footstool before Lady Francesca's chair, the pale pink velvet gown rippling about her. "He did not exactly declare himself, you know," she pointed out meekly. "It was more of a 'testing the waters,' Toby said. A 'supposing this,' or a 'supposing that,' and if such and such chanced, might I then consider him." She smiled tenderly. "Poor boy. He was very careful not to make me feel that we had plighted our troth, so that I could be free if other gentlemen offered."

"*If* other gentlemen offer? Of course they will offer! At the ball last night the beaux were fluttering around, and you have already today receiving two charming bouquets, is it not? Nor dismiss from your mind that very handsome young colonel."

"Colonel Adair is back in France with Lord Wellington. I doubt we shall see him again until the war is ended." Despite this assertion, Consuela knew she must be careful; she was sure her Grandmother really liked Jack, but if she set her mind against him, it would be disastrous. She said airily, "Besides, you may be *à l'aise,* dear *Nonna.* Romance, so they say, is capricious, and a lady seldom marries her first love."

Lady Francesca shook one finger under her granddaughter's small nose and said perversely, "This it is the talk of a flirt, *signorina,* and ladies who flirt have the reputations and sometimes end with nothing more!"

"What about gentlemen who flirt? John Vespa loved another lady once—"

"*Sì.* Long ago. But you know very well he has eyes now only for you. And it is unkind in extremity to tease the young man."

Consuela asked demurely, "Then you think I should accept if he really makes me an offer?"

"No! And—no! A most strong *no!* You will accept him only in despite of my strict disapproval, child."

Startled by such vehemence, Consuela searched the old lady's face and found there a stern resolve. She said in dismay, "But—but, you are most fond of Jack!"

"*Sì.* This it is truth."

"And when Sir Kendrick shot him you helped nurse him and

grieved for his sake, and now we are helping him seek out his real father. Although," she added, forgetting her earlier caution, "I care not a jot whether his father turns out to be a well-born gentleman, or—"

"Or—what, Miss Rattlepate? A highwayman? A footpad? A murderer? Do you care not the jot if your children have inherit the consumptive habit? Or madness? Or the disease that brings sightlessness? What is in the blood will out!"

Consuela was silent. Then she muttered, "As if Lady Faith would have chosen such a one for her lover."

"Ha! Look who she chose for her husband! A pretty monster!"

"True. But her parents chose him, not she. Besides, can one really tell? Sir Kendrick Vespa was to all outward appearances a fine example of aristocracy: handsome and clever and elegant. And inside he was a cheat and a murderer several times over! An honest coal-heaver would have been a better choice for a husband!"

"This also is so. However, one is born to a certain station in life, *bambina,* and no matter what people may say, this it will never change. Was we all to become the coal-heavers there still would be the strongest among the heavers, or the one who sells the most coal would become the Aristocrat among Coal-Heavers and gradually he would pull away from the common herd. It is the way of the world. You loved your papa. Do you thinking he would countenance a marriage between Consuela Carlotta Angelica Jones, of the royal house of Ottavio, and a young English captain who has a haunted and decaying old country estate and expectations of the smallest?" Lady Francesca flung up one hand, silencing Consuela's attempt to comment. "I know what you will say. He was, and I admit this, a gallant and brave soldier. But he also is either the son of the wicked Sir Kendrick Vespa—who was directly responsible for your own father's death—"

"You *know* he is not Sir Kendrick's son," interposed Consuela fierily. "That evil man almost killed Jack as well as my Papa, and—"

"In the which case," overrode the old lady with a daunting frown, "your Captain Jack is the *natural child* of a mystery man about whom we know nothings at all."

"But we *will,* dearest! You and I and dear Toby and Paige, we all are trying to help Jack find the gentleman."

"And if we succeed, how then is it? Your fine captain is too fond of his Mama to shame her by refusing to any longer bear her name."

"Y-yes. Perhaps. But—but if we find that his real father is a fine and honourable man, then you can at least be easy and know what his—his background is."

"And Jack still will be no less of a bastard who will accept neither the Vespa fortune nor the title!"

"*Grandmama!*" Her cheeks pink with anger, Consuela sprang to her feet.

"*Signorina!*" Lady Francesca stood also and drew herself up to her full fifty-seven inches. In her stockinged feet Consuela was four inches taller, but her grandmother's head was thrown back regally, her fine dark eyes could still flash fire, and in that moment she seemed to tower over the girl.

"You will be quiet and pay me heed," she commanded, her voice harsh. "I am knowing of the great service Captain Jack Vespa made us in proving your Papa's murder. I am knowing of the fact that his life he risked and almost lost in saving yours. We are beholden. It is for this reasons I have allowing you to come to London with me, and that I will help him in his quest. He is a good man, *si*. But when *all* the facts are whispered about Town, as soon they must be, he will be a very much disgraced man. *Your* line it is proud. *Your* prospects they are most fine. I would be a poor *nonna* if I allowed you to be shamed by marriage to a man whose only hope for holding up of his head is to leave the country!"

"Oh!" Wrath rendered Consuela almost speechless, and to add to her mental turmoil was the awareness that the old lady loved her and wanted only the best for her. "H-how *can* you speak of him so?" she spluttered. "He is—is one of the most popular young men in London! *Everybody* likes him and has only good to say of him!"

In this, however, she was mistaken. The maid, who at that moment was admitting Captain John Vespa to the suite, neither liked nor admired him, and what she had to say of him to her intimates was far from good. Violet Manning, whose life was not unpleasant, might grumble, as was the fashion, about her 'fussy' employers, but she was also proud of them. She lost no opportunity to point out that although the Duchess of Ottavio was a foreign lady, she was highly born; that Mr. Preston Jones had been among the greatest of Britain's artists; and that his daughter, Miss Consuela, might have had an Italian Mama, but there was royal blood in her veins, and she could look as high as she pleased for a husband.

To Manning it was little short of tragic that her mistress must instead smile upon Captain Vespa. Miss Consuela was perhaps just a bit short of being judged beautiful, and she could get very cross very quick, but she was pretty and full of life and charm, and she had a lovely body. Captain Vespa had a scar down one temple, and he limped. People said he was a fine athlete before he became a soldier. He was not a fine athlete now. Worse, he was evidently touched in his upper works, for why in the world would a sane man refuse his rightful title?

She took Captain Vespa's hat and cloak and scanned without admiration the ally who trotted in after him. Another example of poor judgment. The captain could have adopted his father's bloodhounds; to have such creatures as Solomon and Barrister at his heels might have lent him a bit of interest and dignity. But—no! The great hounds had gone to live in the country with Lieutenant Manderville's father, and the captain was accompanied as always by 'Corporal' a small dog with long greyish-brown hair and no consequence whatever. It was all of a piece, thought Manning resentfully, and opened the drawing room door to announce, "Captain Vespa, my lady."

Vespa sensed the tension in the air when he entered the drawing room. Lady Francesca looked vexed, and Consuela hurried to stand at the window and surreptitiously dab a handkerchief at her eyes.

"Good morning, ladies," he said as he crossed to kiss the hand of the little duchess.

"You are late," she scolded, tapping his cheek with her fan. "We have expecting you an hour since."

"And Paige did not come as he promised," said Consuela, gaining control of herself and turning to face Vespa.

He bowed and, meeting the ardent smile that was then levelled at her, she wondered how Grandmama could be anything but charmed by the hazel eyes so intriguingly flecked with gold, or the strong chin and sensitive mouth, and the way the thick hair— She gave a shocked gasp and flew to touch the gash above his eyebrow. "What now? You are hurt again! I vow I cannot let you out of my sight for one moment but you are into trouble! Tell me!"

"Che orrore!" Lady Francesca threw up her hands. "Have you

none of the manners, Signorina Consuela? Ring the bell! First, we offer Captain Jack coffee and the politenesses. *Then,* he may tell us his tales!"

Consuela's 'politenesses' extended to ringing the bell, but her impatience could scarcely be contained, and the moment Manning had gone off to gather refreshments Vespa was commanded to tell them about his evening's activities. It was not an easy task, for he was interrupted frequently, but when he named the victim of the street attack both ladies were startled into silence. They did not recover their vocal powers until he described his interview at the Horse Guards, whereupon the duchess unleased a flood of Italian during which her small hands were flourished about wildly and expressions such as *stupidita!* and *pazzia!* were so scornfully uttered as to leave little doubt of their meaning.

Unaccustomedly mute, Consuela at length said a puzzled, "But why would they lie about it? And why would Colonel Adair have behaved in such a strange fashion? Jack—you're *quite* sure it was him?"

"Quite sure. Though both Major Blaine and my army surgeon did their best to convince me I'm wits to let."

Consuela asked sharply, "Why should your doctor have been there?"

"That's what Broderick wanted to know. It seems Captain Rickaby is cousin to the major. Perhaps it was pure coincidence that he chanced to be there." He said with a wry smile, "I try, you see, not to let my imagination run riot."

"Well, I think it all most odd. And your surgeon claimed to have seen Hasty— I mean, Colonel Adair, in a hospital in Spain only three days ago?"

"Yes." Very aware of the quick correction, Vespa said, "Not that I believe a word of it."

At this point Manning returned with a laden tray. Lady Francesca poured coffee and when the maid had gone asked shrewdly, "What *are* you believing, Captain?"

Vespa accepted a slice of seed cake, and replied, "That Colonel Adair is most definitely back in England. I didn't imagine our violent encounters. Nor do I think my activities are his major concern."

Consuela said, "But he warned you to stop your search. So, surely, whatever he's about must be in some way linked to what you—we—are doing."

"Shall you stop—as the colonel he demand?" asked Lady Francesca.

"By George, but I won't! I did what I could for Adair and met a brick wall. I'm not on active service now, and barring a straight command from his lordship, I'll keep on."

Consuela nodded. "What about Sir Kendrick's man of business? Might he be able to help?"

"Very likely. But Felton's slippery as an eel. Every time I call at his offices he is very much 'out.' It's clear he doesn't want to see me, and if I did trap him he would likely talk in meaningless circles as those lawyer fellows love to do, so I see no point in wasting my time on him. Toby and Paige have gone off to Bow Street to try and see Adair. I mean to drive down to Richmond and see if any letters have arrived from my mother."

"Good." Consuela slipped a biscuit to the hopeful Corporal. "We have plans for this afternoon also, Jack. Grandmama and me."

He looked at her uncertainly. "You have both been so very good, but—"

"I know. We must not run into danger. You told me that once before."

"Yes, I did." His eyes darkened at the memory. "And had you paid me heed you might not have nigh got yourself killed!"

"Don't go into the boughs. *Nonna* and I mean to—"

"She calls me *Nonna* when she is trying to turn me up sweetly," interrupted Lady Francesca looking far from sweet.

In a stage whisper Consuela told Vespa, "It is merely the Italian version of Grandmama, and I use it because it pleases her. How unkind I should be *not* to want to please my dear little duchess!"

"You are a conniving minx!" declared Lady Francesca, but she could not keep the twinkle from her eye, and Consuela laughed, and went on: "We mean to do nothing more dangerous than to visit the biggest gossip in the southland. But, I had hoped . . ." She glanced rather wistfully at the window.

He said, "You had hoped to see more of London, instead of which you're spending all your time trying to help me."

Lady Francesca said, "You gave up a great deal more than time when you helped us, Captain Jack."

He smiled at her gratefully. "If you don't mean to call on

your gossip till this afternoon, may I now take you both for a drive?"

"In the rain?" Lady Francesca shook her head. "For me, this is not!"

Consuela's blue eyes glowed. "Oh, I should so like to see some more of the city, dearest Grandmama. May I please go?"

"I'll take great care of her, ma'am," Vespa pleaded.

"It is unwise, this," said the duchess meeting his eyes sternly. "There must be no talkings of troths and promisings, you understand? No interest fixings. I will have your word, Captain."

He gave her his word, and said that he was in no position to make such 'talkings,' but his heart sank and he was reminded once again that even if he found his sire to be a most unexceptionable gentleman, his hopes of winning his lady were slim at best.

The dreary weather had kept many people from venturing outside but for Consuela it might have been a summer's day. She had chosen to wear a claret-coloured cloak and hood over a pale pink woollen gown and she came, or so thought Vespa, like a ray of sunlight into the coach. She had seen the more famous of the city's landmarks, and informed him that although she loved to watch the ships on the river, and thought the various parks beautiful, it was a pity more trees had not been planted along the streets. "It is such a sea of bricks and cobblestones. But it is a very exciting place to be, do you not think? All the shops and theatres, and the carriages, and so many people!"

"Less than usual today, because of the rain no doubt, which makes it easier for our coachman to get about."

"Papa used to say that in England if we wait for the rain to stop, we'll never go anywhere. But only look, it *is* stopping! How nice of the Weather Angel to bring the sun out for us! Oh, Jack!" She reached out impulsively and touched his arm. "*Do* look at that lady! What a remarkable bonnet! Are those the new colours? They seem awfully bright."

With difficulty he tore his gaze from the little hand resting so confidingly on his sleeve. The lady in question was indeed clad in bright colours and the umbrella shielding the feathers of her bonnet constituted a distinct hazard to other pedestrians. "A trifle too bright for propriety," he said with a twinkle.

Consuela gave him a questioning look, then chuckled. "Oh. I see. Well, you found a lovely coach for us, and *you* are behaving with great propriety, Captain Vespa."

The smile left his eyes. His 'propriety' was a constant frustration. To have this time with her; to see her vivacity and enthusiasm was delight. To long so to tell her of his love and know he must not, was torment. Her bright glance was fixed on his face. He said, "It was very good of the duchess to allow me to steal you away. She cannot be easy, knowing I— I mean— Oh, Jupiter!"

"What do you mean, Captain Jack?"

Her eyes were so soft, so glowing. Her hand was still on his arm. It was as much as he could do to refrain from seizing and kissing those soft pink fingers, but a gentleman did not break his given word. He wrenched his head away and said hoarsely, "Here—here we are at Cornhill already. You will have a fine view now, Consuela."

It was as well he did not see her tender smile. She said, "Yes, indeed! What is that tower? And why is it called Cornhill?"

"The tower is the Royal Exchange, and Cornhill is so named because it was at one time the site of a corn market." He drew her attention to the famous Tower of St. Michael and the numerous graceful church spires that could be seen. She was interested in everything, especially the fine shops, and the modern architecture of the large houses, and asked if this was a newer area of the city.

"Not really, but much of this section was destroyed during the Great Fire, and the new buildings were marked improvements over the old." He bent his head and leaned towards her side window to point out a fine lantern suspended from a sign that advertised the Manufacture of Writing Desks and Morocco Dressing Cases. "Now we are turning onto Lombard Street," he added, and straightening found his lips scant inches from her chin. He drew back with a gasp. The voice of temptation hissed, 'Fool! This might well be your last chance to be alone with her, don't waste it!' He fought to shut out that all too persuasive voice, but it crept into his mind once more. Where would be the harm in simply begging her to wait? How could there be shame in at least holding her close, just for a little while? 'No one will see you in the coach.'

The struggle for control was won, but he could not keep the yearning from his eyes, and seeing it, and the way his hand trembled, Consuela repented and turned away. "Aha," she said gaily. "Lombard? Now there is an Italian name, no? Does some great family live here?"

Watching the velvety curve of her cheek, the way the light glistened on her dusky curls, he murmured, "What . . . ? Oh! Er, well, yes the Lombards were a great banking or money-lending family, long ago."

"Really? Then Grandmama will probably know them and may wish to pay a call."

"I rather doubt it. I'm afraid they were a rascally lot, Consuela, and did so much mischief that Queen Elizabeth sent them packing."

At once bristling, she said tartly, "From what I have learned of that lady, she made a habit of sending people packing! With or without their heads!"

"You prefer to believe the poor Lombards were pure as the driven snow, do you? Why? Are they kin to you?"

"I don't know. . . ." A new thought banished her irritation, and she clapped her hands. "But—oh, that would be very helpful, would it not? Then Grandmama couldn't very well—" She bit her lip and cut the words off.

"You mean it would be a case of the pot not being able to call the kettle black, I think. As if I would allow my own disgrace to touch you, little *signorina.*"

"You are *not* disgraced!" she declared, her eyes sparkling with anger. "Your war record alone proves you an honourable gentleman! Why should you suffer for what *he* did? You are not of his blood!"

Such fierce defensiveness warmed his heart. He said, "I mean to prove that, just as fast as I can. To which end, Miss Jones"— he tugged on the check-string—"I must take you home to the duchess, and get started to Richmond."

Consuela asked, "Must you drive all the way down there? Surely Thornhill can go and collect any letters that wait for you?"

"He's a fine valet, I grant you, but he has only worked for me a short while. Our butler, Rennett, has been at Richmond since I was a small boy, and there are questions that . . . well, that only I can ask him."

"Ooh!" breathed Consuela her eyes very wide. "What a very good notion, Jack. The servants know *everything!*"

"So good of Consuela to accompany my niece to the lending library." The sofa occupied by Mrs. Monica Hughes-Dering creaked protestingly as she turned to select another sweetmeat from the box beside her. "I would gladly have gone with Minerva," she lied, nudging away the golden spaniel that had settled itself on her foot. "But my constitution is frail, you know, and I cannot like wintry weather. How fortunate that you should have chosen today to call upon me, Duchess. My little London house is close to everything, but I declare none of my friends will venture out in the rain, and I was like to die from boredom till you came. Now, with the girls gone, we can enjoy a comfortable cose."

The 'little London house' was a luxurious mansion located off Dover Street, and was considered by most people much too large to be occupied by one person. However, it had been for many years a Mecca for the *ton* and after her spouse had gone to his reward, the widow had chosen to remain. When she was not receiving her friends, she relied for companionship upon her numerous pets and, to a lesser degree, on whichever indigent relation she could bully into living under her roof. It was a rare afternoon that the elegant drawing room was not crowded with callers come to pay homage to the *grande dame*, and Lady Francesca counted herself fortunate to have found her quarry comparatively alone.

Now, surrounded by five dogs of varying origins, all anxiously watching the path of the sweetmeat, Lady Francesca also watched in fascination as it disappeared into the tiny slit of a mouth. If this tyrant of the *ton* was 'frail' she gave no sign of it. Always, she had been a large woman, but it was some years since they last had met and Lady Francesca was genuinely aghast to note that the dowager had more than doubled in girth. An initial suggestion that they share the sofa was a piece of empty rhetoric, for not even a small child could have squeezed in beside her. The chins that had once been double had quadrupled, neckline and waistline blended into one great bulk, and the eyes were small black beads, almost hidden by the swell of the rouged cheeks.

They were shrewd eyes, nonetheless, and, aware of this, Lady

Francesca accepted the mumbled offer of a sweetmeat and stifled her yearning to enumerate the various means by which
one might put off flesh.

Their 'comfortable cose,' frequently interrupted by loving ex-
changes between Mrs. Hughes-Dering and her unruly pets, commenced with polite enquiries as to old friends and family
members. There was a small disaster when a Pekinese jumped
into the box of sweetmeats, precipitating a battle royal for the
scattered pieces, but once a neat maid had provided another
box the 'cose' resumed. The frightful morals of today's youth
provided an entertaining topic, then Lady Francesca skillfully
initiated a discussion of the terrible discomforts of travel, and
'chanced' to mention that she had come to town under the
escort of a young officer. "I fancy you know of him, dear *Signora*
Monica, for you know everybodys who is anybodys. Captain
John Vespa."

The beady eyes glittered with interest. "Jack Vespa? But of
course I know him. Do you say he is in town already? Poor boy.
Such a dreadful thing when members of the aristocracy can be
attacked and murdered by these dreadful revolutionary ruffians, for that's what they must have been, I am very sure. I
suppose Jack will be sailing off to South America to fetch his
mother home, eh?"

"This it would surprise me not at all. Only am I surprised
the lady she have run off like that. Why do you suppose her
to doing such things?"

Mrs. Hughes-Dering paused for another assault on the sweetmeat box. "Far be it from me, dear Francesca," she said, fend-
ing off the persistently optimistic spaniel. "Far be it from me
to pay heed to the gabble-mongers. You know how unkind they
can be. But—one must face facts. Once a widgeon, always a
widgeon!" She lowered her voice and added confidingly, "To
be honest, Duchess, I often wondered how Sir Kendrick could
abide the foolish creature."

"*Sì.* This I heard. But he was a handsome man, and they say
Lady Faith is a lovely woman. Perhaps she was a credit to him?"

Around the sweetmeat her friend uttered a disparaging snort.
"If he thought so, he hid it well! More than a little bit of a
rascal with the ladies was Kendrick Vespa."

"Ah, but this, it is sad. The poor wife abandoned in the
country alone and unwanted."

The dowager roared. *"Here, lads!"* and hurled two sweetmeats to the far end of the room.

Lady Francesca gave a gasp as a greyhound leapt across her knees. There was a cacophony of barking, scrambling claws, yelps, growls and more warfare. Nobody's fool, the golden spaniel sprang instead onto his owner's lap, or what might be assumed to be her lap. Mrs. Hughes-Dering caught him as he slithered down the slope. "Mummy's little rogue," she cooed, kissing him fondly, and then bellowed, "Elise!"

The maid hurried in, waving biscuits. The canine contingent followed their Pied Piper as though they'd not been fed for several days, even the spaniel abandoning his mistress. "Are they not the dearest creatures?" gushed Mrs. Hughes-Dering. "But they do love Mummy's treats, and I mustn't let myself spoil the little pets. Now—what were we saying?"

"Lady Vespa. Such a sad fate. I feeling for her." The duchess raised her brows enquiringly. "Unless . . . ?"

Mrs. Hughes-Dering giggled. "Oh, yes. There were some of those!"

"Is so? How much of a secret this was, for never did I hear of it. Do you say there was more than one—ah—"

"Side-door lover? Indeed there was, not that many knew of it."

"But you did, clever one!" Pulling her chair closer, Lady Francesca said avidly, "Living as we do in the country, I never hear such stories of romance. Do tell me—ah, but I am silly and these happenings of so long ago you will be forgetting, or perhaps you did not know *who* were these side-door peoples."

It was a challenge no dedicated gossip could refuse. Mrs. Monica Hughes-Dering sat straighter and said, "I *never* forget the *affaires* of the *ton!* Now, let me see. . . ."

Four

The gracious house that sprawled along the banks of the Thames near Richmond had been quiet for weeks but today it hummed with activity. The butler, Obadiah Rennett, had set maids to bustling about with dusters and towels, and bed linen; the fireboy had awoken a fine blaze on the drawing room hearth and was now preparing another in Captain Vespa's bedchamber (Mr. Rennett having been advised that the captain would not move into the suite his late father had occupied); the chef sang happily in his kitchen; and everyone's spirits were lifted because at last the young master had come home.

Not since early summer had John Vespa set foot in this house, and no one could have been happier than the butler when the captain's post-chaise pulled onto the drivepath and he came limping up the front steps. He was unaccompanied, which meant this would be a brief visit. Rennett, who had served the family for most of his life, stifled a sigh and ordered a lackey to collect the Captain's valise, while the first footman was sent scurrying upstairs to serve as temporary valet.

Mr. Rennett had been fond of both sons of the house, and had often marvelled at their mutual devotion, for they were in his opinion very different articles. Mr. Sherborne had been the heir, of course, as handsome as his sire, full of fun and always ready for any prank or escapade no matter how outrageous. It could not be denied that there had been the trace of a 'wild kick in his gallop,' as the saying went, which had displeased Sir Kendrick Vespa, yet a more unaffected and good-natured youth would have been hard to find.

When Sherborne had bought a pair of colours and dazzled everyone with his splendid uniform before rushing off to join a crack Hussar regiment, Rennett had wished him well, and prayed his brother would not follow, for despite the affection in which he held Sherborne, it was Master John for whom the butler would have put his hand in the fire. John had followed, however, and the butler, waiting and worrying, had scanned every edition of the newspapers and trembled over the casualty lists. It had grieved his faithful heart when Sherborne had fallen, and he had grieved even more deeply when John had been brought home a year later, such a shadow of his former self.

It had been a bitter disappointment when the young soldier had elected to live not in London or Richmond, but in the lonely old ruin he'd inherited in Dorsetshire. Today, after one look at Master John's face (he *must* think of him as Sir John now!) the butler guessed the reason behind the prolonged absence, and the lack of mourning dress. The devoted young man was obviously clinging to the hope that Sir Kendrick had managed to survive and would be miraculously found alive somewhere downriver.

'A forlorn hope, poor lad,' thought Mr. Rennett, carrying a tray of decanters and glasses into the drawing room. He glanced about to see if everything was in readiness and swung around when he heard the door close behind him.

Corporal bounced across the thick rug, wagged his tail at the butler and took possession of the warmest spot before the hearth.

Vespa said with a smile, "Everything to your satisfaction, Rennett?"

"We all want to please you, Sir John, and—" There was a slight flinch and an involuntary movement of the master's hand, and Rennett knew he had not pleased. He wouldn't make that mistake again! He said hesitantly, "The staff and I— That is, I am sure you will know, Captain, how deeply we all sympathize with your loss."

"Yes. And I am most grateful." Vespa selected a fireside chair, trying not to see Sir Kendrick sitting in it. "Be so good as to pour me a cognac. Thank you. And now pour one for yourself and come and sit down. I want to talk to you."

Rennett's heart sank. Captain John was going to close this house. He was about to be told to dismiss the staff. He poured a small measure of Madeira and walked to a straight-backed chair.

"No, not there. Over here, man. And for mercy's sake don't sit on the edge as if you cringed before a tyrannical despot." The familiar and endearing smile was slanted at him, and his employer asked, "I'm not one—am I?"

"By no means, sir." Rennett leaned back and waited.

"This—chat must be of a most confidential nature, Obadiah."

'Obadiah!' Mr. Rennett's troubled heart gave a leap. "Of course, sir. If there is *any* way in which I may be of help? Is it about Sir Kendrick's death?"

"Yes. The authorities suspect that there was a—a sort of conspiracy. And I am trying to discover if my—father had any enemies."

The butler's honest eyes widened.

Vespa said hurriedly. "I know there may have been resentments, especially of late years, connected with his various romantic—er, entanglements. But we believe it goes farther back than that. Much farther back."

Thinking a great deal, the butler said with marked hesitation, "Sir—it is not my place to— Perhaps Lady Faith, or Sir Reginald Wansdyke . . ."

"I'm asking you to compromise your high principles, I know. But you see we cannot wait for my mother to come home. To say truth, we've not even heard from her as yet. Sir Reginald was—disturbed by my questions and I'm afraid he's of the opinion I am more than a touch cork-brained." Vespa smiled ruefully. "So I've come to you. I think we have always been friends?"

"I would not presume to—"

"Oh, for heaven's sake!" His patience wearing thin, Vespa exclaimed, "You're a man and I'm a man, and only an accident of birth prevents you being the master of this house and me the butler! Speaking of which, you'll never know how much I needed you in Dorsetshire, Obadiah. I apprehend it's the last place you would want to live, but—"

In an unprecedented interruption, Rennett said fervently, "I would go anywhere with you, Master John!" For just an instant the enigmatic eyes lit up, and the face of this man Sherry had laughingly referred to as 'Mr. Aloof' betrayed a depth of affection that astonished his employer. The butler looked down and a shy flush stained his cheeks.

Touched, Vespa said, "How very good of you. Then will you

help me? I understand and commend your reticence, but this is of the utmost importance, and it is vital to me that you speak frankly."

"In that case, sir, yes, I know Sir Kendrick made enemies. As you say, he was very popular with the ladies, and there were gentlemen—several gentlemen—who resented his—ah, conquests. But none I'd judge so distressed as to resort to violence."

"Then let's try another tack. Do you recall anyone whom Sir Kendrick particularly disliked? I mean *really* disliked. Perhaps long before I was born."

The butler blinked. "I'm afraid I'll be of small help there, Master John— Oh, your pardon! I keep calling you that, when I should say—"

"It's quite all right. You called me that for years. Just don't fling my title at me, if you please. I imagine it is difficult for you to remember what took place a quarter century ago."

"It's not that I cannot recall, sir. The thing is that I wasn't the butler in those days. Mr. Clipstone was still alive, and I was an under-footman, in which position I wasn't privy to—er—"

"To family secrets? Come now, Obadiah. Surely you'd have heard a few pieces of gossip; in the Hall, at least."

The butler met the whimsical grin that was levelled at him, and grinned in return. "Well, I'll have to think back, sir. Let me see now. . . . When Sir Kendrick and Lady Faith first married there were—there always are, you know—those who didn't exactly—ah, smile on the union. One gentleman I do recall was a Mr. . . . now what was his name . . . ? Dilworth! That's it. Very much enamoured of Lady Faith, he was, and even after the wedding he would send her odes and tragic poems and great bouquets of flowers. Sir Kendrick thought it hilarious."

"Whatever became of him, do you know?"

"Yes, indeed. He acceded to his uncle's dignities and became Lord somebody or other. I don't recall the exact title. Perhaps because he enjoyed it for so short a time. He bought himself a yacht. It sank on its maiden voyage, alas."

"With the new lord?"

"Unfortunately so."

Persevering, Vespa coaxed from the butler the identities of several other gallants who had aspired to Lady Faith's hand. One had since passed away, another had been killed during the retreat from Corunna. Rennett was aware of none who had suffered a broken heart or harboured a particular grudge, and to the best of his knowledge most had eventually married other ladies.

Stifling his disappointment, Vespa asked, "What about different forms of enmity? Political or economic strife, for instance. Do you remember anything of that nature? Anyone who might have seriously crossed swords with Sir Kendrick?"

Rennett racked his brains, but without success. Vespa called for their glasses to be refilled and changed the subject, and for an hour the two men chatted like old friends. The afternoon was fading to dusk when the butler stood and began to light candles. "I do wish I could be of more help, sir," he said regretfully. "I'm afraid, if you'll forgive my saying so, Sir Kendrick had such charm, he could win over the most angry men." He paused, frowning at the taper in his hand. "When he really cared to," he added slowly.

There was no more to be had from him; at least, for the moment. Vespa tried not to be downcast, enjoyed an excellent meal, sent his compliments to the Chef and, having leafed through several newspapers, went up to bed.

It had been a long day and he was tired, but Corporal was obviously uneasy in these strange surroundings, so he allowed the dog to come into the room and having commanded sternly that he stay on the bedside rug, fell asleep almost at once. He was awoken by a warning bark and a knock at the door. After the fashion of men who have slept under constant threat of attack, he was at once wide awake.

In answer to his call, a night-capped head, lit by the glow of a candle, loomed around the door. Corporal wagged his tail and accepted a caress.

Rennett said eagerly, "Sir, forgive, but I have remembered something. It's just a small thing, and likely of no help, but I thought I should tell you for fear I forget it by morning."

"Come in, man," commanded Vespa, sitting up. "You've remembered one of my mother's admirers, is that the case?"

The butler hurried in and closed the door. "No, sir," he said, advancing to stand beside the bed. "And, alas, my poor brain won't give me the gentleman's name. He may be dead now. But I remember being awed at the time, because our chef said that if ever there was a man Sir Kendrick detested, it was him, and that sure as check it would someday come to pistols at dawn for them! I never saw the gentleman, and I'd have forgot

all about him, except that Mr. Clipstone was such a great one
for fussy little details, and he asked Chef if he'd noticed that
the gentleman's name had an interesting feature."

Vespa asked intensely, "You mean he was foreign?"

Rennett hesitated. "He may have been, sir. Mr. Clipstone
pointed out that the gentleman had the same two letters in
both his first and last names. Next to each other, if you take
my meaning."

"You mean, if, for instance, his first name was Philip, and
his surname Milbank—the 'il' would be in sequence in both
cases?"

"That's it, sir. I only wish I'd paid more heed, but—it was so
long ago, and I was young and empty-headed."

Vespa said he'd done splendidly, and might have provided
an important clue, and the butler left, beaming.

Disappointed, Vespa lay back and stared at the ceiling. For
a moment, he'd really entertained high hopes, but for all his
efforts he seemed to be getting nowhere. Perhaps he never
would discover his real identity, which would surely spell the
ruin of his hopes. He sighed, which was a mistake because it
alarmed Corporal who at once jumped onto the bed to console
him. It was several minutes before Vespa was able to reassure
the consoler and when he at last fell asleep it was with Corporal—having taken flagrant advantage of the situation—snuggled
close against his feet.

Lady Francesca surveyed the magnificent tapestry that hung
on one wall of the large drawing room, and nodded her approval. She proceeded to wander from the massive and elabo-
rately carven stone chimney-piece, to the great bow windows
that overlooked the back gardens of Vespa House. The marble
statue of Venus and the jade collection on an inlaid table were
viewed critically.

Consuela asked, "Well, Grandmama?"

"Is a fine *casa*, this." The duchess turned to Vespa who hurried to join them. "You will be foolish not to dwell here when
you are in London, my Captain."

He bowed over her hand. "You know I cannot, ma'am."
Crossing to Consuela, his eyes were a caress. "Forgive. The
roads are all mud, and my coach was delayed."

Consuela surrendered her hand and said softly, "I am only

glad you've come home, but I was surprised that you wished to meet here. This is difficult for you."

Difficult . . . Every room, every piece of furniture, even the smell of beeswax and burning coal, held memories of the brother he'd loved and the father who had made devotion into a savage mockery. He said quietly, "Yes. But we have things to discuss, and we must be private. Have Toby and Paige been here?"

"We are now, my pippin!" Tobias Broderick came briskly into the room, bowed to the ladies and went over to the hearth to make a fuss of Corporal, while complaining of the 'beastly cold wind.'

Paige Manderville followed, paying his respects with his customary easy grace and stunning them all with the splendour of a dark purple coat and lavender pantaloons that would have been vulgar on anyone else, but merely enhanced his good looks.

Under the supervision of Rennett, who had accompanied his master from Richmond, two laden trays were carried in. Corporal's attempt to investigate the feast was circumvented, and with a ceremony that amused them all the butler produced a likely looking bone and lured the dog to the kitchens.

"Well," said Vespa hopefully, as plates and mugs of hot chocolate were distributed. "Has anyone been lucky?"

Manderville exclaimed, "Custard tarts! Egad, but I adore custard tarts! You go first, Toby."

Shaking his head, Broderick looked glum and begged that his news come last.

Consuela sprang up, clapping her hands and almost oversetting a tray. "Oh, I cannot wait! Grandmama has been so clever, and has found out—"

"These tells they are *my* tellings!" protested the duchess indignantly. "Sit down, *bambina,* and try to behaving *correttamente!* So. *Now,* we proceed. I, Captain Jack, upon your behoofs, have visit my sometimes friend, Mrs. Monica Hughes-Dering, the queen of gossip, who has, I will say it, become *gross!* How this woman she can allow herself such a great stomach— But—that is neither heres nor theres. She knows *everything,* my dears, about *everyone!"*

Laughing, Manderville said, "Quite true. You went to the proper fountain, my lady, obese or no."

Broderick protested, "No, really, Paige! You cannot scramble syntax in so haphazard a way! I think you mean a well, not a fountain. And how could either be obese?"

"Oh, I don't know, old lad. I've heard there's a fall of waters in the New World that is enormously wide, much like the duchess' friend, so—"

Vespa interrupted impatiently, "Do you say, ma'am, that the lady remembers someone who was particularly enamoured of my mother?"

"No. But—from her I have one little thing learned. If we put it with another little thing, and then some other little thing . . . Who can say?"

"You can," said Consuela, frustrated.

"It is," resumed the duchess with a lofty gesture, "that this *grande dame* of the *ton* have boast and brag of her so *eccelente* memory, but when we put it to the test, pouff! Away it has go!"

"Memory is a fascinating area of study." The learned Broderick appropriated a custard tart and waved it about to emphasize his remarks. "Actually, even today little is known about it, though Aristotle was most interested in concepts formed by reason evolving from sensations which produce memory, and—"

"Unfair!" cried Manderville. "Unfair! We gave you first chance to take the floor, and you refused. So have the goodness to cease your lecturing!"

Vespa said through gritted teeth, "In about one second I'll strangle the pair of you! My lady, are we to understand that the—er, 'Queen of Gossip' had none to impart?"

"But of course she did! She was fairly bubbling over with it! To sort the 'meat from the staff' or whatever this saying is, I learned only one item that is of interest to us. Your Papa—and I mean Sir Kendrick, dear Captain Jack—he had the enemy. The bitter enemy."

"Rennett said as much." Vespa leaned forward. "Was this to do with my mother? Could Mrs. Hughes-Dering name the man?"

"No, and no. It was to do with behaviours. Politics. Ideals—or the lack of them!"

"Ah! Rennett said matters between Sir Kendrick and one gentleman were so strained that a duel was imminent. This sounds a likely customer. Could the lady tell you nothing at all of him? Is he still alive?"

"This she did not know, for the person was outside of England a good deal. Mrs. Hughes-Dering say he had an estate—in Suffolk, she thought, and a castle somewhere, but not in England. And that he lived in those places, when he was not hunting."

"Jove, ma'am!" said Vespa, delighted. "You've done wonderfully!"

Manderville dusted crumbs from his knees and murmured, "What does he hunt? Fox? Wild boar? Stag?"

"Let me tell them, *please*, Grandmama!" begged Consuela. "For it is not important, and so very funny." Receiving a resigned nod from the duchess, she said, her eyes sparkling, "He hunts—*rugs!* Is it not the strangest hobby?"

"*Rugs?*" Manderville shook his head. "Sounds as if he has a vacancy in the upper storey, Jack!"

"Some rugs can be valuable," pointed out Broderick. "In fact—"

"Desist, for mercy's sake," groaned Manderville. "A lecture on rug-making we do not need. What we've to do now is try to put it all together as Lady Francesca said, and see what we've got—do you agree, Captain, sir?"

"I do, but I must tell you first how grateful I am for all the time you've spent, trying to help me."

"Why not?" said Manderville. "We enjoy your hospitality."

Broderick declared, "I don't. Not for much longer, at all events. Been recalled. I was at the Horse Guards this morning, and the doctors say I'm perfectly fit again."

Consuela and the duchess greeted this news with mixed feelings, but Vespa said heartily, "Congratulations! That's good news indeed. Are you for France, then?"

"Next week. I'm pleased, of course, but I don't much like leaving you in the middle of this bog."

"You may be *à l'aise,*" said Manderville. "I shall stand by Jack, staunch and true, as ever. The Army won't have me yet." He moved his arm tentatively. "Shoulder. Still stiff, y'know. And I shall now contribute my *soupçon* of information, which really tells us nothing, yet says a good deal, I think. While Toby was ensconced with the medical monsters, I called in at Bow Street again. You will be interested to learn, Jack, that there is no record of any street brawl the night before last involving your esteemed self; that there was no murder done in London Town; and that Colonel the Honourable Hastings Adair has not set foot on British soil for the last six weeks, at least. In other

words, friends, Romans and so forth, something very sticky is
afoot, and Consuela's colonel is up to his ears in the glue."

Vespa nodded. "Not much doubt of that. Certainly, they
don't want us sticking our noses in whatever it is. Well, at least
we tried to help Adair."

"Who is not *my* colonel," murmured Consuela pertly.

Vespa smiled at her, and went on: "Then we shall leave him
to his own devices and do as Paige suggested. Please interrupt
if you think of something I've overlooked. It seems to me that
the most likely candidate we've found thus far is a gentleman
much disliked by Sir Kendrick, and who is out of the country
a good deal of the time. We have several clues to his identity.
One is that both his first and last names contain the same two
letters in succession. Also, we believe he may have an estate in
Suffolk. And, lastly, his hobby is to hunt—rugs. Not a great
deal, I admit. But it's a start."

Broderick pointed out. "Your surest route would be to sail
at once for South America and try to wheedle the truth out of
Lady Faith."

"Oh, absolutely. But the courier my great-uncle despatched
must surely reach my mother long before I could get there,
and she may well decide to return at once. There is the risk
that if I now sail, our ships may pass each other in midocean,
and"—he met Consuela's eyes steadily—"it would take a year,
at least. I think I do not want to wait that long."

Consuela blushed, and there was a small silence.

Lady Francesca, who had been frowning at Manderville's purple coat, said suddenly, "I cannot like that colour, and I have
find something we forget, Captain Jack. It is the castle. Did not
your man tell you this same gentleman have a castle somewhere?"

"Yes. But he didn't know where, save that it was not in England."

"Still, it's a help," said Broderick. "We can go into Suffolk
and enquire for a landed local gentleman who also owns a castle
that may or may not be in the British Isles."

"Oh, oh!" cried Consuela happily. "We *are* making progress!
And if the castle chances to be *somewhere* in Britain: Wales, for
instance, or Scotland, it would . . ." She stopped suddenly, her
widening eyes flying to Vespa's face.

Lady Francesca demanded, "What is it? What is it? Never

become mute and stiff like the stockfish! If you have thinking of somethings, speak up, Meadowlark!"

Consuela moved hesitantly to stand before Vespa. He stood at once, and she touched his arm and murmured, "I am sorry to speak of that terrible time. I know you don't like to think of it."

His nerves tightened into knots, but he put a hand over hers and said, "Do you mean when we were down in the quarry? It's all right, Consuela. Tell me, please."

She closed her eyes for a second and could see again that dismal mine tunnel, and Sir Kendrick, pistol in hand, so cruelly taunting his son. She shivered, and looked up quickly. "He said," she blurted out in a rush, "Sir Kendrick said something about your having a stubborn Scots streak in your make-up."

Vespa muttered, " 'Miserably dogged Scots streak' were his words, as I recall."

"He *did* say it?" Broderick asked intensely. "You're sure?"

With a travesty of a smile, Vespa said, "Do you suppose I could ever forget that moment?"

"I have to admit he was right," said Manderville. "No offence, dear boy, but you *are* stubborn, you know, and—"

"Very true," agreed Broderick. "Thing is—have you also—"

"Or have the Wansdykes—" interrupted the duchess.

"Any Scots on the family tree?" finished Consuela, breathless with excitement.

Vespa stared from one expectant face to the next. "I know there are no Scots among the Vespa's. I'm not . . . not sure—" He gave an exultant shout. *"No!* I *am* sure! My grandfather, Sir Rupert Wansdyke, was a great one for tradition. Several times when Sherry and I were schoolboys he dragged us through the picture gallery in Wansdyke House and gave us a small lecture on each ancestor. We thought it deadly dull. But I remember that he said they all were of Saxon heritage, most having been born and bred in the Southland, and that not until his daughter—my mother—married a man of Norman origins had anyone from so far afield been brought into the family!" Jubilant, he seized Consuela and swung her around. "Clever, clever one! You've found the best clue of all! My father must have been a Scot!" He gave her a smacking kiss on the cheek. "Thank you! Thank you!"

Lady Francesca screamed and pounded him with her little fists, demanding that he 'unhand' her granddaughter at once, and when he did so, threw her arms around him and collected a kiss of her own.

Manderville and Broderick came to clap him on the back and share his triumph.

Broderick said enthusiastically, "Your puzzle is as good as solved, old fellow! We'll go up to Suffolk at once, and if we can't track down a gentleman who owns an estate somewhere in the county, besides having a castle in Scotland—why, I'm a Dutchman!"

"This, it is so?" asked the duchess, misunderstanding, but beaming at him. "And I am the Italian, and my Consuela is a bit of this and a bit of that, and Jack may be half a Scot." She turned to Manderville. "You, dear Lieutenant Paige, it looks like is the only true Englishman of us all!"

He laughed. "And my many greats-Grandpapa ran afoul of Charles of Anjou in 1257 and had to leave Marseilles or lose his head, so I'm likely as mixed as the rest of you!"

His heart lighter than it had been for weeks, Vespa summoned Rennett and ordered champagne, and they all drank to Suffolk and success.

And never dreamed that Suffolk was just the beginning.

Five

Although a pale winter sun broke through the clouds, the wind that swept in from the North Sea had an icy bite. Vespa drew the collar of his riding coat higher, glanced back along the winding lane, and whistled. Bright-eyed and ears flying, mud on the end of his nose, Corporal scampered from investigating a burrow.

"Keep up, you little scoundrel," called Vespa, and turned his hired grey horse to the west once more.

He had spent three fruitless days scouring the Ipswich area. Friendly inn-keepers, waiters, parlour-maids, blacksmiths, shop-keepers, a cobbler, two muffin-men, a pedlar, a fisherman and a constable had each been only too willing to pass the time of day over a tankard of ale or a cup of tea, but no one knew of any local land-owner who also owned a Scottish castle and was away a good deal of the time. He could only hope that Toby Broderick, investigating Bury St. Edmunds, and Manderville, prowling the area around Stowmarket, had been more success-ful.

In this eastern edge of Suffolk the roads were not as travelled as those in the Home Counties, nor the houses as numerous, but the villages were charming and the country folk kindly. The land was low for the most part, but not flat, rising into occa-sional gently rolling hills. On this bright morning Vespa fol-lowed a lane that was lined by thorn hedges and trees. It would have been deeply shaded during the summer months, but today most of the trees lifted obligingly naked branches that did not shut out the welcome December sunshine. He came to the crest of a rise dignified by an impressive flush-flint and stone church, and as he rode down the slope he entered what was more a

town than another village: a prosperous wool town by the look
of the people and carts bustling about.

He raised his hat to a lady and a little girl passing by in an
open carriage. The lady looked away, and the child stared un-
smilingly. He was accorded the same treatment when he nodded
to two men loading a cart outside a mercantile warehouse, and
an old gentleman in smock and gaiters positively glared at him.
It was the first time he'd encountered an unfriendliness that
bordered on the hostile. The folk hereabouts appeared to have
a distrust of strangers; possibly they took him for a Riding Officer—certainly smuggling was widely practiced along this coast.

Corporal raced past, his little legs flying. Vespa caught a whiff
of woodsmoke and cooking; a laden waggon rumbled by, the
waggonner scanning him with cold suspicion. 'Brrr!' thought
Vespa, and wondered whether the proprietor of the whitewashed inn up ahead would deign to serve him luncheon. The
street dipped into a watersplash through which the grey horse
trod daintily. Corporal had been obliged to swim across and as
the street turned uphill once more he trotted towards a pump,
at which point he paused and looked back for his master.

A young gentleman stood beside the trough, watering his
mount. Vespa's glance flickered over the high-crowned hat
tilted at a rakish angle, the fashionable riding coat and leathers,
the gleaming boots and long-necked spurs, and came to rest
on the tall chestnut horse. It was a handsome thoroughbred
with a glossy coat and a long and waving mane and tail. It was
also, in his opinion, a shade short in the back and too much
inclined to twitch and dance about. 'All nerves and show,' he
judged.

It was then that Corporal decided to shake himself.

For a small dog the amount of displaced water was remarkable. The young exquisite was liberally showered. He sprang
aside and collided with his nervous mount which promptly shot
into the air as if levitated, sending its owner into an ungainly
sprawl. The elegant wet garments became muddy wet garments.

Noting from the corner of his eye that several grinning pas-
sers-by had stopped to watch, Vespa rode up and dismounted.
"I'm so sorry," he began, limping to the rescue.

The victim fairly sprang to his feet. His well-cut features were
scarlet and twisted with wrath. Cursing, he aimed one of his
glossy boots at Corporal. "Damned little *cur!*" he howled.

"Hey!" Vespa's helping hand became a firm tug and the kick landed only glancingly.

"Is that—that apology for a dog—yours?" roared the victim.

As cool as the other man was enraged, Vespa drawled, "I see only an apology for a gentleman."

Somebody hooted.

The dandy's bloodshot eyes narrowed. His heavy riding whip flailed at Vespa's head.

A lithe sway, an iron grip and a heave, and the infuriated young man was flat on his back again.

"Cross-buttocked!" howled an exultant voice. "Limp or no, he cross-buttocked him, by grab!"

"Neat as ever I did see," confirmed another.

Vespa turned to take up the reins of his grey, and Corporal scuttled quickly to his side. Vespa bent to inspect him, but the little dog didn't seem badly damaged.

" 'Ware, sir!"

He straightened at the warning yell. The dandy had regained his feet and although he tended to sway, was lunging into another attack. Growling ferociously, Corporal charged forward and got a good grip on a now considerably less glossy boot.

"Confound the—mangy cur!" The young man's hand plunged into the pocket of his riding coat and emerged holding a small pistol.

"Corporal—*up!*" said Vespa sharply.

The dog released the boot. The pistol shot reverberated in the small valley of the street, and Corporal flew into Vespa's arms.

A small crowd had gathered. There were shrill screams, cries of "Shame!" and "Play fair!"

A matron wearing a splendidly laced cap cried, *"Disgraceful* behavior! To try and kill a poor little doggie!"

"You're damned lucky I didn't hit you, fellow! Whoever you are," advised the dandy rather thickly, and with an uneasy glance around the ring of condemning faces.

Vespa set Corporal down. "If I weren't particular about my acquaintanceships, I'd give you my card." He took out his purse. "Your aim is as uncontrolled as your temper. But since my dog did dampen you a trifle, I'll pay for your garments to be cleaned." He tossed a half-crown contemptuously, and was mildly surprised when this unpleasant but undoubtedly aristocratic individual caught it with a quick snatch.

A ripple of scorn went up from the onlookers.

The dandy said ungraciously, "It's a small part of what you owe me. If you weren't—were not—crippled, I'd call—you out! Be damned if I—'f I wouldn't."

"You'd not get me out," said Vespa. "I only fight gentlemen, and never when they're 'up in the world.' "

Again, the reddened eyes were lit with rage. "I'm not drunk, d-damn you!"

"Go home!" shouted a youthful voice from the edge of the crowd, and other voices were raised:

"You ain't welcome here, Mr. Keith!"

"Go back to the 'big smoke'!"

"Maybe we should show 'un the way, mates!"

"Aye! At the tail of a cart!"

'Mr. Keith' glared at them, but it was clear their antagonism was growing. He swung into the saddle and wheeled his mount so hard that Vespa was almost caught by the chestnut's plunging head. With a snarled threat to 'have the law on the l-lot of you yokels,' the ill-tempered dandy spurred to a gallop and beat an inglorious retreat.

Vespa, however, found himself surrounded by now-beaming faces. He was patted on the back, informed that "We took ye for Mr. Keith's friend, sir!" and was borne into the White Horse Inn very much the conquering hero.

The tap was a cheerful place, mellow with age, and ringing with talk and laughter. Vespa's limp was not mentioned again, but his tidy victory over the evidently much disliked Mr. Keith was a cause for celebration. A tankard of ale was pressed into his hand, and he was begged to reveal his identity.

Before he could respond, a deep voice shouted, "Jack Vespa! As I live and breathe!"

A bronzed young giant with unruly red hair, a black patch over one eye and a broad grin pushed his way through the throng, and swept Vespa into a crushing hug.

"Calloway!" gasped Vespa. "Let be, you old warhorse before my ribs are powder! I thought you were dead! What the deuce are you doing up here?"

Lieutenant Sean Calloway, late of the 71st Highlanders, roared a laugh that rattled the casements. "Farming, Captain, sir! And if it's any consolation, I was *sure* you were dead!" In response to shouts of enquiry, he turned to the gathering and introduced "Captain Jack Vespa, who was an aide-de-camp to Lord Wellington."

Vespa's intent to remain incognito was foiled, but he could scarcely blame this old friend, and he reacted smilingly to the admiring and awed exclamations and the inevitable questions of the company until Calloway broke in to ask, "What the deuce have you done to have caused such a fuss in this quiet corner of England?"

"Cap'n knocked down that there Keith gent, Mr. Calloway, sir," supplied a very wizened old man. "Wanted doin' for ages'n ages. Cap'n done it. Tidy. Eh, lads?"

During the chorus of agreement, Vespa gathered that 'Young Mr. Keith' was 'proper high-in-the-instep,' that he had 'too much Lun'on in his ways,' and ordered folk about 'like we was dirt under his feet.'

Calloway laughed. "If that ain't just like you, Jack! Always up to your neck in some kind of imbroglio! Come over here and sit down, I want to know what you've been about since Vitoria. I got my come-uppance at that little rumpus, as you see."

"Yes. It must be a beastly nuisance for you."

"Oh, well. I'm alive, which is more than you could say for a lot of my poor fellows. Or for that fine brother of yours, eh? You must miss him."

Vespa stared rather fixedly at his tankard, then said quietly, "Very much. We're the lucky ones, Sean, even if you don't see quite as well nowadays, and I don't run quite as fast."

They adjourned to an inglenook by the blazing fire and for a little while enjoyed mutual recollections of their army days and the comrades they'd served beside. The local people relived and chuckled over the morning's encounter, the name 'Keith' being bandied about frequently. Vespa asked at length, "Who is this fellow who's made himself so unwelcome here?"

"Be dashed if I know. I'm fairly new to the county. My mama inherited a small farm here and has been good enough to hand it over to me. She thought I'd soon tire of it, I suspect, but I'm not a Town beau, and country life suits me. I did hear that Keith has a boat moored somewhere along the coast. Don't know if it's truth, but if it is he likely runs tubs or such-like and passes through here en route back to London. He's no local, that's certain."

"Know most of the locals, do you?"

"Most." The solitary blue eye slanted at Vespa shrewdly. "Why?"

"I'm trying to locate a gentleman. I understand he has an

estate in the country, but the devil's in it that I don't know his name." Calloway stared, and he added, "It's a commission my mother sent me just before she sailed for South America. Unfortunately, her letter was rain-damaged and all I have is a most urgent message for the old fellow. I feel I have to try to deliver it, but I've little to go on."

"Gad! Your best chance, surely, would be to contact some of the local squires, or the clergy."

"It would, of course. But—well, to say truth, Sean, the matter's of a rather delicate nature, and . . ." Vespa shrugged.

"Ah. Family business, eh? Well, I wish I could give you an assist. Have you no other description at all?"

"Only that he also owns a castle in Scotland."

Calloway scratched his red head and frowned thoughtfully. "A castle in Scotland . . . hmm. Now what did I hear about . . . ? I know! It was my great-aunt! You don't know the lady, I think. Gad, what a chatterbox! Kindest heart in the world, mind you, but— Well, at all events, she was rattling on to my father about an old friend whom she and my great-uncle used to visit at one time. She was enormously impressed by his estate, which is up near the Cambridgeshire border. Delightful place, to hear her tell it, and with a superb rose garden. There was some sort of family trouble years ago, and the gentleman sort of dropped out of sight. Sounds to me as if he's short of a sheet. Hardly ever in England. I'm sure my aunt said he has a place in Scotland, but whether it's a castle or not, I couldn't tell you."

Jubilant, Vespa exclaimed, "It sounds very promising, Sean! Why do you say he's short of a sheet?"

"Well, it seems he don't spend much time in Scotland, either. Two jolly fine homes, and what must he do but waste his life flitting about the world searching for a mythical rug or some crazy thing. Poor old fellow must be in his dotage, or—"

"That's *him!*" cried Vespa, giving his friend a clap on the back that rattled his teeth. "You've found him for me, bless your clever old red nob! Do you recall his name? Or the name of his estate? Is he a Scot, d'you think?"

Calloway pushed him away and said with mock indignation, "Easy, you madman! I'm a feeble invalid yet! Devil if I know whether he's a Scot, though my great-aunt is, and I'd think she would have mentioned it if he were. Name's—um . . . Cragburn or Kincarry—something like that. Don't remember what his estate's called, but oddly enough the name of the carpet he's after stuck in my mind. It's called the Khusraw. Some Eastern fairy tale, probably. I say, is this your dog? What a nice little chap, but he looks hungry. Don't you ever feed him, you flintheart?"

Vespa laughed. "I suppose you're hinting for me to buy you lunch?"

"I suppose I am."

Vespa did; in fact he bought lunch for everyone in the tap.

A drop of rain fell coldly on her nose. Consuela halted and looked up. The clouds were pulling together now, the occasional glimpses of sunlight becoming less frequent. She had left the cottage to escape her grandmother. A large bunch of hot-house roses had been delivered to the duchess this morning; a gift ordered before his departure by Colonel Adair. Not one to let the grass grow under his feet was Hasty Adair, and knew which side his bread was buttered on. Predictably, the old lady had gone into raptures, singing the colonel's praises and envying the "lucky girl" who would become his bride, until Consuela had been driven to retaliate. A heated Italianate argument had ensued, and refusing the company of her maid, who suffered loudly from corns, Consuela had ventured alone into the chilly early afternoon.

When she'd reached the Widow Davis' Grocery/Post-Office in Gallery-on-Tang there were three letters and a parcel for the duchess and two letters for herself. The widow loved to talk and had told her that Captain Vespa had quite a pile of correspondence waiting to be picked up by his steward, Hezekiah Strickley. One of the captain's letters, she imparted, was from G. L. Manderville, Esq. "That'll be Lieutenant Manderville's father, I do expect, Miss. Likely telling the captain how poor Sir Kendrick's dogs are going on in their new home. And there's another letter, very important it looks too. From the Horse Guards. Do you know when the captain will come home again, Miss Consuela? Such a fine gentleman, and I'm sure we're all sorry for the terrible happenings out at the quarry . . ."

She had launched into a lengthy monologue, during which Consuela chose some wools for a shawl she was embroidering for her grandmother's birthday. Mrs. Blackham, the constable's tall lady, had come in with her booming voice and a

long shopping list, and tucking her purchases and the mail
into her basket, Consuela had managed to escape. Outside,
she'd walked on, thinking wistfully of how she had first met
Jack and of their desperate efforts to uncover the truth of
her father's death. She was too lost in thought to notice that
her steps had turned instinctively towards the old manor, and
when the raindrop interrupted her musings she was mildly
surprised to find herself far past the village and on the Alabaster Royal estate road.

She wandered along slowly, taking note of how much Jack
had done to improve the property. The once pot-holed lane
was now a quite respectable road; the grasses of the wide park,
that had been a mass of weeds, were smoothly scythed, the yew
trees that lined the drivepath neatly trimmed, the overgrown
rose garden weeded and pruned. Her gaze went past the little
hump-backed bridge over the stream, to the manor itself. Alabaster Royal. Long, two-storied, its entrance flanked by the twin
round conical-topped towers that lent it an aura of strength
and invincibility. The exterior was bright with new paint, the
mullioned windows clean and sparkling even under the greying
skies. 'Dear old house,' she mused and with the thought heard
hoofbeats on the road behind her.

Hezekiah Strickley was probably exercising some of Jack's
horses, she decided, but on turning, saw that it was not the
rather cantankerous steward. Instead, a luxurious coach drawn
by four magnificent matched bays pulled up beside her. The
coachman was one of the biggest men she had ever seen; not
fat, but with a great spread of muscular shoulders and powerful hands that stretched the seams of his gauntlets. His hat
was pulled low over his face, and his head was downbent,
concealing his features. A window was lowered. An elegant
gentleman with dead-white skin and lank black hair, leaned
to smile at her.

"Good afternoon, my pretty," he said in a purring and
slightly accented voice. "Have you far to go? There will be rain
soon, I think."

Consuela thought indignantly, 'My *pretty?* How *dare* you address me so?' She was about to respond to his presumption
when two things occurred to her. Firstly, that there was something about this man and his strange coachman that made her
uneasy; and, secondly, that her windblown hair and the basket
she carried, in addition to the fact that she was unaccompanied,

had undoubtedly caused the creature to think she was a village lass. For no reason she could have explained, she bobbed a curtsy. "Good aft'noon, sir. I've just to go as far as the manor, if y'please."

"Then it is that you are a local girl," he said, with a flash of very white teeth, "and can be of assistance to me."

Consuela wondered if this was a French spy. Beginning to enjoy herself, she asked demurely, "How, milor'?"

He swung the door wide, and she drew back as he trod down the step. Goodness, but he was tall.

"There is not the need for alarm," he said. "It is that I have heard Sir John Vespa he seeks a friend of mine. I may be of help to him in this. Do you know if he is at home?"

She blinked at him. "Your friend, sir?"

"No, child. Sir John."

"I don't know, sir."

"But surely, if you are going to the manor you must know whether he is there."

"Oh, I know that, sir. There isn't no Sir John there. Just Captain Vespa, sir."

The black eyes widened a little. "Do you say he does not use his title?"

She wrinkled her brow and said with bovine density, "Most folks calls him Captain Jack, milor', be that what ye means?"

It seemed to her that suspicion came into those deep eyes. Perhaps she had overdone her little imposture. From the corner of her eyes she saw the coachman turn and glance at her. It was a brief glance, but enough to show her a face the like of which she'd never seen. The complexion was sallow, the eyes narrow slits sunk into features that might have been carven from stone.

The tall man's hand reached out, a shilling on the palm. "This is what you want, eh? And, me, I am only glad to pay you for a simple answer, pretty child. I will speak slow for you. Is—Captain—Vespa—at—home?"

"Oh. No, sir. He bean't."

"Ah. We progress. Would you know where he can be found, little cabbage? He will be most pleased to hear what I will say."

Consuela hesitated. Perhaps this odd individual did have news that would help Jack in his quest. Perhaps she could help by telling him that Jack was in Suffolk. And yet—the manor was no more than a half-mile distant. Surely the most natural course would be for the coach to simply drive to the front door. "I did hear summat," she murmured. "The groom said where the master goed. I think . . . he said Caernarvon—or were it? Car—summat."

"In *Wales?*" he exclaimed.

"Be it, sir? No! Cardiff! That's it! Can I have me shilling now?"

He muttered, "Cardiff. I wonder . . ." then tossed the shilling.

Consuela caught it, and like a striking snake his hand flashed out to close around her wrist. "Such a dainty hand," he purred. "One might think it never had scrubbed a floor or milked the cow."

The coachman slanted another piercing glance at her. Consuela was suddenly quite frightened, and she started when she heard another vehicle approaching.

"Miss Consuela! Oh, Miss Consuela!" Violet Manning was perched on the seat of the Widow Davis' delivery cart. "*Here* you are! The duchess is fairly *beside* herself, and desires you to come home at once!"

Consuela jerked her hand free.

Anger glinted in the eyes of the tall man. His lips smiled, but it was a mirthless smile that made her forget her vexation with Manning. He said, "I think you have the little game with me. Is it not so, miss? I do not care to be made sport of. And I cannot but wonder why you should be so devious. Perhaps, next time we meet, this I shall discover."

"Perhaps you will not then be so impertinent as to address me as 'your pretty,' " she riposted haughtily.

A frown, a curt inclination of the head. With a swirl of his dark cloak and a shout to his coachman, he was inside the coach. The door slammed, the team swung in a wide turn and raced away.

The slow-witted youth who now made deliveries for Mrs. Davis said haltingly, "Dicky-boy don't like that there genelman."

Manning, who had been temporarily bereft of speech, cried, "Goodness gracious me, Miss Consuela! Whatever were you *thinking* of to talk with such dreadful people? That coachman made me go gooseflesh all over!"

"He is Chinese, I think," said Consuela, still gazing after the rapidly disappearing coach. "I wonder what they really wanted with Captain Vespa."

The youth reiterated, "Dicky-boy don't like him. Nor his master, neither. Cap'n Jack he wouldn't have no friend like that one."

"I almost thought the gentleman was *threatening* you, miss," wailed Manning. "I vow, 'tis all of a piece! Wherever Captain Vespa goes, trouble follows! It would be so much better if you—"

"If you were to say no more," snapped Consuela.

The lone pedlar had been amiable enough, especially after Vespa had purchased a small cloth doll from him. The Inn of the Black Lamb was 'just t'other side of the village,' he'd said, adding, "Can't miss it. Jest keep going straight, sir." The drifting mist was thickening to fog and reducing visibility so that it had become necessary to ride cautiously along the rutted lane, and Vespa was beginning to wonder if he'd missed the village altogether. Manderville, who had a more than nodding acquaintanceship with Newmarket, had suggested the inn, saying he'd once stayed there during racing season when all the better posting houses had been full, and that it boasted clean beds and a good cook.

"I wonder he could find the confounded place," muttered Vespa. "Of all the hidden-away—"

The grey horse shied suddenly as a lad darted across the lane. With consummate horsemanship, Vespa kept his seat. Ghostly cottages loomed into view. They had reached the village, at last. He whistled and Corporal raced up, tongue lolling, only to stop abruptly and growl at some menacing object on the ground. "Come on," called Vespa, and reined around.

The inn sign hung from a rail extended over the lane. Vespa turned the grey into the yard, and a groom ran to take the reins and scream "House, ho!" in a high falsetto that sent the grey into another shy. Vespa swore and dismounted as a door opened sending a flood of light gleaming across the damp cobblestones.

"Welcome, sir," called the host, a big bluff individual, his ruddy features wreathed in a grin. "Ye'll be my captain guest. I knows ye by yer dog. What've ye got there, you little terror? His toy, is it, sir?"

Vespa's downward glance revealed that Corporal had retrieved something he'd not realized he had lost. He said with a grin, "I must have dropped it. Give it here, you scavenger. That's for little Molly Hawes. Much need you have for a doll!"

Having been advised that his friends awaited him in the parlour, he arranged for Corporal to be fed, then was shown up the narrow winding stairs to his room. It was a tiny but spotless chamber under the eaves, so low-roofed that he had to bow his head when he approached the latticed casement.

A rosy-cheeked maid carried up a ewer of hot water, and a lad hurried in with his valise. In short order he washed, brushed his hair, changed his neckcloth and went downstairs, his spirits rising as he breathed the heady scent of preparations for dinner.

He found the parlour, and his friends stretched out in chairs flanking a roaring fire.

Broderick stood to greet him heartily. "Thought you'd never get here, old lad. What's to do? Any luck?"

Manderville waved a tankard, and yawned. "Too tired to get up, *mon capitaine.* My efforts in your behalf have left me with a blistered heel and an unquenchable thirst."

"And that's all," appended Broderick, pulling up another chair. "He didn't learn a thing."

"Indeed, I did," argued Manderville indignantly. "There's a jug of ale on the sideboard yonder. We saved some for you, Jack."

Vespa filled a tankard, carried it to the fire and sank into the chair. The flames warmed his feet, the ale warmed his inside, and the loyalty of these good friends warmed his spirit. He leaned back, stretching out his long legs. "No luck, eh, Paige?"

"Some. Toby thinks he's bested me, but I doubt it."

Broderick said, "I know damned well I've bested you! All you achieved was to pick a fight with some poor fellow."

"Did you, though?" exclaimed Vespa. "What about?"

Manderville shrugged. "Nothing, really. I'd given up on the Stowmarket area and ridden east. I was making my little enquiries, polite as you please, to the most fruitful sources—"

"Namely—housemaids, dairymaids, nursemaids and pretty maids all in a row," inserted Broderick.

"Which is known as mixing business with pleasure," said Manderville with a grin. "At all events, this stupid dolt took exception. Called me a nosy foreigner, if you can credit it! I punched his head for him, I can tell you."

Amused, Vespa said, "One of your 'pleasures' was his, eh? These country-folk regard anyone from outside the county as foreign, and guard their women-folk from such threats as city men and especially from soldiers like us. You're lucky your 'stupid dolt' didn't come after you with a pitchfork."

"The devil!" exclaimed Manderville. "You make me sound a conscienceless libertine! I'll have you know, Captain sir, that I didn't touch the wench! And besides, he was no countryman. A slippery roué, more like, and didn't deserve her." He paused, looking thoughtful.

"Paige thinks he knows the chap from somewhere," said Broderick.

"Can't remember where." Manderville shook his handsome head and said that he must be getting old. "I've met him before, I'm sure of it. Oh, well. It'll come to me. Go on, Toby. Amaze our captain with your superior achievements."

Broderick leaned forward. "I think I may have solved your puzzle, Jack. Or part of it, at least. I discovered that there's a fellow named Lord Kincraig who owns an estate some distance from Bury St. Edmunds. It's said to be a fine property, but the old fellow travels extensively and is seldom there."

"Jolly well done!" cried Vespa. "Did you chance to learn his given name?"

"Curse me for an addlepate! I forgot to ask. The business of the two successive letters, eh?"

Vespa nodded. "Never mind. My grateful thanks to you both."

Manderville said aggrievedly, "Dash it all, Jack! I believe you already knew."

"Some. Not all. But when we put it together— Now why do you look so glum, Toby? To my mind, between us we've done splendidly."

"Yes. Well, there's just one thing, dear boy. Splendid or not, I think we'd best hope this old duck is *not* your sire. Tell him what else you turned up, Paige."

Manderville said, "His lordship is said to be touched in the upper works. Has some—er, very odd fancies. Sorry, but there it is. Did you turn up anything?"

"Yes, I rather think so. I ran into Sean Calloway in Kersey. D'you remember him? Big chap with red hair. Lieutenant. 71st Highlanders. Lost an eye at Vitoria, poor fellow. He knew of a mystery sort of absentee land-owner with an estate up

here somewhere. The gentleman is said to wander about
Europe collecting carpets, but he's hoping to find one in par-
ticular." He paused as his friends exchanged sombre glances.
"What now?"

Manderville answered reluctantly, "Then it must be the same
gentleman. Did Calloway tell you the old boy is after a *flying
carpet?*" He pursed his lips. "Not very promising, Jack."

"More like a fine case of senility," said Broderick.

"Or an artful dodger," murmured Vespa. They both stared
at him, and he went on: "Well, only think, if this man really is
a collector, he's probably too shrewd to go about advertising
what he's really seeking."

Manderville said dryly, "If he's seeking a flying carpet he'd
do well not to spread that about else he'll find himself in Bedlam with not so much as a dishcloth on the floor!"

"Very probably, but it would certainly prevent charlatans
from trying to foist off imitations or raise their prices when
he's in the vicinity, as they would if word got out that he's after
something very special."

Curious, Broderick asked, "I suppose Calloway had no more
details about this 'special' rug?"

"Only one. It has a name, apparently. I knew I wouldn't remember, so I asked Sean to write it down for me." Vespa tugged
a crumpled piece of paper from his pocket and passed it to his
friends.

Manderville glanced at the paper and remarked that it
sounded like a Polish name.

Broderick however took one look and was galvanized. "The
Khusraw Carpet? Lord save us all! Was Calloway quite sure of
the name?"

"He said his great-aunt told him, and that it had sort of stuck
in his mind. Why?"

"Then it's as we feared! I'm truly sorry, Jack, but this Kincraig
must be mad as a mangle!"

"Is this as bad as the flying-carpet business?"

"Practically. It's a legend almost, going back to about the
sixth century."

"Gad!" exclaimed Manderville. "The rug must be of better
quality than the one my grandmama bought! Hers is only about
fifty years old and already showing moth fang marks!"

"The Spring Carpet of Khusraw," said Broderick, fixing him
with a stern look, "is of Persian origin and was made for the

palace at Ctesiphon. It was said to have been designed to represent an elaborate garden complete with ornamental waters and pathways. And it had a religious significance, in that it also represented Paradise. By all accounts it was exquisitely beautiful, even apart from the fact that the 'dirt' was of woven gold, the border was of emeralds to resemble grass, and all the flowers and trees and what have you growing in the garden were of precious gems.''

Vespa said incredulously, "And people *walked* on this treasure?"

"I don't know about that," said Broderick. "But you're right about the treasure part. It's believed to have been the wealth of the nation, and to have made a profound impression on visiting potentates of the time."

"It would have made a profound impression on me, I can tell you!" Interested, Manderville lost his lazy drawl and asked, "How large was it? Ten by twelve inches?"

"I think it measured about eighty-some square feet."

"Good Lord!" exclaimed Vespa. "It must have been priceless! Even if Lord Kincraig found it, I shouldn't think anyone now living could afford to buy the thing!"

"Well, you're right, of course. It was seized when the Arabs defeated the Persians in the seventh century. They cut it up. The Caliph is said to have been awarded the largest piece, and after him, a few other notables. The balance was distributed among their warriors, and you may guess their shares were not large. Most of them sold their pieces, but even then they were valued at about a thousand pounds each. Fact is, we're talking about something that ceased to exist almost twelve centuries ago, Jack. If any of the segments could be traced today, which I very much doubt, they'd likely be found in museums or locked away in the vault of some sultan or princeling!"

"Why on earth would any rational man go hunting something that no longer exists?" muttered Vespa frowningly.

"Said it yourself, old lad," said Manderville, watching him with compassion. "Best give it up, Jack. Our long-lost lordling cannot be a rational man!"

Broderick shook his head and sighed. "Mad as a mangle! One thing, though. Monteil's lurking about. He's after something."

After a pause, Vespa said, "I suppose it's possible Lord Kincraig really is on the track of a remnant of the Spring Carpet?"

Manderville said, "Anything's possible, but take my advice, dear boy. Let's go home."

Six

Vespa and Manderville rode out alone next morning, Broderick having left them to visit his family prior to rejoining his regiment. The host of the Inn of the Black Lamb had contributed another piece to their puzzle, and they now had the name of Lord Kincraig's estate and clear directions as to its location.

The sky was white and the air frigid but Vespa was elated because he believed his search to be almost ended. East Anglia continued to impress him with its prosperous farms, large flocks of sheep and lush paddocks where thoroughbred horses grazed. "And I'd expected to encounter only desolate miles of fen and swampland," he told Manderville. "When you think that most of this is reclaimed land, it's a real achievement, don't you think?"

"Too flat for my liking," grumbled Manderville, shivering, "and too damp. Water everywhere!"

"It's not so flat as the Low Countries. And do you notice the light?"

Not at his best early in the morning, Manderville squinted about and observed that it was usually light by nine o'clock.

"But not this light. Everything seems so crystal clear. The Kincraig estates are well-named."

"Lambent Grove," said Manderville, and added cynically, "Let's hope it will shed some lambency on the whereabouts of your elusive rug merchant, since you *must* persist in this search for disillusion."

"Hold up a minute." Vespa drew the grey to a halt and dismounted, waiting for Corporal to catch up with them.

"He'd go along better if he didn't haul that stupid doll everywhere," grunted Manderville. "You should take it away from him."

"I did. Twice. But he manages to find it. It's in no condition to give to Molly now, so he may as well keep it."

Corporal arrived, puffing around the cherished toy that was firmly gripped between his jaws, and Vespa picked him up and deposited the dog and doll in the shallow basket he'd tied to the pommel. Mounting up again, he said, "You've been a great help, Paige, but d'you know, I really think I've reached the end of my search. If you were to ride fast you could likely come up with Toby and be back in London tomorrow."

Manderville looked at him obliquely. "Trying to be rid of me, Captain, sir? Well, you'll not. I promised I'd stand by you, and we Mandervilles don't break our given word."

"Even if it kills you, eh? You've been in the doldrums since we left Town, don't deny it."

"I'm concerned, I'll own." Staring fixedly at his horse's ears, Manderville said, "I don't want— That is to say— Deuce take you, Jack! If you must have it, I've a strong feeling you're galloping straight to Point Nonplus! I wish you'd forget about this quest of yours. After all, these are modern times. Nobody gives a button about who was your actual father, or whose natural son you may be. You've built an honourable name for yourself, that's all that counts."

"Thank you." Taken aback by this cavalier view of the almost fanatical emphasis the *haut ton* placed on Lineage and Family, Vespa said wryly, "I'm grateful for the vote of confidence. But— if you had a daughter whom you loved dearly, would you permit her to marry a man who doesn't know who his father might have been? Or—worse perhaps—with a name that at any moment will be disgraced past forgiveness?"

"Nobody could blame you for Sir Kendrick's misdeeds. And Britain has countless 'Fitz's' and 'bar sinisters' who've become great men despite their—er, clouded parentage."

"A nice evasion, Paige. But Lady Francesca has made it perfectly clear that I'm not presently a *bon parti* for Consuela. She's right. No man in my position could in honour propose marriage to such a—a darling girl," He paused, then said huskily, "I won't bring shame to her. I must *know*, do you see, Paige? I *must!*"

Manderville scowled at his horse's ears, and after a pause

grunted, "Well—there it is. You can see the chimneys over that stand of oaks to the—"

Vespa caught his arm in a hard grip. "How do you know? By God, you've *been* here! Why in the *devil* didn't you tell me?"

"I told you I think you're disaster bound. Besides, this Kincraig may not be your man, you know, and—"

" 'Morning, gents." A wiry individual with snow-white hair but wearing green livery watched them from behind tall and delicately wrought iron gates. "Oh, it's you again, sir," he said with a nod to Manderville. " 'Fraid I can't tell you no different today. His lordship's away. As usual."

Manderville met Vespa's enraged glare. "Now I'm properly dished!" he moaned and, spurring his horse, rode back up the lane.

Restraining the impulse to follow and strangle him, Vespa said curtly, "I've an urgent message for Lord Kincraig. Is there a butler or steward in residence who can tell me where to reach him?"

The elderly gatekeeper swung one gate wide while looking curiously after Manderville. "Aye. Mr. Barnard's up to the house. He's the butler. The young master was here yest'day, sir, but I dunno but what he's gone already."

Vespa rode through, and said, "I only hope I've come to the right house. Is this the residence of Lord Peter Kincraig?"

"Nay, sir. Our master's Christian name do be Blair. A odd sorta name, bean't it? Now the family name be Keith—what sounds more like his first name. Only it bean't. Proper contrary—backwards, says I."

Vespa scarcely heard the words. Blair! And the 'ai' repeated in 'Kincraig'! His heart leapt. Another link in the chain? Or was he building too much on coincidence? "Blair!" He realized that in his excitement he had spoken the name aloud. The gatekeeper was staring at him, doubtless thinking he was properly dicked in the nob. Glancing down, his heart gave another lurch and he flung himself from the saddle.

The gatekeeper was deathly white. His hand, shaking violently, clutched at the grey's mane.

Vespa threw an arm about the frail shoulders. "My poor fellow. You're ill!"

The old man mumbled something.

Alarmed by the fear that he had suffered some kind of seizure, Vespa dispossessed Corporal and his doll then helped the gatekeeper into the saddle and led the grey along the winding drive.

The house was quite a distance away. It was a large Elizabethan structure of handsome brown carstone, the main block rising to three storeys, with a two-storey wing jutting to the west. The roofs were high-pitched and contained a row of oriel windows; the windows on the lower floors being tall and narrow. The chimney-stacks were also tall, and elaborate. All the wood trim and the balustrade that edged the steep flight of steps leading to the front entrance were a creamy white. Noting inconsequently that the house and grounds were very well maintained, Vespa eyed that long sweep of outside steps uneasily, and he was relieved when in answer to his hail a neat, darkly clad man appeared from the west side of the house and hurried towards him.

"Your gatekeeper's been taken ill," Vespa shouted. "Are you the butler?"

"I am. Come this way if you will, sir."

Vespa followed the path leading around the west wing and discovered another single-storey wing at the rear.

With the butler's help he guided the gatekeeper from the saddle and supported him into what appeared to be the servants' hall.

The elderly man sank onto a chair. "I'm all right . . . now, thankee, sir." He watched the butler who was pouring a glass of wine. "It were just . . . the shock, Mr. Barnard. Thought fer a minute I seed a ghost."

The butler handed him the glass. "Here you are, Shubb. I thank you for bringing him up here, sir. May I ask . . . what . . ."

The polite words ceased, and, again, Vespa saw a hanging jaw, and a pair of glazed eyes that regarded him in stark disbelief.

"Might I . . . ask your name, sir?" faltered 'Mr. Barnard.'

"It is Vespa. Captain John Vespa. Perhaps I am in the wrong place. I've an urgent message for Lord Kincraig."

Butler and gatekeeper exchanged glances. Barnard regained his composure, but his voice still shook when he said, "Rest here till you feel better, Shubb. Will you step this way, Captain?"

He ushered Vespa through an inner door, past a great kitchen where maids peeped curiously, and up a flight of stairs. They entered a long corridor where parquet floors gleamed, and finely carven chests and benches were spaced about the walls. Next came a very large and luxuriously furnished saloon, and then a smaller but even more luxurious drawing room with one of the finest plastered ceilings Vespa had ever seen. Lowering his gaze, he found the butler watching him intently, and he said with an apologetic smile, "I fancy you are accustomed to rude visitors who gawk at this ceiling."

"It has been featured in several guide books, sir." Barnard gestured towards the hearth. "The painting is also much admired."

Vespa was at first struck by the fine Queen Anne fireplace. A portrait hung above the mantel, and— He stood perfectly still then, staring at the lean face, the strong nose and chin, the sensitive mouth and the wide-set hazel eyes that might be described as 'tawny.'

But for the powdered wig, it might have been a portrait of himself.

The butler's voice seemed to come from a great distance. "You see why Shubb and I were so taken aback, sir. This is a portrait of the late Robert Keith Lord Kincraig, taken in his youth. You'll be—of the family . . . ?"

Vespa stammered, "I came here . . . hoping to—"

"What the devil? Are you gone demented, Barnard? Throw this fellow out! Or I will!"

The bray of a voice cut through Vespa's confusion. The arrogant dandy he'd been obliged to knock down yesterday stamped into the room. The handsome features were not flushed this morning; the hazel eyes were clear and they were of the same unusual shade as his own. Stunned, he thought, 'Jupiter! This impudent lout may be my half-brother!'

"You caught cold at that the last time you tried it, Keith," he said.

"Captain Vespa has brought a message for his lordship, Mr. Duncan," murmured Barnard.

'Duncan Keith,' thought Vespa. 'A Scots name if ever I heard one!'

"Then it should have been left at the kitchen door! Did you not tell him my father is off at his stupid wanderings, again? There's no excuse for having allowed him . . . into . . ." Keith, who had been staring at Vespa, broke off and turned his frowning gaze to the portrait. "What'd you say your name was?"

"It is Vespa. Where may I find his lordship?"

"Vespa . . . I've heard that name before . . ." Comprehension brought a shout of laughter. "By God, but I have! All London is buzzing with it! What's to do, Captain? Do you seek to escape your disgraced name by claiming kinship with us? So far as I'm aware we've no Vespas on our family tree." His grin became a leer. "Not—ah, legitimately, that is! So don't fancy to fill your pockets at my father's expense, or—"

His sudden leap to the rear was much too slow. Vespa's hand was fast-gripped in his cravat, his narrowed eyes blazed into Keith's alarmed face as he said gratingly, "What gentleman in his right mind would have the least desire to claim kinship with a slug like you? I came with—"

Choking for breath, and unable to tear free from that steel grip, Keith kicked out in desperation, his foot smashing against Vespa's injured leg. Vespa swore in anguish, but despite his injuries he was in far better physical condition than Keith, who obviously drank too much and whose athletic pursuits were probably limited to Mayfair saunters and an occasional afternoon ride in the park. With a lithe sway, Vespa eluded another kick and brought his boot heel down hard on Keith's toe. Keith howled and doubled up, and Vespa shoved him violently, sending him hurtling across the room to crash into a sideboard, the impact causing a fine Limoges fruit dish to shatter on the floor.

Gripping his throbbing leg, Vespa said, "I'm sorry about the dish, Barnard."

"Damn your . . . eyes! You'll meet me for this!" gasped Keith, making no attempt to rise.

"I've more important things to do," said Vespa contemptuously.

Barnard said, "I think you're hurt, sir."

"He'll be more . . . than hurt when . . . I'm done with him," raged Keith. "Come and help me up, curse you! You work for *me,* if you remember!"

"No, do not, Barnard," said Vespa. "If you help that creature stand, I'll just have to knock him down again." Ignoring Keith's profane response, he went on, "I *must* find Lord Kincraig! I don't mean to endanger your position in this house, but, if you can help me—"

Keith dragged himself to a sitting position and said with a breathless laugh, "Tell him, Barnard! Oh, by all . . . by all means tell him where my illustrious sire may be . . . found! With luck this . . . silly clod will go seeking him!"

The butler looked from his employer's enraged heir to the slim younger soldier. The resemblance was undeniable. He thought 'if only . . .' and smothering a regretful sigh, he said in his quiet way, "Lord Kincraig is at the moment believed to be—in France, sir."

'France? But—"

"But we're at war with France," jeered Keith. "And you are likely thinking no . . . no sane Briton would attempt to enter enemy territory. Quite correct! But—but you don't seek a sane man, Vespa. My sire is a lunatic who hunts a *rug,* of all things! A rug that was destroyed a millennium since! He's the laughingstock of Europe. But, with luck, old Boney will get him!" He glared at the frowning butler. "I'll be master here then, Barnard. Bear it in mind, if you want to keep your situation! Now—ring for my man, blast you, and kick this slippery bastard off the premises! I've a splendid five-bore duck gun I'd be happy to use on a mushrooming fortune-hunter. You'd best see how fast you can run, Vespa!"

"By all means stand up," invited Vespa coldly. "I'll wait."

Keith's jaws rippled as though he ground his teeth. He snarled, "You heard me, Barnard! And tell Wickes to fetch my new Manton."

Barnard bowed and tugged at an embroidered bell-pull.

Vespa stood there, gazing down at this sullen and spoilt man, and thinking of the gallant half-brother he had loved and lost.

"If you please, sir," murmured Barnard.

"He wants thrashing," said Vespa thoughtfully.

"You'd not dare," blustered Keith.

"For my sake," pleaded Barnard *sotto voce.* "This way, Captain."

Reluctantly, Vespa accompanied him across the saloon, and offered his card. "I've likely done you a poor turn today. If Mr. Keith's hopes materialize, or if you decide on a change of scene, you must call on me."

The butler thanked him and pocketed the card. "I'd fancied a change of scene long since, Captain. But—his lordship is fond of this house."

"And you're fond of his lordship."

Barnard flushed. "I've been in the family's service most of my life. Lord Kincraig is a fine gentleman. He worries for young Mr. Keith. I promised that in his absence I'd try to preserve both the estate and—"

A tall footman hurried toward them and eyed Barnard questioningly.

"He's in the drawing room," said the butler. "He wants Wickes."

The footman nodded and looked at Vespa, curiosity coming into his eyes.

"At once!" snapped Barnard.

The footman fled.

As they walked on Vespa said, "You've done very well with the house and grounds, at least."

Barnard smiled. "Thank you, sir. My efforts in the other direction were doomed, I'm afraid. The damage was done years ago."

"Indulgence?" asked Vespa, as they started down the stairs.

"A beautiful but unscrupulous woman, sir. Lady Kincraig trapped his lordship into marriage even after he'd told her he was devoted to—someone else. I collect she thought she could change him. When she found she couldn't, she chose to think herself ill-used. She was a woman of violent and brooding temperament. Her vengeance was to make her husband's life a hell on earth, and to turn their son against his father."

Surprised by such confidences, Vespa said, "You use the past tense. I take it Lord Kincraig is a widower?"

"Her ladyship was killed in a riding accident two years ago. There had been a particularly acrimonious quarrel. The lady demanded that they return to their home in Scotland. Lord Kincraig had some business to attend to, and would not agree. He urged her to go without him, but there was no reasoning with her when she was in one of her furies. At length he told her he was sailing for Italy that night. She insisted on accompanying him. He refused, and in spite of her threat to shoot him if he attempted to leave her, he drove out. Lady Kincraig followed, still wearing her dinner gown and slippers, and riding her favourite horse: a high-strung animal. There was summer lightning that night. The horse bolted and the lady was thrown." Barnard pursed his lips. "She was killed instantly. Mr. Duncan blamed his father."

They had reached the lower floor and as they entered the servants' hall Vespa said, "One would think that Lord Kincraig might have stayed with his son."

"He did, for a while. Mr. Duncan tormented and vexed him in every possible way until his lordship forbade him this house, set him up in a London flat and gave him a most generous allowance."

"But when Kincraig is away, the charming heir returns?"

"Just so, sir. His lordship knows. In spite of everything he still has affection for the young man, and I think he worries that having his mother's excitable nature, her son will meet a similar fate. He's wild enough, certainly."

Vespa leaned back against the long table. "Duncan Keith is not a pleasant fellow to work for, eh?"

"No, sir. But I promised his lordship. Even if I had not, I've an ailing mother, and Lord Kincraig pays me very well, and allows her to live on the estate."

"I see," Vespa said thoughtfully. "You don't impress me as the man to betray your employer's secrets, Barnard. Why do you tell me all this?"

The butler met his eyes steadily. "The resemblance is so strong, sir. I don't pretend to know how, but—of a certainty you are in some way connected to this family."

"You must have some idea what is that connection."

"It is presumptuous in me to—to dare hazard a guess, Captain, but"—Barnard flushed darkly—"but—forgive, sir. I—er, I do know that his lordship, who is a very gentle person, had an—an almost ungovernable hatred of—of one particular gentleman."

"Sir Kendrick Vespa."

"Yes, Captain. But—I never heard— I mean, her ladyship was half crazed with jealousy. If she'd ever so much as suspected—"

A distant voice howled. "My *gun*, you idiot! And fast!"

Barnard said, "You must go, sir!"

"Never worry. He'd not dare shoot down an unarmed man."

"There are four other menservants in the house. And he has *her* blood. After one or two glasses of cognac, there's nothing he wouldn't dare!"

He was pale. Clearly, he believed what he said.

Vespa swore. "I *must* have some answers! Can we meet? After your work is finished tonight, perhaps?"

"It will be late, and brief, I'm afraid, Captain. But unless Mr. Keith decides to leave for Scotland today, I'll try to slip out. Where will I find you?"

"I saw a fine stand of oaks up near the road. I'll bring a closed carriage and wait there. Quickly, now, is there a painting

of Lord Blair Kincraig I can see? Perhaps a miniature I might
take with me?"

"Regrettably, no, sir. There was a fine portrait of his lordship,
but Lady Kincraig destroyed it in one of her tantrums and he
refused ever to sit for another."

"Blast! Is there some feature that would help me recognize
him?"

"Not any one feature, Captain, but you've only to look in
the mirror and imagine a few lines, and some grey hair at your
temples." The butler's eyes brightened; he asked hopefully, "Do
you really mean to try and find him?"

"Possibly. He *is* in—er, in full possession of his faculties?"

"Oh, most certainly. A trifle eccentric, perhaps, but a highly
intelligent gentleman. His interest in rugs and carpets, especially antique rugs, is of long standing."

"But why would a man of intelligence allow the rumour to
be spread that he's searching for a *flying* carpet? That's so nonsensical!"

Barnard glanced uneasily at the door. "I couldn't say, sir.
Except that his lordship has ever been a rather solitary man,
and not one to care about the opinions of others."

"Is it true that he ventures into France on his expeditions?"

"He travels all over Europe and the Near East. And always
alone. He's had some very desperate encounters, I know. It
worries me excessively. His life has not been happy, and sometimes I fear . . ." The butler looked troubled and left the sentence unfinished. "I believe he has no set route. He goes
wherever he hears of some interesting specimen. I'm sorry, but
there is *nothing more* I can—"

"Barnard? Where in *Hades* are you got to?"

The enraged howl was closer and spurred the butler into
hurrying from the room, turning back at the door to whisper
an impassioned plea that Vespa leave Lambent Grove at once.

Seething with frustration, Vespa yearned to wait and face
down the terrible-tempered heir. But it would result in a turn-
up at the very least. Common sense whispered that he was not
at the top of his form, and with several menservants to back
Keith, he'd likely get himself soundly trounced. Reluctantly, he
abandoned the prospect of such delicious but foolish heroics.
He would see Barnard tonight, and learn as much as possible
about the elusive Carpet Collector. He fought against becoming
overconfident, but with the help of his friends he had learned

so much. 'Consuela, my darling girl,' he thought, 'we may yet stand at the altar together!'

Outside, the elderly gatekeeper was leading the grey horse up and down the drivepath. He accepted the coins Vespa handed him, and relayed the information that the captain's dog had run off and that a gentleman was in the lane, throwing his toy for him.

An unseasonable sun was shining and the air was less chill. Corporal pranced gaily to meet his master. Manderville drew back, throwing up one arm protectively. "Do not strike me! Ah! I am reprieved! How much nicer you look with that dazzling grin, Captain, sir! You must have realized why I didn't tell you about your odd relations."

"Chawbacon! They may be odd, but you're right. There can be no doubt but that my father was Lord Blair Kincraig!"

"One look at Duncan Keith should have told me that, but I didn't realize till today why I thought I'd met the fellow somewhere." Manderville mounted up. "I hope you appreciated my tact in not accompanying you. He's the roué I had to knock down after I left Stowmarket. He don't much like me."

Vespa's smile was rather grim. "I'm afraid I didn't impress him, either!"

Lady Francesca Ottavio's 'cottage' was actually a large house set back from the lane amid venerable old trees and pleasant gardens. It was located a short distance north of Gallery-on-Tang, the Dorsetshire village that had once been part of the estate John Vespa inherited from his maternal grandparents. The village was a delightful sight even under the gloomy skies of a December afternoon, and when Vespa had ridden along its single street he'd been welcomed with such warmth and affection that it had been some time before he could decently break away. Now, he was alone with the little 'duchess' in her comfortable drawing room, his nerves taut as he awaited her reaction to the news he'd brought.

She looked very small and frail in the great fireside chair, but he knew better than to judge her anything but formidable. She wrung her claw-like hands absently, and gazed at Corporal who lay on the rug.

"Why do you allow that he plays with that silly doll?" she demanded. "Is not the proper toy for a boy dog."

"I bought it for Molly Hawes, but he found it, and—"

"You mean he stole it. You should have beaten him."

He said meekly, "I thought I'd leave that to you, ma'am."

She gave him a sharp look and seeing the twinkle in his eyes, advised him that he need not think to bring her around his thumb with his flirty ways, adding, "Consuela you have telling all these things?"

"No, ma'am."

"Why? It might have won you the advantages."

"And had I told her without your approval I'd have been dealt a thundering scold—and deserved it, eh, my lady?"

She smiled suddenly, and patted his knee. "You are the honourable gentleman, and with honour you play the game. What do you mean to do?"

"Are you satisfied with my— I mean, would you think me more acceptable if Lord Kincraig is my father?"

"Acceptable, is it? Ha!" She threw up her hands and demanded, "What is this choosings you now offer me? My great-grandsons they must have fine men in the family to look up to. And what shall they look up to in either a grandpapa who was a murderous black-hearted villain; or an aristocrat with the bent brain, the mad wife and the half-mad son, and who wastes the life the Good God give him by roaming about seeking flying carpets! *Le gioia e della vita!*"

Vespa reddened. "I believe that remark had to do with joy, my lady?"

"*Si.*" She said in a gentler tone, "And me I am being the cynical, which is rude. Very well, you say you love my little Consuela. If I leave this decision in your hands, you would now with happiness make the offer for her—yes?"

He frowned, then said resignedly, "No. Had I been able to question the Lambent Grove butler privately, as I'd hoped, I might have sufficient information, but Duncan Keith took a sudden whim to leave for Scotland that very afternoon. So I still lack many of the answers I need. I must find Lord Kincraig, and see for myself what kind of man he is, and whether he will acknowledge me."

"Ah! This is good and I know you would doing it. Now—you really think he is in France?"

"I think that is where I must commence my search."

She gave a derisive snort. "Madness! What have the handsome tailor's delight he say to this?"

"Manderville? Oh, he's dead set against it. Says I could never hope to find his lordship. But we traced him to Suffolk, in spite of all the gloom-merchants." His jaw set. He said a vehement, "I'll find him!"

"Jack!" Consuela hurried into the room, her eyes alight, and hands outstretched to him. She still wore her cloak, and the wind had tumbled her curls and brought roses into her cheeks.

Vespa's heart gave its customary lurch, and he sprang up and took her cold little hands eagerly.

"Oh, but I did not know you had come home," she cried, searching his face. "You must stay to dinner, must he not, Grandmama? Is Paige here also? What news have you?"

"Sit down and your gabbling stop," commanded the duchess testily. "And you may sit next to my granddaughter, Captain, if you will be propriety."

Consuela allowed Vespa to take her cloak. Briefly, his strong hands tightened on her shoulders. She looked up, her sparkling eyes meeting his ardent ones.

Lady Francesca snapped, "No fondlings, no fondlings!"

They sat dutifully on the sofa, side by side and a little distance apart.

"I am so anxious to know," said Consuela eagerly. "What have you discovered, Jack?"

He glanced at Lady Francesca.

"He has lost Lieutenant Paige, who have gone wandering off about his own businesses," imparted the duchess. "And he have find this man he thinks may be his sire. Who is mad."

"Oh, never say so!" Aghast, Consuela gripped her hands tightly. "Are you sure? Who is he? Where is he? Have you met him, Jack?"

"He is Lord Blair Kincraig, and I haven't met him—yet. But—"

"How can he be meeting him when this lordling is gone to France? Which proves he is mad."

Dismayed, Consuela said, "To *France?* What on earth . . . ?"

Vespa smiled at her. "He is, I believe, eccentric. Nothing more."

"Hah!" said Lady Francesca. "Only that he hunts two carpets, *bambina.* One that fly like the bird; and the other made of jewels that was cut up more than a thousand years since! Eccentric, you say? Hah!"

Intrigued, Consuela demanded the whole story and listened

raptly while Vespa told her of the Spring Carpet of Khusraw, and of his visit to Lambent Grove. "Good gracious," she said, when he came to the end of his account. "Lord Kincraig does sound a—a rather odd gentleman. Whatever do you mean to do now?"

"What would you suppose?" interposed the Duchess. "Our Captain John Vespa he follow this mad father to France, which it show the madness he has inhibited!"

"Inherited, dearest," corrected Consuela. "And, of course you cannot even think of going, Jack."

Her proprietary air warmed his heart. He said, "I must, but—"

"We will *not* hold the hands," warned the duchess.

Sighing, Vespa snatched his hand back. "My apologies. And I *must* go, Consuela. Heaven only knows how long it may be before he returns to England."

"I had sooner you wait than have you go to France and be shot as a spy!"

"Very right, and we will speak no more of foolishnesses," agreed Lady Francesca. "Now, Consuela has something to tell us, that she keep the big secret. Speak up, meadowlark."

Consuela said eagerly, "Oh, yes. I have wanted to tell you, Jack. I met an—er, admirer yesterday, who—"

Vespa stiffened. "Has that confounded colonel been slithering around you again?"

"Languages!" shrilled the duchess, clapping her hands over her ears.

Vespa apologized for his lapse, and Consuela said with a trace of annoyance, "La, sir, do you fancy I have but the one admirer?"

Hastings Adair was the rival Vespa most feared and his wrath cooled a little. "I can visualize regular armies of 'em," he acknowledged. "Nor could I blame the poor fellows."

"Why 'poor'? Perhaps you think their choice is ill-considered? I'll have you know—"

"Come down from the boughs, *Signorina* Consuela Carlotta Angelica Jones! Tell me about this latest of your beaux."

She was always amused when he reeled off her complete name, but although she smiled, there was a look at the back of her eyes that disturbed him. His unease grew while she told of the strange man who had questioned her on the estate road, and at the end a cold fear gripped him.

Horrified, the duchess exclaimed, "Foolish, *foolish* child! You should have tell me this at once! Do you knowing these mens, Captain Jack?"

He frowned. "I hope I don't, but you'll remember I spoke of the very powerful fellow who tossed Hastings Adair about when we were attacked in Town. Toby thinks their descriptions would fit a fanatical Swiss art collector name Monteil. He has a very large Chinese servant, and a decidedly ugly reputation."

"If this it is so, then these are very dangerous peoples," said the duchess, wringing her hands agitatedly. "And now they make the threats on my meadowlark? *Dio ce ni scampi e liberi!*"

"That means 'God forbid,' Jack," translated Consuela.

"Amen," he said fervently. "But our prayers would not be necessary had you not seen fit to tease them."

Consuela had been eager to share what she had found out, and she gave a gesture of exasperation. "Oh! Is that the thanks I get? If it is not typical of a man to never give a lady credit where it is due! It does not occur to you that I was all alone when they came up behind me, and yet—"

"My God, but it occurs to me! You will persist in—"

"—and yet I managed to convince them I was a villager and—"

"If you had Manning with you, child, there would not have been the need to convince them of anythings," put in the old lady, her eyes glinting with a mixture of alarm and vexation. "Ah, *San Pietro!*"

"Saint Peter was likely helping me, *Nonna,* for I'd almost succeeded in sending them off in the wrong direction. If that silly Manning had not come wailing up and spoilt everything—"

The picture of what might have happened if Manning had not come, made Vespa break out in a cold sweat. "You might have got your pretty neck wrung!" he said harshly. "I'll not have you taking such chances, Miss Independence! It is as unwise as it is improper for—"

"You will not?" She sprang up in a flame. "What right have you to censure me, John Wansdyke Vespa? We are not betrothed—nor ever like to be if this is how you bully and browbeat a lady!"

His own cheeks flushed, Vespa stood and faced her. "A lady does not wander unescorted about the countryside, inviting the attentions of any womanizing makebait who chances her way, as—"

"In—*inviting? Oooh!* How—"

"—as I've told you before, ma'am. No! Be still! It is one thing, and a very dear thing, for you to want to help, but quite another to deliberately make mock of a man who you admit alarmed you."

She said with a rebellious little pout, "He was insulting, and deserved a set-down!"

"And you gladly administered one, did you not? The truth is that you plunged recklessly into another of your jolly adventures." He checked. She was angry now, and she had meant well, and was so young and sweet and innocent, and he loved her so much. His tone softened. "There are men, Consuela, with whom one dares not play games! Who are far less civilized than the deadliest jungle serpents. I'd hoped you had learned that lesson."

"From whom?" she riposted furiously. "Your father? How *frightfully* disappointing for you that I am such a widgeon as to try to be of assistance! Only think, Captain, you almost offered for a girl who is as—as stupid as she is *improper!*"

"That—will—do!" Lady Francesca's voice was ice.

Feeling beset on every side, Consuela half-sobbed, "You are as—as bad as he is! You both think I am a silly child, but I am *not!* I try to help. I *have* helped, but for all the appreciation I get, I had as well not bother!"

"What you had as well to do is go to your room, at once, *Signorina!* I do not wish to be seeing your face again this day!"

Blinded by tears, Consuela was already running for the door.

The duchess turned to Vespa, who was as pale as he had before been flushed. "You will please not to heed her, Captain Jack. When she is angry—well, you know she do not always mean what she sayings." She shrugged expressively. "She is Italian."

He took a steadying breath. "And as she said, I had no right to censure her." He sat down wearily. "But—Lord, ma'am! She's as brave as she can stare, and so fearless there's no telling what she'll do next. Hastings Adair warned me that my enquiries concerning the—the rug fancier had been noted. Heaven knows I never dreamed I would involve Consuela with a man of Monteil's stamp! I'd sooner die than put her in danger!"

"She is a proud lady, and the Swiss man he was a rudesby. But I cannot really think he would harm her only because she have chastize him."

Vespa said gravely, "It's more than that, my lady. In Town I thought they were after Adair, but now here they come, very obviously seeking Lord Kincraig. They must know I also am searching for him, and now Consuela has tried to send them off on a wild-goose chase. I've no wish to alarm you, and I hope I am borrowing trouble, but you must be aware of the business—just in case."

"I *am* alarmed! Which it is as well. We should not keep the secrets, you and I. Is best to be prepared. Perhaps I need this man you set to guard us when those bad men steal our paintings?"

"Cobham. Yes, he's a good man. I'll hire him before I leave." Vespa ran a hand through his hair distractedly. "How *can* I leave? If I'm not here to protect her, she'll run herself into danger, sure as check! Almost, I wish her wretched colonel *was* slithering about!"

"Perhaps I should take her into Town. Better yet—take her back to Italy!" The duchess was briefly silent, pondering. Then she exclaimed, *"Mama mia!* Now have I not the fine notion to which you must give your ears! If you follow your mad lordling you will surely be caught, for you have much too fair the hair and skins to pass for a Frenchman. Me, I am Italian, and a duchess. My name, my family, they are known and respectful. My wanting for many years has been to take Consuela to meet her relations in Italy. Now, who is to notice if while travelling across France I have on my coach a footman who does not speak—or do you have the French?"

Answering her in that language, Vespa exclaimed, "By heaven, you're as reckless as she is!" Reverting to English, he declared vehemently, "If you imagine that for one instant I would allow you, or Consuela, to accompany—"

At her most regal, the duchess came to her feet and interrupted, "Again, you have overstepping yourself, Captain John Vespa! Francesca Celestina, Duchess of Ottavio, is not spoke to in such a ways! You may apologize."

Standing also, Vespa faced her and said quietly, "I have the greatest respect for you, my lady, but I think you have not considered. I am a British officer. If I should be caught, out of uniform, in enemy territory, I would be tortured and eventually shot as a spy. If I was lucky, it would be over quickly. Forgive that I must speak of such things. But if you and Consuela were in my company, you both would merit the same fate, or worse.

No, pray do not tell me of the fine French gentlemen you know
who would never resort to such barbarism. I also have friends
in France whom I value highly. But we are at war, ma'am, and
although the war seems far away to most people in England, I
promise you that suspected spies, male or female, are shown
no mercy by either side. *No*, Lady Francesca! You are a very
dear and brave woman, but—I'll have none of it!"

The little duchess blinked up at him. "Well," she said, for
once at a loss for words. "Well, now . . ."

Paige Manderville burst into the room, grinning broadly and
obviously much excited. "Excelsior!" he cried. "How d'ye do,
ma'am?"

"Pray come in," she said with daunting sarcasm.

"Eh? Oh, yes, well you must forgive me, for I've grand news!
I came upon one of my sergeants, Jack. He's been sent home
because he lost a leg. Had blisters on his heel and if you can
believe— But never mind that. Thing is, he's a wheelwright
now, and he told me he worked on a large cart yesterday morning. The cart was full of *rugs!*"

Vespa stiffened and the duchess uttered an excited gasp.

Manderville said, "The owner was a cultured gentleman but
clearly wits to let. He claimed to have just come back from
France, which so astonished my sergeant that he asked how
ever the gentleman was able to travel there in these times. The
rug dealer said he's well known to be a 'collector' and everyone
knows him because over the years he has brought back some
fine specimens!"

"By George!" cried Vespa, his heart pounding rapidly. "Did
your man know where this 'collector' is going next?"

"Apparently the gentleman likes to chat, and while he was
waiting for his wheel to be repaired he said he'd intended to
stay at his home in *Suffolk* for a while, but—"

"Suffolk!"

Manderville grinned. "Yes, dear boy! Suffolk! But he's apparently learned that a *flying carpet* has been discovered near
Antwerp, so he will go there as soon as he unloads his cart. It
must be Kincraig, don't you agree? I mean, there couldn't be
two of 'em!"

"Not likely!" exclaimed Vespa. "What tremendous luck!" He
wrung his friend's hand. "Bless you, Paige! I'm deep in your
debt!"

Manderville rubbed his numbed fingers and stared at Vespa

in an oddly embarrassed fashion. "No, no, my boy," he protested, his face very red. "Glad to be of assistance."

Elated, Vespa scarcely heard the mumbled words. "I'll warrant Kincraig plans to sail from East Anglia. I'll leave at once!"

"Not now, you won't," said Manderville. "There's fog rolling in. It was all I could do to find my way here."

Vespa strode to the window. The gardens were wreathed in a white blanket. He swore under his breath. "I'll have to wait till morning then. But if he's driving a laden cart to Suffolk it shouldn't be hard to come up with him before he embarks for Belgium."

"I'm going with you," declared Manderville. "Wouldn't miss it for the world!"

Seven

Consuela's hope that she could enjoy her misery in private was doomed. When she reached her bedchamber she found Manning sitting before the fire, replacing a button on her dressing gown. Consuela hesitated in the doorway, and then realized the woman was fast asleep. Sighing, she crept in and sat on the bed.

Why had she said such a dreadful thing? Poor darling Jack had so much to bear, and for her, of all people, to turn on him, was inexcusable. It was her horrid temper: the bane of her existence. Try as she would, she could not seem to behave in a cool, poised and dignified way, as an English lady should. On the other hand, Jack and *Nonna* gave her no credit. It was the same as when she'd followed that horrid man into the Alabaster Royal quarry in September. She'd not *meant* to be caught. She'd been trying so hard to help. Instead of which . . .

Manning's snores were getting louder. Consuela looked at her maid resentfully. She could wake her, of course, but if she did she would either be treated to another homily on the unwisdom of a young lady talking to strange gentlemen, or endure a report on the condition of Manning's corns. If she sent the woman away, Manning would at once run to Cook and wail that Miss Consuela was upset, and Cook would tell Grandmama, and there would be a fuss. She suffered a guilty pang. Manning was often tiresome, but she was also loyal and impeccably honest. She had suffered a bad head cold last week, and she really did look tired.

There was no refuge up here, it seemed. She took her warmest cloak from the press and ran lightly downstairs. The drawing room door was closed but she heard the murmur of voices.

Grandmama and Jack were likely discussing her shocking want of conduct. The entrance hall was empty. From the kitchen passage came a rattle of crockery and cook's merry chatter, interspersed by deeper male tones. Watts, their elderly coachman, had probably come in for a cup of tea.

Wanting only to be alone, Consuela went outside and closed the front door quietly. It was chilly this afternoon, with mist drifting about. A fine setting, she thought, for her gloomy mood. She wandered in the garden miserably, and was startled when something struck her foot. Corporal had deposited his doll on her shoe, and sat regarding her hopefully. She bent to stroke him. He picked up the doll, pranced away, and stopped, looking back at her. She smiled and dried her tears.

"You want to go for a walk, do you?"

His little tail vibrated, and a muffled bark came from around the doll.

"Very well," said Consuela. "But it must be a short walk, my friend. I think we are to have real fog, and I dare not get into any more trouble."

She set out, glad enough of the little animal's company, and throwing the doll when it was occasionally presented for her attention.

The stricken look on Jack's dear face haunted her. She had loved him very soon after their first meeting. It had been a tempestuous meeting. She and *Nonna* had moved into the then empty manor house at Alabaster Royal, hoping to discover what her beloved father had learned there—the secret that had led to his death. Jack had arrived and surprised her, and during her struggles to escape, *Nonna* had hit him on the head with the frying pan. She smiled nostalgically. Those had been adventuresome days. Dangerous days at times, but there had been gaiety, too. And comradeship. And by the time it was all over, her heart had been given completely and irrevocably.

The fog was becoming quite thick. She had given the dog a nice long walk, but now she must turn back.

There was no sign of Corporal. She called him repeatedly, but the fog muffled her voice. And then, from somewhere nearby she heard him whine. He must have heard her, but had not come. Usually, he was very good about— There he was, foolish creature! Why was he crouching down like that? She peered at him curiously. One might think he'd been turned to stone.

A feline voice rang out nearby. An orange and white cat trod daintily towards Corporal, its tail high-held in a friendly fashion. It was a very large cat. Not too long ago Corporal had been badly frightened by a similar creature and, even as Consuela called to him, he snatched up his doll and ran away, his little legs flying.

Consuela's calls and commands were ignored. The cat, having found a playmate, joined the game merrily, its pursuit lending wings to the terrified dog.

Exasperated, Consuela tried to discourage the cat while demanding that Corporal "Come!"

Refuge appeared when least expected. A large coach, apparently abandoned, stood at the side of the Alabaster Royal road, one door wide, and the steps down. Having discovered such a familiar haven, the dog sprang up without an instant's hesitation and vanished inside.

"Oh, my *goodness!*" panted Consuela, clapping her hands at the cat. "Now see what you have done, you bad moggy!"

The cat had lost all interest in such a silly game, and sauntered away with fine feline nonchalance.

Consuela peered about. Even though the brake was probably set, the owner of the carriage must not be far off. There was no sign of a coachman, but one of the four horses had been taken from the traces. It had likely thrown a shoe or gone lame, and had been led to Young Tom, the village blacksmith. She ran quickly to the carriage. Corporal was crouched, trembling, under the seat. She reached out for him, but he shrank away. "This is not your master's coach, you silly creature," she scolded. "The cat has gone, and you must get out at once, or we'll be in disgrace. Come!"

Instead, Corporal scuttled back. With a moan of exasperation Consuela hurried up the steps and tried to catch him, but caught only the doll. She threw it into the road, urging Corporal to "fetch!" but he only whined and looked at her soulfully.

She was stunned then as a vaguely familiar voice with a French accent declared, "That blacksmith, he is a slow-witted fool. I cannot wait about. This is a good enough animal. I shall ride ahead. Dyke will bring our hack."

"You finish with people here, master?" This asked in a frightening deep growl.

"It was a sorry waste of my time! The yokels would not have refused my money had they known anything. Save that young woman. *Certainement* she knew more than she pretended. Could I but get my hands on her . . . !"

Consuela gasped with fright and prepared to jump from the coach. It was too late. Their figures were already looming up through the fog: a very tall man mounted on a fine bay horse, and his companion, incredibly broad and powerful looking, striding at the stirrup. There could be no doubt; it was the same pair who had tried to question her on Wednesday afternoon, the Swiss whom Jack thought was very dangerous and his great coachman. She shrank down, expecting to at any moment be confronted by a dead-white face and piercing black eyes, and trying to think whatever she would say to him.

Another horse came up at reckless speed, almost colliding with the Swiss who unleashed a flood of profanity at someone named Lieven who was evidently a dolt and a clumsy block.

The newcomer panted in French, "A thousand pardons, Monsieur Monteil! It is that I am told to rush, and do not expect to find you here. Ah, but you have suffered a mishap with one of your hacks?"

"A shoe it is lost, merely. The animal is now at the village smithy. When you feel so inclined no doubt you will give me your message."

"Your pardon, monsieur. It is that the Big Bertrand has word of him!"

Monteil snapped, "Where? When?"

"He was seen in Belgium some time since, and again last week near Rennes."

"Ah! How persistent he is!" Monteil's soft laugh held a chilling edge of gloating. "A long way for an Englishman to travel alone on French soil. And dangerous in the extreme. It were a kindness for us to assist him. Especially if he has found his flying carpet."

Consuela's heart gave a jump of excitement. Then these nasty creatures *were* looking for Lord Kincraig, just as Jack had suspected!

She heard a rumble of sound that might have been amusement, and then the growling voice of the coachman:

"Fog thick very far way, Lieven?"

"No, Ti Chiu. A mile or so to the south it is still clear."

Monteil said, "Then I shall ride on to the coast and find a boat." He issued crisp instructions as to the disposition of the various horses, there was the chink of coins, and he said, *"Adieu. With luck, we shall sail tonight."*

With luck, thought Consuela, her heart beating very fast, she would now slip out of this coach and run home to tell Jack his quarry was in Rennes and that the sinister Monsieur Monteil and his terrible Chiu coachman were hard after him. Why that should be so was baffling. Horrid as he might be, this Monteil did not sound like an idiot. And who but an idiot would really believe in such mythical objects as flying carpets? Unless . . . Might they suppose the eccentric Lord Kincraig had actually found a piece of the ancient and legendary carpet—what had Toby called it? The Spring Carpet of . . . Poonah or was it Basrah?

Someone was riding away. Monsieur Monteil, no doubt. She peeped from the window, then jerked back with a shocked gasp. Only a few feet away the messenger named Lieven had dismounted and was unbuckling his saddle girths. He was a stoop-shouldered individual with a lined face that was set into a sour expression, and he grumbled that it was very well for 'Monsieur' to commandeer his horse for the carriage. "Much he cares that it is cold and damp and I've to trudge all the way to the village in these riding boots!"

The carriage lurched. Consuela saw Ti Chiu's bulk approaching. She crept to the left side and reached for the door. This would be her best chance, before they finished poling up Lieven's horse and while they were both on the right side of the coach. The latch was very stiff. Struggling, she gave a yelp of fright as something touched her elbow.

She whipped around. Corporal had jumped onto the seat and now panted at her sociably. "Little beast," she whispered. "You frightened me half to death! No, do not dare bark! Were it not for you, we wouldn't be in this terrible pickle!" She glanced at the far window apprehensively. The two men were beyond her range of vision, but she could hear them: Lieven grumbling, and the mighty coachman offering an occasional unsympathetic grunt.

She turned back to the door handle again. Hurry! She must hurry!

* * *

A breeze came up at about eight o'clock, strengthening to a wind that began to disperse the fog until, by nine, the evening was clear. It was very cold. A three-quarter moon sailed up the sky, threw shadows on the quiet village street and turned the river to a silver thread.

Slightly more than a mile to the east the manor of Alabaster Royal, bathed in its brilliance, seemed almost a fairy-tale castle, its twin conical-topped towers standing guard majestically on either side of the entrance. Several of the windows glowed with amber candlelight, including three on the upper floor, for Vespa meant to retire early so as to be ready to leave at sunrise. He was at the moment seated at his desk, writing a note to Consuela. Manderville had stayed on at the cottage, accepting the duchess' challenge to a game of chess. Lady Francesca had refused to reprieve her granddaughter, saying it would do her good to stay quiet in her bedchamber and let her temper cool. Nor had Corporal appeared; Consuela was fond of the little dog, and had probably kept it with her for company.

His hand slowed, and he gazed dreamily at the unfinished note. Her rages were usually brief, for her nature was too sunny for her to sulk or hold anger. She was probably unhappy at this moment, bless her, regretting her hasty tongue. Or perhaps she was asleep, if her maid had left her in peace. He smiled the fond smile of lovers and, taking up his note, put it down again as rapid hoofbeats clattered over the stone bridge. If this was Paige returning, he must be foxed to gallop his prized horse, Trouble, at such a rate.

Candlestick in hand, he limped to the stairs, unease touching him now, because the clamour of the bell was accompanied by Paige shouting his name. That was no drunken outcry. Something was wrong.

Thornhill, the large and majestic major domo at Alabaster, hurried across the entrance hall and flung the door wide. Manderville strode in, shivering with the cold and clearly agitated. "Has the master retired, Thorny?"

"No." Vespa came quickly to join him. "What's amiss?"

Manderville searched his face in an oddly desperate fashion. "Is Consuela here?"

"Of course she's not here!" A part of Vespa's mind registered the fact that Thornhill was poking up the fire in the drawing room. The implications were obvious. Trying not to panic, he said, "Come. I'll get you some brandy. You look half frozen."

"Only half?" Manderville's laugh was short and strained. Pulling off his gauntlets he crossed the big room to warm his hands at the fire.

Vespa offered a glass of cognac. He was pale now and deeply apprehensive. Marvelling at the steadiness of his hand, Manderville said, "You staff officers! You're a breed apart!" He took a mouthful of the liquor and sprawled in a chair. "God! I'd prayed she was here!"

"You're quite certain she's not at the cottage, I take it?"

"We've searched it from cellars to attic. There's not a sign of her. That wailing woman of hers had fallen asleep in her room and didn't wake until Consuela's supper tray was carried upstairs an hour ago."

'Steady! Steady! Keep your wits about you,' thought Vespa, but his voice was harsh with strain when he said, "She was upset. She likely went for a ride and stopped to call on someone."

"The hacks are all accounted for. But her new winter cloak is gone, and— The dog, by George! Has Corporal come home?"

"No. If he's missing also I expect she took him for a walk." But if that was the case, she wouldn't have stayed out after dark. Unless she had fallen . . . The spectre of the quarry rose up to haunt Vespa. She wouldn't go there, surely? Not after the nightmare they'd all lived through in those ghastly tunnels!

Watching him, Manderville said, "We've half the village out searching, Jack. I made a detour at the quarry on my way here. The tunnel's still boarded up."

"Thank God!" But Vespa was plagued by a dread vision of his little love lying somewhere, alone in the dark, hurt and afraid, needing him. He turned to tug on the bellrope, but glanced up to find his small staff gathered by the door. Thornhill, the tall and majestic former actor; Harper, short, bow-legged, ex-Navy, who had come close to starving before becoming Alabaster's manservant; Peg, 'fair, fat, and forty' as she described herself, and who had led the chequered life of a barmaid before joining the household as parlourmaid; and the very stout Henri, the latest addition to the staff, who had tumbled down a steep bank while poaching two rabbits and, fully expecting to be hanged, had instead been hired upon revealing that he had once been a chef *'Par excellence!'* The back door creaked open and hurried footsteps announced the arrival of Hezekiah Strickley, formerly the caretaker and now steward/head groom. The thin, harsh-featured man looked around the gathering and asked, "What's to do, Captain?"

"Miss Consuela is lost," said Vespa. "She was at her home this afternoon, but has not been there since about four o'clock. Have any of you seen her?"

No one had seen her.

Manderville said, "Corporal was with her. Is he somewhere about?"

Heads were shaken. Corporal had not been seen either. They all looked apprehensive.

"The village people are out and looking for her," said Vespa. "It's late and it's very cold outside, but there's a bright moon and we dare not wait for daylight. You men go and dress warmly, and we'll join the search. Hezekiah, we'll need lanterns and torches."

They dispersed at once.

Vespa stood motionless, his eyes blank. Manderville gripped his shoulder. "We'll find her, old fellow. Never worry so."

"I keep thinking . . ." Vespa's hands clenched hard. "I keep thinking of that rogue who tried so slyly to pry information from her—about Kincraig. If Imre Monteil has—taken her . . . !" He drew a shaking hand across his eyes.

Manderville's grip tightened. "Steady, old lad! She needs you now."

"Yes." The bowed shoulders were squared, the fair head came up. "Thank you, Paige. I'll get a pistol."

"I have brought one, sir." Thornhill paced in carrying Vespa's cloak, boots and gloves. "Hezekiah is saddling up Secrets, and Peg is preparing hot soup."

"You are all—so good," said Vespa.

Settling the cloak carefully across his shoulders, Thornhill boomed with rare brevity, "We are your people, Captain."

Manderville thought, 'And they all would die for him! He hasn't got my looks, or Toby's brains, or a great fortune. How in heaven's name does he do it?'

"You'll stay at Alabaster, if you please, Thorny," said Vespa. "I want someone here in case Miss Consuela should come. Or Corporal."

The valet looked worried. "I should be with you, sir. Peg will be here."

"Yes, but I don't want her left alone. Ready, Paige?"

Thornhill swung the front door open. "God go with you, Captain!"

Consuela whispered, "*Nonna* is likely talking to Saint Peter by now, but I am asking *you*, dear Mama. How I fall into these dreadful scrapes I do not know, but if you could contrive to bring me safe out of this one, I would truly be very grateful!"

Her attempt to escape before the carriage drove away had failed miserably. The left-hand door latch was so stiff it might as well have been nailed shut, and all she'd achieved was to break three fingernails in her attempts to open it. Desperate, she'd taken off her boot and hit the silly thing. It had been the magical solution. As if cowed, the handle had yielded easily to her next attempt. Overjoyed, she'd started to open the door, only to hear Lieven's voice, very close by, saying he thought he'd heard something. Monteil's cold words, 'Could I but get my hands on her . . .' had seemed to thunder in her ears again, and she'd hidden under the rug. A moment later the carriage had lurched and started off. Helpless, she had hugged Corporal and prayed they would stop somewhere so that she might slip out.

It had begun to get dark, but they had left the fog behind and the team had increased its pace. The steady pound of hooves and the rocking of the carriage had made her drowsy. If they'd stopped anywhere she hadn't felt it, and had been bewildered to awaken to shouts and moonlight. Peeping from the window she'd glimpsed a quay where fishing boats bobbed and sails flapped and men ran about with lanterns or wind-whipped torches. A horse had been led past, and someone had shouted, "Look sharp, mates! We'll have the Riding Officers down here 'fore the roach can run!" There had been no sign of an inn or tavern. Frantic, she had wrenched the door open. Corporal had jumped out and gone scampering off, but before she could follow, the big coachman and two rough-looking seamen had come clumping up, and she'd had to swing the door shut quickly. Men were all about the coach then, chains were being lowered, and she'd had to return to her refuge under the rug lest someone should glance inside and see her.

There had been a horrible lurch, a rocking sensation, howls

of "Keep clear o' the mast, you stupid block!" and "Ye be too far to starboard!" and, more terrifying than the rest: "Careful, dang yer eyes, or ye'll swing right over the side!" Flung about dizzyingly, preparing to faint, Consuela had been plunged into deeper darkness, landing with a thud that had rattled her teeth. She'd huddled under her rug, trembling, grateful to be alive, knowing that the carriage was now in the hold of some large fishing boat, probably setting off on an illegal run for France.

Now was her chance! The boat must have a captain. She could appeal to him for help, and Monteil would not dare . . . But seamen laboured all about the carriage, cursing and straining to load boxes and crates and heavy objects that shook the floor. By the dim light of a lantern their faces looked dark and villainous. In her agitated state she thought they were probably all smugglers who would fear she'd report them to the authorities and be more likely to throw her overboard than to help. Peeping out, she caught sight of the great Chinese coachman, watching. And she was too afraid to move.

For an eternity the uproar had continued. Before it eased the sudden jolts had settled into a steady rising and falling motion. With a sob Consuela realized they were putting out to sea. Her chance to get away was gone. She was all alone in this beastly coach, with not even Corporal to keep her company, and she was cold and very hungry and in great need of a room with a washbowl and towel—and other amenities.

It was chill and stuffy in the hold, the only light coming from a lantern that hung swaying beside a ladder, and was too far from her to do much to alleviate the gloom. Horses were stamping and snorting somewhere. She felt utterly helpless and for once her resolute spirit was daunted. She thought of her beloved Jack, so far away, and of Grandmama and Paige, and even Manning, all worried and searching for her, as they would certainly be by this time. Whatever was to become of her? Who would protect her? If that horrid Monsieur Monteil caught sight of her he would certainly either hand her over to the authorities, or kidnap her away. 'Could I but get my hands on her . . .' She shivered. And what possible chance would she have against him and his gigantic Chinese servant?

She found that she was crying. Disgusted by such weakness she dashed her tears away with the heel of her hand. One might suppose she had never been in danger before, that she must

now turn into such a weak-kneed watering pot! Only a little
while ago she'd been trapped in a hideous quarry with men
who were even more evil than Monsieur Monteil—at least, she
hoped they were. Whatever else, she didn't think Monteil had
murder in mind. So why was she snivelling?

What she must do was behave as Grandmama and Papa
would have expected. She had, so *Nonna* insisted, royal blood
in her veins. It was time to start living up to it! First of all, she
would get out of this revolting coach. She opened the door
cautiously. Ti Chiu had gone at last and there were no other
men to be seen. The hold was crammed with boxes and bales,
great coils of rope, large barrels and smaller tubs. There was
very little space between the coach and what appeared to be
an empty horse-box with steel bars comprising the walls and
roof. She squeezed through the coach door, and was trying to
push it shut again when a warm breeze blew on the back of
her neck. Paralyzed with fright, she stood utterly still. The
breeze blew at her again. She thought numbly that whoever
was behind her had very nasty breath. Perhaps, if she moved
quickly enough, she could elude him. He said something in a
growl of a voice. It must be that giant coachman, she thought
with an inner moan of despair, and how could she run when
there was scarcely room to move? If she bribed the great brute,
perhaps he would take pity on her.

She gathered her courage, jerked around, and came nose to
nose with a very big brown bear.

She was not conscious of having screamed, nor of having
moved, but somehow she was kneeling on top of a bale, a good
ten feet from the cage. The light was a little brighter here and
she saw the bear drop down to all fours and mutter to itself
disconsolately. Even as her heartbeat began to ease to a gallop
she realized that there was something else alive nearby. Strange
snuffling sounds were coming from below her bale. She peered
through the gloom. A small figure lay writhing about on the
floor.

"Good gracious!" she exclaimed. "Are you ill?"

There came a heart-rending wail. The small figure resolved
itself into a boy. Consuela climbed from the bale and bent to
offer a helping hand. He sat up and leant back against the
bale, drying his tears, and moaning feebly.

"Poor boy," she said. "I'll go and fetch help."

"I never . . ." he gasped, "saw anyone move so quick . . . in all my life!"

Indignant, Consuela drew back. "You are laughing at me! Horrid creature!"

"Well, anyone would. You were so—funny." He sighed, and dabbed at his eyes again. "Why did you stay in the coach? Are you a stowaway?"

"No. I am just hiding from—from somebody."

"Who? The Excisemen?"

"From a very unpleasant person."

"Oh. I thought I heard someone crying. I 'spect it was you. Girls are always crying about something or other."

"I'm afraid it was me. I've been in that horrid carriage for hours, and—I'm so cold and hungry, and—if I could just go to a cabin and wash and tidy myself, I think I could bear it." She knew she'd sounded forlorn and added quickly, "What are you doing down here?"

"Oh, I'm hiding too." He sounded miserable. "My uncle said he had come to my school in England to take me home to Paris, but I heard him paying a man to throw me overboard."

Horrified, Consuela exclaimed, "My goodness! We must tell the captain at once!"

"I tried to, but my uncle's with him. He's very rich, now. Till I grow up."

"Is he your guardian, then?"

"Yes. He wants my fortune. I've tried to tell them, but they won't believe me. He gets whatever he wants. He's a very bad man. I'm doomed."

"Indeed you are not," she declared, stroking his thick hair comfortingly. "But you must have some help. You're much too young to fight him all alone."

He said staunchly. "No I'm not. I'm—er, twelve!"

He looked more like eight. His coat was well-cut, his shirt gleamingly white. Lurid as it was, his tale might very well be truth. She said, "I'll help you if I can. But—would you be brave enough to help me first?"

" 'Course I would. Come on. I'll take you to my cabin, and I'll get you something to eat." He looked at her skirts dubiously. "You'll have to climb up the ladder. Can you?"

Consuela assured him she could, and followed as he went up the rungs with the nimble ease of childhood. At the top, he pushed back the hatchway with much huffing and puffing, and peeped out.

Consuela smelled sea air, cold and fresh, and heard voices, flapping sails and ropes and the thud of the bow slicing through the waves.

The boy turned his head. "What does your nasty man look like? There's a great big fellow hanging over the rail in the stern. I thought he was a pirate, but he can't be, 'cause he's seasick. My uncle says he's Chinese."

"Is there a very tall man with him?"

"No. But there was when we came aboard. He was all black and white. I 'spect he's in his cabin. Do you want to try it now? I'll help you."

Consuela nodded, and clambered up eagerly. There were several men on the deck, but they were farther forward and not looking her way. She held up her hands and the boy steadied her until she stood beside him looking forlornly at a great expanse of dark tumbling waves.

"Quick, now," he said, and guided her through an open door into a narrow passageway lit by two hanging lanterns. He flung open another door and announced, "This is our cabin."

Willy-nilly, Consuela was pulled inside. The cabin was large and surprisingly comfortable, with two bunk beds against the walls, a washstand with soap and towels, and a small writing desk. There was no other occupant, but some large portmanteaux were stacked behind the door, and there were shaving articles on the washstand.

She turned to question the boy and was momentarily struck to silence as for the first time she saw him clearly. He was the most beautiful child she had ever seen, with deeply lashed green eyes, auburn curls burnished in the lamplight, a pale and clear skin and finely etched features. She thought, 'Paige must have looked like this when he was a boy.'

"I'll go and see if I can get you something to eat." He opened the door, stuck his head back in and said warningly, "You best be quick 'fore my uncle comes. He's very wicked. Especially with ladies. There's a commode under the washstand."

Consuela's face flamed.

The boy shrieked with laughter and slammed the door.

* * *

"Oh, but that was just delicious!" With a contented sigh, Consuela set the empty plate aside and dabbed the napkin at her lips. She had been completing her hurried toilette when the door had swung open and the boy had returned carrying a tray of cold chicken, a hard-boiled egg, several slices of buttered bread, two large servings of crumb cake and a mug of lukewarm chocolate. Enraptured, she had at once proceeded to enjoy this feast which she'd told her youthful benefactor was 'fit for a king.'

He had helped her dispose of the crumb cake, and while she ate had told her more of himself. His name was Pierre de Coligny. He was an only child and his life had evidently been a lonely one. At his birth his British-born Mama had extracted a promise from her husband that her son would be educated in England. He was seven years old when both parents perished in a fire and he was placed in the care of his uncle. That heartless individual had been only too willing to pack his unwanted charge off to school in England. Pierre had hoped to find friends there, but instead had been subjected to the endless beatings of the seniors, and the ridicule of the younger boys.

"Poor child," said Consuela sympathetically. "What a horrid time you have had, to be sure. But at least now you are going back to your own country."

"If ever I reach there alive," he sighed.

She put down the mug of chocolate and stood, shaking out her skirts. "I mean to make sure of that!"

"Where are you going?"

"To report this business to our captain." She clung to the end of a bunk as the vessel slid down a wave.

He stared at her. "Do you not feel sick? After eating all that, I would think you'd be green."

"Oh, no. I'm a good sailor. My father used to take me with him when he went fishing. Sometimes, it was very rough. Shall you be all right while I am gone?"

The boy stammered uneasily, "Suppose—he comes back?"

"Hide. Once I've told the captain about that wicked man, he'll never dare touch you, and if—" She paused, it occurring to her that the captain might be surprised to hear such a tale from a lady who had no ticket and was really no more than a stowaway on his vessel. Her heart jumped when somebody jerked at the door handle.

"Here he comes!" cried Pierre shrilly.

Consuela gave a gasp, looked around desperately for some kind of weapon, and snatched up a silver-handled umbrella.

The door burst open. A tall, handsome gentleman came in, taking off his hat and ducking his auburn head as he stepped over the threshold. His fine eyes widened as they fell upon Consuela, umbrella raised threateningly.

"Qui êtes-vous, Madamoiselle?" he demanded with a frown.

"Do not dare attack this child!" cried Consuela, swinging the umbrella higher.

Pierre screamed, "Papa!"

"What?" gasped Consuela.

The boy raced to throw himself into the newcomer's arms, shouting in French, "I found her hiding in the hold, Papa! She made me bring her here and buy her food! She is an English spy!"

Eight

Dawn crept in while the men were still searching. They were all tired and cold, but there was no thought of giving up hope. Vespa was scouring the wilderness area lying between his land and the preserves of Lord Alperson. He was hoarse from calling Consuela's name, and tormented by fears that grew ever more terrifying as hour after hour passed without a trace of her. Plunging into dense shrubs and copses had made riding impractical, and he'd been on his feet for most of the night, a lantern held high, his red-rimmed eyes narrowed, his ears straining to hear the faintest answer to his calls. Weariness and despair were ignored as was the steadily worsening pain in his leg. He refused Manderville's pleas that he rest, as the other men had been obliged to do. When his friend persisted, warning that he would surely collapse if he didn't at least sit down for five minutes, he swore at him, and strove on, driven by his overwhelming need to find her.

Little Signorina Consuela had come unbidden into his house, rearranged his life, and taken possession of his heart so gradually that he'd not realized for a time how much she had come to mean to him. She was not his first love; yet in a sense she was, because his love for her was so deep, so right, so much a part of him that he knew he had never really loved before. Certainly, he had never known a lady like her. He smiled yearningly, seeing in his mind's eye her sparkling blue eyes, the soft and often unruly curls, the lovely mouth that could be so wilful and proud, or so tender, the rich curves of her beautiful body. Consuela Carlotta Angelica Jones. Hot-tempered, impulsive, irrepressibly mischievous, prone to act in an outrageous fashion—and a perfect little darling, who he knew beyond question

fully returned his devotion. If he lost her now . . . "Dear God!"
he whispered. "Please . . . Please!"

As if in answer, Manderville came running, shouting his
name excitedly, and flourishing something.

"Jack! See what we've found! See here!"

Vespa's hand shook as he took the ragged little doll.
"Where?" he demanded.

"It was lying on the estate road."

"Show me!"

Together, they ran across the wilderness and through the
park.

Vespa panted, "Have—have you had time to search the area
where you found it?"

Also breathless, Manderville said, "I didn't find it. Your ex-
Navy tar did. Sharp eyes has Harper, to have seen it with all
this mist about. They'd started to search both sides of the road
when I came to find you."

The light was brighter by the time they reached the spot
where Harper waited. The bow-legged little man touched his
brow and said eagerly, "Hezekiah's gorn over to that there spinney to have a look, but I knowed you'd want me to stay here,
sir. Pure luck it was that I stepped on it. Lying right there, it
were. The dog musta been here recent, 'cause I see him carrying it yesterday."

Vespa slapped him on the back. "Good man!" He bent to
peer at the ground. "There's been a coach here."

Manderville wheezed, "So there has . . . by Jove! And a heavy
one at that."

"Stood here for some time, sir," said Harper. "A four-in-
hand, I reckon."

"Someone rode off this way, alone." Manderville pointed towards the village.

Vespa said, "Yes. But the coach drove . . . south."

He felt icy cold and as he stood straight the world tilted and
he reeled drunkenly. For a moment he lost touch with things.
He heard Manderville swear, and found his friend's arm tight
around him and a flask held to his lips.

"I warned you, damme if I didn't!" fumed Manderville.
"Prancing about for hours on that game leg! And still not fully
recovered from the pistol ball you took in September! Who the
hell d'you suppose you are? Goliath?"

Vespa said brokenly, "They've got her, Paige! God help her! That miserable bastard's . . . taken her!"

"Lor' luvvus!" exclaimed Harper. "Gypsies, you reckon? Never say so, guv!"

Manderville tightened his arm about the stricken man. His own face unwontedly grim, he said, "Not gypsies, Harper. And we can't be sure it was him, Jack. But I'll go after the coach at once, and you can—"

"No!" Vespa pulled himself together. He turned to Harper. "You've done splendidly, and I know you need some sleep, but I'll ask that you first ride into the village. Go to Young Tom at the smithy and find out if he shod any coach-horses yesterday, and if he did, everything he can tell you about their owner. Come back as quickly as you can, please."

Harper nodded, and ran off to get his horse.

Manderville asked, "Do you mean to call off the search, now?"

Vespa shook his head. "I may very well be wrong, Paige."

"Exactly. That's why you should stay here while I—"

Vespa stopped that offer with one flashing glance.

As they started towards the manor side by side, the sun came up, painting a roseate glow on small scattered clouds.

"I understand, dear old boy," said Manderville kindly. "You mean to follow that coach yourself. I don't blame you, but have you thought this through? If you go haring off after Monteil, you'll lose Kincraig."

Vespa rounded on him fiercely. "Do you suppose anything weighs more with me than to find the lady I love?"

"No, of course not. Don't eat me! But—but this is your best chance to catch him, and I can follow the coach as well as—"

"Have done! I'll come up with Lord Kincraig after I've found Consuela."

"Be sensible, man! Look at yourself! You're properly wrung out. Most of us took a few minutes for a bowl of Peg's soup at least, but you haven't stopped once. Can't keep on like that. You'll fall over and lose the pair of 'em."

Chafing at the delay, Vespa bowed to common sense. "Very well. We'll breakfast while we wait for Harper's report. Then you can go on up to Suffolk for me."

"Devil a bit of it! I'm going *with* you! If it is Monteil and his Coachman Colossus, you'll need help."

Vespa gripped his arm briefly. "Thanks, Paige. There's one

thing in our favour—the ground is so damp that the coach left a clear trail. With luck, we'll be able to follow it far enough to have an idea of their eventual destination." He scowled and muttered through gritted teeth. "Lord help that filthy swine if he's hurt her! I'll kill him!"

Watching that anguished face, Manderville did not doubt it.

Two hours later, Vespa's eyes searched the ground as he walked slowly back to where Manderville waited with the horses. "Confound that miserable bastard! He could have turned off half a mile back, or more!"

Manderville said, "They're heading for the coast, Jack."

"Small doubt of that. He means to carry her into France. But—why? What can he possibly hope to achieve by—" Vespa interrupted himself, groaning a frustrated, "Why do I waste time with such nonsensical questions? Perhaps we should just make a dash for Weymouth. It's pretty much in line from here, and we could start our enquiries there, though I dread the waste of time . . . if . . . " The words trailed off. Initially they had followed a poor thoroughfare, potholed and muddied by the rains, and not much travelled. The latter condition had helped them in their enquiries and several farmhands and a gatekeeper had recognized their description of Monteil's coach. They'd come to a busy crossroads then, and a better-maintained road. With the increase in traffic both their sources of information and the wheel tracks had disappeared.

Plagued by indecision he gazed along the road ahead. From a distant hill a farm waggon was crawling towards them. He tensed. "Paige!"

"What? I don't see—"

With an imperative gesture Vespa said sharply, "Listen!"

Straining his ears Manderville could hear only bird calls and, faint with distance, a dog barking.

Vespa walked forward, his eyes beginning to brighten. "By God!" he half-whispered. "I think— Hey!" He began to run.

Leading Secrets, baffled, Manderville followed, and then he too saw the small shape bounding past the waggon.

"Corporal!" shouted Vespa.

"Be damned!" exclaimed Manderville.

Another minute and the dog was close enough to hurl itself

into Vespa's arms, writhing with joy and licking his chin frenziedly.

Hugging the little animal, Vespa looked up at his friend through blurred eyes and said brokenly, "Thank the Lord! Now we know which way to go!"

They lost no time, but having reached the coast and investigated several likely-looking coves, they had still discovered no trace of Monteil's coach. They were both very tired when they rode into the yard of a tiny cliff-top hedge-tavern to rest the horses. Manderville stumbled into the tap and called for luncheon, then had to be awoken to eat the thick coarse bread, sliced cold beef and pickles that were offered. He was dozing over a tankard of ale, and Corporal was fast asleep, when Vespa went outside, fretting against the delay.

There was a cold wind and the clouds were dark, but occasionally a ray of sunlight peeped through. 'Afternoon, already,' he thought wretchedly. The picture of Consuela forced to endure another night in Monteil's hands was like the turn of a knife under his ribs. Wandering across the cobbled yard, he sank onto a hay bale, and bowed his head in despair. Gradually, he became aware of a heated discussion nearby.

". . . wuz, Oi tells ye! Din't Oi see him, an' me Pa, too?"

"An' he were bigger'n a bull."

"Wiv a yeller face, an' no eyes."

Two of the country voices dissolved into laughter that was abruptly stilled as Vespa limped towards them. All three sprang from the fence where they'd perched. Hats were snatched off, and brows knuckled respectfully. They were youngish men, the eldest among them not over forty, their broad faces aglow with health, their eyes friendly.

"I heard you talking about a big man," said Vespa without preamble. "No—pray don't be alarmed. Which of you saw the fellow?"

Uneasy glances were exchanged.

Vespa lied, "The thing is, there's a reward for anyone with news of him."

"There be, zur?"

They crowded around eagerly.

"How much?"

"What's he gone and done, milor'?"

"The reward is not large, I fear." Vespa took a quick mental inventory of the funds he'd brought along. "Five guineas to the man who can tell me where he went."

"Cor!" Clad in the smock and gaiters of a farmhand, his bronzed face crowned with a shock of very blond hair, the youngest of the three exclaimed, "Five *guineas*?"

The older man, who appeared to be a fisherman, had been eyeing Vespa shrewdly. "Why?"

Clearly, to these simple folk five guineas was a vast sum even split three ways. Equally clearly, they were not sure of him. "I put it up myself," he elaborated. "My name is Captain Vespa. The big man you saw is Chinese. He works for a Swiss gentleman named Monteil. They have stolen an English lady. The lady to whom I am betrothed. I'm very afraid"—his voice cracked slightly—"I'm afraid they mean to carry her over to France."

The brief, shaken words won them over as no amount of involved explanations would have done, and provoked an outburst of shocked wrath. That a foreigner would dare to make away with an Englishwoman was as insulting as it was horrifying.

"Oi couldn't but notice as ye look proper pulled, zur," said the fisherman. "Nor Oi cannot blame ye. If ever Oi heered o' such wickedness! Oi be Ezekiel, zur. This here"—he pulled forward a small and painfully shy individual who appeared to be an ostler—"this be Ed. And the big lad wi' all the yeller hair— that's Samuel. Ye best tell the Cap'n, Ed."

Thus encouraged, Ed stammered that he had indeed seen such a strange chap. "Hugeous big, he were," he said, throwing out both arms to emphasize his remark. "Nigh to seven foot tall, Oi do rackon. And broader'n Farmer Stowe's bull! Axed me summat as Oi couldn't no-wise make out. But me Pa were along o' me, an' he tells this here giant as how the other gent had rid through a hour afore."

Vespa's breath was snatched away. Then he gasped, "What other gent? Not a very tall man with black hair and dead-white skin?"

"Ar." Ed nodded.

"I see *that* 'un," the blond Samuel chimed in eagerly. "Riding of a neatish bay mare, he wuz."

"Bravo!" exclaimed Vespa, elated. "Was my lady with him? She is small and very pretty, with dark brown curls and big blue eyes and the sweetest smile anyone—" He caught himself up, feeling his face redden.

The loverlike description won sympathetic smiles. Samuel said with regret that he had seen no such lady.

"Me Pa says as the big giant fella axed for Willy," supplied Ed, hopefully.

"That'll be Willy Leggett, zur," clarified Ezekiel.

"Willy were lying off White Cove yestiday, but—" Samuel stopped, looking scared.

His heart pounding with renewed hope, Vespa said quickly, "Never fear, I'm no Riding Officer. Mr. Leggett is a free-trader, I take it. Show me where his boat lies, and I'll make it nine guineas you divide between you!"

Willy Leggett's 'fishing boat' was at the moment 'at sea.' George Leggett, his brother, conveyed that information to Ezekiel, who had accompanied Vespa and Manderville to the large quay that ran out from a cove that was as if tucked into the cliffs. Ezekiel had at first approached Leggett alone and had held an earnest discussion with him, during which Leggett's enigmatic gaze had shifted constantly between Vespa and Manderville, while the straw he gripped between his teeth jerked as constantly from one side of his mouth to the other.

He was a sturdy man of late middle age, his skin red and leathered from years of exposure to wind and water. At first suspicious and reluctant to talk to these strangers, he was much shocked by the tale Ezekiel told, and Vespa soon managed to win his confidence. He admitted that Willy was on a run to France, and had sailed with the previous evening's tide, bound for Brittany.

Startled, Vespa exclaimed, "Brittany! Do you know whereabouts?"

"Aye," said Leggett, retaining the straw.

"Was there a lady passenger? A very lovely young lady?"

"One or two ladies. I wouldn't 'zackly say 'lovely.' But that tall gent were aboard, and his gert hulking servant with him."

"You're quite sure the gentleman did not drive away in his coach?"

"Couldn't of. Coach went too."

Vespa glanced along the quay. Several fishing boats were tied up, and a good-sized crane was unloading bales from the hold of a merchantman.

Manderville said, "Jupiter! Your brother must have a large boat, Mr. Leggett."

A faint sly grin curved the thin lips. "Aye."

"Is she very fast?" asked Vespa anxiously. "Have I any chance of coming up with her?"

Leggett viewed him thoughtfully. "Might. The *Saucy Maid*'s heavy laden. Low in the water. Touch and go it were, whether she'd clear the sand bar. If Willy spies any Coast Guard cutters, he'll likely hide in the Islands 'fore going on."

"Which would give me a chance to catch up?"

"Might. If you wasn't 'bliged to hide as well. Either way, ye'd be needing a fast boat, sir."

"Only tell me where to find one!"

Leggett took the straw from his mouth and considered it. Once again his keen gaze flashed from Vespa to Manderville. "Both on ye?"

Manderville said quickly, "Both of us."

Turning to him, Vespa argued "Paige, this will be enemy territory. I'll not ask you to—"

"*Both* of us," reiterated Manderville.

Vespa clapped him on the back gratefully. "I must send off a letter to the duchess at once. And then—what d'you say Mr. Leggett?"

"Enemy territ'ry, right enough," said Leggett. "Risky. But if this here Frenchy stole your lady, Cap'n—well, we can't have that now, can we?" With an almost-grin he replaced his straw and started to stroll along the quay. "Foller me, gents, and meet my *Lively Lace*, the fastest yawl on this or any other water!"

The *Lively Lace* was fast, all right. Clinging to the rail near the aft mizzenmast and watching her mainsail and two jibs crack in the wind, it seemed to Vespa that the yawl fairly flew, her bow throwing up billowing clouds of spray as it sliced the waves.

George Leggett had been quite willing to convey them to the port on the Brittany coast where his brother would hopefully have dropped anchor. The fee was surprisingly low. George had said with a twinkle that since he'd not be carrying any contraband for once, if a Revenue cutter did challenge him, he could claim that he was simply ferrying passengers to the Channel Islands. "Put their noses proper out of joint, it will," he'd chuckled, as he showed them to the small cabin below decks. There were bunks in the cabin, and within minutes two were occupied. Vespa had slept for almost seven hours, awakening to the familiar pitch and roll of a ship and the heavenly aroma of frying ham that wafted from the tiny galley. A wash and shave and a hasty meal, then, leaving Manderville still sleeping like one dead, he'd come up on deck feeling a new man.

A bright moon escaped the clouds from time to time and was reflected on the endless expanse of heaving waters. The cold air blew salt spray in his face. He thought yearningly, 'I'm coming to you, my love. God keep you. I'll find you soon.' Leggett, at the wheel, had watched his approach approvingly and called that the captain had his 'sea legs' all right.

Vespa crossed to his side and shouted, "I've done my share of sailing. Can we hope to reach France tonight?"

"If this wind holds, sir, I'll have you in Brittany by dawn—give or take sunrise."

Vespa nodded and returned to the rail. Time passed, and he was joined by the tall yellow-haired Samuel, who Leggett had explained sometimes sailed as 'crew.' Samuel offered an oilskin coat with the warning that Cap'n Vespa would get 'soaked through' without it, because it looked like 'weather' was blowing up.

He was right. Within an hour, Leggett and Samuel were struggling to shorten sail while Vespa took the wheel. Manderville came reeling up, shouted something unintelligible, lost his balance and shot across the deck. Vespa gave a horrified yell, secured the wheel and ran. Manderville was hurled over the rail but somehow managed to clutch it. He hung on for dear life while Vespa dragged him back onto the deck.

Bracing himself, Vespa gasped out, "Devil of a time . . . for a swim, Paige."

Manderville clung to him and groaned, "What . . . I don't risk . . . in the name of . . ."

"Of—what?"

"Of—er, friendship, of course. And—curse you, you've torn my—new coat!"

"Ingrate," panted Vespa, staggering back to the wheel. "D'you want a turn at this?"

"Certainly not! I'm a soldier—not a damned merman! When dare we hope to reach—to reach dry land again?"

"Dawn—so Leggett says, if this wind keeps up."

"*Wind?* I thought it was a hurricane!"

Hurricane or not, when the pale fingers of dawn streaked the eastern clouds the *Lively Lace* was following the Normandy coastline towards Brittany, just as George Leggett had promised. Vespa had seen several distant lighthouse beacons, but not so much as a glimpse of a Revenue cutter. The seas were treacherous here; great plumes of spray boiled up around offshore rocks, and the dark water surged in swift and deadly currents that only a skilled mariner could hope to navigate.

The wind having dropped, Manderville risked another climb to the deck. One glance at lowering skies, heaving seas and a great mass of black granite that suddenly reared up beside the bow, and he flung a hand over his eyes and retreated, moaning.

For Vespa it had been a night of backbreaking effort, but the battle against the elements, bruising as it was, had given him the chance to put aside, for the moment, his crushing anxieties, and he had the satisfaction of knowing his health was steadily improving and that he'd managed to be of real assistance.

Peering at the looming ridges of Brittany, he stood at the wheel beside Leggett, and asked, "Are you sure of your brother's destination? That coastline ahead looks very wild. I never saw so many coves and inlets, and each guarded by offshore rocks. Might he not choose an easier route?"

"He got no choice, Cap'n. with that there coach to off-load, he'll need a port with a crane, but he's got to take care. The French navy don't amount to much since our Nelson met up with 'em, but they got a few ships of the line and some Customs cutters, and Willy being English they'd be main glad to send him to Davy Jones' Locker!"

"I haven't seen much in the way of towns. This area's pretty sparsely populated, isn't it? Would it be worthwhile for French naval ships to patrol here?"

"Not in a reg'lar way, sir. But the more lonely it is, the more chance for free-traders and such to slip in and out." He shouted suddenly, "Hi! Sam! We're going in! Shorten sail!"

The yawl slowed, and turned landward. For some minutes Vespa had heard a dull roaring, and now, looking ahead, he caught his breath. Here again, the coastline was guarded by clusters of rocks like so many jagged teeth snarling against shipping, the waves thundering and foaming around them. "Good Lord!" he muttered.

Leggett's hands were strong on the wheel, his keen eyes fixed on the tumultuous seas. "If it weren't for that there dratted coach . . ." he muttered.

The *Lively Lace* began to buck and leap like a fractious horse. Vespa clung to the rail and marvelled at the skill of these men who could pick their way through such treacherous currents. Black-green water hove up along the side, then suddenly fell away; the roar was deafening, and for a heart-stopping few seconds the deck seemed to drop from under his feet and he was sure they were going down. A moment later the yawl drifted easily on a surface with scarcely a ripple.

Leggett shouted, "Good for you, Cap'n! Ain't many landlubbers could keep their nerves steady through that. This is where I put you off."

"Here?" There was nothing in sight but a deserted beach backed by low, barren-looking cliffs. "I cannot see the *Saucy Maid* or any other shipping. Where are we?"

"As close as I can bring ye to Brittany, sir. Sam'll row you and Mr. Manderville ashore and set ye down on the beach. You see that headland, yonder? Go 'round that, and you'll find the fishing port. It's called La Emeraude, what means emerald, on account of when the sun shines on 'em, the rocks and the sea looks green. Not today, they don't. But there's times they does. They got a nice deep harbour and a crane." He winked. "Cater to The Gentlemen, they do."

"Free-traders, you mean."

"Aye. Them. Likely, Willy will be already tied up and offloading. He's knowed here, and he's got plenty of Frenchies aboard what had no business going to England, any more than you got going to France. More'n I dare do to sail in right under their noses with two Englishmen aboard, and one of 'em a army captain! You take care, sir, and don't speak nought but French. It ain't exactly what they speak here, but better they should think you French than British. Been a pleasure having you on the *Lively Lace*. Good luck finding your lady!"

"Thank you. You'll be sure to send my letters off, and keep my dog safe till I return or my people call for him?"

Leggett gave his solemn promise to do as asked. Manderville came up in response to Vespa's hail, and having shaken hands with Leggett, they climbed into the dinghy and were rowed ashore.

"How do we get home, once we find Consuela?" asked Manderville, eyeing the departing dinghy uneasily.

"We'll arrange that with brother Willy."

"If he hasn't already sailed."

Vespa didn't respond. His thoughts were all on finding Consuela and settling accounts with Monsieur Imre Monteil.

The sun was up now, but concealed by a grey overcast. The air was dank but not as cold as it had been in Dorsetshire. They were both wearing riding boots which made the long walk tiresome. Manderville said morosely that he didn't believe there was a port at all, but Vespa's faith in Leggett was justified when they rounded the headland and a little forest of masts came into view. A moment later they saw the port. It was not much more than a village; some clusters of pale granite houses and on the outskirts quite a number of whitewashed cottages set well apart from each other, their steep thatched roofs and the unfamiliar shapes of the chimneys appearing alien to British eyes. On a nearby hill a church spire rose among sparse trees. There were few people on the cobbled street; an old lady wearing severe black except for the tall and snowy lace cap on her head carried a covered jug to a nearby house; three small boys were running down towards the quay, where Vespa's searching gaze had discovered several fishing boats and men already at work repairing nets.

Manderville muttered, "Don't see no *Saucy Maid,* do—"

"The crane. See—there!"

And there she was, a large two-masted vessel, with some half-dozen passengers gathering their luggage on the deck, and four or five children watching in great excitement as a fine travelling carriage was hoisted from the hold. Observing this procedure critically was a tall, elegant gentleman with jet-black hair and very pale skin.

"Hi!" cried Manderville. "Jack! Hold up, you lamebrain!"

He was too late.

With an inarticulate growl of rage Vespa was already sprinting up the gangway to the deck of Willy Leggett's *Saucy Maid.* In another instant an astonished Swiss gentleman was whirled around, an enraged young face glared at him murderously, a strong hand was ruining his perfectly arranged neckcloth, and a very British voice was snarling a demand to know what he had done with 'her.'

Unaccustomed to such treatment and considerably off-stride, Imre Monteil gasped a bewildered, "With—who?"

"You know who, you murdering bastard," raged Vespa, tightening his grip on the neckcloth. "Tell me, or so help me God, I'll—"

"*Jack!*"

However shrill, there was no mistaking that beloved voice. Vespa's heart leapt and he jerked around, whispering a prayerful, "Consuela!"

Her face aglow with joy, she rushed to him.

Monteil, half throttled, gasped, "Let . . . me . . . go, you curst imbecile!"

"So you *did* take her! Damn your eyes!"

Vespa's deadly right was brought into play and Monsieur Monteil ceased to complain.

Ignoring the resultant uproar, Vespa crushed Consuela to him and with his cheek against her silky curls half-sobbed, "Thank God! Thank God! My little love!" He held her away, scanning her frantically. "Did he hurt you? Did he dare to touch you?"

"No." Her radiant eyes searched his face. "I am perfectly all right. Oh, my dear, how ever did you find me? How worn you look! I must tell you that—"

His overwhelming relief turned perversely to anger. He shook her, and snarled, "If *ever* you deserved a good spanking! Wandering off alone again! Frightening us to death! After I'd *told* you—"

They were wrenched apart.

"*Ma foi,* but this one is of a violence!" cried a Gallic voice.

Two of the deck hands who'd been working with the crane gripped Vespa's arms, and told him in an odd French dialect that he was fortunate Monsieur's servant was a victim of *mal-de-mer* else he would assuredly by this time be very dead.

Manderville ran up beside a stocky young man who bore a strong resemblance to George Leggett. Several of the male passengers gathered around, ladies were shrill in their condemnation of such bestial behaviour, various saints were called upon for protection and the air rang with questions and expostulations.

Leggett waved his arms about and spoke loudly in the language that sounded like a mixture of French and Gaelic. It was hard to follow, but Vespa identified enough words to realize that the onlookers were being informed this was a simple case of mistaken identity, and that no great harm had been done.

The two deck hands released their prisoner reluctantly.

"This wild one he is *sans doute* from Paris," declared one.

His companion nodded scornfully. "There, they all are mad."

Vespa slipped his arm about Consuela's waist again. "I suppose you would be overjoyed if your lady was stolen," he said in French.

They stared at him, obviously taken aback.

The small curious crowd that had gathered began to disperse, and the deck hands carried the awakening Monsieur Monteil off—presumably to his cabin.

Willy Leggett said in low-voiced English, "They was right, sir. Your friend tells me as you sailed here with George. I can't hardly blame you for cutting up rough if he stole your lady, but you'd be wise to stay least in sight for a while. If I knows Monsieur Monteil, he'll be out for blood! Was you wanting to make the return voyage on the *Saucy Maid*?"

"Yes," said Vespa emphatically.

"No," said Consuela, even more emphatically.

Someone shouted urgently for Willy.

"You people best get below," he said. "And make up yer mind, sir. I don't stay hereabouts a second longer'n I must. The *Saucy Maid* sails with the tide."

He hurried away, Manderville following and enquiring uneasily as to the likelihood of interference by French port authorities.

"No, we cannot go," said Consuela, tugging at Vespa's arm and leading him into a narrow passageway. "Do come quickly. Oh, I wish you had not struck that horrid Swiss man!"

"I should have wrung his scrawny neck," he growled. "You're of an extraordinarily forgiving nature, Consuela."

"There is nought to forgive. Monsieur Monteil never touched me. He didn't even know I was on board." She flung open a cabin door. "This gentleman has been taking care of me."

Bewildered by her revelations, Vespa was more bewildered to face a steadily aimed pistol in the hand of a tall and distinguished individual.

"*You!*" he gasped.

"*Mon Dieu!*" exclaimed de Coligny, recoiling.

"Shoot him! *Shoot* him, Papa!" urged Pierre, jumping up and down in excitement as he rushed into the cabin. "He is English! I heard him when he knocked down that funny black and white man. He called him a murdering bas—"

Consuela clapped a hand across his mouth.

"Well, he did!" squealed Pierre, wriggling free. "He is a *spy*, Papa! Just like her! I told you—"

"You will cease to tell me," said de Coligny in a no-nonsense voice that silenced his son. He reached out. "My dear fellow!"

The two men exchanged a firm handshake, and de Coligny gestured to Pierre to close the cabin door.

"You are—acquainted?" asked Consuela, sitting on a bunk beside Vespa. "But—Monsieur Gaston, you never said you knew my betrothed!"

The Frenchman put the pistol aside and said with a twinkle, "It is, you might say, a passing acquaintanceship. Besides, Miss Jones, you did not tell me his name."

"I never thought my Papa would cry friends with a perfid'us Englishman," grumbled Pierre, disappointed.

"He is *not* perfidious!" protested Consuela.

"I believe that is from Napoleon Bonaparte's name for us," said Vespa. "Perfidious Albion." He glanced at the Frenchman's left hand, immobile and encased in a leather glove. "So you lost your hand, after all. Were you then exchanged?"

De Coligny nodded. "I was sent home. Did your shoulder necessitate your own separation from the army?"

"It was a—contributing factor."

"Ah—you fought together," said Consuela, the light dawning.

"But on opposite sides," qualified Vespa.

Pierre was sitting on the floor watching sulkily, but at this he sprang up, exclaiming, "Now I know, Papa! This is the British officer you told me of! The man who shot you!"

"Fair exchange, rather." Vespa turned to Consuela. "The Chevalier de Coligny was with D'Erlon at Vitoria. We encountered each other on the field, and were unhorsed by the same shell. Only one hack survived and, in the struggle to capture it, each of us was wounded."

De Coligny explained. "My shot took Jacques in the shoulder."

"And he shot off your hand," cried Pierre, scowling at Vespa.

"Not quite," said his father with a smile for that fierce resentment. "Although he was himself hurt, Captain Vespa was so good as to apply a tourniquet to my wrist. Else, my son, I should not be here now. Unhappily, the infection it set in." He shrugged fatalistically. *"C'est la vie.* And I am fortunate. I have not to earn my living, and with the help of my family and my good servants, I contrive. I am only glad, *mon capitaine,* that I was not responsible for your demise, for I had heard it that you were killed."

"Wars!" said Consuela, who could picture the battlefield scene all too well. "How utterly stupid they are. If women ran the world we would outlaw the silly things!"

"Perhaps, someday, you will," said de Coligny.

"In the meantime," said Vespa, still holding Consuela's hand tightly, "Will somebody be so kind as to tell me how it comes about that my lady seems to be—ah, travelling under your protection?"

Simultaneously:

Consuela said, "I was trapped in that horrid Swiss man's coach!"

Pierre said, "*I* found her, hiding with a bear!"

The Chevalier de Coligny said, "The lady slept in my cabin!"

"Did she, indeed?" Vespa seized on the final incomprehensibility. "I think you must explain that, monsieur!"

"*Certainement,* I must!" agreed de Coligny hurriedly. "But I pray you will not look upon me with such ferocity, *mon cher Jacques.*"

"He is very ferocious," put in Pierre. "And he is an English spy also, Papa. What are you going to do with him?"

The two men looked at each other.

"Ah," murmured de Coligny. "Now that is the question."

Nine

The chevalier, who had begun to look grave, was much relieved when Vespa assured him that he was in Brittany only to retrieve his lady. Consuela told her tale with typical Latin drama. Vespa paled when she spoke of her "flight through the air" as the coach was loaded into the hold of the fishing boat, but was won to laughter by Pierre's exuberant description of her encounter with the bear. "So it is Pierre who has rescued your Miss Consuela," the boy boasted proudly.

"And it is Pierre to whom I am very deeply indebted," said Vespa, bowing to him.

"Such a terrifying experience for a gentle lady," murmured the chevalier, who was still not a little shocked by such behaviour. "I am very sure my dear wife would have swooned away."

Consuela stared at him. "She would? But it was a great adventure. Though, I'll admit I was a little bit afraid. Just now and then, you know. And I am very glad that Jack has come and everything turned out so nicely."

"Oh, are you?" said Vespa, feigning indignation. "I take it that you care not a button that I have knocked down an innocent gentleman!"

"Not the tiniest button," agreed Consuela, her eyes sparkling at him.

"And I must question the innocence of that particular gentleman," said de Coligny. "He has the reputation most unsavoury."

"Yes, indeed." Having kept her most exciting piece of news to the end, Consuela said, "And now you must listen closely, Jack, for I have learned something of the greatest importance, that you will be very happy to know."

He smiled at her tenderly. "I can think of nothing so important as to know that you are safe, my little Signorina."

For a moment there was silence as they exchanged glances that betrayed their love with more eloquence than mere words could have done.

Amused, the chevalier coughed politely behind his hand.

Vespa started and flushed with embarrassment.

Consuela said, "Oh, dear! Now what was I saying?"

"It cannot have been so very important if you've already forgot," said Pierre, bored, and went out onto the deck.

"But it is!" said Consuela. "Jack—Lord Kincraig is *here!* In Brittany! That's why Imre Monteil came. He means to find him!"

"What?" he said incredulously, "But are you quite sure? Manderville heard that he was gone to Suffolk."

"No, no! I was hiding in the coach when the messenger brought the news to Monteil! He said the 'Crazy Carpet Collector' had been near Rennes last week, and Monteil was very pleased! Isn't it wonderful that we've found him?"

"That *you've* found him, clever girl! And it's wonderful indeed, if—"

"So here you are!" Paige Manderville stepped into the cabin and closed the door quickly.

"Yes." Vespa stood, his mind a whirl of excitement and new hope. "Has Imre Monteil reported us to the authorities?"

"Don't think he found any to report to! He seems to think you've gone inland, and the silly clunch has taken his monstrous coachman and gone haring off after you. Jolly good luck to him! I've arranged with Willy Leggett for our passage home. I fancy you'll want to go ashore, de Coligny?"

The chevalier confirmed this, and Vespa also declared his intention of going ashore.

"Consuela has been telling me how she came to be in Monteil's coach," he explained, responding to his friend's astounded expression.

"The man is a scoundrel, no doubt of it," said Manderville. "But to follow and demand satisfaction would be the height of folly, dear old boy."

"I've no least intention of doing either. Though, I suppose he is entitled to a meeting. I did knock him down, after all."

"Stuff! You'd every right to knock him down. But if you don't mean to follow the villain, why do you wish to go ashore? Ain't much of a place, so far as I can see. No offence intended, de Coligny, but there's not much here outside of granite and sand and a lighthouse every few miles."

"There will be," declared the chevalier. "We've plans to improve roads and transportation and to plant crops to enrich the soil. Soon, this will be a grand agricultural centre."

"And besides, I found out that Lord Kincraig is here," put in Consuela. "Isn't it marvellous?"

Manderville gave a snort of derision. "Marvellous fustian! What on earth gave you that notion? Kincraig is in Suffolk—and likely even now preparing to hop over to Belgium. Someone's been filling your ears with treacle, Consuela."

"No such thing!" she argued fiercely. "I heard a courier tell Imre Monteil that the 'Crazy Carpet Man' is in the vicinity of Rennes! It is *your* informant who is wrong, Paige Manderville!"

"In which case," said Vespa, "we're closer than we've ever been, and I mean to lose no time in—"

"In—what? Running your head straight under the nearest guillotine? You're as bacon-brained as he is!" Exasperated, Manderville declared, "I tell you, Jack, Kincraig's nowhere near Rennes!"

Vespa said dubiously, "I suppose Monteil's man could have erred."

De Coligny said in his courteous fashion, "Forgive that I interfere, but may I know why you would wish to find this poor mad gentleman?"

Consuela and Manderville both looked to Vespa and were silent. He improvised quickly. "It is a family thing, Gaston. My mother believes this carpet collector may be her long-missing cousin, and she has charged me to find him."

"Ah," de Coligny nodded sympathetically. "It is a sad task, that. I cannot help, for I know very little of him. From what I have heard of Imre Monteil, his people would not dare to bring him false reports. But Lieutenant Manderville speaks truly, Jacques. Even had you the means, to venture into France would be to write your death-warrant."

"That does not appear to weigh with Lord Kincraig," said Vespa.

"No—because he is, you will forgive, demented, and knowing this, people do not pay him heed. With you, it would be otherwise. And of a certainty you must take Miss Consuela out of harm's way."

"Paige will escort her home for me, won't you?" said Vespa, turning to his friend.

"We both will take the lady home," argued Manderville stubbornly.

"You will do no such thing," said Consuela, her little chin setting. "Whatever you say, Jack, I know what you mean to do, and I am not going to be packed off home to worry myself into a decline while you rush out and get yourself slain! No, and no!"

His heart warmed by this declaration, Vespa said fondly, "You are very dear, but you must see that I can't drag you about all over France, with not the whisper of a chaperone. Even if your lovely head were not forfeit, your reputation assuredly would be."

"Look about you, Captain John," she commanded. "Where are the crowds? The leaders of the *ton?* The gabsters and gossips and rumour-mongers? Who will know I am here? Rennes is not very far away, and you certainly do not mean to journey through France wearing a scarlet uniform—"

"Blue," corrected Manderville absently.

Consuela swept on, "—you will go in some sort of disguise, no? And I shall be your sister—or your affianced, or the Lady Consuela of Ottavio, whom you escort to the duchess, her Grandmama, and who would be an asset, rather than—"

Someone pounded on the door and bellowed, "All ashore what's goin' ashore!"

Vespa led Consuela to the door saying in a lowered voice, "My little love it will not serve. I have no coach, and may have to ride on a donkey if I can hire one, or travel many miles afoot. To be always responsible for your precious self would be a constant worry at a time I'll need to keep my wits about me. You must allow Paige to take you home so that I can know you'll be safe."

" 'Fraid not," said Manderville. "If you go, Jack, I'm going with you."

Consuela clapped her hands and did a little jig of delight.

Dismayed, Vespa said, "But I can't let her go back to England alone! That would really cause an uproar!"

"I agree. So abandon this foolish plan and you'll find I am in the right of it."

"It is *not* a foolish plan! Don't listen to him, Jack," said Consuela. "We will journey to Rennes, you and I, and find your carpet collector!"

Vespa shook his head. "Whatever the case, your safety must be my first consideration," he said firmly. "I'll take you back to your Grandmama, and then come—"

She gave a wail of mortification, and said she had been so eager to tell him her wonderful news and now that horrid Paige Manderville had spoiled everything.

Manderville looked aghast and hurried off to advise Leggett the decision had been made.

Pierre came back and with a disgusted look at Consuela said, "What? Crying again? What watering pots you ladies are!"

The chevalier told his son to apologize at once, and then sent the boy off to call their coachman to come and get the luggage.

The next few minutes were not pleasant for either of the remaining gentlemen. Consuela wept bitterly and lamented between sobs that she was now the cause of Jack losing Lord Kincraig. Vespa's attempts to comfort her were to no avail, and he could not have been more relieved when de Coligny's coachman and footman arrived to collect the portmanteaux.

The chevalier murmured excusingly, "She has endured much, the little lady."

"She has indeed. There's no end to her courage and resourcefulness, but I fear she is quite exhausted. It is as well she'll be able to rest on the return passage." Vespa took Consuela's arm. "Come, my signorina. I'll see what Leggett has arranged for your cabin, and you can say adieu to your new friends."

The wind was rising when they went on deck. Consuela clung sadly to Vespa's arm, but thanked the chevalier for all his kindness to her, and waved goodbye to Pierre, who had followed the bear's cage onto the quay and was leaping about "as though," said his amused sire, "he went on springs!"

Shaking de Coligny's hand, Vespa said, "I shall never be able to thank you for taking such good care of her, Gaston. If ever—"

He was interrupted by Consuela's shriek. A chorus of shouts went up, interspersed by squeals and screams and a frenzied scattering of those on the quay.

Consuela squeaked, "Pierre has let that terrible bear out of its cage!"

"Mon Dieu!" gasped the chevalier, and ran for the gangplank.

"Oh, heavens!" exclaimed Consuela. "Pierre thinks he can play with the creature!" Vespa was already limping rapidly after de Coligny, and she called, "Jack—do be careful!"

Willy Leggett roared a frustrated, "I ain't a'waiting, Captain Vespa! If we're to catch the tide we must leave—*now!*"

Vespa scarcely heard him; his entire concentration was on the distraught father who, in an effort not to further alarm the bear, was now walking smoothly towards his son.

Pierre was prancing about in great excitement and advising the bear to "cut and run" while he had the chance. Misunderstanding, the bear reared up onto its hind legs. Beside the small figure of the child, the animal appeared enormous.

De Coligny drew his pistol and aimed it.

A shabby looking little man raced up and sprang in front of the chevalier. "What do you intend for my beast?" he demanded with wrathful indignation. "Your child, he release my poor Étudiant with much malice, and in return you seek to destroy the dear soul! My very livelihood! Such wickedness!"

Scanning the bear, who stood at least six feet tall, Vespa thought he had seldom seen a less promising 'student.'

De Coligny said, "If that brute touches my son . . . !"

The little man called, "Come to Papa, Étudiant, my dear. We will not suffer these evil men to harm you. Come!"

The bear snorted and snuffled and threw its head about a few times, then dropped to all fours and ambled to its master, the long nose searching out a likely pocket. Something was withdrawn from the pocket and deposited into a front paw, that was, Vespa noted, well equipped with very long claws. 'Papa' said with some embarrassment, "He likes the currant buns. It is that he have only four teeth, you know."

The chevalier snatched up his son, and snarled something that abruptly dampened the child's exuberance.

Recalled to his own interests, Vespa glanced to the *Saucy Maid*.

She was moving!

"Oh, Lord!" he groaned, and rushing to the edge of the quay made a desperate leap for the vessel. He landed safely, but was unable to hold his balance on the rolling deck and fell to his knees.

In his ears was a beloved voice, shrieking his name.

From the quay!

He clambered to his feet. Consuela, looking far from exhausted, stood beside the chevalier, waving frantically.

Snarling English, French and Spanish curses, Vespa ran back a few yards and again launched himself across the widening band of dark water.

He landed hard, wrenching his damaged leg painfully, which did not improve his temper. Some people who had recovered from their terror of the toothless and now-leashed Étudiant set up a cheer.

De Coligny steadied Vespa while imploring him to exercise some self-control.

Impressed by the Englishman's athletics, Pierre was applauding even as tears of mirth glinted in his eyes. "These English, they move from one place to another very swiftly, Papa," he chortled.

Consuela's mischievous face peeped from behind the chevalier. "I am truly sorry, dear Jack," she pleaded, with not a tear in sight and her eyes alight with laughter.

"Yes, I can see you are," panted Vespa, scarlet with embarrassment and momentarily forgetting how he had grieved and worried for his exasperating love.

"Jack!" Running along the deck to the stern of the *Saucy Maid*, Paige Manderville howled, "What the *devil* are you doing over there?"

"Sorry, Paige," shouted Vespa breathlessly. "But— *No!* You maniac! It's too far!"

It was. Manderville jumped, notwithstanding.

Fortunately, he was a good swimmer.

Ignoring the hilarious onlookers, and Pierre, who had crumpled to the ground and was rolling about, convulsed, Vespa rushed to assist Manderville onto the quay. Such selfless devotion was astounding, and gazing in awe at his gallant but drenched comrade, Vespa said, "My dear fellow! How very good of you! But—oh, egad! Your new coat!"

Manderville dashed salt water from his eyes and peered down at the disaster. "My . . . new . . . coat!" he wailed through chattering teeth.

Vespa took off his cloak and wrapped it about the swimmer. "I must get you out of this wind, before you catch the pneumonia."

De Coligny waved imperatively, and a small carriage drawn by four ill-matched horses was driven to them.

A liveried footman opened the door. Pierre clambered onto the box beside the coachman, and de Coligny ushered Consuela, Manderville and Vespa up the steps, then climbed in to sit beside Vespa. "Shall you wait for the next boat?" he enquired, as the footman closed the door.

Consuela, who was chafing Manderville's icy hands, said, "No! Jack, I will *not* have you lose this chance to find Lord Kincraig, only so as to escort me home! Besides, with that horrid Monsieur Monteil after him the gentleman is in great danger, and must be warned! You cannot turn your back on a kinsman! We are *here!*"

"Y-yes. And dash it all, C-Consuela, we shouldn't b-be!" complained Manderville. "Use your—your wits, Jack! The people on the quay know we're British! We'll be l-lucky to get away from here alive, l-let alone go farther inland!"

Troubled, Vespa turned to de Coligny. "Have I already put you at risk, Gaston?"

The chevalier shrugged. "Long ages past the Bretons migrated here from your land, did you not know it?"

Vespa nodded. "From Cornwall and Wales, I believe."

"Yes. Which is why this peninsula was once called *Petite Bretagne*—or Little Britain. The common folk dislike foreigners, Parisians especially, for throughout our history France has often tried to conquer us. You will think it odd, but I believe my Bretons would be less likely to arrest you, or to blame me for your presence, than they would if you had come from Paris. Still, Manderville is right. To leave my area and travel inland will involve much risk for you, *mon ami.*"

"Perhaps. However, Miss Jones is dark-haired and part-Italian, which would, I believe, guarantee her safety and not endanger you or your family. Gaston—may I impose on you to guard her for me while I go on to Rennes?"

De Coligny looked thoughtfully from one to the other of their anxious faces. He said slowly, "I owe you my life, Captain John Vespa. And as I have said, I am a Breton. Even so, I fought for Napoleon. I will have one thing from you before I answer: your word of honour that your quest has nothing whatsoever to do with this war, and that for France it holds no threat."

Vespa said fervently, "On my honour, and as God be my judge, I swear it!"

"In that case," said the Frenchman with a smile, "my home

is but three leagues distant, and I am very sure my wife will be delighted to have Miss Jones' company."

Manderville threw up his hands. "You're *all* mad!" he declared. "S-stark, raving l-loobies!"

The drive to the Château de Coligny was far from comfortable. The road was poorly paved and full of potholes, and the terrain was very ridged. It seemed to Consuela that she was constantly either almost jolted from the seat when the coach was moving down some steep slope, or in danger of having Jack deposited in her lap when they were climbing one of the innumerable hills. The bumpy ride did not disturb Manderville; evidently tired from his impromptu swim, he soon fell asleep.

Vespa wanted to hear more about Consuela's meeting with de Coligny, and the chevalier told laughingly how he had been terrified by her threat to attack him with his own umbrella.

"My lady is an Amazon, *véritable,*" said Vespa, his eyes saying something very different.

Blushing because of that look, Consuela declared, "It was all because of Pierre. He told me *such* a story! He said Monsieur de Coligny was his wicked uncle, who had arranged to have him thrown overboard."

"In order to seize control of his fortune, no doubt," said Vespa, amused. "I wonder you believed the little scamp, Consuela."

The chevalier shook his head ruefully. "He has too much of the imagination, alas."

"He was certainly very convincing," said Consuela. "And one does hear of such things. Only think of the little Princes in the Tower, poor boys. I remember when *Nonna* told me about them. . . ." The words trailed off into silence.

Vespa said gently, "You're thinking of your Grandmama."

"Yes." Her lips trembled. "She is—frail, you know. And she will be terribly worried."

"So I thought, and I left a letter for her with Willy Leggett's brother. With luck it will be in her hands tomorrow."

"Oh, Jack, how *very* kind."

He leant forward to kiss the hand she reached out to him, and said with a smile, "I agree that Lady Francesca must have

worried. But as for her being frail—never! She is resilient as
steel, and I've no doubt that the moment she reads my letter
she will have old Watts drive her down to retrieve Corporal."

"You *found* him?"

"Say rather that he found us, and it is thanks to him that
we were able to follow Monteil's coach."

"Dear little fellow! Then *Nonna* will trust you to rescue me
once again, for she will assuredly question Mr. Leggett. Thank
heaven! Now I may be easy."

She was indeed greatly relieved and her buoyant spirit reas-
serted itself. She was with the man she loved, and things were
going so well. Her frightening ordeal in Monsieur Monteil's
coach had turned out to be a blessing in disguise. Rennes was
not very far away, and with luck, between them they would find
Lord Kincraig and their troubles would be over.

It was typical of her to be undismayed by the fact that she
was far from home, in an enemy country, and without a
chaperone; that she had not so much as a toothbrush or a
comb for her hair, and only the clothes she stood up in. She
was in Jack's hands and he would take care of everything.
Within weeks, perhaps, she would be his betrothed. The one
shadow to mar her pleasant scenario was the presence in Brittany of Monsieur Imre Monteil. But once the silly man accepted
the fact that the Spring Carpet of Khusraw—ah! She'd remembered the name!— Once he acknowledged that it was no longer
in existence, he would take himself and his frightening servant
away.

She glanced at her beloved. He and de Coligny were engaged
in a low-voiced discussion about Brittany and the plans for its
development. She listened drowsily, amused by the expertise
with which Jack drew out his companion so that the chevalier
did most of the talking. They would probably, she thought, become lifelong friends. Certainly, de Coligny was convinced that
Jack had saved his life on the battlefield, and now he was taking
a considerable risk in helping them. He was older than Jack by
about a decade probably. He was very handsome and must have
been hotly pursued during his courting days. If she had met
him when he was single . . . She smiled to herself at such nonsensical thoughts. She liked him very well, but she found him
a shade too stiff and rather studiedly dignified. There was no
doubt but that he took himself very seriously. She pictured him
sitting in judgment in the local *cour d'appel*, if they had such

courts in Brittany. He would be grave and distinguished, and look splendid and all the ladies would sigh over him. She wondered what his wife was like, and if she ever did impulsive and reckless things that a lady should not do. Perhaps she was as dignified as her husband.

Glancing at Jack, her heart warmed. He was quick-tempered at times, and might not match the chevalier for looks or dignity, but he was blessed with an underlying strength and compassion. And he had besides a ready sense of humour. How glad she was that he was the man she meant to spend the rest of her life with.

She caught herself up. To be criticizing de Coligny while she sat in his carriage, en route to accept his hospitality, was surely the height of ingratitude. She turned her attention to the window and looked into the grey morning.

She was struck by a pervading impression of emptiness. For mile after mile the land appeared barren, with only sparse vegetation and stunted trees growing in the stony soil. Yet there was no shortage of water, for streams and busy little creeks were rushing about everywhere. Houses were few and scattered, and despite the fact that they were usually situated all alone in the middle of some field or meadow, they were enclosed by low walls with thick hedges growing from the tops as if jealously forbidding the approach of any invasive neighbour. These Bretons, one gathered, liked their privacy. Frequently, a cross loomed up atop some hill, but when she asked de Coligny where so many churches found their parishioners, he replied that most of the crosses indicated only a wayside shrine or small chapel. "They are convenient for travellers or country folk," he said. "But the *bourg,* or village, churches are very well attended on Sundays."

Manderville woke up and mumbled sleepily, "Is it Sunday already?"

They all laughed.

Peering through the window he said, "So we're off on Consuela's wild-goose chase, and my sound advice has been rejected. Much chance you have of catching Kincraig now. Don't say I didn't warn you!"

Consuela shivered. It was weak-kneed and silly, but sometimes she was afraid. Her every hope for happiness rested with a mysterious wanderer who was at the very least eccentric. If he should turn out to be hopelessly insane, or if he refused to

acknowledge Jack, *Nonna* would never give her consent. To go
through life without him . . . It did not bear thinking of, and
she would not dwell upon such terrors. She thought resolutely,
'We will find Lord Kincraig, and he will be a good and sensible—'

"What a jolly fine animal," said Vespa.

A man riding a tall black horse came into view briefly, then
was gone.

"He must be going in the same direction as we are," said
Consuela. "I saw him soon after we left the port."

Manderville said, "I see three more riders over there."

"Your people, de Coligny?" asked Vespa.

"No." The chevalier looked grim. "They are robbers, most
probably. This is not a very safe place to be riding alone."

"Deserters?"

"Some, yes. But times are hard, the crops are poor, and there
is little in the way of law and order here. But have no fears,
Miss Jones. My servants are well-armed, and we will be on my
preserves in but a few moments. I promise there will be wine
and a warm fire, and for poor Manderville, a hot bath."

"And some breakfast?" asked Consuela, who had suddenly
become aware that she was ravenous.

The chevalier said with a smile, "This, too, there shall be."

When first she saw the towers looming on the hilltop Consuela exclaimed, "Oh, my! It is a castle!" The estate road was
better-maintained and they passed through wide fields where
men and women laboured at weeding or digging out rocks.
The men touched their caps respectfully, and some of the
women waved, or bobbed a curtsy as the coach rumbled past.
She heard Pierre screaming a demand to be allowed to blow
up a hail on the yard of tin. His efforts were faint and discor-
dant, and his father chuckled and said that his son's lungs must
grow a trifle before they could master the art. A moment later
a strong note was sounded, the coachman having evidently reclaimed the horn.

The carriage jolted into a cobbled courtyard and grooms
came running to hold the horses and let down the steps. The
walls of the château soared upward, grey and cold and somehow disdainful. A manservant, the butler no doubt, and a
footman flung open the front doors. As Consuela was handed

from the coach, a lady ran down the steps, and with a glad cry of "Gaston! Gaston! At last!" threw herself into the chevalier's arms.

Surprised that such a passionate embrace would be enacted in front of strangers and the servants, Consuela glanced at Vespa. He grinned, and winked at her. The chevalier looked embarrassed. He murmured something to his wife, and ushered his guests up the entrance steps and into a very large hall where he performed the introductions.

Madame de Coligny was a tall lady, slender and beautiful, with great brown eyes and lustrous dark hair. She responded politely, but she was clearly taken aback by the arrival of unexpected company. Her gaze held on Vespa a shade longer than was proper, then she turned to her husband and exclaimed, "But—Gaston! They are *English!*"

"Yes, my love," said the chevalier. "Captain Vespa is the man who saved my life at Vitoria, and—"

"Ah!" She held out her hand to Vespa again and said throbbingly, "Then I must be ever in his debt!"

'Hmm,' thought Consuela.

"I will tell you the whole later, Thérèse," said the Chevalier. "But see, here is our Pierre, come home to us."

He gestured, and the boy, who had been hanging back, came forward and bowed. *"Maman,"* he said politely.

Madame Thérèse looked at him appraisingly, and remarked that he had not grown at all. "Nor did your letters tell us very much," she added. "Did you not like England?"

"More than here," he said, with a defiance that spoke volumes.

It seemed to Consuela that little swords flashed in Madame's eyes. De Coligny looked annoyed and suggested sternly that his son would want to inspect his room again.

Manderville sneezed and apologized into his handkerchief. Madame edged away from him uneasily. The chevalier gave orders that his guests be shown to suitable apartments and murmured an aside to his butler concerning the preparation of a hot bath.

Following the footman up the winding stone staircase, Consuela heard Madame Thérèse exclaim a shocked, "They are not *wed?*" She paused, frowning, but Vespa's hand caught her own, and she thought, 'She does not understand. The chevalier will tell her what happened.'

En route to the first floor she looked about curiously. De
Coligny could scarcely be a poor man, but the château had
a stark look; walls were unadorned by paintings, and there
were no works of glass or sculpture or pottery. The only deco-
ration appeared when they turned on a half-landing where a
large crucifix was hung on the wall. At the top of the stairs
a long passage stretched out, silent and chill and grey. Vespa's
strong clasp on her hand tightened and she clung to him
gratefully.

The bedchamber into which she was shown was small and
spotlessly clean, but rather dark, with only two tall narrow
windows to admit the light. The bed had a medieval-type
headboard that reached to the ceiling and was painted in dark
greens, black and browns. The floor was bare of rugs, the
walls were an unrelieved stone, and the one painting was a
Calvary, the detail so gruesome that Consuela had to look
quickly away.

"Good gracious!" she exclaimed involuntarily.

His eyes glinting with laughter, Vespa told the footman to
go on ahead with Monsieur Manderville. He murmured as
they walked away, "Yes, I know what you are thinking, my
little rogue, but you will be safe here. And I may be at ease,
for Gaston is a perfect gentleman, and will see that you are
well cared for."

"What of his lady?"

"A beautiful creature, don't you agree?"

"A beautiful creature who wishes me at Jericho."

"No, no. Gaston says that she gets lonely here at times, and
will be only too glad of your company."

"She looked anything but glad just now."

"I daresay she was surprised to have all of us descend on her
with no warning. But did you notice how devoted she is to her
husband? I thought it most affecting."

'Men!' thought Consuela. "I wonder if Pierre thought it affecting," she said tartly.

"He's a changeable rascal. One minute trying to have us all
arrested as spies, and the next telling his step-mama that he
likes England better than La Belle France."

"His step-mama? Madame Thérèse is the chevalier's second
wife?"

"Yes. I thought Pierre had told you."

"He told me he was an orphan, the little wretch!"

He laughed. "He's full of spirit. The sort of youngster who will grow into a son any man would be proud of."

She stood on tiptoe and kissed him on the chin, and heard a smothered gasp as a chambermaid carrying a pile of clean linens edged past and hurried into the bedchamber.

Vespa whispered, "What was that for, you forward hussy?"

"It was for—for just being you. Oh, see. The footman is waiting."

"So he is, the marplot!" To have found her, to be with her again was unutterable relief. He didn't want to leave her, even for a few minutes. And their minutes would be few, because very soon he must tear himself away. To love so deeply was a blessing, but it carried with it the pain of parting. He lifted her hand and pressed it to his lips, and with a twinge of guilt remembered the promise he had given to a trusting old lady. He sighed and knew he must be very careful, or his honour would be sullied beyond redemption.

In the room he was to share with Manderville a hip bath had been set in front of a hastily laid fire. De Coligny's valet, shaking his head over the crumpled wreckage of the once-magnificent coat, carried it away together with Vespa's garments. A footman came in with a ewer of hot water. He was the first of a continuing line of water carriers so that Manderville was very soon able to enjoy the promised bath, while Vespa washed and shaved.

The fire began to warm the cold air. Another footman brought heated wine and biscuits and advised that Chef was preparing a hearty luncheon. The valet returned with their clothing neatly brushed and pressed, and Manderville's new coat much restored. "Although," its owner said between sneezes, "it will never be the same."

Lost in thought, Vespa stood gazing out of the window and made no comment.

"You're very quiet," said Manderville. "What's churning in that clever brain-box of yours?"

"I was wondering how that rider we saw came to own such a fine horse."

"Because he's a horse thief, of course."

"Perhaps."

"What d'you mean—perhaps? There's no other explanation."

"I expect you're in the right of it. But you know, I've the

impression that de Coligny's the principal land-owner here-abouts."

"What has that to say to anything?"

"Only that I looked in his paddocks and stables as we drove in. I saw not one hack to compare with the one our thief straddled. And if it wasn't stolen from here—it would be interesting to know where it did come from."

"Why?" said Manderville. "More importantly, let us collect your lady and seek out this alleged hearty luncheon. After which, you'll be anxious that we continue on to Rennes, I sup-pose?"

Vespa looked at him from the corners of his eyes.

"No!" said Manderville.

Vespa smiled.

Ten

"Where is it that you are born?" The shabby and angular wanderer peered at Vespa suspiciously over the slice of dried beef he held in a hand that was lacking three fingers.

Vespa tossed another branch onto the small fire he'd built in the shelter of the woods and took his time about replying. He had left the Château Coligny shortly after two o'clock the previous afternoon, riding the sturdy little piebald mare that the chevalier's head groom had assured him would be more sure-footed in the wilderness country than a larger animal. Parting from Consuela had been wrenching; the sweet girl had tried not to weep, but her trembling lip and tear-wet lashes haunted him and he had made Paige promise to take her home if he did not return within two weeks. De Coligny had provided a razor, strop and soap, together with clothing less likely to attract attention than his own well-tailored garments, and the head groom had drawn a rough map and given him directions that had proven a godsend. He had spent the night in a little hollow, wrapped in his blanket with fallen leaves piled over him, the cold and the myriad night sounds of the open country carrying him back to the Peninsula Campaign. Up with the dawn, he had travelled all day towards the southeast, walking occasionally to rest the mare, and seeing only a farmer driving a cart westward, and a group of boys gathering firewood, all of whom he had avoided.

He'd reached the lonely little shrine to the Lady of the Sea just before the light failed. It had not been an easy climb, and that he'd found the spot at all was largely due to the fact that the shrine had at some recent date been painted white, and it had shone rather eerily against the surrounding darkness of the trees. A stream ran close by, as de Coligny's groom had said, the icy water clear and sweet. He'd tended to the mare whose name was Bruine. This, he felt was a misnomer, for, as he told the animal, she might be the colour of drizzle, but she was a willing little lady with an affectionate nature. Having built a fire he had settled down to enjoy the now rather stale but still good loaf, and the remains of the cheese and smoked meat Gaston's chef had packed for him. And then this tall unkempt fellow had arrived with his equally unkempt donkey and invited himself to share the fire.

"I was born in *España,*" lied Vespa. "Not that it is any of your affair."

Despite his brusque growl the answer appeared to be satisfactory and his unwelcome guest started to slice mould from a hunk of cheese and said with a nod, "That will explain the way of your talk. I knew you were no Breton."

"Nor are you," said Vespa.

The knife stilled. "Why do you say this?"

"Because Bretons like their privacy."

The pale eyes stared unblinkingly. Then, a grin twisted the wide mouth. "A man gets enough of their standoffish ways, I won't argue that point. Me, I like company. That's a nice little beast you have."

"It is. And I mean she shall remain *my* little beast."

"So. You likely have a *pistolet* in that pocket, eh, Monsieur *l'soldat?*"

"*Very* likely. Why do you suppose me to be a soldier?"

"I saw you walk. You have the limp, but you have the shoulders and the movement of the man of action. You fight for our 'Little Corporal,' eh? Where did you earn your limp?"

"Vitoria. Where did you lose your fingers?"

"Badajoz. Aha—this is the bad word for you, I see. It was a most terrible battle. You have perhaps suffer another wound there?"

"I lost my brother there." Vespa put down his bread and reached out. "I am Jacques."

They exchanged a handshake and the shabby man's face lit up. "Me, I am Paul. It is a good thing for two old soldiers to meet and to talk, no? *Nom de Dieu,* but this Brittany is the lonely place. It cause much discomfort to my poor stomach, which I will tell you is a most delicate machine. How may one talk with these people when one cannot understand what they say even when they *will* speak? At least you have the proper French. What do you here, *mon ami?*"

"Obey my master. He is desirous of meeting with some strange old fellow who goes about buying carpets."

"What, the Crazy Carpet Man?" Paul gave a hoot of laughter. "I wish you joy of him." He tapped his temple. "I think much of the time he knows not where he is."

Vespa's heart gave a lurch. "You've seen him?"

"But—yes. Yesterday? The day before? I forget. *Les enfants,* they like him, you know. I hear them squeak and shout, and there they are, all around his big waggon. And what a grotesquerie!"

His hopes sinking, Vespa said, "The man?"

Paul chuckled. "The waggon—or cart, or whatever it is. People, they laugh and call names. But he is a good-natured old fool. It is sad, eh?"

That sounded more promising. "You have a kind heart, Paul. Can you tell me where I may find him?"

"But of a certainty I can! He is likely no more than a day's journey to the south and you will have but to enquire in Rennes. Everyone knows him and *les enfants* in especial will point you the way he goes."

So his clever little love had been right, after all. 'God bless her!' thought Vespa. 'Tomorrow I may meet my father, at last!'

It rained in the night. He awoke to darkness and a clamorous wind that scattered a flurry of raindrops from the tree above him. *Bruine* stamped about restlessly. Vespa slid the pistol from under the saddlebags that served as his pillow. Moving as silently as a shadow he went to the mare, but his suspicions were unjustified; she greeted him with a soft whicker and there was nothing to indicate that Paul had attempted to appropriate her. The man's bed, composed of a thick wool blanket that smelled strongly of sheep, was still spread out beside the dead fire. Vespa turned back to his own bed but was momentarily dazzled as lightning's blue glare lit the makeshift camp. The trees seemed to leap up. Bruine gave a snort of fright. Vespa moved quickly to hold her nostrils, for something else had leapt into view: two men stood by the stream. Even that brief glimpse revealed this to be a furtive meeting. Their conversation, evidently conducted in whispers, was quite inaudible, and although he caught a whiff of burning oil, their lamp was now extinguished.

He slipped back to his own blanket and arranged the saddlebags to resemble a man sleeping, then took up a position behind a nearby tree, the pistol gripped in his hand and his eyes fixed in the direction of the conspirators. He was faintly disappointed. He rarely misread his man, but he had evidently done so in this instance. Still, he'd been prepared and had slept lightly. De Coligny had said poverty dwelt here, and poverty had a way of breeding thievery and murder.

Lightning flashed once more, this time followed by a clatter of thunder.

Ignoring his own bed, Paul crept towards Vespa's blankets and reached out.

Vespa's grip on the pistol tightened. He watched and waited for the slash of a knife.

"Monsieur Jacques," called Paul softly, nudging the blanket. "Wake up! Monsieur—"

"I'm over here." Vespa walked forward.

"Sacré bleu! You take no chances, eh? I think I am insulted."

"I saw you talking to someone. It is as well to be cautious. *I* think you and your friend are free-traders, but I ask no questions."

"This it is the best way, *mon ami.*" Paul began to roll up his blanket. "You have allow that I share your fire and we talked together. So. Now I must go, for these woods they are become too crowded, which is bad for my poor stomach, you will understand."

"Crowded? I saw scarcely a soul."

"No more did I. But my friend, he says there are strangers about who stop people and ask odd questions. They ask many questions of my friend, which make him most nervous. Paul, he also does not care to be questioned. Perhaps he might not have the right answers, eh?"

Vespa watched him secure the blanket roll across the back of his little donkey. "Did your friend tell you what it was that these men wanted to know?"

"Two of them, they have pretend to search for an Englishman, but this it is not the case, of course. As if even an Englishman would be such a fool as to journey into France while we have this war! Unless he is as demented as the Crazy Carpet Man! So they really look for something else. And with all the uproar over the great robbery causing innocent men to be regarded with suspicion, this Paul he does not wait to find out!"

"What robbery? I've heard nothing of it."

"I thought every living creature must know of it. At some great mint in Belgium it happened, and a young guard most savagely killed. They are saying there was no need to have murdered the boy, and that thousands upon thousands of gold *louis* were made off with. Not one piece did Paul have knowledge of then, or ever will. But—try to convince the police or the military blockheads of it! So I go away from where questions are asked."

Vespa had enjoyed the man's company and was sorry to see him go, and Paul embraced him as emotionally as if they had been old friends. Soon after he had said his farewells the storm drifted away. The little clearing seemed lonely now, and since it was almost dawn Vespa packed up his own belongings and rode out with the first light.

He journeyed more cautiously than ever. That those who trailed him were Imre Monteil's hirelings he had no doubt. The Swiss was the only person who knew he might be in France—aside from the chevalier, of course, who would not have betrayed him. Still, it was odd: Monteil had left the fishing village before him and, with the advantage of a coach and four fresh horses, plus freedom from having to keep out of sight and guard against arrest, he should have reached Rennes last evening at the latest. If Rennes was his destination. Perhaps he was intent upon demanding satisfaction from the man who had knocked him down. Whatever the case, it would be interesting to know what was his business with the Crazy Carpet Man.

The sun came up, setting the clouds afire with pink and red and mauve, and turning the droplets left by last night's rain into countless glittering gems. When the celestial display faded the skies were overcast but bright and although the air was chill it was a crisp cold. Vespa rode with eyes and ears alert for other travellers, but an hour later he had seen only a solitary boy herding some two-score sheep. He was hungry and risked enquiring about a tavern or inn where he might buy food. The boy stared at him with great solemn dark eyes and spoke in the odd Breton tongue that had so much in it of Gaelic. So far as Vespa could decipher, he was being asked the same question as to whether he was from France. When he answered that he was a citizen of Italy the boy evidently understood, because a smile brightened his face, and he pointed to the southeast and

said something that Vespa translated as indicating the route to
an inn 'with a good wife.'

He thanked the young shepherd and rode on. The boy
shouted, and turning back Vespa waved. And far beyond the
boy he saw on the crest of a ridge a bright flash, such as might
be made by a rifle barrel—or a telescope. Or perhaps merely
some traveller's frying pan.

The 'inn' turned out to be a small farmhouse sadly in need
of paint. The 'good wife' was a thin, sour-looking woman who
stood in the doorway wiping her hands on the apron to which
a small girl clung timidly. The woman eyed Vespa with suspicion. He gave her a warm smile and begged that the 'gentle
madame' would forgive his poor knowledge of the language
since he was Italian-born and could but do his best.

Some of her hostility faded. She sniffed, pushed away the
child with one hand and tidied her stringy hair with the other.
Her name, she imparted, was Madame Forêt. "It is that m'sieur
wants breakfast, eh? When my stove is yet barely warm!"

"And you are very busy, madame. One can see that so sparkling a kitchen must have a peerless lady to rule over it, a lady
whose fame as a cook I have heard much of. Might I be permitted to wait? Perchance the little one would care to sit on
my lap? I will tell her a story. Your first-born, madame?"

Since the lady was obviously nearing fifty, this was rank flat-
tery, but having been named a peerless cook and housekeeper
in one breath, as it were, her hostility was quite gone. She
beamed at Vespa. He was permitted to enter her kitchen, the
'little one' flew to clamber on his lap, and at once they were
the best of friends.

Vespa told small Anne-Marie the story of Corporal and of his
fear of cats and the troubles this had caused. Both the ladies
were enchanted and squealed with laughter. As a reward, Vespa
was given permission to wash and shave at the pump behind
the house. He stripped to the waist and used soap and towel
vigorously, the icy water setting his blood tingling. As was his
habit, he sang while he washed, taking care to choose a French
ballad. Anne-Marie giggled and jumped up and down and while
he shaved did her innocent best to teach him how to carry a
tune.

Afterwards, he enjoyed an excellent breakfast of a *baguette,*
the long round loaf still hot and fragrant from the oven, an

omelette served with fresh mushrooms and goat cheese, and a mug of superb coffee.

Madame Forêt washed dishes and hinted gently at his reason for coming to Brittany, and he told her his tale of having been sent to find the 'Crazy Carpet Man.' Both mother and daughter were excited by this confidence. Anne-Marie lisped that the Carpet Man was her especial friend, and Madame said smilingly that the poor depraved one had given her daughter sugared almonds when they had journeyed to Rennes. "If you wish to come up with him, Monsieur Jacques," she said, "you will be wise to swing south of the city, for he was travelling in that direction."

Vespa thanked her and at once made preparations to depart. When he slipped several coins into her hand, Madame gave a little nod as though she had reached some decision, and to his surprise put in a plea that Anne-Marie be permitted to ride Bruine once around the yard. Vespa hesitated; the child was ecstatically eager, but she was very small. He lifted her to the saddle and prepared to walk beside Bruine. However, Madame Forêt insisted that her daughter was quite able to ride without assistance. Clearly, the lady wanted to speak to him alone.

As soon as her little girl was out of earshot, Madame Forêt leaned to Vespa's ear. "You are the good man," she said softly. "But you must beware. You ride a dark path, and you are sought."

He stared at her, but when he attempted to respond she waved her hands impatiently. "This I will say, although I know you are not Italian, but an Englishman, like the crazy one, and the others, who are of a rudeness and speak the so-bad Bretagne."

Taken aback, Vespa said, "Englishmen have been here seeking me? Did they perhaps leave a message?"

She shook her head. "I think they do not wish you well. It is perhaps that you are the spy, and I have too trusting the nature. But my ancestors came from your place called Cornwall. This Bonaparte who calls himself our Emperor, he send his great soldiers to tear all our young men away and force them to go and fight. They have not come back. Not one. And what is he? An upstart! Do I like him? No, I do not! Do I have need of him? Again, I have not! What has he done for Bretagne? Nothing! But you, Monsieur Jacques, you have the kind heart

and have made my poppet laugh, who has been sad since her
brothers are gone off to the war. And so now I warn you. Guard
your back, and keep always among the shadows! And now, be
off with you! And *Dieu vous bénisse!*"

Vespa thanked her for the warning and for her blessing and
bade an affectionate farewell to little Anne-Marie. An hour later
he was pondering Madame Forêt's remarks, and heeding her
warning to be alert for ambush.

He was drawing closer to Rennes now. There were more
houses and farms, more people to be avoided, more and better-maintained roads. As far as possible, he kept to by-ways and
wooded areas, pausing often to scan the countryside behind
him, but detecting no sign of pursuit.

It was as he dismounted and led Bruine to a stream that
Madame's warning proved justified. He heard a high-pitched
metallic whirr. His reaction was very fast, but even as he
crouched and whipped around something jerked sharply at
the cape of his cloak. A solid thud, and silence. No following
attack; no triumphant shouts; no glimpse of anyone. For a
split second he stared at his cloak, the cape pinned to the
trunk of a tree. It was a young tree. The bolt had transfixed
it. He thought in astonishment, 'Crossbow! Be damned!' And
tearing his cloak free, he sprang into the saddle and sent
Bruine off at a gallop.

He had not anticipated that Monteil would order his death;
in fact, he'd suspected the Swiss wanted information from him.
If they'd intended to capture him, a fine marksman could have
used a rifle to bring him down without inflicting a fatal wound.
But a crossbow—while admittedly having the advantage of silence—offered little in the way of precision, even in the hands
of an expert. Whoever had fired that bolt must have known
that a hit might very well result in death. And if he died, Monteil would lose the opportunity to either force Kincraig's whereabouts from him, or to make him lead them to the baron. It
was puzzling in the extreme—unless the Swiss had already
found Kincraig and was determined to keep him away. But in
that case—why bother? He was riding alone and would pose
small threat to the man, especially if Monteil had his giant servant at his side.

He bent low over the pommel and urged the mare to greater
speed. Now that he had been found he must detour, for whoever these enemies might be, he had no intention of leading

them to Lord Kincraig. He turned eastward, therefore, and rode for an hour, leaving a clear trail until at length he guided Bruine into a stream and they splashed along for over a mile before leaving the water at a low spot in the bank where the soil was mostly rocks and pebbles and the mare's hooves left no imprint to betray them. Turning in a wide sweep, Vespa headed south once more. Just before noon, he was riding through a copse of poplars at the crest of a rise. It was not a high hill, but it afforded a fine view of the surrounding area. He saw three men riding slowly along the stream he had left and obviously searching for tracks. They were too far away for him to identify them, but as he'd hoped, they were proceeding eastward. He smiled grimly and reined Bruine around. With luck, he'd find Kincraig before the would-be assassins realized their error. With more luck, he'd whisk his lordship safely back to Château Coligny and within a day or two they'd be back on British soil.

"It is the best notion I've heard of for the past two days," declared Consuela, her eyes sparkling. "Of course we should leave! I will—"

Seated beside her in the chill château library, Manderville roared a sneeze into his handkerchief, groaned, and whispered, "Hush! They'll hear you! And I did not say *we*—I said—"

"If you think for one instant, Lieutenant Paige Manderville, that you are going to leave me here with that revolting female—"

He put a hand over her lips. "For heaven's *sake!* Madame Thérèse is very beautiful, and—"

Wrenching away, Consuela said scornfully, "She would agree with you, I am quite sure!"

"Anyone would. And she has been more than kind. Own that she has provided us with food and lodging—"

"Only because her husband insisted upon it!"

"And she gave you a toothbrush and tooth powder, and even loaned you some of her garments—"

"Her garments?" Consuela spread her arms and wailed, "Can you suppose Madame would ever have worn *this*? It is *hideous* and it does not even smell nice! I know I am no beauty, but this rag makes me look absolutely dreadful!"

Manderville eyed the faded brown round gown sceptically. It

had seen better days, certainly, many better days; and along the way had been clumsily darned here and there. The colour made Consuela look washed out, and the style or lack of it concealed her ample curves and gave her a dumpy appearance. He was rather surprised that Thérèse de Coligny would offer even an uninvited guest such a shabby frock, but striving to pour oil on troubled waters, he said, "I don't think the chevalier is exactly plump in the pockets, you know; times are hard for these people. I expect that—er, dress was intended to serve only while your own clothes are being laundered. It was—er, probably made for Madame in her youth."

"Stuff! It is from some old cast-offs she had gathered to donate to the poor—I heard her giggling with her maid over it! She said I was not tall enough to wear her gowns, and would look ridiculous if I were to try and do so. Oh, Paige, I am not an ungrateful girl! I do not expect to borrow her *best* gowns, but surely she must have something better than this. I offered to wash and iron my own things, but they were taken away and each time I ask for them I am told they are not drying properly. The truth is that she had a spark in her eye for Jack, and she thinks it will be a grand joke for him to see me in this monstrosity when he comes back." Consuela gave a little sniff and said in a forlorn voice, "I tell you, Paige, she fairly *loathes* me."

"Now why on earth should she do so? I have seen her smile at you most kindly, and she has never by the least hint suggested—"

"Oh, no. She is all polite sweetness to me in front of you and the chevalier, but when I am alone with her, she is perfectly horrid and treats me as though I were a—a fallen woman!"

Manderville groaned. "*Do* try to be reasonable. I know you're worried about Jack, but you must not let your imagination run away with you."

"I have done no such thing! You silly creature, have you not noticed how Madame Thérèse is absolutely obsessed with her handsome husband? I believe she resents anyone—including poor little Pierre—who dares intrude on their privacy."

"You just said she liked Jack, which—"

"She liked him better than she likes me, certainly. And she cannot resist fluttering her eyelashes at any male. But I believe that if she could, she would kidnap her prize Gaston away to a cave somewhere and shut out the whole world!" She scowled and muttered stormily, "There are women like that, you know. It is a form of madness."

Manderville threw up his hands in frustration. "How you can have taken the lady in such aversion is beyond me."

"Yes, because you are a man," she said, rounding on him. "And men are great awkward creatures who clump around in—in china-shops and are blind to everything under their noses—unless it is a woman's bosom!"

With a grin, Manderville said, "Very well, I'll stay here with you, *petit coquin* that you are. Likely my unease is nonsensical and old Jack is going along splendidly." He looked down, but watched her from under his long lashes as he added, "Lord knows, he's faced enough dangers in his life and managed to survive."

Consuela had been preparing to deny that she was a 'little monkey,' but at this she was all contrition and, seizing his arm, demanded, "But you said you have the feeling he needs you. If that is so, we must leave this place at once!"

He shook his head and said reluctantly that he had promised Jack to stay with her and be sure she was safe. "He would never forgive me if I took you into danger, so if you will persist in accompanying me, then I cannot go, do you see?"

She did not see, and when he resisted all her arguments with unyielding determination she flew into a rage and left him. Climbing the stairs to her cold bedchamber, she paused on the half-landing and gazed miserably out of the tall narrow window. It was as grey outside as it was in here, and the leaden skies gave promise of rain to come. Her beloved was out there some-where, facing who knew what perils, while she fussed and grum-bled like a spoiled child about—about trifles, and thus prevented Paige from going to help him.

She sighed. It was all her doing. Jack had not wanted to come here, nor had Paige. She was the one who'd insisted that Lord Kincraig was in Rennes and who had deliberately missed the return voyage of the *Saucy Maid.*

Even so, Madame de Coligny was not a kind person. Con-trary, as usual, Conscience whispered that a lady more gently natured than herself would likely have been able to deal with the horrid—with Madame. The fault lay with Consuela Jones, and her wretched temper. When would she ever learn to hide anger behind honeyed words and glittering smiles? Her beloved Papa, striving always to teach her to be more in control of her emotions, had said lovingly but with regret that her nature was volatile.

She'd once asked Jack if he thought her volatile, and he had answered that she had plenty of spirit which would help her over life's rough spots. Darling Jack. She squared her sagging shoulders. Well, she would not let him down this time. She would be meek and humble and behave politely and properly so that Paige could leave her here, and—

Her resolve interrupted by soft laughter, she looked up. The chevalier and his wife were walking slowly towards the top of the stairs. Madame, looking—one had to admit—ravishingly lovely in a pale pink gown of the soft wool called cashmere, was saying that she was sure that Pierre was happily occupied.

"But he particularly asked that I go for a walk with him," argued the chevalier, looking troubled. "I'd forgot the *curé* and Mayor Dubois are to call, and I must be here to discuss the rot in the church roof. Would you object to taking the boy out, my dear?"

Consuela gave an inward chuckle and could not resist waiting to hear the answer before revealing her presence.

"But how should I object, Gaston?" trilled Thérèse. "It is merely that I have so much to do today. I shall find someone to take him, I promise you. Perhaps Captain Vespa's woman can make herself useful."

Captain—Vespa's—woman? Consuela gave such a snort of rage that she wondered flames did not issue from her nostrils.

The chevalier's glance shifted to her. He looked aghast and his face reddened as he stammered helplessly, "Ah—Mademoiselle! I—er, we were just—er, wondering if—er—"

"Yes." Consuela's brand-new resolution shattered to unmourned fragments. She said with her sweetest smile, "I would be overjoyed to repay Madame for her—kindnesses—although I know such deeds are rewarded in heaven. But, fond as I am of Pierre, for he is the very dearest child, surely he would value his mama's company over that of a comparative stranger."

"Very true," said the chevalier, blind to the glare his wife slanted at their guest. "And I have the ideal solution. You can surely spare a quarter of an hour, Thérèse, and if Miss Jones will be so kind as to keep you company, you can get to know one another."

"Oh, that would be lovely, sir," gushed Consuela.

She could all but hear the beauty's teeth grinding, but Madame Thérèse controlled her annoyance and said nobly that she would by all means spare a half hour for the boy's sake.

De Coligny dropped a kiss on her cheek and told her she was all consideration. "If you two lovely creatures will wait just a minute I'll call for wraps for you both."

"Foolish one," purred his wife, secure in her warm gown. "You know I am so healthy I never feel the cold. But we had best provide a cloak for you, Miss Jones. Your nose is quite red, poor dear. It looks as if you might be catching poor Monsieur Manderville's cold."

Consuela allowed that remark to hang on the air all by itself. Surely the chevalier was not so besotted as to miss his wife's spiteful barb, but even if he was that dense she had scored so gratifyingly that she was willing to allow Madame her petty hit.

"Papa said he would go with me," grumbled Pierre, when they walked out onto the front steps.

"I am going with you," snapped Madame, finding that the wind was far more chill than she had anticipated. "Can you never be satisfied?"

"All right," he said. "So long as Miss Jones comes, too."

They set out, following the drivepath, the boy between them. The few remarks Madame uttered were tinged with malice. Away from the constraints imposed by the presence of the gentlemen, Consuela entered the verbal duel, wording her responses in such a way that Pierre would be unaware of the invisible swords that engaged over his head. Soon, he saw a friend in the field and went racing off. Madame Thérèse, whose teeth were chattering, gave a relieved exclamation when a large coach came trundling up the drivepath. She waved to the occupants to stop. This was misunderstood. An elderly gentleman returned her wave, and shouted admiringly that she was the kind *maman* to play with her son on such a day, and the coach went on.

"Imbecile," muttered Madame under her breath. A moment later it began to drizzle, and she declared with relief that they must go back. "It is raining. Pierre! Come here at once. You must not get wet and take a chill."

"This is not rain. It is but drizzle," he called, chasing after his friend's dog. "You go back, *Maman*. Miss Jones doesn't want to go in yet, do you, Miss Jones? Come and meet Henri's dog!"

"I would love to meet Henri's dog," said Consuela, pulling the warm wrap closer about her.

Madame cried angrily, "No! Do you not hear me? I wish to go back!"

"Then by all means you should do so," said Consuela. "I promised the chevalier I would walk with Pierre, and English ladies never break a promise." Pleased with this fallacious sally and ignoring a stamp and a shrill demand that they both come *'at once,'* she hurried across the field and gathered up a stick to throw for the playful sheepdog.

Furious, Madame Thérèse hesitated, then followed them, her commands that they return drowned by the barking of the dog, the happy squeals of the boys and Consuela's laughter.

Five minutes later the drizzle abruptly changed to a downpour and everyone ran for shelter. The field became a sea of mud. Madame's wails were interspersed with expletives that ladies seldom uttered in public, and Pierre began to giggle uncontrollably.

As they reached the château, the front door was thrown wide, and the chevalier, accompanied by Manderville, the *curé* and several distinguished-looking gentlemen hurried outside opening umbrellas.

"My poor drowned ones," exclaimed de Coligny.

"I am *drenched!*" wailed his wife.

"We came back quicker than we went," laughed Consuela, dashing rain from her eyes.

"Wheee!" screamed Pierre at the top of his lungs. "Look at *Maman's legs!*"

Every eye flashed to Thérèse. The charming cashmere gown had succumbed to the assault of rainwater. The hem had shrunk to mid-calf length. It was painfully evident that not only had Madame very skinny legs, but her feet were far from dainty.

The *curé* uttered a muffled snort, threw a hand across his mouth, then hurriedly closed his eyes.

One of the gentlemen let out a quickly stifled guffaw.

Pierre screamed, "What big feet you have, *Maman!*"

Consuela's besetting sin got the best of her and she squealed with mirth.

Madame de Coligny had seldom known humiliation. Aware that she looked both ridiculous and disgraceful, she was shocked and embarrassed, but to be laughed at rendered her livid with fury. In a lightning reaction she snarled, "Revolting brat!" boxed Pierre's ears, then turned her wrath on Consuela. "You wicked little trollop—this was your doing!" she screeched.

"Sharing my husband's cabin like any woman of the streets! Coming here with your lover! You are as shameless as—"

"You forget yourself, Madame de Coligny!" said the chevalier in a voice of ice.

He wife turned to him, her face twisted with passion. The onlookers stood in shocked silence. With an enraged sob, she pushed through them and ran into the house.

Eleven

Vespa's attempt to elude his pursuers had evidently been successful; unhappily, it also resulted in a considerable loss of time. He turned Bruine to the west and rode as fast as he dared, seeing no one until he came upon a solitary cottage and then a track that led past a farm. Soon, the track was crossed by footpaths; a group of women carrying baskets stopped chattering and stared at him as he passed. They probably knew he was a stranger to the neighbourhood. He touched his hat to them politely, and they subsided into giggles. A man driving a dog cart pulled up and waved his arms violently. Vespa tensed. The man began to shout dire warnings of the dangers lurking on the road ahead. Monsieur must have his knife sharpened and he could give a good low rate—a pittance merely—for so vital a service. Amused, Vespa shook his head and rode on, followed for some distance by howled offers to render scissors, daggers, swords, bayonets or cutlasses razor sharp.

The track widened, more travellers appeared, most passing with scarcely a glance. Vespa slouched in the saddle and kept his head down. There were scatterings of houses now, and the track was replaced by a quite respectable road. Carts and riders were more frequent and soon he glimpsed the sparkle of a river, and beyond it a cluster of spires and towers. Rennes! At last! The old city seemed to be thriving and, at least from this distance, showed no sign of the disastrous seven-day fire that had gutted its centre in 1720.

His nerves tightened when a troop of *cuirassiers* clattered towards him, their steel helmets and breastplates gleaming. He drew aside with his fellow travellers to make way.

It seemed that every eye in that troop was fixed on him; that every soldier must hear the thundering of his heart as the youthful officer in the lead threw up his arm and the troop came to a halt.

The officer stabbed a finger at Vespa. "You. Come here."

The onlookers stared in silence.

Vespa rode forward reluctantly.

"Dismount, and take off your hat."

Had they realized he was British? If they had, was there any way out of this? He could seize this arrogant young bully and use him as a shield. If he had to resort to that his chances wouldn't be very good, but—

"Did you hear me?"

The roar could have been heard in Rennes, thought Vespa. He swung from the saddle and snatched off his hat with a subservient bow.

The officer said jeeringly, "Let's have a look at you."

A corporal grabbed Vespa's chin and jerked his head up, then jumped back as he met the sudden glare in the hazel eyes. "This one is dangerous, sir," he exclaimed.

The officer rode back and scanned Vespa appraisingly. "Age?"

"Five and twenty, sir."

Glances were exchanged among the onlookers.

The officer tapped Vespa on the shoulder with his riding whip. "Perhaps you can explain why you are not in uniform."

"I was, if you please, sir," said Vespa in as humble a voice as he could summon. "I served as *sergent* with General d'Erlon's forces at the Battle of Vitoria and was wounded when we tried to keep the village of Margarita. They sent me home because—"

The officer's eyes had widened. The French defeat at Vitoria was still large in the public mind, and he interrupted peremptorily, "I believe not one word of it! You look well enough to me! Where are these wounds that keep you from military service with the rest of France's patriots?"

"My head, sir. And my shoulder—here. And my leg."

It was ordered that Vespa's shoulder be bared. The officer looked at that scar and the other than ran down his temple. "We will see the leg," he snapped. "All of it. Roll down your breeches."

Incredulous, Vespa glanced around at the spectators. "Here—sir? But—there are ladies."

"He's shy," jeered the corporal. The military men all

laughed. The spectators did not laugh. Many of these Bretons had sons and husbands who had been forced into the army, and French soldiers were not popular here. Reminded of this, the officer's grin became a scowl. He barked out orders and his men dismounted and stood around Vespa, providing a human screen. Embarrassed and furious, Vespa struggled with his temper, but complied. The officer bent and inspected the scars that spread from calf to thigh. He glanced up at Vespa's grim face, and stood straight. *"Mon Dieu!"* he muttered in awe. "Were those all bullet wounds?"

There was fear in his eyes now, and Vespa thought, 'He's never been in an action.' He answered, "Grape shot, sir."

The officer had lost some of his colour. He stared at the scars and whistled softly, then as if recalling his wits, he said briskly, "Yes. Well, I am pleased that you are a true patriot who has served France. You may make yourself respectable."

Vespa fastened his breeches.

A sudden salute was offered.

Without another word the soldiers mounted up and the troop rode on looking stern and formidable, bound no doubt for their regiment and the war zone.

Several of the spectators grinned and nodded at Vespa. An older man spat in the direction of the *cuirassiers*.

Vespa could breathe again. It had been uncomfortably close, but another hurdle had been crossed successfully. His resentment faded and he chuckled to himself, wondering what that pompous young ass would do if he discovered he'd named a British captain 'a true patriot who had served France.' Still, he could almost feel sorry for the boy. He'd seen several of that type—all starch and bluster until the first cannonball screamed past, and then as liable to turn and run from the field as to be capable of following orders.

His next challenge came soon afterwards when some caravans approached with two men on dapple-grey horses riding alongside. They moved from one caravan to another and were clearly questioning the occupants. Taking no chances, Vespa turned aside into a patch of woodland, and kept to the trees while staying parallel with the road.

The two men with the caravans were not part of the group he'd tricked into following a false eastward trail; none of those three had ridden dapple greys. Perhaps he was getting jumpy and the caravan pair had no least interest in the affairs of Jack

Vespa. On the other hand, he was sure that the solitary rider on the black horse was following him. Why, was another mystery, but at least the fellow kept his distance and did not seem murderously inclined.

If all six were after him—again, why? Had word gone out that he sought the Crazy Carpet Collector? And even if that were the case, why would so many savage but presumably relatively sane people pursue a confused old gentleman? Unless they were witless they must know the poor fellow would never find his 'flying carpet.' And there was Imre Monteil who was very far from witless. For the Swiss to track Lord Kincraig with such determination could only mean that he was after *something* of value; perhaps there really was a fragment of the fabled Spring Carpet of Khusraw still in existence. Such a find would certainly be a treasure that greedy and unscrupulous ruffians would kill for. But it was so unlikely that— He was jolted back to awareness as Bruine stumbled.

For the third time he'd been obliged to detour around impenetrable clumps of trees and undergrowth and now it seemed to be getting dark. He looked up and found that the sky was hidden by dense branches. It was the trees shutting out the light, not storm clouds as he'd supposed. He had been so lost in thought that he'd not paid sufficient attention to his route; as a consequence, he was completely surrounded by trees and there was no longer a sign of the road. It was the sort of lapse that would have provoked him into dealing any of his subordinates a sharp reprimand. Vexed and frustrated, he informed Bruine that she was being ridden by an idiot and reined her to the left, his sense of direction telling him he wasn't far off his route. Instead of dwindling away, however, the trees and shrubs became ever more dense so that he was forced into more detours and had to acknowledge at last that this was no small patch of woodland, but a forest.

Dismounting, he led the mare back the way they had come. They had left no tracks on the thick carpet of leaves and twigs and he saw nothing he recognized as having passed before. The trees met overhead in a dark canopy, and the quiet deepened to a hush that was oddly oppressive. That he should be delayed by this stupid predicament was infuriating, and he was bedevilled by the awareness that unless he found his way out soon, the rogues following might come up with Kincraig before he did. But with each passing moment the more the trees closed in, the more crushing became the quiet.

He was greatly relieved to come suddenly upon a well-worn path. If people travelled this way he would have to risk asking for directions. Preparing to mount again, he saw Bruine's ears perk up and she stood quite still, gazing ahead fixedly. Faint sounds drifted on the air . . . strange sounds; a low bubbling sort of moan, followed by a very soft and chilling ripple of laughter. He saw something from the corner of his eye and, looking up, beheld a pale shape that floated among the branches. The hair on the back of his neck began to lift. For most of his life he had scoffed at tales of the supernatural, but a recent and uncanny experience at his ancient manor house in Dorsetshire had defied all logic and forced him to revise his opinions. Even so, he drew the pistol from his coat pocket and walked forward boldly. "Come down here, else I shall fire," he shouted.

The result was chaos. Howls and oaths rang out. He had a fleeting impression that ruffians were materializing from behind every tree. The pistol was smashed from his hand. He struck out instinctively and a yelp added to the uproar. Brutal fists grabbed him. He twisted free and landed another solid right, but they were too many. Blows were raining at him. Trying futilely to protect his head, he was down. Boots spurned him. A fierce voice yelled, "Kill the filthy spy!"

He thought numbly that he had been found out, and for a moment the scene dimmed before his eyes. . . .

They were hauling him up again. Peering dazedly, he did not seem to distinguish military uniforms.

Someone groaned, "Break his accursed nose! He has broken mine!"

Another voice exclaimed, "I have seen him. This, it is the same wild man who was attacking everyone on the *Saucy Maid!*"

Vespa was shaken hard, which hurt his head. A harsh voice snarled, "Speak—curse you! How did you find us? Who sent you?"

But when he tried to explain they were evidently offended by his halting words, and he was shaken more violently.

"He is foreign! Listen to his ugly accent!"

"Kill the *saleté!*"

"Cut his lying throat!"

Glancing up, Vespa saw something white hurtling at him. "Hey!" he croaked, and threw out his arms.

For what seemed a long time, he did not hear them any more. Then, a boyish voice was crying, "But he *saved* me, Papa! He saved my whole life!"

Vespa opened his eyes, and gasped faintly, "Is—is that you—Pierre?"

"It is I. Alain. I was the ghost in the tree. I am a good ghost, but my sheet caught on a branch and I fell. Most bravely you have caught me, monsieur."

He had . . . ? It had been an instinctive attempt to fend off whatever was falling on him. However . . . least said soonest mended. . . .

A great unkempt brute of a man with very long moustachios appeared before him, and growled, "This, it is truth. This *canaille* saved the life of my son. So what now must I do?"

He was the recipient of a chorus of advice on the various and gruesome methods for despatching the spy, and there was no lack of volunteers willing to administer the 'despatch.'

"If you mean to—to kill me," said Vespa faintly. "I think you might at least offer me some brandy first."

This was evidently considered to be a reasonable request. He was dragged to a tree and allowed to lie propped against it while a bottle was produced.

The large father of Alain thrust it at him. "You first, spy. And likely it's your last," he growled.

It was excellent brandy. Vespa's initial conviction that he had been rolled over by several gun carriages began to fade.

The bottle was taken and they all sat down and stared at him while the brandy made the rounds.

Alain's father demanded, "Why were you fighting everyone on the vessel?"

Simplifying matters, Vespa answered, "A rogue stole my lady."

They appeared to accept this as logical enough, but . . .

"Who sent you to spy on us?" snarled a fierce young man with very black hair and dense jet eyebrows.

"Nobody. I was trying to find—"

A thin bald man cried angrily, "Why do we talk and talk? He will lie, whatever we ask. It is truth that he caught your son, Jules, but he cannot be allowed to go free, you know this!"

There were shouted responses—most approving.

It seemed to Vespa that he was trapped in another of the very strange dreams he'd experienced while convalescing from his war injuries. Here they all sat, in this hushed forest clearing, the birds twittering blithely, Bruine placidly munching at the grass and these men contemplating his murder even as they shared their brandy with him. But it was not a dream, and he knew quite well that his life hung in the balance. He thought of Consuela and prayed he would see her dear face again.

A tall man with a deeply lined face said with authority. "Léon is right. Restore him to his feet for the trial, Jules."

The boy rushed forward. "No! You cannot! Papa! He saved—"

Jules said gruffly, "Go to the tents, boy. This is man's work."

Vespa was pulled to his feet, and the boy was led away, protesting bitterly.

The tall man said, "If you have any last words, monsieur, this is the time."

"I work for the Chevalier de Coligny," said Vespa, and seeing their scowls added hurriedly, "I regret if my speech is confusing. I was born in Italy and my Bretagne is not good."

"How did you find us?" demanded the man called Léon.

"I wasn't trying to find you. I am not here to spy on you, but to try and find the man who goes about collecting carpets."

This drew derisive hoots and the consensus that even a pompous ass like the Chevalier de Coligny would have no use for a lunatic. A husky individual wielding a gory handkerchief reiterated, "He broke my nose, the villain! Kill him!"

"He saved Alain's life," argued Jules, scowling.

"You'll not exchange it for mine!" The eyebrows of the fierce young man met like a bristling black bar across his nose, and he flourished a long knife and glared at the prisoner murderously.

His sentiments won enthusiastic approval. Trying to speak, Vespa was shouted down, and rough hands wrenched his arms behind him.

"Are you all gone mad?" A newcomer pushed his way through the angry group. "I could hear you a mile back. What is all this— *Jacques!*"

Vespa's uninvited overnight guest gazed at him in astonishment.

"Paul!" he said breathlessly. "For Lord's sake, tell these fellows—"

The tall man demanded. "You know this one, Paul?"

"But of a certainty," said Paul. "We fought in the war together. This is the man who shared his fire with me when you found me last night, Raoul. What are you doing here, my Jacques? Did you come seeking me?"

The tension eased, there were mutterings of relief and the bruising hands relaxed their grip.

Vespa said ruefully, "I wish I could say I had. The truth is, I was trying to avoid a pair of ruffians who were following me—at least, I think they were. I dodged into some trees, and suddenly found myself in this forest. I'm no woodsman and in no time I was blasted well lost!"

"They all wanted to kill him, Uncle Paul," cried Alain, wriggling through the onlookers. "And he saved my life!"

Aghast, Paul picked up the boy and hugged him. "This is so, Jacques?"

It did not seem the moment for absolute truth. Vespa said modestly, "Well, I—er . . ."

"He caught me," declared Alain proudly. "I was at the time the ghost of King Arthur, but I fell from the tree, and Monsieur Jacques caught me, and I knocked him down, and then they all tried to—"

"Be still," said his father. "What is your business here, Monsieur Jacques?"

"It is as I told you. I am sent to find the crazy man who collects rugs."

Alain said shrilly, "Ah! My friend!"

"Why?" asked Léon suspiciously.

Vespa shrugged. "I do not know. I think it is Madame who wants him."

"Ah . . . Madame . . . !" Grins, nudges, and knowing nods were exchanged.

"If I don't find him," sighed Vespa, "I shall be in much trouble."

"If Madame wants him and you *do* find him, the chevalier will be in much trouble," quipped Léon.

This was received as a great witticism.

Alain started to jump up and down and, over the howls of laughter, shouted, "I know where he is! He has heard of a flying carpet and is even now on his way to buy it! He promised to take me for a ride in the sky when he gets it!"

"They should clap up that one, before he does someone

harm," grunted the bloodthirsty young man, sheathing his knife.

"Indeed, they may do so," agreed Paul. "Those fellows who ask all the questions—I told you of them, Jacques—they also are seeking your Crazy Rug Collector. They mean to collect *him*, I think."

Vespa said, "Then I must find him first. Can you direct me, Alain?"

The boy looked uneasily at his father. "I can tell you he took the St. Just road," he said. "But I cannot guide you out of the forest, monsieur. It is—the ghosts, you see. And there are the menhirs, which I do not at all like." He added solemnly, "One chased me, on a time."

This claim was greeted with scornful laughter, and Jules said with a broad grin that he wished he might have seen a great block of stone chase anyone.

"You must not make up the stories, *mon petit chou*, or they might come true," warned Paul. "I'll show you the way, Jacques. The ghosts do not trouble me."

Curious, Vespa asked, "What ghosts?"

They all stared at him. Jules said, "Why, Sir Lancelot and Queen Guinevere, of course."

Bewildered, Vespa said, "Here? But I thought—" He cut off his knowledge of the British legend hurriedly.

"Long ago, they lived here," said Alain. "And Merlin, also— eh, Papa?"

Jules nodded. "I think Monsieur Jacques knows little of the Forest of Paimpont and of our great King Arthur. But then, I know nothing of Italy, so there you are. Go with Paul, monsieur." From somewhere he produced an intriguing bottle which he slipped into Vespa's saddlebags. "And—thank you for my son's life."

Bruine was led up and, having taken a solemn oath never to betray their meeting place, Vespa mounted cautiously, very aware of the various bruises he had collected. He turned to the individual named Raoul. "When you came to my camp last night Paul told me you'd seen men asking a lot of questions. By any chance did one of them ride a black horse?"

Raoul nodded. *"Mais oui!* There was a man alone mounted on just such a horse. A very fine beast."

"Ah. And the rider also was seeking the Crazy Carpet Man?"

"No, Monsieur. That was two other men—very wicked ones—

the kind who would sell their mother for a bottle of brandy! They rode dapple-grey horses; nice, but not to compare with the black animal."

"Then what did the owner of the black horse want?"

"He asked about strangers in the district. But he was a stranger himself. A Parisian, I guessed. So I did not answer, of course."

"Of course," agreed Vespa and, waving goodbye to Alain, followed Paul from the clearing.

Vespa pushed Bruine hard after he left the forest. Soon he could again see Rennes in the distance and was considerably surprised to note how far to the southwest he had wandered. The early afternoon was bleak, a chill wind sent low-lying clouds racing and carried the scent of rain. The road was bustling with traffic. Fretting against all the delays he rode on long after his injured leg had become a relentless ache and his head throbbed as viciously. But he could not ignore the needs of his faithful little mare and, following Paul's advice, he turned off the road at length and walked the tired horse into the yard of a small villainous-looking inn that huddled under a solitary and leafless tree as if trying to hide from the public eye.

The ostler stared blankly and seemed quite baffled by Vespa's accent, but at last shrugged and led Bruine away kindly enough. The innkeeper, a fat little man with crafty eyes and a perpetual smile, ushered the new guest into a spotlessly clean parlour and accepted unblinkingly his explanation of his accent. Vespa relayed Paul's recommendation. The smile broadened, and the innkeeper laid a finger beside his nose and purred that he knew Paul Crozon well, and Monsieur need not be troubled, for it was his habit to ask no questions. There was a fine bed available for Monsieur, in a room he could share with a glass-blower who had come from Rome to help with the reconstruction of St. Peter's Cathedral. As Monsieur knew, this cathedral it had survived the great fire only to fall down forty-two years later. "You two sons of sunny Italy will have much to chat about," he said, beaming.

Since Vespa's knowledge of Italian was limited to the phrases used by Consuela and the duchess, he was much relieved to learn that the Roman glassblower was not expected until sunset. He declined the offer of the bed, but followed the host to the tap. When the door was thrown open he was aghast to find the room crowded with men who all seemed to talk at the top of their lungs until he entered, whereupon conversation ceased. In the sudden hush every head turned to him. Fortunately, he had not removed his hat, and he pulled it lower over his fair hair, and kept his head down. The host smirked knowingly and led the way to a corner table far from the window and the glowing hearth. Vespa sat on the high-backed settle and ordered a baguette, cheese and wine. The innkeeper nodded and patted his shoulder. "You may be *à l'aise, mon ami.* There is not an Excise Officer for at the least twenty kilometres!"

This remark was overheard. Grins were exchanged and conversation began again. Thereafter, Vespa might have been invisible. He ate quickly, anxious to be on his way as soon as Bruine was adequately rested, but it was shadowy in his corner, the room was warm and his head started to nod.

He awoke to hear someone grunt disparagingly, ". . . says he is French, but me, I have the French, and his—*voyons!* But it is execrable!"

Another voice muttered, "Well he is no Breton, that I'll wager! It would surprise me not at all if the fellow is a spy! He looks more English than French with that light hair, did you not remark it?"

Vespa tensed and gauged the distance to the door.

The first man said, "I remarked that I do not like him. I do not like his loud voice, or his strange talk, or his manner, which is of an arrogance, and his friends are cut-throats if ever I saw any!"

This bore investigating. Vespa stood and slouched across the room. A serving maid hurried to him, and said his horse was ready, and he paid his shot and went outside.

A large coach and four had arrived. The ostler and stableboy were busy and nobody seemed to notice when Vespa led Bruine around to the back of the barn. An old rusted bed-frame, some splintered fence-posts, a bucket with a hole in the bottom, a sagging mangle and other debris littered the area which was evidently a home for discarded items. A warped door was propped against the barn. Vespa tied Bruine's reins to the latch and found a knot-hole in the wall through which he could glimpse part of the interior. Three men were in there, arguing loudly in French.

Their horses were led out and while the ostler and stableboy were saddling the animals the trio moved closer together. They were facing the open doors and Vespa could only see their backs, but they were speaking English now, and he was able to make out the words.

". . . and if that stupid block was right, my unwanted kinsman has wandered into the *Forêt de Paimpont!*"

The voice was unmistakable. Duncan Keith! Vespa swore under his breath.

"Or he followed the old man in there," this suggestion offered in a soft Welsh drawl.

"You're right, by God!" exclaimed Keith. "What better place than a haunted forest to search for a flying carpet?"

They laughed, then a thin nasal voice said, "They'll likely fall foul of the thieves and free-traders who lurk about there."

"Or get lost. They say some folk who've gone into that forest never have found their way out. The little we saw of it made my flesh crawl, I don't mind admitting."

"Either way, we can forget the business and go home."

Keith said silkily, "Can we, indeed? Idiots! D'you think I paid you such a price for anything less than a certainty?"

"You have paid us not a damned farthing yet," the Welshman grumbled.

"The devil! What about the sixty guineas I gave you in London?"

"That was to cover our passage and expenses. We're risking our necks in this business, Keith! And—"

"Keep your voice down, damn your eyes! You'll get the rest of your blood money when I'm sure he's dead! That forest will be a fine place for you to play with your favourite toy, Rand. Perhaps you'll even manage to aim your next bolt accurately!"

There was a nasal curse and mocking laughter, then the ostler called that the horses were ready, and the three hopeful assassins hurried outside.

Vespa gave them a few minutes, then followed. He was in time to see them ride around the bend in the road that led back to Paimpont and the forest.

"Bon voyage," he muttered sardonically, and turned Bruine towards St. Just.

So Duncan Keith was the leader of the group of three. He'd almost had a face-to-face encounter with them. It was pure luck that he'd arrived when he did. Now at least he had identified one enemy; a man who was not above putting a cross-bow bolt through his half-brother. It was curious that the local inhabitants either ignored him or accepted his story, while the real dangers appeared to have followed him from England. The man on the black horse was perhaps another agent of Imre Monteil, who would eventually have to be reckoned with. Who the two riders on the dapple greys worked for and why they sought him was baffling.

He had other things to think about, and with an impatient shrug dismissed the matter from his mind. Alain had spoken with his 'friend,' the Crazy Carpet Collector, only a day earlier. From what the boy had said, the waggon was heavy laden, in which case Kincraig could not be far ahead.

A carriage rumbled past heading north at a spanking pace. The coachman looked vexed and was complaining loudly to the guard about 'mountebanks.' Vespa glimpsed the feathers of a lady's bonnet inside the coach and at once Consuela's lovely and loved face was before his mind's eye. What would she be doing on this grey afternoon? Taking tea with Madame Thérèse and friends, perhaps, or playing some children's game with Pierre. The dear little soul was so kind and warm-hearted, it would be like her to try to amuse a lonely child. He sighed wistfully.

The flow of northward-bound traffic thinned and then ceased altogether. It was not a good sign. There may have been an accident, or a hold-up, or—worse—there might be a military search party ahead, perhaps made up of the 'mountebanks' who had annoyed the coachman. The road skirted a lake fringed with weeping willows and as they rounded the bend his forebodings were confirmed. Several carts, a waggon and a carriage were drawn up blocking the way and travellers were halted in both directions. Voices were raised in anger, and arms were being waved about. Some of those arms were clad in military uniforms. Vespa whistled softly between his teeth and looked about him. A lane led off at right angles to the road and he could see a cross and a small shrine some hundred yards distant. He could stop there, then go back the way he had come without making too obvious a change of direction.

He was turning Bruine onto the lane when a lady's voice rang out over the deeper voices of the men. She was berating them in a mixture of French and Italian. Stunned, he thought, *'Consuela?'* But that was impossible. It *could not* be!

". . . are truly a *bruttura!* An imbecile! A great *stupidita!* Have

I not say it these three times and more? Unfasten your ears, my good fool!"

Vespa moaned, "But it is, by God!" and, ignoring the indignant shouts of the people waiting to get through, he sent Bruine cantering forward.

Gaston de Coligny's smaller coach was at the centre of the dispute. The coachman sat huddled over on the box, a figure of dejection. The door had been flung wide and a small but officious sergeant was arguing with Consuela, who stood on the step, facing him haughtily.

"Never mind about my ears, mademoiselle. You admit you are foreign. How do I know you are who you claim to be? No, it will not do! I *must* have proof of your identity! Since you have none, I've no choice but to detain you."

Vespa's mind raced. This sergeant was far from being a model of a French fighting man. He was sorely in need of a shave, his uniform was ill-fitting and much creased. Probably, a poor man and a conscript. And as such—corruptible. Vespa reached into his saddlebags and took out the bottle Jules had given him.

Consuela was in full cry. *"Non dire cretinate!* Have I not said I am the Lady Consuela of Ottavio? Have I not told you that my *grand-mere* is the Duchess of Ottavio, to whom I now return? Have I not get it through your so dense brain-box that my papers they are carried by my courier, Pietro, who has lost himself? Is it that you are quite *pazzo*? My *grand-mere* is well acquainted with your General Napoleon Bonaparte, and I promise she will be in touch with him about his disgraceful—"

The sergeant was unintimidated. "I will tell you this, Lady Consuela," he bellowed, "that there is a large reward for the apprehension of foreign spies. Your deaf coachman he cannot vouch for your identity. You have no papers to show me, and nobody here has heard of you—or your alleged *grand-mere!* I know my duty, and I demand—"

Vespa's blood ran cold and he spurred Bruine into a gallop, the crowd scattering before him. Two troopers in rather sorry-looking uniforms presented crossed bayonets to halt him.

He shouted, "Signorina! My Lady Consuela! Pietro have come! See, I have find the wine!"

Consuela's head jerked towards him and her pretty mouth fell for an instant into an 'O' of surprise. She wore a long cloak and a hood protected her dark curls, and he thought her the loveliest sight he had ever beheld. His mind whirled with con-

jecture as to how she came to be here, and his heart was torn
between the delight of seeing her again, and with fear for her.
He did not have to try very hard to appear frantic, and improvised, *"Mi perdoni?* I am—er, *chicchi-richi!"* 'Mi perdoni' he knew
meant 'I beg your pardon.' He was less sure of *'chicchi-richi,'* but
he'd heard Consuela say it, so thought himself safe, and there
were no surprised comments or challenges of his proficiency
in Italian.

Consuela's eyes, which had sparkled with delight, now became very round, reflecting an emotion that startled him. He
dismounted and bowed before her and, recovering her wits,
she burst into a torrent of Italian, while belabouring him furiously with an umbrella.

This behaviour appeared to reassure the onlookers, and one
of the soldiers said audibly, "She's Italian, right enough! I've
heard about their hot-tempered women!"

Ducking the flying umbrella, Vespa caught a glimpse of the
coachman's grinning face. Manderville! If they got out of this
bog, he thought ragefully, he'd have a word or two with that
hare-brained varmint for putting Consuela at such terrible risk.

A few onlookers were grumbling about his chastisement, and
the sergeant seized the umbrella, and bellowed, *"Assez,* Signoriny or lady or whatever you are! Have done, I say!"

Turning in an exasperated fashion to the cringing Vespa, he
demanded, "Who is—" His gaze shifted. "What is that you have
there?"

"A purchase my lady desired me to make," said Vespa. "It
is for—"

"A likely story! There has been no tax paid on this, I think."
The sergeant seized the bottle and slid it into the pocket of his
cloak. "It is my duty to impound it. You will tell me what the
signoriny said."

"My lady is most displeased with me I fear, sir," moaned
Vespa, massaging his battered arm. "I have not the very good
Bretagne, but—"

"She says you have her papers," snapped the sergeant. "You
will now produce them!"

"Do so, you lazy, good-for-nothing blockhead," screeched
Consuela. "Do not dare to waste another minute of my time.
Show this foolish man what he demands. *Vite, vite!* I shall then
see that the duchess will write to his superior *and* to his General!"

The sergeant began to look uneasy. The crowd was losing patience; there were angry demands to be permitted to pass, and that he get done with this terrible-tempered foreign aristo lady. Vespa watched Consuela as if petrified with fear of her and stammered that he had been attacked and beaten on the road and all his papers stolen.

"What?" shrilled Consuela, swinging up the umbrella once more. *"Imbecile!* Dolt! You allowed them to take my papers?"

Dodging the flailing umbrella, Vespa mumbled that there had been five armed men, and he all alone. Sympathetic protests arose from the onlookers, and the sergeant threw up a restraining hand. "This fellow he is bruised, as any fool can see. One might think you would have more compassion for him, Signoriny. *Voilà, qui est louche!* And me I do not like things that look suspicious. Corporal! These people you will escort to that barn over there and guard them until I can spare the time to properly question them."

Obedient to the corporal's gestures, Manderville guided the chevalier's coach and pair into the barn. Vespa, and the still protesting Consuela, escorted by stern troopers with fixed bayonets, were made to follow and the doors were swung shut.

"It wasn't my fault, you bloodthirsty hedgebird!"

Outside, the corporal could be heard arguing with the angry farmer whose barn had been appropriated. Inside, Manderville threw up his coachman's whip to hold Vespa at bay, and dodged around a hay bale.

Consuela hung onto Vespa's coat-tails and cried, "Do not, Jack! Paige is right. It was that horrid female, and poor Paige—"

" 'Poor Paige' is going to eat some hay!" Infuriated, Vespa sprang forward, wrenched the whip away and unleashed his lethal uppercut.

Consuela squeaked and beat at his back furiously. "Oh! How savage you are, Captain John Wansdyke Vespa! That you would attack the good friend who rescued me from—"

His eyes blazing, Vespa turned on her and said through his teeth, "Sit . . . down and . . . be quiet!"

Consuela blinked, backed away and sat on the carriage step.

Vespa bent over the fallen. "You swore to me that you would keep her safe! You know what she is! You *swore* you'd not let her run into danger!"

"I had . . . no choice," moaned Manderville, feeling his jaw tenderly. "Damn you, Jack, you've cut my lip!"

"Why do you just lie there like a limp crêpe?" demanded Consuela, disgusted. "Why do you not jump up and strike the ingrate?"

"Because half Wellington's army knows about Vespa's right," he answered without a trace of shame. "He'd just knock me down again. What I should do, of course, is call him out."

"And what I should do is to cut your feeble heart out," snarled Vespa. "Where the blazes did you think you were taking her?"

"Taking her?" The picture of outraged innocence, Manderville sat up, sneezed, and said stuffily, "The chevalier sent me after her when she went tearing off—"

Consuela ran to kneel beside him. "You have taken such a cold, my poor Paige. But what else could I do, after that horrid female called me 'Captain Vespa's *woman*—' "

"And said you were a trollop," put in Manderville helpfully.

Taken aback, Vespa demanded, "Why on earth would a well bred and gracious lady like Madame Thérèse—"

"She forgot to be gracious and well-bred when she got wet," said Consuela tartly.

Manderville grinned. "By Jove, but she did! Wet as a whale! But you'll have to admit, Consuela, if you hadn't giggled—"

"I tried to stop myself," she said with a remorseful sigh. "But how could I help it with her standing there in half a gown, while the Mayor and the curé and all those other gentlemen gawked at her—er, limbs."

Vespa gasped in horror, "Gawked—at—*what*? Oh, egad! Whatever did you do to the poor lady?"

"I did *nothing,"* snapped Consuela, scowling at him.

"It came on to rain, you see," explained Manderville. "Madame Thérèse was wearing a charming woollen dress—"

"And—it shrank," said Consuela.

"And—*shrank,"* wheezed Manderville.

"Up . . . and up . . ." squeaked Consuela, overcome.

For all the world like two naughty children they clung together at Vespa's feet, laughing helplessly. Watching them, his wrath faded. He sat down on the hay bale. "All right, you two rascals. Tell me the whole."

He could not restrain a chuckle when the tale was told and,

knowing his lady's mercurial temperament, he could understand her indignation.

"It's too late to change now," he said to Manderville. "But why—once you'd come up with her, did you not take her back to the château?"

Consuela said stubbornly, "Because I would not go! And besides, I was so worried about you, Jack." She reached out and he pulled her to her feet. Touching his cheek anxiously, she said, "And I was right, do you see, Paige? Only look at his poor bruised face."

Vespa hugged her tight. "Are you surprised, after beating me so mercilessly with that murderous umbrella?" She smiled and leaned to him. She was soft and yielding in his arms. Gazing down at her, he forgot all about danger and disgrace and jewelled carpets, until an angry shout outside brought him back to earth. Reluctantly, he put her from him, and said, "But it was well done, little meadowlark, and properly fooled our pompous sergeant, I think."

"Then I am glad I was such a shrew. We have told you why I ran away, Jack. Now I want to hear what happened to you."

He gave them a brief account of his journey. "They're not amateurs," he said, holding up the torn cape of his cloak. "This was skewered by a crossbow bolt."

Consuela clung to his hand and said in a shaken voice, "Merciful heaven!"

Manderville's brows went up. "There's a bounty on spies. D'you think that's what they're after?"

"I do not. I think there are several interested groups. Monteil, we know about; the fellow on the black horse, who keeps his distance but is definitely tracking me; two men riding dapple-grey horses, who question travellers about Kincraig; and another three, two of whom are hirelings, and the third—the unkind Mr. Duncan Keith, who has instructed his man with the crossbow to shoot straight next time!"

"Jupiter! Your half-brother?"

"He apparently believes that to be so. Though what he stands to gain by my death, I've no notion."

He went to the door and peered through a crack in the weather-beaten boards. The trooper stood guard, augmented by a farm-hand with a long-tined hay fork. He and Manderville could probably overpower the pair without much trouble, but then the hunt would be up, and Consuela deeply involved.

"Monsieur Corporal," he called. "My lady is anxious to be on her way. We must—"

"You must do as the sergeant orders," interrupted the corporal harshly. "If you and your mistress are placed under arrest, you will be taken to the barracks at Rennes."

"Confound it," muttered Vespa. "I *must* get on!"

Consuela said remorsefully, "Were it not for me, you would slip away and find Lord Kincraig. Well, you go, Jack. Paige will take care of me, and—"

"And who's to take care of Paige?" demanded Manderville. "If you mean to abandon us, Jack—"

"As if I would, you great gudgeon. Now tell me how you contrived to pass me by. You must have made excellent speed."

"For one thing we had a pair of horses, and we didn't have to lurk about and avoid roads, as you did." Manderville chuckled. "Consuela was really splendid as the arrogant Italian *grande dame,* and had everyone bowing and scraping."

"I believe that," said Vespa, lifting her willing hand to his lips. "Thoroughly enjoyed your charade, did you not, my rascal? But how did you know where I was?"

"We knew you would most probably ride towards Rennes," she replied, "so we went straight to the city and made enquiries for the Crazy Carpet Man. Every child in the area seems to know him. It was the children who told us he'd gone to St. Just, so we left the city on that road, guessing you'd follow the same path."

Manderville put in, "Good thing you come up when you did. That confounded sergeant was within Ames-ace of flat-out arresting us."

"Yes, and if he were under my command he'd be a private! He was so interested in the bottle I'd brought that he made no effort to verify *my* identity. What a blockhead!"

Consuela said with a saucy glance, "You should thank your stars that blockhead did not know any Italian, Captain Jack!"

"I thought you looked hilarious when I came up," he said. "Doesn't *mi perdoni* mean 'beg pardon' or something of the sort?"

"It means 'will you forgive me?'—which was quite *convenable.* But when you said that you were *chicchi-richi*— Oh, my poor Jack! How I kept my countenance I do not know!"

Manderville asked curiously, "Why? What did he say?"

"Jack said he was"—she gave a choke of mirth—"he said he was 'cock-a-doodle-doo!' "

Manderville howled, and Vespa clapped a hand over his eyes and groaned that he'd never live it down.

A familiar voice was raised. "If you are finished with your quarrelling, may I please have something to eat? I'm fairly starved."

They all whipped around.

Standing beside the boot of the carriage, Pierre de Coligny watched them hopefully.

Twelve

"Why should I not run away?" Pierre said with defiance, "Miss Consuela did. She knows what it is like there! Madame, who is not my *Maman*, hates her. As she hates me."

"Your poor Papa will be frantic," said Consuela, dispensing with insincere reassurances.

Vespa said, "And searching for you."

Frowning, Manderville nodded. "And if he blames us, as he probably will, he'll likely tell the authorities who we are and we'll have every soldier and policeman in France after us!"

"I doubt that," argued Vespa. "Too many people know we were his guests. De Coligny would incriminate himself. Consuela, you and Paige must take Pierre home."

"No!" said Consuela, Manderville and Pierre, emphatically and in unison.

"You've got too many enemies," Manderville declared.

Consuela pointed out, "You may need help. And how can Paige drive me back to the château, when we've told this silly sergeant I am returning to Italy and my Grandmama?"

"In which case, you should be turning east," said Vespa worriedly. "You are heading towards Spain, rather!"

"I wish you will all stop arguing and find me something to eat," complained Pierre.

There arose a sudden flurry of shouts and activity outside. Manderville made a wild leap onto the box of the carriage and Consuela scrambled inside. Pierre ran for the barn door, and Vespa caught him just as it was thrown open.

The sergeant stamped inside and halted abruptly, staring at the boy. "Hello, hello, hello! What's all this?"

"I am the farmer's son," lied Pierre. "And these bad people have kidnapped me."

His accent gave him away. The sergeant said with a chuckle, "Oh, ho! You'll not hoax me with such a tale, fierce one. Your talk is more of Paris than St. Just, and those clothes on your back were never worn by a poor Breton farmer's brat."

Vespa met his enquiring glance and said, "He is Lady Consuela's nephew, sir, and she fetches him from his school in Paris to see his great-grandmama." He added, low-voiced, "He's a rare handful!"

"This I can see." The sergeant's gait was slightly erratic as he moved closer. "Well, he comes by it honestly, I'd say. Now—" he hiccupped, and then called, "Are you awake, Lady Signoriny? I'll have the truth of it all, if—if you please."

There was a strong aroma of brandy on his breath. Vespa gave a mental cheer. His little ploy with Jules' bottle had born fruit. If the fellow was half-foxed, he'd be easier to outwit.

Consuela said, "Leonardo, what have you been telling the sergeant?"

"My name is not Leonardo!" Pierre scowled. "It is—"

"Come, that's no way to talk to your aunt," scolded the sergeant, wagging a finger under his chin.

"If you had but half a brain in your head—" began Pierre haughtily.

"Be still!" said Consuela, frowning at him. "You have my apologies, Sergeant. My nephew is rude."

"He is young, madame." The sergeant rocked on his heels and gave Pierre an indulgent smile. "I didn't know you'd a boy with you. I've sons of my own. Four. And scamps, every one. Now, I feel sure we can come to a quick resolution of our problems. Tell me, young Leonar-ardo. What is the full and real name of this lady, and where do you live?"

Vespa held his breath and from the corner of his eye saw Manderville preparing to leap from the box.

Pierre folded his arms across his chest and said heroically, "I shall tell you nothing, my good fool. Lead me to Madame Guillotine!"

The sergeant's jaw dropped. Then, with a shout of laughter he turned to Vespa. "You were right, *mon ami*. He's a handful. Since you are the Lady Signoriny's servant, you *assurement* can confirm for me her full name and where is her home."

"She is the Lady Consuela Carlotta Angelica of Ottavio, sir.

And I escort her to her grandmother, the Lady Francesca, Duchess of Ottavio."

"Bon!" The Sergeant snapped his fingers. "At long last we arrive at the answer. So you may be upon your way, and I can get to my own fireside. Do you see how simple it is, Lady Signoriny? Had you but told me the truth to begin with . . ." He clicked his tongue, shook his head at her, and reeled from the barn.

Vespa was inclined to believe Pierre's claim that Madame Thérèse had no love for him. He was sure however, that the chevalier was deeply fond of his son, and he was troubled by the awareness that the poor fellow was probably frantic with anxiety. Even if de Coligny did not at once guess that Pierre had run away, he would certainly by this time have instituted a thorough search. Vespa liked and respected the Frenchman and, under normal circumstances, he would not have hesitated an instant before turning about and taking both Pierre and Consuela back to the château. But the circumstances were far from normal, and he was torn between the need to catch up with Lord Kincraig and his responsibility for the safety of Consuela and the boy.

To an extent she was correct in believing herself protected by her Italian heritage and, if she was apprehended again, the chances were that at worst she would be ordered to leave the country. But if he and Paige should be challenged and it was revealed that she was travelling with two British officers it would be a very different story. The possible outcome made the sweat start on his brow.

As they left the barn and turned onto the road once more, Manderville watched him and called ironically, "Second thoughts, *monsieur le capitaine*? Justified. If we keep on this road much longer you're unlikely to persuade anyone that we're bound for Italy."

"What do you suggest?"

"When we started this journey you told me that your first concern was for Consuela's safety. If you really meant it, we should at once make a dash for the château. That, or turn east towards the Franco-Italian border."

Irritated, Vespa said, "Do talk sense! Every minute we're in France we run the risk of discovery. To travel clear across the country would be madness. And you know very well that to attempt to cross the Alps in winter is unthinkable."

"Why? The really hard winter weather don't set in till after Christmas, and—"

"Very true," interjected Consuela, leaning from the window. "But the terrible mistral can come down without warning, and with a howl like thunder. My dear *Nonna* told me her Mama used to say that one day the duchy would be blown clear across Italy and become a suburb of Padova."

Pierre squeezed into the window beside her and declared that he had seen the mistral. "I was little then," he boasted. "And the wind it picked me up and carried me off so that my uncle had to run for ten miles to catch me again!"

"What a rasper," snorted Manderville, "But our options are clear. To turn east is unacceptable. To continue towards St. Just is to invite sure disaster, so it's a race for the chateau and the coast."

"No!" shrilled Pierre. "I will *not* go back!"

"We are so close now," pleaded Consuela. "One more day only, and we should come up with Lord Kincraig. It is our future we fight for. Please, *please,* dear Jack, do not give up."

It was true that their every hope to marry depended upon his locating the elusive peer who might be his sire. If only he could in some way get Consuela and the boy to safety. To attempt to reach the Italian border was out of the question, as Paige knew very well. He'd likely only suggested such a ridiculous route because his cold was dulling his wits. As risky as it was to follow Kincraig they *were* close now; he could feel it. They'd risked so much—another day wouldn't make much difference, surely? If they didn't come up with Kincraig tomorrow, they would turn to the west and make a dash for the château.

Consuela's anxious eyes were fixed on his face. He said, "Very well. One more day. But one day only!"

She squeaked and clapped her hands, and Pierre shouted "Hurrah! I am still free!"

Manderville looked disgusted, but whipped up the horses. Vespa reined Bruine beside the carriage and they turned south on the road to St. Just.

The afternoon was well advanced and the chill wind carried a steady drizzle. It developed that Pierre was not the only 'starved' member of the little group. When Vespa learned that

in their haste to find him Paige and Consuela had not stopped
to eat, he pulled into the yard of the first farmhouse they came
to and was able to purchase a cold roasted chicken, the inevitable baguette—sliced and buttered—and a bag of black plums.
Pierre ran into the big kitchen demanding to know if there was
any cake, and the farm wife laughed and graciously added some
bread pudding to their lunch.

She allowed them to eat in her warm kitchen and they were
soon on their way again, Vespa riding escort, and constantly
scanning the road ahead for any sign of a waggon and an elderly gentleman. They passed a group of the menhirs; the great
standing stones that might well have been erected by the same
ancient peoples who'd left them in Cornwall and Stonehenge.
Vespa pulled back to draw Consuela's attention to the strange
monoliths. She was fascinated, but Pierre hid his face against
her, crying that the menhirs were well known to be evil men
who'd been turned to stone for their wickedness, and that it
was very bad luck to look upon them.

The miles slipped away and still Vespa saw no sign of a likely
looking waggon. His heart stood still when a young officer in
a showy blue uniform rode up and ordered them to pull off
to the side. Obeying, but prepared to make a run for it, Vespa
was able to breathe again as a troop of artillery clattered past
escorting a gun-carriage. Readying for the next action, he
thought, that would come in the spring if Wellington could
muster the forces and supplies he needed. He grinned faintly,
picturing the great man's impotent rage at all the rain.

They were allowed to move on then, encountering tinkers
walking by the side of the road with great packs on their backs;
ponderous rumbling wains; rickety donkey carts; a brightly
painted caravan from which a very old woman leered at Manderville and screeched an offer to tell 'the handsome young
citizen's fortune'; a family evidently moving, their goods bundled and lashed to four mules, the husband leading the way
and his lady walking beside the last mule, holding the hand of
a small girl and keeping an eagle eye on a cradle perched pre-
cariously atop the overloaded animal's back.

Vespa's concerned gaze was on that cradle when the inevitable happened: The mule stumbled over a pothole in the road.
The cradle slid, but on the far side of the lady, who let out a
terrified screech as she made a fruitless grab for it. Vespa had
already spurred Bruine. He caught the tumbling cradle in the

nick of time, but it was all he could do to keep the infant from falling, and its howls were scarcely less piercing than those of its mama.

The husband ran back to snatch the cradle. The wife retrieved the baby and began to rock it and croon soothingly. Vespa said, "I think that is not a safe place for your infant, madame."

The husband levelled an affronted glare at him, restored cradle and child to their precarious perch and ran back to his place at the head of the column.

As they passed with not one word from the family, Manderville said in French, "That'll teach you to be a knight errant, Captain, sir!"

"The baby might have been killed," said Vespa indignantly. "What would you have done? Galloped over it, I daresay."

"You're in no case to gallop over anything, *mon ami*. Your heroic deed did not benefit your trusty mare. She's favouring her left front leg."

Vespa swore and dismounted at once. Pierre hung from the coach window and informed them that Miss Consuela was asleep. He also spoke without finesse of his own needs which were, it seemed, of an urgent nature. Vespa turned off the road and into a grove of poplars and evergreens. Pierre ran off, and Vespa and Manderville inspected Bruine's damaged leg. Fortunately this only amounted to a thrown shoe but, until she was reshod, she could not be ridden.

Vespa told her she was a good little lady, and unbuckled the saddle, depositing it in the boot. Pierre had left the carriage door open, and he peeped in at Consuela. She was fast asleep, her hood fallen back and an errant curl nestling against her sleep-flushed cheek. One hand lay, palm up, on the seat. How dear she was; how intrepid and resourceful and high-couraged. By Society's rigid standards she was an incorrigible minx, but how many ladies of the *ton* would have taken such risks to help him in this desperate search? How many would have so bravely endured the perils and hardships she had faced with never a whine or a whimper? Aching with love for her, yearning to take her into his arms, he kissed his forefinger and very lightly transferred the kiss to her soft little palm.

Behind him, Manderville sang hoarsely:

> " 'When is the time a maid to kiss?
> Tell me this, now tell me this.
> 'Tis when the drizzle turns to rain.
> 'Tis when Pierre's run off again.
> Is—' "

Flushing hotly, Vespa whipped around. "The devil! Have you called him?"

"As you'd have heard were you not so entranced by—"

"Confound the boy! You'd better go and search for him." Manderville sighed and turned away, but Vespa had seen the weariness in his face and the dark circles under his eyes. Catching his arm he said remorsefully, "I'm an insensitive clod, and you've a beast of a cold. I'll bring the young varmint back, it shouldn't take above a minute or two, then I'll drive and you can get some rest."

His 'minute or two' stretched to ten, at the end of which, fuming, he had searched through several thick clusters of fern and shrubs while his calls went unanswered. He was beginning to worry and he climbed to a high point to look about. As he approached the top he heard shouts and squeals, seemingly coming from the far side of this rise. Real alarm seized him. Pierre was the son of a chevalier of France; it was not beyond the realm of possibility that this time he really had been kidnapped! Impelled by visions of enormous ransom demands, a heartbroken father and his own failure to have protected the child, he began to run. At the top of the rise, he halted, and stood there motionless while the raindrops fell unnoticed on his bare head.

At the foot of the slope a large waggon of unusual design was drawn up under a wide-spreading tree, a tent pitched beside it. He could see the smoke of a campfire and he heard a man's deep laughter, but neither man nor fire were visible, for the waggon was surrounded by children. In an oddly remote fashion he wondered where they had all come from. They crowded in, squealing, jumping up and down with excitement, and waving small paper-wrapped objects triumphantly.

'My God!' he thought. 'Oh, my dear God!' Perversely, at the instant of success he was afraid; afraid of discovering that the Crazy Carpet Collector was indeed crazy; afraid of an infuriated denial or of being contemptuously rejected; afraid that—like

Duncan Keith—Lord Kincraig might fancy him to be an opportunistic fortune-hunter, or despise him because his mother had married the man he loathed.

Pierre's shrill voice cut through his trance-like immobility. "Here he is, Capitaine Jacques! Here is the Crazy Carpet Person you search for!"

In the midst of the crowd a man stood straight and turned towards him. He said something, and the uproar faded and ceased. The boys and girls began to drift away, some scowling at Vespa resentfully, then running with the quick adaptiveness of childhood, shouting about the rain and home and supper.

The man by the waggon still stood there. A rifle was propped against the wheel beside him, and there was a guardedness in the way he watched the newcomer.

Pierre came leaping up the slope, waving a handful of sweetmeats. "See what I've got, Capitaine! He gave me—"

"Go back to the coach." Vespa did not raise his voice, but the boy checked, gazing up into his stern face curiously. Then he ran off without a word of protest.

Kincraig called in fluent French, "Good day, monsieur. You have been seeking me? What may I do for you? Have you perchance a carpet to show me?"

Vespa limped down the slope. How did one open a conversation under such circumstances? 'Oh, hello, sir. I think I may be one of your by-blows?' Or, 'How d'ye do, my lord? Your bastard son has come to call?' He thought an irritated, 'Idiot!' And drawing closer, realized there was no need for words.

He had expected to confront a much older man, but although Kincraig's fair hair was streaked with grey, his figure was trim, his chin had not sagged, and he looked to be only a year or so past fifty. The features were so similar to his own that it was indeed like looking into a mirror of the future. The cheekbones were slightly more finely etched, the mouth almost too sensitive. There were lines in the face that spoke of suffering, and although he smiled tentatively, deep in the eyes Vespa thought to glimpse a hint of sadness. And it was the eyes that sealed their resemblance; in shape and hue, even to the amber flecks, they were identical to his own. He saw that Kincraig was staring and had become very pale. He said in English, "Good afternoon, my lord."

"Who . . ." croaked Kincraig, "who the—the deuce are you?"

"Until recently I thought I was John Wansdyke Vespa, but—"
He sprang forward to support the man who sagged, white to
the lips, against the waggon. "And I'm a sorry fool," he added
repentantly. "Let me get you out of the rain."

He all but carried Kincraig to the tent and deposited him
on a camp bed. Several crates had been piled on their sides to
create a makeshift cupboard. Among the objects on the top
'shelf' was a bottle of greenish liquid that he eyed uncertainly.

"Yes—please," whispered Kincraig. "Medicine."

Vespa took out the bottle and following his lordship's sig-
nalled instructions measured two inches into a mug and handed
it over.

After a minute or two some colour returned to the waxen
features, the eyes opened again, and Kincraig said more steadily,
"That's better. My apologies, sir. Didn't mean to . . . to throw
such a scare into you. A slight nuisance with my health, is all.
If you will excuse my crude hospitality, there's . . . some fair
cognac in the lower box. I'm afraid my folding chair will have
to serve for a sofa."

Vespa settled for both cognac and chair, and having occupied
the second and sampled the first, he met Kincraig's searching
gaze and said, "I'm so sorry. This has been a shock for you,
and—"

"Never mind about that." The baron made a gesture of impatience. "My God, but you've my father's eyes! And mine, of
course. To say I'm astonished is a masterpiece of understate-
ment, but there's nothing to be served by tippy-toeing around
the issue. Your name and your face tell me all I need to know.
The fact that you've come to me says you must know it also.
Or—some of it?"

"Not much, sir. But—I think we are—er, related."

"I'd say that is a certainty. Did Lady Faith send you? How is
she, bless her heart? How did she know where I was?"

"My mother is well, but she's out of the country at the moment. She never breathed a word of the true state of—of the
matter to me. When I learned that Sir Kendrick Vespa was not
my father, I decided to try and find out who was. With Mama
away, it—er, hasn't been easy."

"I'll wager it hasn't! A tricky business for you, I've no doubt.
And you likely judge me a proper rogue." Kincraig waved a
hand as Vespa attempted to reply. "No, don't answer. How
could you think otherwise? I've no intention to try and wrap

it up in clean linen, but I'd like you to know that I was deep in love with your beautiful mother and it was my dearest hope to make her my wife. After she married that— Well, I stayed away at first, of course. But poor Faith was neglected and so unhappy. We began to meet in secret, and I tried to cheer her."

He sighed nostalgically, then went on: "Inevitably, it became an *affaire de coeur.* I won't say I'm sorry. We were as much in love as ever. We belonged together and should never have been separated. Sir Kendrick found out, eventually. I don't know what he said to Faith, but when I confronted him he refused to meet me in a duel—he has a horror of scandal, as I'm sure you know. He was icy cold, and—I'm sorry, but truth is truth—he warned that if I ever came near Faith again, she would suffer a fatal accident. He meant it. And I know he's capable of—"

He slanted a glance at Vespa's enigmatic countenance, and said apologetically, "Well, I must not say more on that head, save that I haven't seen her since. I was too distraught to stay in England and removed for a time to a property I own in Scotland. But it was lonely and when I realized I was sinking into melancholy I began to travel abroad. I blundered into a marriage that was not happy, which spurred me into extending my travels, but whenever I was in Britain the Society pages of the newspapers kept me fairly well apprised of Faith and her sons. I never dreamed one of them . . . might be mine."

He drew a hand across his eyes, then asked, "Well, young man? Now you have my story, are you here to demand satisfaction because of my disgraceful conduct?"

Vespa said with a slow smile, "If my mother did not judge your conduct disgraceful, sir, I scarcely have the right to do so."

"Aha! You've a silver tongue, I see. Which shouldn't surprise me, since I believe you served as one of Wellington's staff officers?"

The voice was clear and incisive now, the eyes sparkling. Lord Kincraig showed no sign of either denial or rejection, and if this was a lunatic, he was indeed a complex one. Heartened, Vespa replied, "Yes, sir. Until Vitoria."

"By Jove! How splendid! Then you're no green boy. Still, it was likely a shock for you, as well. Egad, but there's so *much* I want to know! Firstly, how and when did you find out that Sir Kendrick is not your father; and why in Hades wasn't I told of your existence?"

"I believe Mama was frightened into keeping silent, sir."

Kincraig frowned darkly, "Yes. He'd do that, the proud bas—" He bit his lip and cut the words short. "I'm sorry. You are likely fond of him."

Vespa said quietly, "I loved him. He's dead, my lord."

"Great heavens!" Staring in stupefaction, Kincraig gasped, *"Kendrick Vespa? Dead? Recently?"*

"Very, sir. And suddenly."

"But he was always the picture of—Did some public-spirited citizen call him out, or—What on earth—No! Never say it was an accident? Your dear mama was not—"

"My mother was abroad when—when it happened. We wrote to advise her of my—of Sir Kendrick's death."

Bewildered, but trying to take it all in, Lord Kincraig said, "Yet you're not in mourning, and you're—Good God! Where are my wits gone? Do you realize what will happen if you're unmasked as a British officer? You can't go jauntering about France in time of war! Why are you here?"

Vespa said with a slow smile, "I might ask you the same, sir."

"My carpets! Oh, egad! I must see to them!" Distracted, his lordship sprang up and hurried from the tent, Vespa following.

Kincraig stopped, turned back, and asked rather shyly, "May I request an embrace? A man don't gain a fine young son every day, you know."

Vespa's heart gave a joyful leap and he returned a crushing hug. His eyes rather dim, he asked brokenly, "Then—you don't mind, sir?"

"Mind!" Kincraig leaned back and searched his face. "My dear boy! I cannot tell you how—how proud— Oh, Jupiter, the back is open! He ran to the waggon and Vespa helped pull the double rear doors closed. The waggon was even larger than he'd at first realized, and sturdily built, with a wooden roof and sides so that it resembled an outsize caravan with overhanging eaves. There were many rolls of carpet inside, all neatly disposed, but that would, he realized, constitute quite a weight.

Kincraig said with a proud smile that the waggon had been built to his own design. "I have to keep the rain out, you know. And if I find many treasures on one expedition, the load can get extremely heavy. You see my team over there?" He gestured to where four big cart-horses were loosely picketed and munching contentedly at the contents of their nose-bags. "Strengthy beasts, and there are times—But never mind that. John—may I call you John?"

Sir Kendrick had called him John. He said, "By all means, sir. But I'm Jack to most of my friends." His friends! Dismayed, he exclaimed, "Oh, Jupiter! I've left my coach and my—er, people fast asleep! Forgive, but I must—"

Kincraig looked over his shoulder and said inexplicably, "I think you had best let me deal with this, my boy."

Gaston de Coligny's coach was moving cautiously down the slope, escorted on either side by a rider, each of whom was astride a dapple-grey horse. Manderville was flushed and tight-lipped. From the window, Consuela's eyes flashed an unmistakable warning. 'Damn!' thought Vespa. This was the same pair who had been questioning the people in the caravans and whom the free-trader had spoken of. Seen more closely, they looked grim and dangerous. Certainly they knew their trade, for they'd lost no time in coming up with him. He pulled a low-trailing branch aside and stepped forward as they rode up side by side.

"Good day," called Lord Kincraig. "What have you brought me, my friends?"

"This!" A wolfish-looking individual with a profusion of bushy greying hair reached behind him and dragged Pierre forward.

The boy was white-faced, his eyes big with fright. He said quaveringly, "I did not do anything naughty, Monsieur Jacques."

"But—no," confirmed the intruder, regarding Kincraig with a broad grin. "So you will want him back. He is your grandson, eh?"

Kincraig said in bewilderment, "He was with the children who come for their sweetmeats, but I do not know the little fellow. Perhaps, he is the lady's child?"

The wolfish man shrugged. "You evade. It is of no importance. We will see your waggon now, Monsieur Collector."

"Ah," exclaimed Kincraig, rubbing his hands happily. "You are interested in rugs, is that the case? Come, then! I will show you my harvest! It is always a joy to meet an *aficionado*. But—these beauties they are not for sale, you understand."

He trotted towards the waggon. The two intruders exchanged a slightly perplexed glance.

Pierre struggled and demanded to be put down at once.

"Quiet, scrap," said the leader, and as the boy kicked and wriggled, he added a harsh, "Stop your squirming, or I'll—"

"Ow!" howled Pierre. "Capitaine Jacques . . . !"

Vespa released the branch he still held. It flailed out with a great scattering of raindrops. The dapple greys took the brunt of it and reared with shrill neighs of fright. The man who held the boy fought against being unseated, and Pierre jumped clear. Vespa ran to snatch up Kincraig's rifle. The intruders regained control of their mounts to find themselves staring down a long barrel held in a pair of very steady hands.

Pierre ran to clutch Vespa's coat. "These are very bad people," he cried vehemently. "They are rough with Monsieur Manderville, and they frighten your lady!"

Vespa darted a glance at Consuela.

"I am not hurt," she called. "But they struck Paige and took his pistol."

"Which I will now have back," said Manderville.

"Come and take it," jeered the second man. His face was a mass of pimples and he was shorter and more stockily built than his companion, but looked just as ruthless.

"You will do well to shoot them first, Capitaine Jacques," advised Pierre.

"An excellent notion," said Vespa, taking aim and drawing back the trigger.

Perhaps judging others by his own standards, the wolfish individual cried, "What a bloodthirsty villain! All we wanted was to see the flying carpet."

"A desire we share," said Kincraig with a sigh. "Alas it eludes me, but I have several very fine specimens I will be glad to show you."

His finger steady on the trigger, Vespa said, "If all you wanted was to see this gentleman's carpets there would have been no need to bully my friends and the child. I should warn you that my hand is tiring. And when it tires my fingers tend to cramp. Drop your weapons."

They both glared at him murderously. He allowed the rifle to jerk slightly. With lightning speed two horse pistols thudded to the ground, followed by Manderville's pocket pistol. This smaller weapon had a hair trigger, and the impact caused it to fire. The shot set the horses rearing and squealing and the ball ruffled Vespa's hair, startling him into losing his aim.

Thinking him wounded, Consuela screamed.

Pierre gave a piercing howl.

The two intruders seized the moment and departed at a gallop.

Consuela threw open the carriage door and flew to Vespa's side.

Manderville jumped down from the box and began to gather the weapons.

Pierre demonstrated the benefits of a British classical education by leaping up the slope after the departing ruffians and screaming, "Good riddance to bad rubbish!"

Seemingly bewildered by the sight of a pretty young lady embracing his newly acquired son, Lord Kincraig looked from one to the other, and shook his head. "What a pity," he remarked despondently. "What a pity."

Manderville sniffed, and asked stuffily, "Your pardon, sir?"

Kincraig gave him his gentle smile. "Those two gentlemen," he murmured. "I think they really were interested in my carpets."

Vespa said quietly, "My lord, may I present Miss Consuela Jones, the lady I hope to make my wife."

"Good gracious," exclaimed Kincraig, as Consuela curtsied before him. "Do you say you are travelling together, but not married? What a pretty creature you are, my dear. Your parents must be very broad-minded, but I'm afraid you'll find me rather old-fashioned."

Consuela blushed.

With an edge of steel to his voice, Vespa introduced Manderville, and said, "There is so much for us to discuss, my lord. But our first concern must be to find a safer campsite. Unless I mistake it those two rogues work for an ugly customer named Imre Monteil. I don't know what he wants of you, but he's ruthless and persistent."

"Oh, yes. Monteil. I know of him. A greedy gentleman who collects art works whether or not people wish to sell them. He'd travel to the ends of the earth for a fragment of the Spring Carpet of Khusraw. I can't let him have it, you know. Such a sad waste of his time. But—I suppose it gives him something to do." Nodding to himself, he trotted back into the tent.

Vespa and Consuela looked at each other. She said staunchly, "We cannot blame him for misjudging us, Jack. Anyone would think the same. I'm sure he will understand when you explain everything."

Manderville asked, "How much have you told him? He must have noted your resemblance, surely? Does he admit your, er—relationship?"

"He was very kind," said Vespa, his chin high. "And seemed delighted to acknowledge me."

"Ah. Well, that's a step in the right direction." Manderville added dubiously, "I suppose. Well, don't glare at me like that. You were warned that he's—ah, eccentric." He chuckled. "He's that, all right."

"Damn you," said Vespa. "Come and help me pole up his horses."

Whatever Lord Kincraig's mental shortcomings, he knew the countryside. At dusk they were snugly settled into a wooded hollow having the benefits of a shallow stream with a level but stony bed along which the horses and vehicles passed without leaving telltale tracks. Vespa had brought up the rear of their little cavalcade and had stayed for twenty minutes on the highest ground, alert for signs of pursuit. He was lured to the campsite by the smell of bacon frying and found Consuela busily cooking over a small fire, and Manderville and Kincraig settling the horses for the night.

Pierre fell asleep when he finished his supper. Consuela could scarcely keep her eyes open and Vespa carried the boy and walked beside her to Kincraig's tent, which had been assigned to them. Pierre mumbled sleepily when he was laid down on the pile of rugs that was his makeshift bed for the night.

Vespa turned to draw Consuela into a long-awaited hug. She snuggled close and with his hand on the back of her curls and her soft shapeliness pressed against him, he yearned with every fibre of his being to kiss her. It would not be dishonourable now—would it? He'd publicly stated that she was his betrothed; she had as publicly confirmed it. Besides, if word got out that she had travelled unchaperoned in his company, the duchess would likely demand that they marry. But the word might not get out, and it would be a shabby trick to take advantage of a possibility, before the fact as it were. The inescapable truth was that he'd given his word to the old lady. To break it would not be the act of a gentleman, and to break it while her granddaughter was far from home and under his protection would most definitely be dishonourable. Sighing, he forced himself to draw back.

"I think Pierre had better not be undressed. Just his coat and boots. We may have to move again." He looked uneasily at the camp bed with its rough blankets. "This is Turkish treatment for you, Consuela. Will you be warm enough? Shall you be able to sleep?"

She assured him she could sleep through an earthquake, but despite her indomitable smile she looked very tired. He stroked her cheek. "You've been so good through all this, poor sweet."

"Yes," she agreed. "I really think my dear Papa would not be ashamed of me." She caught his hand then, and said urgently, "Jack, I'm so glad you've found your father. But he seems very set in his ways. Will you be able to persuade him to come home now? Grandmama will want to meet him."

"You may be very sure that I mean to try." He pressed her fingers to his lips, and in response to her indignant look, he pointed out, "I gave your Grandmama my word not to try and fix my interest. And even if I had not, I've no wish to trap you into matrimony, little meadowlark."

She said with a sigh, "Sometimes, I wish you had not such a high sense of honour, Captain Jack." And knew that not for the world would she change him.

Thirteen

Outside, Lord Kincraig was still sitting by the fire, but Manderville had said his goodnights and taken his cold and his blankets to his assigned 'bed' in the coach.

"You must be worn to a shade, my boy," said his lordship kindly. "Are you sure you're not too tired to talk tonight?"

Vespa assured him that he was not at all tired. "I've waited a long time for this moment, sir."

"In that case, we will not delay it." Kincraig gestured to a nearby crate. "Pull up one of our elegant 'chairs' and we'll try to discover each other."

Their 'discoveries' were at first superficial, both reluctant to put the more harrowing events of their lives into words. Kincraig spoke of his home in Suffolk and his Scottish castle, of which he appeared extremely fond. He was very ready to laugh at some recountings of the youthful exploits of Jack and Sherborne. Soon, however, the conversation turned down a path Vespa dreaded to follow. Despite his denial, he was very tired, but it occurred to him that for all his eccentricities, his lordship possessed a remarkably keen mind. He wanted to know the details of the final tragedy in the quarry at Alabaster Royal. Vespa took refuge in evasions, but it was no use. Always, however gently, Lord Kincraig brought him back to the subject, and at length he capitulated. He kept a tight rein on his emotions, but his brief account and the clipped restrained words painted a clearer picture than he guessed. Kincraig, who had pushed for the truth, had suspected fraud and skullduggery; he had not expected brutality and murder. He saw the sheen of perspiration on the grim young face and for a moment was too horrified to comment.

Vespa slanted a glance at him and said haltingly, "You likely think me a blind fool, but Sir Kendrick was a consummate actor. All those years, and I had not the slightest suspicion that he wasn't really my father. We didn't see him often at Richmond, but when he was there he could scarcely have been more kind— to both of us, although everyone knew he favoured Sherry."

Recovering his voice, Kincraig asked, "You did not resent that fact?"

"Was I jealous? Oh, yes. Of course. But . . . well, you'd have to have known my brother—I expect I should now call him my half-brother. Sherry was such a—a splendid fellow. We were— very attached."

The rain had stopped and the clouds had drifted away. The air was cold and clear, and the moon had come up, throwing its soft radiance over the hills and dappling the ground with the shadows of the trees. Lord Kincraig stood and wandered to where he could watch the horses still cropping at the grass. Seeing none of the pastoral scene, he said in a voice that trembled slightly, "I can scarce credit that even such a one as Kendrick Vespa could have shot you down so callously. It was because he hated me, I've no doubt."

"Not entirely, sir. Quite unintentionally I had discovered his scheme. I didn't know it was his at the time. But I did know I couldn't allow it to go on, and so—well, I stood between him and a great deal of money."

"So you implied. But you don't say how he expected to make such a fortune."

"No." A pause, and Vespa said, "I'm afraid I'm not at liberty to discuss that."

Kincraig swung around. "Good God! Do you say you've been *ordered* not to speak of it? Then it must be a matter of national security! Is Lady Faith aware of all this?"

"She knew nothing of it. But if she has received the letter my great-uncle sent off she may be on her way home, and I must be there when she arrives. And now, my lord, it occurs to me that you've very adroitly fished out a great deal of my life history, but have told me very little of yours. Fair play, you know."

His mind still on the appalling events this newly found son had survived, Kincraig hesitated, then sat down again and said with a forced smile, "I've told you most of it. You know that I loved your beautiful mother, and that my own marriage was disastrous. I suppose it was my unhappy home life that drove me to plunge deeper into research concerning my hobby. Eventually, my fascination with rugs and carpets induced me to spend much of the year seeking out rare specimens."

Vespa said carefully, "But you're not really hoping to find a—er, *flying* carpet, are you, sir?"

"That would be a find, to be sure!" Kincraig chuckled. "No, Jack. But it's a useful ploy. When I began my wanderings the news got about that a rich collector was searching for fine rugs. I was besieged by would-be sellers bringing me everything from small mats to very large carpets, and most at ridiculously inflated prices. Since I've spread the rumour that the rich collector is seeking a flying carpet, most of the opportunists have decided I am demented and they certainly have no such item to offer. Thus, I am less overwhelmed with merchandise that is useless to me."

"What about the Spring Carpet of Khusraw? Is that why you continue your search?"

Gazing into the flames, his lordship said dreamily, "Who knows? As I recall it was Robert Herrick who wrote: 'Attempt the end, and never stand to doubt. Nothing's so hard but search will find it out.' "

"You certainly seem to have found many fine specimens. The waggon cannot take much more weight, I'd think. You must be ready to go home."

"Home. A beautiful word, Jack."

"And you've a beautiful home, sir. Yes, I've seen Lambent Grove. I went there seeking you."

"Did you now?" Kincraig turned his head and looked at him thoughtfully. "You likely found the place closed up, which is a pity. It's a nice house."

"Very nice. Your butler was kind enough to show me a few rooms."

His voice expressionless, Kincraig said, "If Barnard was still there, I fancy my son Duncan was in residence."

"Yes."

"And you didn't see eye to eye. Not surprising. I suppose Duncan noticed the family resemblance?"

"Yes."

His lordship's smile was brittle. "You can say a lot with one word, Jack. The boy was offensive, I gather."

"I'm afraid we had a—er, a small turn-up, sir."

"Which you won, of course." Kincraig shook his head and said with a sigh, "Poor lad. Poor lad. It's not his fault. His mother . . ." He shrugged and the words trailed off.

Vespa waited through another silence then said, "You will think this vulgar, my lord, but—I have a small inheritance from my mother's parents. I won't touch the Vespa funds or properties, but I've an old house in Dorsetshire I'm fond of, and I have no need— That is to say—I mean—I am not a pauper."

"Duncan accused you of being a fortune-hunter, did he? What nonsense. I've more than enough for both of you."

"But I don't want anything from you, sir. Except, perhaps, your affection and—and acceptance. If your son could be made to see that—"

"I'm afraid he cannot. To an extent I understand his resentment. You see, when my wife died, I was involved in a rather chancy business. I made a new will, under the terms of which, upon my demise everything would go to my legal heir—Duncan. Although you cannot be named a legal heir, I mean to acknowledge you as my son, and make suitable provision for you. No! Please do not argue. It is my wish, and my right. Duncan knows me. He knows what I will do. His nature is such that— Well, I'm afraid he won't like it!"

No, Duncan Keith wouldn't like it, thought Vespa. Unless perhaps his man with the crossbow shot straighter next time.

The morning dawned bright but cold. Vespa rose early, started a fire and carried a bowl of hot water to the tent. Consuela answered his call drowsily but then demanded that he wait, and next instant her tousled head appeared through the tent flap, and her eager eyes were searching his face.

"What did he say? What did he say? I tried to keep awake so that you could tell me, but I was too tired, and you must have talked the night away! Is he willing to acknowledge you?"

He tugged on an errant curl. "He doesn't seem averse to the notion."

She squeaked and gave a little leap of excitement, causing the tent to rock ominously. "Oh, how splendid! *Nonna* will give us her blessing then, I am sure! Now why must you look troubled? Ah! You think his lordship may not approve of *me*, is that the case? Well, let me tell you, Captain John Wansdyke Vespa, I have done *nothing* of which I am ashamed, and in fact—"

He laughed and tweaked her little nose. "Get dressed, Signorina Fiero! It should not take you above an hour, do you think?"

"Monstrous man! I shall be cooking breakfast in ten minutes!"

A quarter of an hour to complete a lady's toilette, he told her, would break all known records. Her indignant vow to make him eat his words followed him as he went down to look at Bruine, his heart light and his hopes high.

He had ascertained that there were no pebbles or stone bruises on the mare's hoof and was preparing to feed the horses when Manderville joined him, looking flushed and sleepy and speaking in the stuffy voice that accompanies a cold. Scooping oats into a nosebag he said, "Well? Well? Are you the acknowledged son and heir?"

Vespa grinned at him happily. "I am. One of 'em, at all events. Do you know, Paige, the dear old fellow really seems pleased to welcome me to the family."

Manderville slapped him on the back and said he couldn't be more pleased. "This means your path to the altar is clear, at last. Have you persuaded Lord Kincraig to turn for home now?"

"He says he cannot: that he's to meet a fellow who really may have a scrap of this fabulous Khusraw carpet. It's nonsense, of course, but I must tread carefully. Still, I hope to persuade him to change his mind."

While the men shaved, Pierre was assigned the task of being their lookout in case any strangers approached, and Consuela prepared a breakfast of coffee, rolls and omelettes. She was timid with Lord Kincraig until he bowed and kissed her hand with stately gallantry, and told her his 'son' had explained matters. "I gather it is thanks to you that Jack found me, my dear," he said. "I can only hope that my future daughter-in-law will forgive me for my hasty judgment."

She was overjoyed and, to his great delight, his lordship was hugged and a kiss pressed on his cheek. She was, he told Vespa when the two men were poling up the cart-horses, a darling of a girl, sunny natured and full of spirit. "To see the way you look at each other is heart-warming. I think you have found a love that is not given to many. It reminds me of when your dear Mama and I—" He broke off, then finished quickly, "Don't let it slip away, Jack. Guard her well."

"I mean to, sir. And in that connection, I want her back in England as fast as may be."

"Excellent! She can say what she likes about being protected by her Italian ancestry, but she is at high risk here. You must leave at once."

"Very good. Do you think it safe for us to all travel together? Or shall you lead the way while we follow?"

Lord Kincraig chuckled. "Blandly said. But as I told you last night—"

Vespa raised a delaying hand. "Your pardon—father." The word came unbidden to his tongue, and for a minute he was too moved to continue. Then he asked shyly, "Do I—presume too much, sir?"

Kincraig also was overcome, and stretched out an unsteady hand which Vespa took and held strongly. "If you *knew*," said his lordship. "Of course, you cannot know, but— Consider your little signorina and how deeply you love her."

"More than my life, sir."

"That is how I felt about your mother. To discover that she bore me such a fine son . . . There are no words, my dear boy! I shall be proud to have you name me so!"

Such a display of emotion was an embarrassment to both British hearts, wherefore they avoided each other's eyes and became very much occupied with straps and buckles and harness. As soon as he could master his voice, Vespa said, "Thank you. But—you must know that Consuela refuses to go home unless I do. And I have no intention of leaving until you come also."

Kincraig turned and looked at him squarely. "So soon, you challenge me," he said with a faint wistful smile.

"I have been pursued, shot at and beaten, since I commenced to search for you," said Vespa, meeting his gaze steadily. "It's very obvious that several groups think you have found your jewelled carpet and mean to have it. With all due respect, my lord, I have had the deuce of a time finding you, and I will be damned if I will now run the risk of losing you!"

Kincraig gave a shout of laughter. "I see how it will be. So long as I behave myself I will be 'father,' but if we don't see eye to eye, I am doomed to exist as 'my lord'!"

Vespa reddened. "No, really, sir! My apologies if I spoke harshly. I've no thought to challenge your authority, but—"

"But you demand that I do as you wish."

"Not demand—never that! Only—I do beg of you to recon-
sider. No carpet ever woven is worth your life—or worth risking
Consuela's life. How you've managed to wander about Europe
like this in time of war is beyond me, but no man's luck holds
forever. It's long past time that you were safe home in Suffolk—
or Scotland."

Kincraig looked worried. "The girl presents a problem, no
doubt of that," he muttered. "And you're quite right. I shall
go home. Just as soon as I've met my friend. No—don't argue
with me, Jack. I have no alternative, you see. He waits a scant
three leagues away. I gave my word to meet him, and I've never
broken my word yet."

Vespa's jaw tightened. "Then you leave me no choice but to
accompany you, sir."

"Nonsense! Your first thought must be for your lady. Take
her home, lad. Take her home."

And so it went, the young staff officer using every wile and
stratagem at his command, the nobleman smiling and genial
and immovable, until Manderville came to join them with
Pierre leaping along behind him. "Is this a private quarrel?"
he enquired with a grin.

"May I have a sweet?" cried Pierre.

"One only," said Kincraig. "You know where they are."
Pierre jumped onto the tail of the waggon and clambered over
the rugs to a crate at the far end.

"It isn't a quarrel at all, Paige," said Vespa sharply. "I've
merely been trying to persuade his lordship to come back to
England with us."

"Jolly good," said Manderville. "The only sensible thing to
do. And I think we shouldn't delay. Those are thunderheads
unless I mistake 'em."

One glance at the threatening skies and Kincraig scurried
for the tent saying in that odd, shrill voice so different from
his usual manner, "I must strike camp! If we get much rain it
will be difficult . . . very difficult!"

Vespa looked after him uneasily.

Manderville said, "I wonder you convinced him, he seems
so determined to go his own way."

"I didn't convince him. Dammitall, he's stubborn as any
mule!"

"You resemble him in more than looks, I see," said Manderville with a grin.

"I'm glad you find it so blasted amusing. You won't object to taking Consuela home."

Manderville's response was pithy and profane.

Vespa said intensely, "Paige, you *must!* I daren't leave him—not with that unholy crew at his heels!"

"It appears to me they're at *your* heels. And he has gone on very well by himself these many years, from what I can gather. Come now, own he's dished you. You've done what you could, and he'll have none of it. You cannot compel him to your way of thinking, and if he's given his word of honour—"

"To do—what? Meet some cloth-head who fancies he's found a piece of that confounded ancient rug? It's not *possible*, you know that as well as I!"

"Lord Kincraig don't appear to know it."

Vespa muttered, "Small wonder they call him crazy. I've a damned good mind to take him home by force, if only to protect the dear man."

"You'd catch cold at that, I think." With rare austerity Manderville said, "I for one would have no part in such a scheme, I promise you."

"Confound you," exclaimed Vespa, turning on him angrily. "Then why did you come if you meant to refuse your help when most I need you? If Toby were here, I'll warrant he'd—" He broke off and ran a hand through his hair. "No—forgive me. I don't mean that. You've been very good, Paige. It's just that—I'm at my wit's end. I *must* get Consuela safely home, and I cannot abandon my—my father to his probable death! *Please!* If you will just—"

"Do what?" interposed Consuela, who had come up unnoticed. "Bundle me off again? Paige won't try it, for he knows very well I'd get away and follow you."

"Not if I tied you up and threw you in the coach."

Her blue eyes widened. "Jack! You wouldn't!"

"To protect you from yourself? Oh, my dearest girl, be sure I would!"

"Then it would be a coach you'd have to drive," said Manderville.

Lord Kincraig screamed, "Why do you all stand there? Can you not see there is going to be a storm? Tend to your horses, quickly!"

The clouds were heavier and ominously dark. Even as they all looked up great cold drops began to patter down. His lord-

ship was carrying crates and blankets to the waggon, Vespa ran
to help him and Manderville hurried to harness his own bor-
rowed pair.

Jumping up and down, Pierre shouted, "What about Bruine?"

Vespa was reminded that the little mare must be reshod. He
called, "Hold up, sir. I'll get Manderville on his way, then ride
with you till I can find a smithy."

Lord Kincraig nodded and proceeded to strike the tent. The
rain threatened to become a deluge. Consuela pulled up her
hood and retreated to the carriage with Pierre. As soon as de
Coligny's animals were harnessed and poled up, Vespa went to
Bruine who was grazing farther down the slope. He started to
saddle her, hearing in his mind Kincraig's words, 'A scant three
leagues away . . .' Three leagues; nine or ten more miles of
enemy territory for Consuela to risk, and they were not a great
distance from the war zone. No, it would not do! She and Pierre
must be returned to the chateau immediately. He frowned,
thinking that if Manderville refused to help, he'd resort to his
army rank and *order* the thimble-wit to take her back. He
himself would accompany Kincraig on what appeared to be this last lap,
and that was all. His lordship had promised to go home after
he met up with his friend, and by heaven, but he'd see that
promise was kept, even if he had to resort to dragging the old
gentleman back to England by force!

Deep in thought he finished saddling Bruine, and led her
up to the camp. It was deserted. Both waggon and carriage
were gone. Knowing he would not ride the mare, they'd slithered off and left him to manage as best he could! It was Consuela's doing, of course. The little minx knew he would follow
Lord Kincraig and she had no doubt persuaded Manderville to
drive out before he could insist that she and Pierre be sent
back to the chateau. That blasted weak-kneed Paige! The silly
block should have known better, but he was like putty in her
hands!

It was as well his beloved was not within earshot as Captain
John Wansdyke Vespa voiced his reaction to such dastardly conniving in furious and unrestrained barracks-room language.

He had trudged less than a mile through the now-driving
rain when he came upon a commotion. A goose girl hurrying
to shelter with her flock had incurred the wrath of a farmer
whose load of apples had shifted when he swerved his waggon

to avoid the geese. The farmer was bellowing, further frightening the geese; the dray horses were stamping about agitatedly; the girl was in tears as she ran about trying to gather her flock together; and apples were strewn across the muddy road. Vespa stopped to help pick up the apples, and managed in the process to calm the distraught girl and placate the farmer by buying a bag of his fruit. The girl left him with a tearful smile and a blessing, and the grateful farmer directed him to a forge located in a lane "just a scant distance to the south—two hundred meters at most."

For once the directions proved reliable, Bruine was soon being shod by a gregarious blacksmith who had no objection to a foreign accent and in no time Vespa was able to ride out in pursuit of the dastardly conspirators. He came up with them a quarter of an hour later. The carriage was pulled off to the side of the road and barely discernible through the grey curtain of the rain. Manderville had climbed down from the box and was blowing his nose and peering despondently at the right rear wheel.

As Vespa rode up, he said unrepentantly, "Well, it's past time you arrived!"

"No thanks to you, my good and loyal friend! You succumbed to the signorina's blandishments again, didn't you!"

Manderville gave him a resentful look. "You try and gainsay her! I wish—I wish . . ." he sneezed, groaned and finished, "I wish you joy of it!"

He looked quite haggard and was getting thoroughly soaked. Vespa thought 'I'll have him down with the pneumonia if I'm not careful!' He said in a kinder tone, "What's the difficulty now?"

"A damn great blade from a broken pair of scissors or something of the sort has stuck itself in the wheel. I'm afraid it'll split if I don't get it out, so—"

Consuela called from the open window, "Jack! I am so sorry, but we have lost his lordship again!"

He stared at her then asked Manderville, "*Lost* him? How the deuce could you lose him in bright daylight?"

"It ain't all that bright. He drove around a bend in the road and when we came up, there was no sign of him. He's slippery as any eel, and could have hidden himself in any of a dozen spinneys we passed."

"Stay here," said Vespa tersely. "I doubt you'll be noticed in this deluge. I'll come back as soon as I can."

Manderville grunted, and from behind his handkerchief enquired, "What does that mean? A sennight from Wednesday?"

Ignoring him, Vespa reined Bruine around. Consuela watched him penitently from the open window. "I know you are cross, dear Jack. Have you decided to abandon me?"

"Yes," he said, fighting the urge to kiss her rosy but drooping lips.

She giggled and clapped her hands. "Your eyes give you away! I am very naughty, but you still love me. Where are you going?"

He had remembered that when he'd left the forge he'd noticed some deep ruts in the lane. Lord Kincraig's waggon left just such marks. He said, "I passed a lane where his lordship might have turned off. Keep out of sight, and do please try to be good."

"For a change?" she prompted mischievously.

He nodded. "For a change."

"Be careful," she called after him.

He rode fast but not so fast as to draw attention to himself. Traffic was lighter in the rain but he scanned each coach and rider going south, alert for a fine black horse, or two dapple greys, or Duncan Keith's unlovely trio. The wheel tracks were still visible when he reached the lane and he turned Bruine down it. Paige had been right about his lordship hiding; there was a spinney ahead and the tracks led right in amongst the trees. It was rough going for Bruine; for the big cart-horses to haul the heavy waggon over such muddy and rock-strewn terrain must be downright murderous. Why on earth his lordship would come this way was—

Vespa's irritation was banished abruptly. The waggon was just ahead, balanced on the two left wheels and tilting crazily against a tree. His first dismayed glance told him that Kincraig had been driving along a narrow track when the weight had caused the ground to give way under one wheel: probably a rabbit warren or some such thing. The horses did not appear to be harmed and were standing patiently, but there was no sign of Kincraig. Vespa rode up quickly, calling his father's name. He thought he heard a faint response from under the waggon and he threw himself from the saddle to peer underneath. His lordship lay sprawled a few feet from the tilting side. Vespa raced around the horses, his eyes flashing to the tree that was the only thing keeping the waggon from toppling. It was a young birch and it was leaning perilously. At any instant it might snap under the weight, or be uprooted, and Kincraig would be crushed. He fell to one knee beside the inert figure. "Sir—I must get you out of here! Are you hurt?"

Kincraig blinked up at him, then smiled weakly. "Found me, did you? Found me . . . in a pickle. No, don't move me. I was thrown clear. Not—not hurt, but I think I'll—just rest here for a—"

A root of the tree was torn from the earth. The waggon jerked with an ear-splitting creak.

"I think you won't, sir," said Vespa and, gripping Kincraig by the shoulders, dragged him clear and propped him against a boulder. "Now you can rest," he panted. "I'll get the horses unhitched in case the waggon goes down."

It looked to be in imminent danger of doing just that. He worked feverishly to get the team un-poled and led them off to the side. Securing the harness straps to a low branch, he ran back to the waggon. It was even more tilted now. He knew how heavy it was and that to venture onto the far side and try to push it up would be not only useless but likely suicidal. Even if he found a sturdy fallen branch and tried to lever it erect, he'd never prevail. The ground to the right of the track sloped down a little but it wasn't impossible. He led the two leaders to the waggon and tied their harness straps to the two right-hand wheels, then guided the horses down the slope. They were fine big animals, but their combined strength failed to do more than shake the waggon. Frustrated, Vespa thought, 'The wheels are too low, dammit!'

An idea occurred to him; the kind of crazy idea that his army comrades would have expected of him. He tore open the rear doors of the waggon, praying Kincraig would be carrying what he needed. His prayers were answered; on one wall hung a neatly coiled length of rope. "Excelsior!" he exclaimed and appropriating it, tied the end to the harness of one animal. Holding the rest of the rope, he climbed cautiously onto the driver's seat. The waggon let out a sound like a groan, and shifted. He hung on, watching the tree and holding his breath. The birch was young and supple and held firm. Moving cautiously, he clambered onto the roof, trying not to notice how the waggon lurched under him. The surface was wet and slippery, and too slanted for him to stand upright, so he lay down and fed the rope around the back of the tree trunk.

Climbing down again, he secured the free end of the rope to the harness of the second horse and set the pair in motion again. He had to stop them twice while he adjusted the length of the rope so that the pull on the tree would equal that of the harness straps secured to the wheels. The third time he started off again, the horses leaned into their collars and strained their powerful muscles with, at first, little apparent effect. Suddenly, there was a jolt. The waggon had shifted slightly. Elated, Vespa urged the pair on. The waggon jerked. He could only pray the tree would not snap. The waggon swayed and began to tip. Gradually, the roof moved upward, the tree straightened. Then, with a crash, the right wheels hit the ground and the waggon bounced upright. "Whoa!" cried Vespa, and the cart-horses halted.

There came a burst of applause. Lord Kincraig, still lying against the boulder, exclaimed admiringly, "Jolly well done!"

Flushing with pleasure, Vespa praised and petted the pair, then poled up the team again. "You've got some splendid cattle here, sir. Now, what may I do to help you? You said you weren't hurt?"

"No. Not at all. The wheel went down into a pothole I suppose, and I was hurled from the seat when the waggon tipped. Must have knocked the wind out of me for a minute or two."

Despite his cheery manner he was pale, and made no attempt to get up. Vespa asked anxiously, "Why did you go off like that? It's too dangerous for you to jaunter about alone. You could have been badly hurt and with no one near to help."

"Pish! I'm as fine as fivepence. If I could—er, just have my medicine."

"Oh, egad! Of course, sir."

Vespa hurried to the waggon, Kincraig calling instructions as to where his medicine could be found. The accident had resulted in the contents of the interior being scattered about haphazardly. Vespa righted two crates before he found the bottle and reached for it, relieved that it wasn't broken. Something cold touched the back of his neck. He stood rigidly still, thinking that it was either a pistol muzzle or a knife. He was struck lightly, this time on the head. There followed an odd chinking sound.

He said harshly, "Well? Who is it?"

Silence; followed by more metallic chinkings.

He withdrew his hand and the medicine from the crate, and this time was hit squarely on the wrist.

He stared down at a gold piece. A French *louis*.

"What on earth . . . ?" He looked up, then ducked aside as a veritable rain of the coins showered from a wide crack in the roof. He set down the medicine bottle and a glance at the rolls of carpets made him gasp. Gold glinted everywhere. He scooped up two handfuls and realized he held the equivalent of thirty guineas. There must, he deduced numbly, be at least another hundred *louis* scattered about. Frowning, he thought, 'The old fellow is *really* out of his mind to carry such a sum with him!' He remembered then and, tossing down the coins, took up the medicine and hurried outside.

There was no sign of Lord Kincraig. He had wandered off again. But had this latest disappearance anything to do with accident or illness, or had the old gentleman simply slipped away to meet his friend? If that were the case, out of simple courtesy he might at least have said something before he left. Irritated, but still uneasy, Vespa searched about for some time, dreading to come upon his lordship lying collapsed somewhere. He made no such sad discovery, nor were his calls answered and he concluded at length that wherever his father had gone, he would return at his own convenience. It was, he thought glumly, another instance of Kincraig's eccentricity.

He climbed back into the waggon, and scowled up at the roof. No more coins were cascading down, but something else could be seen. He climbed onto the carpets, crunching gold pieces under his boots. A piece of sacking hung down. He gave it a tug and it came away together with several more gold pieces. Evidently, his lordship carried his purchasing funds concealed in a sack in the roof. It must have split from the impact with the tree—or perhaps when the ceiling boards had ruptured.

He began to gather up the scattered coins. It took quite a few minutes and when they were all collected, he had counted out two hundred *louis*. Murder had been done for much less than this! His lips tightened into a thin, determined line. If anything had been wanting to convince him he must force his father to return to England, this piece of folly turned the trick. The very thought of Kincraig jauntering about all alone in an enemy country, with a great bag of gold hidden in his waggon, made his blood run cold.

He piled the coins on the torn sack, but there was no way
to tie it securely. If his father had purchased all these rugs there
might be an empty sack he could use. He stood on the carpets
again and reached up. The splintered board gave slightly when
he tried to move it aside and another hard shove opened a
loose section he was able to slide back. Now, he could reach
inside. He groped about, and he had guessed rightly, for he
felt another sack. Only it wasn't an empty sack. It was solidly
heavy. "Jupiter!" he gasped. "However much is the old fellow
hauling about?"

Tugging and struggling, he could feel two more sacks, but
how many were up there he couldn't tell. He was really alarmed
now, for such a risk must surely be unwarranted even for a
gentleman who was slightly unbalanced. He sat on the carpets
and stared blankly at the golden glitters all around him. And
unbidden and unwanted came the memory of the free-trader
Paul who had shared his camp and told him of the robbery at
the Belgian mint and the young guard who had been needlessly
murdered.

Disgusted with himself, he muttered, "Nonsense! He is an
honourable gentleman! As if he would do such a thing!" Besides, Lord Kincraig was a rich man. He'd said, "I have more
than enough for both of you." But how had he amassed his
fortune? Could it be that this was the real reason for the years
he'd spent roving about Europe and spreading his silly rumours
of jewelled and flying carpets? Had Duncan Keith tried to put
a period to his unwanted half-brother not because he coveted
the entire Kincraig fortune, but because he was afraid Jack
Vespa might discover that their father was—

Such disloyal thoughts were disgraceful. It couldn't be true!
It *couldn't!* But his eyes were drawn back to the sack. And he
saw that it was indeed the kind of sturdy container that money
houses tended to use. Struggling to dismiss the suspicions that
were so horrible and yet so inescapable, he found that he was
gathering the coins together once more. He stood on the carpets and began to stuff the *louis* and the torn sack back through
the aperture in the roof. He tugged the splintered board as far
closed as he could, then jumped down from the waggon and
closed the doors.

The rain had stopped. Lord Kincraig was nowhere to be seen.
He walked to where Bruine was grazing and secured her reins
to a shrub. And he thought wryly that it would appear he might

have exchanged a sire who was a murderous traitor for one who was a murderous thief. The duchess would be a great deal less than delighted to welcome him into her proud 'royal family' if that was the case. The only hope would be that his lordship had some perfectly logical explanation.

With a cynical shrug and a heavy heart, he sat on the tail of the waggon to wait.

Fourteen

Perhaps because he was so troubled, Vespa found the wait intolerable and after some minutes had passed he went in search of his father. The rain had given way to a misty overcast that did nothing to lighten his spirits. He left the spinney but Lord Kincraig was nowhere in sight. About two hundred yards to the south another copse of trees bordered a stream and he started in that direction. As he drew nearer, he heard men's voices. His lordship, it would seem, had met someone. A comrade in crime, perhaps? He swore under his breath, and moved cautiously into the trees.

There were two of them and they were conversing in English, but so softly that he could detect only a word or two: ". . . damned chancy, but worth . . . if we can bring it off!" That was Kincraig, and speaking with an irked briskness quite unlike his often vague ramblings.

His companion muttered, ". . . hot after you . . . I'll try to find out where . . . Don't like . . . no choice . . . *con Dios!*"

It was the farewell, and in Spanish. Vespa sprinted forward, his steps muffled by the pound of hooves, and was in time to catch a glimpse of a fast vanishing rider. A rider mounted on a splendid black horse. 'And that,' he thought bitterly, 'properly drives me to the ropes!'

He walked quickly back to the waggon, not much caring whether Kincraig saw him or not. He was adjusting the team's harness straps when Kincraig joined him.

"Been looking over my fine fellows, have you?" he said, resting a hand briefly on Vespa's shoulder.

"I can find no injuries, sir."

"Thank goodness for that! I was sure the waggon must go

down. Only thanks to you it did not. Where did you learn that trick?"

So it was to be all lightness and business as usual. Somehow, Vespa found a grin. "Army training, I suppose. We were very often obliged to be inventive so as to win free from some tight spot or other. Do you still want your medicine, sir?"

Kincraig stared at him vacantly.

"You had asked me to get it for you," he reminded. "But when I brought it out, you'd gone. Are you feeling better?"

"Oh—yes. Much better, I thank you. Sometimes, you know, I become a little confused, and I suppose the fall rattled my poor brains a trifle."

Vespa's lips tightened and with an ache of the heart he entered this sad sparring match. "I shall have to keep a closer eye on you. I expect you'll want to inspect your waggon, but I think it's no worse for the accident."

Kincraig glanced at him obliquely then went to the rear of the waggon, peered about inside, and closed the doors. "You're right. No harm done that I can see."

"Then if you've completed your business here, we can go on. Consuela and Paige likely think we're at Jericho!"

Kincraig said ruefully that his joints seemed stiff after his fall, and Vespa helped him onto the seat and handed him the leathers.

Kincraig enquired, "What business?"

"Eh?" Mounting Bruine, Vespa said, "Oh, I thought perhaps this was where you were to meet your friend."

A pause while his lordship guided the team expertly into a wide turn. Then he replied, "He said he might leave a message here if he was delayed. There's an oddly shaped boulder in those trees over there. It serves as our post office. I walked over, but there was no message."

"Ah. Then your friend has not been delayed and will be waiting for you?"

"I hope so." For just an instant Kincraig's expression was very grim, then he said brightly, "Let's go and make sure."

They returned to the lane, Vespa riding beside the waggon and trying not to abandon all hope. After a while, he tried again. "Don't you have locks for your doors, father?"

Kincraig turned and smiled at him. "No, my dear boy. I've never felt the need."

'Good God!' thought Vespa.

"These people are very honest, you know," his lordship added. "And what are they going to steal? My carpets?"

"You did say that some of them are very valuable. And thieves who know of your collection would also know that you must carry funds to pay for whatever you decide to buy."

"No, no. I carry very little cash. All my purchases are by bank draft. I've an account at the Bank of France in Paris—" He saw Vespa's astonished expression and said roguishly, "under another name, I'll admit, but all perfectly legal. So you see, I've little to fear from robbers."

Vespa thought miserably, 'Except for a waggon roof that is practically solid gold!'

They did not speak again until they came up with the chevalier's coach. Manderville and Consuela had waited inside and hurried to meet them. Pierre shouted from the branch of a tree that he had found a bird's nest, but there were no eggs inside.

Vespa dismounted and took the hand Consuela reached out to him. "No uninvited guests?"

She shook her head. "You were gone so long, I was worried to death."

"We were just about to go in search of you," said Manderville, scanning Lord Kincraig narrowly. "Had some trouble, have you, sir?"

"A small *contretemps* with a wheel." His lordship shrugged. "Luckily, my enterprising son was able to solve the problem. Shall we proceed?"

Consuela was watching Vespa, and as he handed her back into the carriage, she asked softly, "What is it?"

He assured her she was finding trouble where there was none, but although he smiled there was an emptiness in his eyes that she had seen all too often during his convalescence and had prayed never to see again.

They resumed their journey. Kincraig led the way, and Vespa, who was driving the carriage, stayed a good quarter mile back, so as not to give the impression they were together. When they stopped at a wayside tavern to rest the horses Consuela and Pierre went inside to buy lunch, and Manderville complained that he was unable to sleep and might as well drive, because the boy was not still for an instant. When Vespa, lost in thought, made no comment, he asked, "Well? Now what are you mulling over?"

"You wouldn't believe me," answered Vespa shortly, and limped across the cobbled yard to where the cart-horses were being fussed over by an elderly ostler with whom his lordship was chatting earnestly. It struck Vespa that the old man's French was unusually faultless, but it was broken off as he came up, and the ostler hurried into the stables.

Vespa went in search of Consuela, wondering if the ostler was in league with the gang of thieves, and which of them had so viciously murdered the young guard at the Mint. To think such evil of the father he had just found and to whom he was so deeply drawn brought a pang of anguish. If only his suspicions proved to be unfounded. Heaven grant that was the case, and he was letting his imagination run away with him, and shooting at shadows.

They left the farm with baskets of bread, cheese and pickles, and a bottle of wine in each vehicle, plus a jar of milk for Pierre. Of necessity Lord Kincraig drove out first. Manderville volunteered to be coachman and, since the rain had stopped, Pierre sat on the box beside him, so that Vespa was able to join his lady for their 'luncheon.' He ate sparingly, but he cherished these moments when he could hold Consuela's hand now and then. She chattered happily about their marriage and their life together, and he gazed at her, responding appropriately and adoring her, even as he railed helplessly at the Fate which had dangled the promise of a joyous future before his eyes, only to snatch it away again.

He was watching her profile, framed by the opposite window, when he realized they were turning through a broken-down gate and into what appeared to be an abandoned farm. There was a grove of sycamores beside the gate, and a stony track led across a field that looked as if it had never produced a crop of anything but weeds. The carriage bumped along the track which gradually sloped downward, ending in a yard shaded by dense trees much in need of trimming. It was a gloomy and silent place. Vespa felt an odd shiver between his shoulder blades. Consuela's hand tightened on his. He opened the door, said, "Stay here, love," and jumped down.

Some tumbledown outbuildings clustered near a wreck of a house sadly out of plumb and looking as if a strong breeze would topple it. Kincraig's waggon was drawn up outside a large and crumbling barn.

Pierre was already leaping off to explore the house.

Vespa started towards the barn, and Manderville howled, "Wait up, Jack! I'll go with you!" as if he were a mile away.

Vespa glanced at him but walked on and into the barn.

His lordship was there. On his knees. A man lay sprawled before him. One look told the story. Momentarily speechless with shock, Vespa halted. Then, he took off his hat and said curtly, "He's dead, sir."

"Yes." Kincraig bowed his head into his hands. "Poor fellow! Oh, the poor fellow!"

Manderville ran up. "Oh—Egad! What happened?"

Vespa bent over the dead man. "Shot. But he was beaten first: savagely. It's murder, Paige."

They had both seen death in many terrible forms on the battlefield but like Vespa, Manderville had a reverence for life. "Poor devil!" he exclaimed, paling. "This was your—er, friend, my lord?"

Kincraig nodded and said brokenly, "My very good friend. Known Ivan . . . all my life. God! I didn't bargain for . . . for anything like this."

Disgusted, Vespa thought, 'Well, you should have!'

Manderville said, "He's been dead for some hours, I'd guess. We'd best have a look round. The killers may have waited for us."

Kincraig shook his head. "They'd have attacked when I drove in. No, I fancy this brave gentleman sent them off on a false trail, bless him."

"If he came in a waggon, whoever did this has made off with it." Vespa added ironically, "And presumably, his fragment of the Khusraw Carpet. There are cart tracks leading away to the south."

"What do you mean to do, sir?" asked Manderville.

Kincraig looked very shaken. "I—don't know yet. I must—"

"Have done," interrupted Vespa harshly. "This fiasco has gone on long enough! You've led me on a merry chase, my lord, but I am not so blind as you appear to think, and I'll brook no more of your devious little games."

Kincraig sighed heavily, but did not respond.

Manderville said a bewildered, "What fiasco?"

"The one I have foolishly drawn you into," said Vespa, "for which I apologize. But it is over now and I'll not subject Consuela to one more unnecessary hour of peril. We will turn west at once, and make a run for the nearest port."

"What d'you mean—west? If we're to restore Pierre to his home, we'll have to strike north!"

Vespa was driven by two emotions: the oppression of this gloomy place, and a strong premonition that time was running out. He said tersely, "Too far. We'll find a boat and a captain willing to sail around to the *Golfe de St.-Malo.* I want Consuela off French soil by tomorrow!"

"We'll still have about a thirty-five mile journey overland," said Kincraig glumly. "Two or three days, at the least."

"If we push the horses hard we can get there in half that time," rasped Vespa.

Staring at him, Manderville said, "I don't pretend to guess what bee you've taken into your bonnet, *mon Capitaine,* but you can't push horses hard when they're hauling a load like his lordship's waggon. They'll have to be rested and—"

"Whoever murdered this poor fellow is after what Lord Kincraig is carrying," snapped Vespa. "They'll be searching for the waggon so it must be abandoned. You'll not object, my lord." His smile was humorless. "Since your late friend here evidently failed to bring you his piece of the legendary carpet."

Lord Kincraig met his contemptuous gaze wistfully. "You're perfectly right, my dear boy. The waggon must be abandoned."

"What?" gasped Manderville.

Vespa had been sure his father would protest, and waited for the next stratagem.

"But it must be carefully hidden," appended Kincraig.

Vespa muttered, "I wonder why that doesn't surprise me. First, we'd best find some shovels."

While Manderville and his lordship went in search of these necessary items, Vespa hurried to the carriage and warned Consuela. She was horrified by the new tragedy, and hurried to the house to find Pierre and keep him away from the grim scene.

They buried the dead man under a small apple tree. The soil was soft from the rains and very soon their task was accomplished. Heads were bowed while Kincraig offered a reverent prayer for his friend, then Vespa and Manderville left him alone by the grave to say his last farewells.

Walking over to the waggon, Manderville said low-voiced, "What a ghastly thing. What kind of ghoul would kill a fellow like that?"

"The kind of ghoul in search of information—at any price."

"I suppose so. Poor Kincraig blames himself, that's clear to

see. You were beastly short with him, Jack. He's hit hard, and
you might at least have tried—"

"I'm trying now," said Vespa. "Trying to guess how he'll manage to hide his damned great waggon."

Consuela hurried to them. She was pale and shaken, and to
turn her mind from its horror of the murder, Vespa told her
of their latest problem. She gazed at the waggon and said hesitantly, "It will be very difficult, I think, because it is so big."
Lord Kincraig came up, and she asked, "Perhaps there is a cave
or—or gully nearby where we could conceal it, sir?"

"I wish I knew of one, m'dear. But as you suggest, there must
be a hundred likely hiding places; I'm sure we'll come upon
one."

"What are we going to hide?" asked Pierre, approaching with
a hop and a skip.

Consuela said, "We can't take the waggon any further, dear.
Bad men are trying to steal Lord Kincraig's carpets."

"Oh." The boy raced off and ran twice around the waggon,
then came leaping back to announce that he knew just where
to hide it.

Manderville ruffled his curls. "Tuck it in your coat pocket,
eh, scamp?"

"Don't be silly," said Pierre, jerking his head away. "It's the
best hiding place in the world! If I tell you, will you buy me
some sugar cakes?"

"What you are, my lad, is a rogue! Sugar cakes, indeed!"

"We must leave at once, your lordship," urged Vespa. "If this
was the work of Monteil's bullies, they may very well come back.
You'd best get your personal effects together."

Kincraig nodded and went over to the waggon.

Pierre tugged at Vespa's coat. The boy had taken to regarding
him with hero-worship in his eyes, and now said anxiously, "I'll
show you, *mon Capitaine.* Please do come; it will only take a
minute. One minute, only!"

Vespa could not resist that pleading look, and exchanged his
irritated frown for a smile. "If it's a good hiding place you shall
have a dozen sugar cakes," he promised.

"Wheee!" squealed Pierre, and taking his hand led him to
the house, then stopped.

"Around the back, do you mean?" asked Vespa. "I'm afraid
it would soon be found, Pierre."

"No it wouldn't, *Capitaine,* because this farm was accursed, and people do not come here. But I don't mean that we should hide it *behind* the house. I mean *in* the house!"

Vespa hadn't really expected anything much, but this piece of folly caused his brows to lift, and he said, "Oh, you do! Have some sense, lad. How do you suppose we could get that monster inside? Through the front door?"

Pierre giggled and tugged him at the run around the side. There had once been a sort of wooden lean-to at the back that had evidently served as a wash-house, but a big branch had fallen and caused part of the outer wall to cave in. Vespa frowned at the ruins thoughtfully.

Consuela had followed, and she slipped her hand into his. "I'm sorry, Jack. Pierre means well, but this is silly; houses are not built to accommodate waggons."

"Exactly so." He lifted her hand and kissed it absently. "Which fact might work strongly in our favour. I judged it mad at first. But do you know . . . it just might serve. I'll go in and have a look."

He climbed over the branch and, brushing away webs, made his way inside. Pierre went after him eagerly, but Consuela waited, saying she would forego the delights of mould and mice and spiders.

They emerged in a minute or two, and a look at Vespa's face caused her own to brighten. "It will serve?"

"I think it may! It's a dirt floor, so there's no fear of boards collapsing from the weight of the waggon." He patted the exuberant Pierre on the back. "Jolly good work, young fellow! If you were under my command, you'd get a promotion out of this!"

"I am a sergeant!" the boy howled. "Monsieur Manderville! Your lordship! Your problem is solved by Sergeant Pierre!"

Kincraig and Manderville were incredulous at first, but Vespa pointed out that if they moved the branch and cleared away the buckled rear wall they could back the waggon inside, then replace wall and branch so that the waggon was concealed from view. "If we take care to cover any betraying wheel ruts," he said, "who would ever think to look inside a house for such a vehicle?"

Manderville pursed his lips. "To abandon his lordship's beautiful carpets is too chancy by half, in my opinion."

"It is," agreed Kincraig. "And if I could but think of a better solution, I would take it. The pity is—I cannot. I have lost my—

my dear friend, and the most important thing now is to get
Miss Consuela and Sergeant Pierre to safety."

With strict instructions to keep out of sight, Pierre once again
became their lookout, and went skipping off full of his own
importance. Consuela reconnoitred the front of the house to
be sure that, once inside, the waggon would not be visible from
either of the small windows, and the three men set to work.
The fallen branch was heavy, but between them they were able
to move it aside. They took down the rotted wall in sections,
and then dragged an old tub and a rusted mangle into what
had been the kitchen/parlour. Much accumulated rubble had
to be cleared from the lean-to before the waggon could be
backed through the gap in the wall. It would be a tricky ma-
noeuvre for there were scant inches between the roof and the
top of the waggon. Kincraig knew his horses and spoke reas-
suringly to each one, then stood beside the leaders, assessing
the gap they must negotiate.

Vespa said, "We're fortunate that the ceiling is so high. Even
so, once inside it will be a tight fit. The tail will be right against
the far wall. If there's anything more you need to take with
you, now would be the time to get it, sir." He waited cynically
for his father to reclaim at least one sack of the stolen gold,
but Kincraig said he had already removed his "necessaries" and
that Manderville had been so kind as to store them in the boot
of the chevalier's coach.

Consuela clung to Vespa's hand nervously. "It's going to be
terribly difficult to back it into such a narrow space. If only he
could just drive it in."

"Even if he could, the inside door is on the wrong wall, and
we wouldn't be able to get the horses out. But they're fine
animals, and if you will be so good as to guide him from this
side, and Paige from the other, I think his lordship will manage."

She was only too glad to be given a chance to help. Vespa
watched as the challenging process began, then slipped away.
He went quickly to the carriage. Kincraig's belongings had been
packed into two boxes. He inspected each item, even feeling
in the pockets of the garments. There was not a single *louis*.
So all the gold was to be left in the waggon. To be retrieved,
of course, either by his lordship or an accomplice; probably,
the man riding the black horse.

There arose a deafening screeching sound as he closed the

boot, and he limped rapidly around the side of the house. The
waggon was backed halfway into the lean-to, the horses rolling
their eyes in alarm and Kincraig trying to calm them. Vespa
was struck by the incongruity of the scene—the giant waggon
looking for all the world as though it was being extracted from
the house.

Manderville was on the top, struggling to break away a portion of the roof of the lean-to that had sagged down, blocking
any further progress. "Where did you get to?" he demanded
irritably. "The waggon is fairly stuck! Can't budge it back or
forward, confound it all!"

Vespa retrieved two of the shovels and handed them up, then
climbed to join him. The sagging portion of the roof had
scraped across the top of the waggon, leaving deep gouges before it dug in, halting any further progress. He said, "If we use
the shovels as levers, perhaps we can raise the roof enough for
the waggon to move." He called down to Lord Kincraig to be
ready to back the team again, then he and Manderville attempted to lever the roof up. It was hard going and he wondered cynically what would happen if the pressure of the shovels
broke through the top of the waggon. He was denied that scene
as the obstructing section of the roof suddenly buckled and
broke off. He and Manderville cleared away the debris and
climbed down and Kincraig once more inched his team backwards. Within minutes the waggon was inside and halted by the
far wall.

The cart-horses were lathered from their efforts and Manderville walked them away to allow them to cool down.

Consuela, his lordship and Vespa stood gazing at the remains
of the lean-to.

Kincraig said, "It's very tight, but once we replace the wall
and that big branch, I do believe it will show not a sign."

"Except for the pole, of course," said Vespa. "It will have to
come off, and should slide underneath—or is that not possible,
sir?"

"The work of a few moments, merely. When I designed my
waggon, I tried to anticipate any predicament, you see."

"You did indeed." Vespa met Kincraig's gentle smile but did
not return it and wondered how many 'predicaments' his lar-
cenous sire had surmounted these past few years.

Consuela exclaimed, "Oh, my goodness! What about the
horses?"

At last that dilemma had been mentioned. Vespa thought
with bleak irony. 'Well? Speak up, my lord!'

Kincraig said, "Oh, they'll fend for themselves well enough.
We'll simply turn them loose."

"If we do that, sir," argued Vespa, "anyone coming upon
them will surely realize there's a cart or a waggon somewhere
about."

"Or steal them," said Consuela. "They're beautiful animals."

Kincraig made light of such objections. He would leave instructions with a peasant who dwelt nearby. The old man would
be glad enough to earn a few pence in exchange for making
sure that the cart-horses were taken care of and kept from the
hands of thieves.

Vespa thought, 'And kept available for your friends!'

The roof and walls were propped and nailed more or less
together again, the branch hauled back in place and another
branch added to brace it and conceal a hole in the wall. Manderville and his lordship led the cart-horses off to the peasant's
hut, and Consuela worked beside Vespa to obliterate the ruts
left by the heavy wheels.

"When people conceal things, my Captain," she said, wielding a large rake industriously, "other people are apt to imagine
much worse things."

It was true. And it would be kinder to tell her now than to
let her go on dreaming her dreams of their happy future. He
slanted a quick glance at her face; none too clean after this
hectic day, the wet dark curls straggling about her flushed
cheeks, and her blue eyes watching him with such trust and
devotion. No complaints that she was tired and cold and her
clothes wet from the rain; no moans about missing her Grandmama, or the need for her maid and a comfortable bed and a
chance to bathe and change clothes. She was the bravest and
loveliest creature he had ever known, and he loved her so much
it was an ache inside him.

His jaw set, and he went on raking with swift angry strokes.
How could he tell her their last hope was gone? How could he
bring her such grief—especially now when her beloved *Nonna*
was not here to comfort her? Besides, he did not really *know*
that his suspicions were justified. Suppose it developed that his
lordship was an innocent dupe? After all, he'd been ready
enough to leave the treasure waggon—perhaps he wasn't aware
of what the roof contained. But that was grasping at straws, of

course, and a foolish attempt to delude himself. There were too many pieces that fit the puzzle, too many coincidences for there to be any—

Consuela leaned on her rake and pushed back a curl that had tumbled down her forehead. "What has he done, Jack?"

Startled, his eyes flashed to her face again.

"My poor dear," she said tenderly. "Don't you know yet that you cannot hide your sorrows from me? Oh, I admit you do very well at concealing your feelings from others. But when you are distressed, I can feel it. And you have been deeply distressed ever since Lord Kincraig's waggon almost fell over. Something happened then, I know it. Won't you tell me? Perhaps I can help."

A lump came into his throat and his eyes blurred. He said brokenly, "My precious little Signorina . . . I don't deserve—"

"Capitaine! Capitaine!" Pierre galloped down the slope at reckless speed, knees flying. "Bad . . . people! A great black coach with . . . with the coachman and a footman in black livery. The coachman was that seasick pirate from . . . the ship!"

"Ti Chiu!" whispered Vespa. "Then Monteil's found us! Outriders?"

"Oui, mon Capitaine! There are two other men besides."

"The same pair we chased off yesterday?"

The boy's eyes became very round. "But—yes, sir! With the grey horses. How did you know?"

"They're coming here?"

"No. They went on past, but the great giant coachman looked this way. Oh, but my heart it stand still! And the black and white man he put his head out of the window and give a shout, and the great giant slowed the coach. But then he saw it, and I saw his face, and I thought, 'No, Sergeant Pierre! He is very afraid. He will not come here!' And I was right! He drove on. Fast. Just as I knew!"

"What did he see?" asked Consuela curiously.

The boy led the way from the yard and pointed up the slope towards the lane. "There! That is what frightened the giant! I did not see it when first we came, but it is why this farm died and why nobody comes here!"

Vespa said, "It's another of the menhirs."

"Where?" asked Consuela. "I do not see it."

"There, by the sycamore trees. And it's one of the larger specimens."

At first, she could only discern the trees, but then she realized that the shadows in the centre were not shadows, but instead one of the great standing stones left by the ancient people. "How fascinating they are," she said.

"And how lucky we are that Imre Monteil's coachman is superstitious," said Vespa. "But he's much too close. We daren't give him another chance."

He managed to imbue them with his sense of urgency, and very soon they were back on the lane. This time Kincraig had volunteered to drive the carriage, noting kindly that poor Manderville was worn out from his cold and lack of sleep. He had obtained excellent directions from his peasant friend, he said, and now knew the quickest route to the coast. "A most excellent fellow! He was even able to tell me where a likely fishing boat lies at anchor."

Riding Bruine beside the coach, Vespa said, "Was he, indeed. And did his excellence cost you enormous largesse, my lord?"

Kincraig laughed. "What a cynic!"

"What's a 'cynic'?" asked Pierre, who had claimed a seat on the box.

"I am," said Vespa dryly. "And we should put 'em along now, sir. It's liable to rain again at any minute, and there's little enough daylight left."

Kincraig cracked the whip, the horses leaned into their collars and the coach bounced and jolted over a surface poor to begin with, but made worse by potholes and mud.

The afternoon was drawing in and Vespa's hope to drive through the night had to be abandoned when the clouds darkened and an icy rain began to patter down once more. He shouted, "Hold up a minute, sir. Our sergeant must go inside, else we'll have him down with a cold also!"

The boy was wet and shivering and raised no objections. Vespa swung him from the box and handed him in to Manderville. Consuela looked wan and tired, but she had a smile ready, and set to work at once to dry Pierre's curls.

Vespa asked, "Are your pistols loaded, Paige?"

Manderville nodded. "Trouble?"

"Perhaps not, but I've twice thought someone was behind us."

"We'll have to stop, even so, old fellow. Won't be able to drive after dark. Not one of us knows these roads."

Another half hour and Vespa saw a ribbon of smoke rising

above a rolling hill some distance ahead. If it came from the hearth of an inn, it might be their last chance of shelter for the night.

He called, "My lord, are there are any inns or *pensions* along—"

There came a high-pitched metallic twang. It was an evil sound, and one he knew. For an instant of stark terror his mind warned that a crossbow bolt could go right through the back of the carriage! Dreading to hear a scream, he heard instead a choking cry. His gaze flashed to the box. The reins had slipped from Lord Kincraig's hands and he was slumping forward.

Rage seared through Vespa. He leaned perilously from the saddle and caught the leathers. Drawing the team to a halt, he turned Bruine and rode to the window.

"Help his lordship!" he shouted, then drove his spurs home.

It was a hurt the little mare had not expected from this man. Ever faithful, she sprang into a gallop. Vespa crouched low over the saddlehorn, retribution in his heart, pistol in one hand, the wind whipping at his face and his narrowed eyes fixed on the distant rider who had left the lane and now plunged at reckless speed across the meadows.

Fifteen

There was no doubt in Vespa's mind but that the fleeing assassin was one of Duncan Keith's hired bullies and that he was now making a frantic dash to rejoin his comrades. The awareness and with it the knowledge that he himself might very well be riding straight into an ambush did not for an instant weigh with him. All that mattered in the white heat of his fury was that he bring down this cowardly murderer.

His quarry left the lane and headed across country. Vespa followed, not slackening his speed. The assassin turned and glared back at him. It was a costly move for at that moment his mount stumbled. He was a good horseman and retained his seat and the animal recovered almost at once, but the distance between them had shortened. A moment later the useless cross-bow was flung aside. Again, the assassin turned. Vespa saw the flash before he heard the shot, followed by the hum of a bullet whizzing past. They topped a rise and he saw the gleam of water below. The other man was looking back to see if his shot had gone home, and he turned too late to avoid the lake.

With a howled curse, he wrenched at the reins. Frightened and confused, his horse tried to change direction only to flounder and go down with a tangle of legs, a shrill neigh of fright and a great splash.

Vespa was on the bank then, pulling Bruine up and hurling himself after his adversary who had been thrown a short distance from the shore.

The water was like ice. It was hip deep when he reached the assassin, but the man seemed dazed and was evidently finding it difficult to stand.

"Murderous cowardly swine!" Vespa pushed his head under the water.

Strengthened by terror the assassin fought and struggled madly. He succeeded in breaking free and his head shot from the surface. Vespa grabbed his hair and forced him down again, avoiding the arms that flailed in frenzied attempts to beat him away. The desperate struggles weakened, and then ceased. Vespa let his head come up and he sagged, choking for breath and gasping out faint pleas not to be drowned. The temptation to deal him just such a fate was strong, but Vespa wanted information. Dragging the half-conscious rogue by the hair, he waded to shore. His prisoner tried feebly to crawl out, but he was too weakened. Vespa hauled him onto the grass and kicked him onto his back.

The face was pale and half covered by strands of wet hair. But even in the fading light there was no mistaking him.

"You accursed fool," panted Vespa. "You've just murdered your own father!"

"But—m'sieu," wailed the proprietor, wringing his bony hands and trotting along the narrow passage beside Vespa, "you both are very wet! And it is that I have floors, you comprehend! And rugs, m'sieu! They will be ruined, m'sieu!"

"Where are my friends?" Vespa had tied Keith's hands and now used the crossbow he'd retrieved to prod him towards the stairs of this small hedge-tavern.

"I cannot," moaned Keith, swaying drunkenly. "I shall . . . fall down."

"Then I'll have the pleasure of kicking you until you get up," said Vespa grittily. "I saw our carriage in your yard, host," he added. "Don't make me drag this carrion up your stairs to no purpose!" He flourished the crossbow and the host recoiled eyeing the weapon in horror.

"No, m'sieu! I mean—yes, m'sieu! The poor gentleman is above-stairs and my girl but a minute ago finished washing the blood from the floor, and now, m'sieu—"

"You will be well paid."

At these magical words the host brightened. "It will be the second door to your right hand, m'sieu. Madame Lannion, my wife, is with the young lady."

Vespa nodded and urged Duncan Keith on. "Move, dog's meat!"

The stairs were steep and winding. At the top the second door in a short passage was partly open and Vespa shoved Keith inside.

Manderville and a tall middle-aged woman, Madame Lannion no doubt, were bending over the bed. Kincraig lay on his side with his eyes closed, the crossbow shaft still transfixing his right side just below the armpit. Consuela, pale but composed, was taking his lordship's shirt as the woman cut it away. She looked up when Vespa entered, and said unsteadily, "Thank God you've come!"

"Is he still alive?" asked Vespa.

She nodded, staring at Keith.

Vespa experienced an overpowering sense of relief, but there was a lot of blood and, remembering his lordship's medicine bottle, he knew death lurked nearby.

Manderville turned his head. "Caught the bastard, did you?" he said, forgetting the presence of ladies. "I wonder you troubled to fetch him back, if—" He broke off, staring at Keith. "Good Lord! It wasn't *him?*"

"My murderous half-brother." Vespa shoved Keith hard and the man staggered to the wall and slid down it to sit sprawling on the floor.

Consuela gasped, "Oh! How wicked!"

"Yes. A new low point in depravity, would you say?" Advancing to the bed, Vespa asked low-voiced, "How bad is it?"

"The poor gentleman is not so bad as wouldn't be better without all the evil words and violence," said Madame Lannion severely. Glancing at Vespa, she saw the crossbow and uttered a muffled shriek. "Ugh! Take that wicked machine from my house!"

Pierre, who had been perched in the window-seat, jumped up and volunteered to take the crossbow away.

Vespa handed him the weapon and looked up to find Kincraig's eyes on him. "I'm very sorry, my lord," he said gently, bending over the bed. "I knew we were followed. I just didn't think it was this particular group of ruffians."

Manderville sneezed and went into a bout of coughing, and Madame Lannion eyed him uneasily, then handed another strip of cloth to Consuela and stood straight. A handsome woman with a proud face and a splendid bosom, she met Vespa's anxious gaze levelly. "This I do not at all like," she said. "I help the Gentlemen where I can, but—" she shrugged, "This young man is ill, and—"

"Who—me?" Manderville wheezed indignantly, "Sound as sixpence!"

"—and I will not be responsible for the death of the Carpet Collector," Madame swept on. "You must tend him yourselves."

She had said 'the Gentleman'—the widely-used term for free-traders. Vespa took a chance. "I was counting on you, ma'am. Paul said if I came this way I must stop and say good day."

She checked. "Paul? You know Paul Crozon?"

"I but left him two days since. He was with Jules and Léon and the rest, and his nephew sends you his love."

"Ho!" she said with a flash of her dark eyes. "That one! A rascal is what, and will grow up to be as foolish as his Papa. Ah, but this changes matters, Monsieur . . . ?"

"Jacques, Madame."

She smiled. "No last names, eh? It is as well. I will do what I may. With luck our farrier is in the tap. He is a finer doctor than most who have the title, and he will know what is to be done. Try to keep your poor friend quiet." A nod, a swirl of voluminous skirts, and the door closed behind her.

Kincraig whispered, "Crossbow . . . Then—then it was—" His gaze fell on the sullen features of the man on the floor, and he groaned, "Duncan—did you . . . hate me so much?"

Vespa said quickly, "He didn't mean to hit you, sir. It was me he aimed at. Missed again, didn't you, Keith!"

"Oh, no," sneered Keith.

Kincraig's wound was bleeding sluggishly. Bathing it as best she might, Consuela exclaimed in horror, "You really meant to kill your father?"

Kincraig tried painfully to lift himself, but Vespa eased him back down. "You must lie still, sir. We'll have help for you in only a minute or two."

Keith laughed. "No, you won't, fool! You can't push the bolt through, nor pull it back. He's as good as dead."

"Shut your mouth," snarled Vespa, turning on him in a fury.

"No," gasped Kincraig. "I want to know . . . Why, Duncan? I'd have left you a rich man, even . . . allowing for Jack's share of the inheritance."

"Well, now I'll be a very rich man, won't I? You won't live to acknowledge him as your bastard, or to change your will, and, more importantly, you won't have time to enjoy a son who'd suit your antiquated notions better than I do. A gallant soldier, a fine athlete, a man of noble principles. What pitiful stuff! And only look at what's left. The gallant soldier has been discarded. The fine athlete is now a cripple. And his ridiculous principles will keep him from enjoying the Vespa fortune and estates—if there are any left."

Manderville started forward, fists clenched. "Why, you filthy wart! I'll—"

"No!" Pale with fury, Vespa held his friend back. "We'd as well hear it all."

Keith grinned, and added, "On the other hand, there is your legal son, Papa, who is hale and whole and has done quite well in the Trade. Didn't know that, did you? I've been a smuggler for years. Brandy, scent, guns—right under the noses of the stupid Excise men."

Manderville said stuffily, "What you mead is that in addition to your other revolti'g qualities, you're a traitor!"

"Not to myself," said Keith, laughing.

Vespa saw the glint of tears in Lord Kincraig's eyes. He said, "My apologies, Consuela," and crossed to where Keith sprawled. His half-brother's bravado vanished, and he cringed against the wall, babbling, "You can't hit me! My hands are tied! You must play fair!"

Bending over him, Vespa said softly, "One more word out of you, disgusting whelp that you are, and when we get that bolt out of my father, I'll use it on your own slimy hide! And you had better pray he lives, for it he dies—be assured that I'll do it anyway!"

Keith saw death in his eyes and recoiled, whining that he was freezing cold and sure to become a victim of pneumonia.

Madame Lannion hurried back into the room carrying a tray of medical implements and followed by a stoop-shouldered nondescript-looking man wearing a knitted cap and clutching a bottle of brandy. "This is our good Monsieur Aunay," she said. "He will help the poor gentleman."

Frowning, Vespa reached for the bottle. "I think you won't need this, monsieur."

"No," said the farrier in a deep boom of a voice. "But—he will!" He poured a generous portion and said, "Lift him. A little. No, not you, monsieur! You're soaking wet!"

Vespa drew back and Manderville and Madame Lannion

raised Kincraig to the point that he could sip the brandy. Clearly, he was in much pain, but he didn't utter a sound while the farrier inspected the wound.

Leading Vespa aside, Aunay said, "We have two chances, monsieur."

"You m-must cut it out," said Vespa, through chattering teeth.

"That is our second choice. The first is a seldom-used tool of surgery." The farrier nodded to Madame Lannion, and she brought him a pair of heavy pruning shears. "Do not look so appalled, monsieur," said the farrier with a smile. "Fortunately for us, the bolt has the cruel steel barbs, but a wooden stem. If it were a steel bolt, I would have no alternative but to cut it out."

Vespa eyed the shears uneasily. "If it's wood, couldn't you just saw through the beastly thing?"

"I could try, but I had rather not. It would be more trying for my patient. With luck, one or two hard snaps with these, and we can pull out the bolt. One thing in our favour is that it is so far to the side. I think it has not touched the lung, but the gentleman—your father, sir?"

"Yes. He is not young, is that what you're th-thinking?"

"He is, I can see, a brave man. But it will be a shock. You accept that I am not a *bona fide* surgeon, monsieur?"

"You come highly recommended. I am sure you will do your best."

"As you wish." Aunay looked pleased. "Then—we proceed. The young lady she must leave while we remove your papa's garments, and I wish you will swiftly find dry clothing, or I will have two patients on my hands!"

"Th-three," moaned Keith.

Vespa ignored him and turned back to the bed. Looking into the haggard face of the injured man, he knew suddenly that whatever his crimes, the bond between them was deep and binding. He said, "No tricks please, Father. I want you to dance at my wedding."

Kincraig said nothing, but his eyes brightened and the white lips twitched into a smile.

It was still dark when Consuela ran down the stairs. A fire was burning on the hearth of the tiny coffee room and breakfast

had been set out on a table. Vespa stood with one hand on the
mantel, gazing down at the flames, and she ran to him, saying
anxiously, "What is it? When I left you last night he seemed
peacefully asleep at last."

He turned with a smile and took both her hands. "And how
incredibly brave and kind you were, to stay with us as you did.
Our clever amateur apothecary had given him some laudanum,
so he slept through much of the night."

"Which is probably more than you did." She touched his
tired face worriedly. "Have you seen Monsieur Aunay this morning?"

"Yes. He looked in just now and told me my father goes
along nicely. I wish to heaven we could leave him here, but we
must be on our way at first light." He led her to the table and
pulled out a chair.

She sat down and said, "You never mean to take him with
us? Jack, you cannot! He endured that dreadful ordeal very
bravely, but the poor man is in no condition to travel."

Vespa had already snatched a hurried meal, but couldn't resist the chance to share these few minutes. He poured her coffee and moved the butter and jam and the bowl of hot rolls
closer, then sat beside her. "He will be in worse condition if
we don't get away from here quickly." With a grim look he
went on, "My delightful half-brother won free in the night!"

"Oh, never say so! I thought you had him securely tied in
the cellar?"

"I did. Like a fool! I should have kept him under my eye.
He managed to persuade a gullible kitchen maid to loosen the
ropes, and was free in jig time. I came down on the run when
I heard her screeching. Keith had turned out all the horses. I
tried to stop him but he went off at the gallop on a fine hack."

Dismayed, she said, "And will bring back his nasty friends, I
suppose."

"No. When I hauled him out of that lake yesterday afternoon
he was in a rage because his hirelings have deserted him. Apparently, there are dragoons out searching for us, and his men
were English and decided the risk was too great."

Spreading jam on a roll she asked, "Then—why must we
leave so quickly? You and Paige could deal with Keith, surely?"

"Most assuredly we could. But the unnatural varmint promised to find the dragoons and send them after us. He's sure to

implicate his lordship. It would present an ideal way to be rid of him."

"Oh, what a *horrid* creature he is! But surely they'll not believe what he says? Lord Kincraig has wandered about the continent for years and everyone knows—forgive me, Jack—that he's more a joke than a threat."

"They'd change their minds in a hurry if Keith should fabricate some tale about my father being a British spy." He thought, 'Or a ruthless bank robber!' "And I've your precious self to consider." He ran a finger down her cheek lovingly. "I dare not risk it, Consuela. We must make a run for the coast. Paige is poling up the horses. Poor fellow, he really has a brute of a cold. Madame has been changing my father's bandages. I'm going up now to help him get dressed. Will you see about young Pierre?"

She nodded, but said worriedly that it might be as well to leave the child here so that he could be restored to his family. "The Lannions seem to be good people."

"Yes, I'm sure they are. But the boy is my responsibility, you know."

"Indeed he is not! I was the one who gave him the chance to run away."

"And it is thanks to me that he was not sent back at once. Besides, if we leave him, like as not he'll run away again and try to find us, and get thoroughly lost in the process. No. I must deliver him to Gaston myself."

Consuela had to admit the logic of what he said, but much to her exasperation, she was unable to fulfill the task he had set her. The truckle bed in the room Pierre had shared with Manderville was empty and the boy was nowhere to be found. She gathered her few belongings together and carried them down to the stables. The carriage was ready, the horses harnessed and stamping impatiently. A yawning ostler said that he had seen young Master Pierre carrying the crossbow "like a soldier," but didn't know where he was now. Consuela asked him to put her bag in the boot, and wrapping her cloak tightly around her, went outside.

Dawn was brightening the eastern skies, the air was wintry but, at least at the moment, it was not raining. She went around to the side of the tavern and called, but there was no sign of Pierre. Vexed, she muttered, "Wretched child. Where have you got to now?" Jack was so anxious to get an early start, and he

certainly would not leave without the boy. She walked up the
lane a short way, calling, and peering through a swirling ground
mist for a glimpse of a small figure carrying a crossbow.

She heard Pierre before she saw him. His answering calls
were broken by sobs and she began to run, fearing he had
fallen and hurt himself. She traced the cries to a cluster of yew
trees some distance across the field. No sooner did she enter
their shade than Pierre sped to throw himself into her arms.
He was still clutching the heavy crossbow, but raised no objections when she removed it. The defiant warrior had vanished,
and he was just a very frightened little boy who clung to her
whimpering a plea to go home to Papa.

"But of course you shall, my dear," she said, holding him
tight. "Captain Jacques is even now preparing to leave. Why
ever did you not come when I called you?"

"Because . . . because of—*them.*" He half-whispered the
words, his big eyes peering around in terror.

The hedge tavern was out of sight. Consuela thought of the
wicked Duncan Keith and his scoundrels, and of Imre Monteil
and his terrible coachman, and tried not to look frightened.
Lowering her voice she asked, "Who, dear? I cannot see anyone."

"There!" He pointed impatiently. "And there, and—there!
Oh, but they are all around! I didn't see them when I came in
here to practice with the crossbow. But it began to get lighter
and there they were. Watching me!"

Consuela saw also. An impressive circle of the megaliths with
the trees as if clustered to conceal them. With a sigh of relief,
she said, "But they are just some menhirs, Pierre. Nothing more
than great slabs of stone. They cannot harm you. Only think
how clever the ancient people were, to manage to bring them
here and make them stand upright."

He shook his head vehemently. "This, it is not possible! People today cannot move them. I know, for my Papa and some
of his friends tried once. They were big and strong, but it was
no use. And if modern men who are clever can't do it, how
could cavemen who were stupids? It was magic, Miss Consuela!
And they are here, weaving evil spells all—all around us!"

In his abject fear his voice had risen shrilly. Consuela said
with decision, "Nonsense! That is just silly superstition. Now
come and—"

"No," he wailed, tightening his hold about her. "Only look

at the bad things that have happened. Yesterday the Carpet Collector went to meet his friend, and found him killed stone dead near that great big menhir. And then the old gentleman was shot and is going to die—"

"But—no, Pierre! Lord Kincraig is much better this morning. Only come and you will—"

"No! I cannot! He is brave, the old Carpet Man. But he will die, and I like him and it was only because we came near these menhirs it all happened. Do you see how many there are? Oh, I tell you, they are demons, and—"

"That's enough!" The note of hysteria in his voice caused her to say sternly, "Whatever would your papa and Captain Jacques think if they saw you blubbering like a baby over a silly old piece of rock? Pick up your crossbow like a brave boy, and come with me at once." She had to pry his arms away and he struggled and looked up at her piteously, his face tear-streaked and his eyes reddened. Hardening her heart, she said, "Hurry, now. We are going to find a ship to take us back to the village near your papa's château. If you don't want to come I shall have to go without you."

He gulped a sob, but took up the crossbow and walked as close to her as was possible, trembling with fear at every step.

Consuela rested a hand on his shoulder, and as they stepped out of the circle of yews, she said comfortingly, "There now. That wasn't so bad, was it? And we are quite safe in spite of those silly menhirs."

But glancing up she saw that she had spoken too soon.

Manderville was dismounting as Vespa rode at the gallop into the yard, and the two men exchanged shouts of "Any luck?" The host ran from the tavern and looked from one troubled face to the other. "The luck there is not," he mourned. "But you have been searching for three hours, *messieurs*—how can they have gone so far?"

"How, indeed." Vespa handed Bruine's reins to the ostler. "There has been no letter for me, Monsieur Lannion? No message?"

The host shook his head.

Manderville looked at Vespa sharply, but said nothing, and sneezed his way up the steps.

The host trotted along beside them. "My spouse she says we

should perhaps restore your papa to his bed, Monsieur Jacques. Elegant as it is, he does not rest so comfortably on the sofa."

The window shades were still drawn in the small parlour, and the room was dim. There were no customers at this hour and a maid hovered about dusting half-heartedly.

Fully dressed, propped by several pillows and with a blanket thrown over him, Kincraig lay on the sofa that only a deter-mined optimist could describe as 'elegant.' Vespa scanned the drawn white face and, as if the injured man sensed his presence, the hazel eyes opened. The glow of affection dawned at once. Vespa knew too well the after-effects of wounds, and he took up the glass of water on the occasional table and offered it. Kincraig drank gratefully. Vespa asked, "How can we make you more comfortable, sir?"

"By leaving." The voice was weak but clear. "You should— should have gone at sun-up."

"If you mean, without you, that is not to be thought of. I'll confess I've a heart of stone, sir. I'd have packed you in the coach and driven out long ago. Unfortunately, the boy and Miss Jones have wandered off somewhere. The lady has a habit of— of disappearing."

His lordship's head jerked up, he flinched painfully and lay back again. "You never think . . . Duncan?" he gasped.

"Your son spoke of dragoons, sir," said Manderville, carrying in two mugs of coffee. "But we've seen no sign of military."

Vespa accepted one of the mugs with a nod of thanks. "They were on foot," he said, his eyes bleak. "We searched every area they might conceivably have reached. Pierre's an enterprising rascal. He doesn't want to go home and he might well have led Consuela a merry chase, but—"

He broke off as the ostler ran in, flushed and excited and waving a note. "This it is left for Monsieur Jacques!"

Vespa was across the room in two long strides, and tearing the letter open.

Manderville asked, "Who delivered it? Did you see?"

The ostler shook his head. "I walk the little mare to cool her down and when I come back, the letter it is stuck on a nail on the stall. I see nobody."

As if turned to stone, Vespa was staring at the paper he held. Manderville asked hoarsely, "Well? What does it say?"

Vespa neither moved nor spoke.

Manderville took the paper from his hand. The writing was neat and clear:

> *This time your lady visits me by invitation. You have one hour to exchange her for the location of the waggon. If you prefer to keep the waggon, I will give her to the dragoons who are everywhere now, and collect the reward for foreign spies.*
>
> *Do you think she will be shot—when they finish with her?*
>
> *Or guillotined?*
>
> *How sad it would be for such a pretty head to fall into the basket.*
>
> *My coach will wait by the shrine on the west side of the lake.*
>
> I.M.

Manderville swore and handed the note to Lord Kincraig.

Deathly pale, his mouth set in a tight line, Vespa walked to the door.

Manderville sprang to seize his arm. "What are you going to do?"

Tearing free, Vespa said harshly, "D'you think for one instant that I'd trade Consuela's dear life for that damned waggon?"

"You mean to tell him where it is?"

"Be assured of it!" He started for the door again.

"No!" Coughing, Manderville sprang to block his way and said breathlessly, "You cannot!"

"Like hell I can't! Stand aside!"

"You don't understand! The waggon holds more than carpets! The roof—"

"Is full of stolen gold. Oh, yes, I knew. I didn't think you did. Perhaps that explains your 'devotion' to my search, eh?" Vespa said bitterly. "I should have guessed. But if you think I'll exchange the life of my precious lady for a few hundred gold *louis*—" he shoved Manderville aside and reached for the door handle.

His lordship, dragging himself to one elbow, panted, "Jack! Wait . . . you don't—"

"Sorry, sir. But you'll have to get along without your ill-gotten gains!"

Manderville seized his shoulder, wrenched him around and struck hard and true.

Vespa measured his length on the floor.

Dazed and astonished, he gasped, "Why, you . . . damned blackguard!" and started up, only to pause as Manderville's small pistol was levelled at him. Even now, he'd not expected this. "You . . . wouldn't," he said.

"I will. If you leave me no choice."

Staring into his friend's unwontedly stern face, and noting the blurred look to the eyes and the high flush, Vespa muttered, "You . . . really are ill!"

"No. But I daren't take the chance you might level me with that confounded right of yours."

"You'd shoot me—for a few filched bags of gold?"

Lord Kincraig said faintly, "We'll have to . . . tell him, Paige."

"You're in it together," said Vespa, sitting up and wiping blood from the corner of his mouth. "My God! Well, nothing you could tell me would make a difference. You'll have to pull that trigger, Paige, because I'm going after my lady."

"The gold wasn't . . . filched, Jack," said Kincraig. "I—I rather suspected you thought it was."

Manderville said, "And it's not a few bags."

"I'd guess about four hundred *louis,*" said Vespa contemptuously, kneeling and watching for his chance.

"Try guessing about forty thousand," said Manderville.

Staring at him, Vespa gasped, "You're out of your mind! The roof wouldn't hold that much weight."

"No, but the waggon also has false sides and a false bottom."

"And some of the carpets have—have gold sewn into the backings," said Kincraig.

"Great heavens! How long have you been in the bank-robbery business, sir?"

Manderville sat down wearily and blew his nose. "Wrong business, Jack."

Kincraig explained, "I am . . . by way of being a—a courier, you see."

A courier? Vespa thought, 'What kind of courier would take such a fearful risk as to haul a fortune in gold *louis* across France? Towards Spain . . .' And it all fell into place at last. He groaned and slumped back on his heels. "Oh—my God! *Wellington?*"

Kincraig said weakly, "The Field Marshal hasn't been able to pay his men and—he is desperately in need of funds. Without them, he faces sure defeat in—in the spring."

"And you work for him?"

"Not exactly. I—at present—work for Nathan Rothschild, who—who made the loan. We had to get the gold to Wellington somehow."

"And I'm under orders." Manderville stood and put up his pistol. "Have been from the start." He reached out and pulled Vespa to his feet.

Manderville's stubborn insistence that Lord Kincraig was not in France, his persistent attempts to turn them aside and then his determination that they keep together made sense now, and Vespa exclaimed, "Damn you, Paige! Why didn't you tell me?"

"Sworn to secrecy, old boy. I wouldn't have broken my word now, if this hadn't happened. You can guess the need for it to have been kept so desperately quiet. We had to ship £800,000 in gold under Bonaparte's nose, you might say."

"Eight . . . hundred . . . *thousand?*" Vespa tottered to the end of the sofa and sat there, trying to take it all in.

"I am but one of many couriers," explained Kincraig, holding his injured side painfully.

"Your father has taken some really horrendous risks." Manderville broke into another spasm of coughing. Wiping tearful eyes, he wheezed, "He was supposed to rendezvous with a British warship off Belgium, but a trap was set and he had to make a run for it. Afterwards, he took the chance of trying to get through to Wellington direct. When you began to sniff around in search of your family tree, Wellington was horrified, and assigned me to try and head you off."

"*Head me off?* Why in hell didn't he just *order* me off?"

"I don't pretend to know, dear boy. He's been heard to remark that you were one of his finest staff officers. He knew about—er, Sir Kendrick, and that you'd been wounded again. Perhaps he sympathized, or perhaps he thought you'd never get this close. At all events, Hasty Adair said the great man's hand was over you. To an extent."

Vespa was briefly silent. Then he said slowly, "You've been splendid, sir. And I've been a proper fool. I am so sorry!"

"Nonsense. You reacted exactly as—as you ought. I knew you wouldn't blame me . . . once you learned the truth." Kincraig held out his hand.

Vespa took it and held it firmly, then he stood and offered

a short and rather shy bow. "I'm very proud to be your son, sir. But—I'm afraid I must leave you now."

Manderville, who had moved back to lean against the wall, stepped forward. "I'm with you, Jack. What d'you mean to do?"

Vespa smiled. "Why, I'm going to tell Monteil where the waggon is, of course."

"No!" Aghast, his lordship protested. "You *cannot!* I—I know how much your lady means to you, Jack, but—if Wellington loses this war, Bonaparte will enslave all Europe, and Britain! The prospect—"

"Is terrible indeed, sir. But, tell me, if you will, do you think it possible that Imre Monteil knows what you carry in the waggon? Or is he drawn by the lure of your legendary Spring Carpet?"

Kincraig hesitated, then replied slowly, "I really believe that the only men who know the truth of it are Rothschild's people, who are, I would stake my life, incorruptible; and Field Marshal Lord Wellington."

"Yet—Manderville knew. Who else, Paige?"

"Prinny, of course. Cannot very well keep our next monarch in the dark. Hastings Adair, and one or two other high-ranking officers, probably."

Vespa frowned thoughtfully. "You said you were one of many couriers, sir. Have the others run the gauntlet successfully?"

"I've no idea. The reason I failed was that, as Manderville said, I was prevented from keeping the rendezvous with our warship."

"You were able to keep other rendezvous, though." Kincraig looked puzzled and Vespa said, "The fellow who rides the black horse. I think you had a chat with him after the waggon toppled. One of our people, is he?"

"We have him to thank for leading Monteil astray," said Manderville. "Otherwise we'd have had him and his Chinese juggernaut on our heels before we ever reached Chateau Coligny."

Vespa nodded. "And your friend who was killed at the meeting place, sir?"

"Poor Ivan . . ." Kincraig sighed. "Such a good, brave man. A ship has been despatched to take me up. Ivan was to tell me where to meet it."

"He was badly beaten, sir. Did he know what you carried?"

"You mean—might the secret have been forced from him? I think not. He was of the Intelligence Service, and those poor fellows are seldom given the full story, you know. He—er, he did manage to leave me a message, however."

"He did?" Startled, Manderville asked, "How?"

"He must have still been alive when his murderers abandoned him. He'd managed to scratch a sign in the mud. An arrow. Pointing southwest."

"By Jove, but here was gallantry!" exclaimed Manderville, awed.

"Gallantry, indeed," agreed Vespa. "One last quick question, Father. You said there were *louis* sewn into some of the carpets. Would that constitute a great sum?"

"There are fifty in each of two rugs."

"A hundred pounds, roughly. Hmm. Well, we must be off or the hour will be up." Vespa gripped his father's hand once more. "Don't wait for us, sir. Get to the coast and a ship as soon as you're able."

Lord Kincraig said fervently, "Come back safely, my dear boy. God be with you both."

As they hurried to the stables, Vespa outlined his plan. Manderville said dubiously, "It's not much of a plan. D'you really think it will work?"

"It *must* work! I'll get Consuela out of that bastard's hands, or—" Vespa paused, looking very grim.

"Yes, of course," Manderville cuffed him gently. "Sorry, old fellow." And he thought wearily, 'We might have a chance—if only we can get rid of the juggernaut!'

Sixteen

A bitter wind had come up by the time Vespa approached the lake. The tree branches were tossing about and a few remaining leaves scattered down. On a distant hill a great castle loomed majestically against the flying clouds, the slate rooftops of a village clustering about it.

He rode fast, praying that he could bring this off and wondering if Paige, who was beginning to look quite pulled, would get through. Ever alert, his eyes searched for Monteil's coach, but before he reached the lake he was surprised by two men astride dapple-grey horses who charged from a hollow, drew rein at the last possible instant, causing Bruine to shy nervously, and then pulled in on either side. It was the unlovely pair they had encountered before. They had probably hoped to unseat him, but he was a consummate horseman. He stroked the mare's neck to quiet her, and watched them in a contemptuous silence.

"Mark you, Bertrand," jeered the bushy-haired individual, looking as wolfish as ever. "Is he not the strong and silent soldier boy?"

His friend seemed to have acquired even more pimples. He giggled, and said, "He is—now, Étienne, but monsieur will have him chattering like a magpie in jig time." He added tauntingly, "If he wishes to see his lady again."

Vespa said, "Doubtless, Monsieur Monteil is accustomed to wait while you two exchange clever witticisms."

Étienne laughed and brought his whip down hard across Bruine's nose. The mare reared with a shrill neigh of fright and pain. Bertrand swung the grip of his horse pistol at

Vespa's head, smashing him into a blurred world of echoing voices and laughter.

In a remote fashion it dawned on him that they were moving again. The old head wound and the side of his jaw throbbed with pain. He slumped forward over Bruine's mane as if barely able to stay in the saddle, while gradually his mind stopped spinning and confusion was replaced by rage.

They were slowing. The bushy creature—that would be Étienne—called in his nasal voice, "Wake up, Monsieur-the-so-dashing-Capitaine!"

Bertrand sniggered, "I'll dash him!"

Vespa was ready. As a heavy riding whip flailed at him, he ducked, caught the thong and heaved. Bertrand uttered a surprised yelp and disappeared under his horse. Étienne cursed furiously and swung up a pistol. Vespa spurred Bruine straight at him so that he had to rein aside.

A harsh voice rang out: "Enough! *Imbeciles!* Did I not say that I wanted him unharmed?"

Imre Monteil's luxurious coach waited beside a grove of trees. His Chinese coachman, arms folded across his massive chest, was at the heads of the leaders. On the box, a liveried guard held a musket aimed steadily at Vespa.

Watching frowningly from the open window of the coach, Monteil said, "My apologies, Captain. I had hoped we could deal as civilized gentlemen, but I see my men have been rough with you."

Vespa said coldly, "Never send an animal to do a man's work."

Bertrand crawled to his feet, his narrow eyes glaring hatred.

Monteil shrugged. "You appear to have dealt with my 'animals'—what is it you English say?—deedily? And now, Captain, you and I must deal together. Where is the waggon of your illustrious sire?"

So the Swiss knew Lord Kincraig was his father. Vespa countered, "I will tell you after Miss Jones and the boy are released and I have your word they will be allowed to leave."

The Swiss called, "Ti Chiu!" and the Chinese coachman trundled to the far side of the carriage and swung open the door.

Vespa started around the coach, but the guard on the box shouted, "You will stay where you are, monsieur!"

Halting, Vespa said angrily, "If you think I'll tell you anything until Miss Jones is beside me, you're all about in your
head, Monteil!"

The white hand resting on the window gestured.

Vespa heard a low growl of rage followed by running footsteps. He flung himself from the saddle in time to catch Consuela as she rushed into his arms. He held her close, and she
half-sobbed, "Oh, Jack! Oh, Jack! They have hurt you! I did
it again, didn't I?"

"You're safe," he said huskily. "Just at the moment that's
all I care about."

Ti Chiu came around the coach, limping slightly, and growling at Pierre as the boy ran past, sticking out his tongue with
gleeful derision. The coachman made a snatch for him and
Pierre squealed and hid behind Vespa. "I kicked him. Hard.
And I am not sorry," he declared, and keeping a wary eye
on Ti Chiu, he went on: "And it was not Miss Consuela's
fault. She came to help me, Capitaine Jacques, because I was
captured by some terrible menhirs. I am a brave boy, but I
was very afraid, I will say it!"

"You were well justified." Vespa gripped his shoulder comfortingly while slanting a glance at the Chinese. Stark horror
was written on that usually inscrutable countenance. "And
Miss Consuela was very brave to go to you." He looked steadily into Consuela's eyes. She managed a tremulous smile that
wrung his heart and that faded as he added, "Because I know
how very much she fears those megaliths."

She had never said such a thing, but she sensed that this
was not a joke, and answered cautiously, "You do not like me
to be superstitious, but—"

Pierre interrupted excitedly, "Everyone knows they come to
life at night! They wouldn't let me go, and they made evil
spells round and round us. That's why these bad people
caught us! But Miss—"

"Enough!" said Vespa. "Did these varmints hurt you, Consuela?"

She shook her head. "They wanted me to tell where Lord
Kincraig left the waggon, but I didn't know how to direct
them properly, so they were angry and made all kinds of horrible threats."

"Harsh words," said Monteil with a sigh. "And when I have

with much patience allowed you the friendly little talk. I find your conversation not entrancing. We will now drive on."

It was exactly what Vespa had expected, but he protested indignantly that Monteil had promised to release Consuela in exchange for the location of the waggon. "You did not stipulate that I was to lead you there!"

"But you see," explained Monteil with the thin smile that never seemed to reach his dull black eyes, "People are so sadly devious these days. You will surely not expect me to release the lady until I am sure you have kept your part of the bargain. Besides which," his smile broadened, "you are so much outnumbered, *mon ami,* and you must bear in mind that you have incurred the displeasure of my men. They would be pleased, I am sure, to help you understand my point of view."

His two bullies expressed their willingness to make things clear to the Captain. They were so willing, in fact, that Vespa felt Consuela shiver. He said, "I think you have an exaggerated notion of the worth of that waggon. I'll take you there, but then Miss Jones and the boy go free. It is agreed?"

Monteil nodded and purred blandly, "But by all means, Captain Vespa."

The last time Vespa had ridden this road, Lord Kincraig had led the way and his own mind had been preoccupied with other matters. As a result, it was as much as he could do to recall the route, and he was relieved when the road narrowed as it wound through a ravine-like break in the hills, which he did remember. After that, for a while memory failed him, but he was again reprieved when they came to the river, crossing it at length over a tall-sided wooden bridge whose strange construction made it quite a landmark. And so he went along, feeling his way as it were, from one vaguely familiar spot to the next, until they came at length within sight of the broken gate leading to the abandoned farm.

Monteil had insisted that Consuela and Pierre return to the carriage, and Étienne and Bertrand rode on each side of Vespa. His nerves were taut as he rode onto the stony track and past the grove of sycamores. There was no shout, no sign. He sent up a fervent prayer that his plan would not fail; Paige

had been right, it was so appallingly simple it could not really
be termed a plan. If he could just get Consuela safely away . . .
if he could just keep the waggon from falling into Monteil's
greedy paws . . . if only Manderville was in place . . . His
father would never forgive— There was a dispute behind him.
His heart leapt. He thought, 'Aha!'

Monteil howled. "Vespa! Halt!"

The carriage had come to a stop. Ti Chiu was climbing
down from the box. Through the open window Monteil raged
at him. "You bovine idiot! What d'you think you're about?"

His henchman strode back onto the lane and stood there,
facing away from the farm, arms folded across his chest, massive, forbidding, immovable: for all the world like another
menhir. His master's commands were as if unheard; insults,
curses and threats were completely disregarded.

Vespa called innocently, "Is this far enough, Monteil?"

"How do I know, curse you? I see no waggon!"

"You'll find it further along this track. You'll come to—"

"We will come nowhere without you lead the way! Guard!
You drive on."

"But—what about Ti Chiu?" enquired Vespa.

Monteil's response made Consuela cover Pierre's ears. One
gathered that Ti Chiu refused to go any farther towards a
farm that had been abandoned because of the menhirs who
dwelt there. He was an ignorant dolt, an imbecile, and he
could stand there like the block he was until they took him
up after they'd found the waggon! "And it had better be
here," snarled Monteil.

Riding on, Vespa was cheered by the thought that the first
step in his plan had succeeded. For the moment, at least, the
greatest menace was out of commission.

When they stopped in the yard, Étienne ran into the barn.
He came out a moment later to report that there was "no
waggon, monsieur," and leered hungrily at Vespa.

Monteil said softly, "I warned you, Captain!"

"And I warned you. The waggon is here. Let Miss Jones
and Pierre down and I'll show you."

Bertrand picked at his unlovely countenance and said, "He
make the big bluff, but I will beat the truth from—"

Monteil stepped down from the carriage. "You will keep

the lady here, while our captain fulfils his part of the bargain. Étienne, you come with me."

Consuela and Pierre left the coach and stood together, holding hands.

Tearing his eyes from his beloved, Vespa said, "This way."

Monteil and the wolfish Étienne followed. When they reached the back of the farmhouse, Vespa paused, astonished. He'd not dreamed Paige could have done so much in such a short time, but the branch and the smashed wall had been moved aside, the waggon was out of the lean-to, and the pole connected once more.

Monteil exclaimed, "*Sacré bleu!* Kincraig he is crazy indeed! He leave his treasure of carpets standing here like this? Unguarded?"

Vespa gathered his wits. "As you know very well, my father was shot by your killer with the crossbow. We had to get help for him quickly."

He was afraid the Swiss would realize his answer made little sense, but Monteil was too eager to inspect the waggon to analyze the remark and the reference to a killer with a crossbow disturbed him. "I have no such person in my employ," he said, with an uneasy glance at the dismal farm and the distant menhir. "Open the door of this ugly cart."

Praying, Vespa threw the doors wide.

A French *cuirassier* in all the glory of luxuriant whiskers, great steel helm and breastplate, a sabre in one hand and a musket in the other, leapt from the waggon, howling at the top of his lungs, "Traitors! Murderers! Thieves! Now I have you caught in my fist! I arrest you in the name of *l'Empereur!*"

There was a concerted gasp. Impressed by Manderville's resourcefulness, Vespa whipped around, and his right jab sent the gawking Étienne into collision with his employer. Monteil thrust him away and they retreated at the gallop. From the corner of his eye Vespa saw another *cuirassier* hot after Bertrand, whose knees had a fine fast action. Although puzzled by the reinforcements, Vespa was not one to let opportunity pass by. He snatched the bugle that hung about Manderville's neck and blew a fairly creditable 'Advance at the double' on the dented instrument. The retreat became a rout. Carriage, Swiss and Bertrand tore up the stony track, Étienne running weavingly after them, with the second *cuirassier* in hot pursuit.

Laughing, Vespa said, "Paige, when I asked you for a diversion, I never dreamed—" Turning to his friend, the blithe words died away.

The musket was still aimed at his heart. The *cuirassier* who held it so steadily was scarlet with wrath.

Whoever he was, he was not Paige Manderville.

"Whoops!" said Vespa.

"You have blow on my bugle!" the *cuirassier* roared, putting first things first. "You are not of La Belle France! You, I arrest as the English spy!"

"I apologize for your bugle, monsieur," said Vespa politely. "But—who is this?"

Instinctively, the *cuirassier* turned his head. Into Manderville's fist.

"Gad," said Vespa, easing the Frenchman down. "What happened? And how on earth did you get the waggon out of—" Again, his sentence went unfinished.

The four cart-horses were being shepherded across the field by a solitary rider.

"Damn!" exclaimed Vespa, and snatched up the *cuirassier's* musket.

"Easy, Captain, sir! Easy!" croaked Manderville, pushing the weapon aside. "I'll own I've been tempted from time to time, but . . ."

For the first time Vespa had a clear view of the man on the black horse. Incensed, he curtailed his lusty swearing as Consuela ran to join them.

Her reaction was quite different. "It's *Toby!*" she cried joyously. "Oh, how lovely! We are all together again!"

Vespa took her outstretched hand, his eyes softening, but he said, "Of all the bacon brains, Broderick! Trailing me all over Brittany! Why didn't you identify yourself? I thought you were one of Monteil's ugly crew. I'd have blown your head off if you came close enough!"

"Exactly why I kept at a safe distance, my tulip." Grinning, Broderick dismounted, clapped Vespa on the back, and flushed shyly as Consuela hugged him.

"That'll be enough of that," said Vespa, pulling her to him. "I allowed it only because I am told you kept Imre Monteil off our heels for a while."

"Then I'm entitled to another hug," said Broderick. "I've found us a short-cut to the Lannions' hedge-tavern."

"Have you, by Jove! Jolly good, Toby. But there's no time for more rewards. Our French friend here is probably part of a scouting party. The rest of his troop is liable to come calling at any moment! We must be least in sight, but *vite!*"

The men worked swiftly to pole-up the cart-horses. Consuela and Pierre bound the hapless *cuirassier* and he was dragged, barking out ferocious threats, into the house. Within five minutes the waggon of the Crazy Carpet Collector was speeding along under wind-whipped trees.

Broderick led the way, following a rutted track that he assured them would bring them onto the road leading to the hedge-tavern. Vespa rode Bruine, keeping close to the waggon, and Manderville drove, with Pierre and Consuela perched on the seat beside him. There was little talk, even the boy sensing their tension although nobody voiced the fears that were uppermost in all their minds: that the French military were much too close on their heels; and that Imre Monteil knew exactly where they would go.

Broderick's 'quickest route' began to seem very much the long way round. The heavy waggon bumped and jolted over the uneven surface, and the wind became a near gale, blowing a cold drizzling rain into their faces, and sending branches and leaves flying.

They'd been travelling for half an hour when they turned west onto the road to the Lannion hedge-tavern. The river was running high now, the water roiling and full of debris. Vespa realized belatedly that the oddly constructed bridge was a comparatively flimsy wooden structure. If it could not bear the weight of the heavy waggon . . . He glanced uneasily at Manderville, and saw apprehension on the handsome features. "Hold up!" he shouted.

Manderville pulled up the team.

Vespa sent Consuela and Pierre across the bridge on foot. Broderick and Manderville rode, and Vespa—over Manderville's hoarse but indignant protests—drove the waggon. The cart-horses trod onto the timbers and began to snort and toss their heads uneasily. The bridge creaked and it seemed to Vespa that it swayed. He thought, 'Please God, we're so close now!' If the waggon crashed into that muddy boil of

water below it would be the end of his father's brave struggle
and he would have failed his General. On the far bank he
could see Consuela looking pale and frightened, watching him
and clinging to Manderville's arm. The bridge creaked even
more menacingly. There was a sudden loud crack and the off
wheeler neighed and pranced in the traces. Vespa's heart
jumped into his throat. A large carriage approaching from
the west stopped, and pulled off to the side of the road. Rain
sheeted down blindingly. 'Nothing ventured,' he thought and
in desperation whipped up the horses. They plunged forward
and the bridge definitely swayed, but then there were shouts
of triumph, the wheels thudded onto solid ground, and he
could breathe again.

Consuela flew to climb onto the waggon seat and hug him.
"Wretched Englishman," she half-sobbed. "As if anything was
worth taking such a chance! I had rather see the stupid waggon swept away than have you go down with it!"

"To say truth, love, so would I," he admitted, kissing her
forehead. "But Wellington and England are desperately in
need of my father's 'Spring Carpet!' "

He ordered Consuela and Pierre to travel inside so that
they could keep dry, and then they were off again, this time
with Manderville bringing up the rear. The afternoon was
wearing on and the wind seemed ever stronger. After a while
Manderville galloped to the front of the waggon, and tried
to shout, but his voice was now quite gone. He gestured urgently to the east. Vespa leaned to the side and peered back.
Far off he saw the glitter of light on metal.

Breastplates and helmets.

"Here comes the cavalry," he muttered grimly, and cracked
the whip over the heads of the team.

The cart-horses leaned into their collars and responded gal-
lantly, but they were handicapped by the bulk and weight of
the waggon. Each time Vespa glanced behind them it seemed
to him that the troop of *cuirassiers* was closer. It was a race
now, and one they had little chance of winning unless in some
way they could give the French military gentlemen the slip.

Their chances shrank when they reached the section of the
road that wound between the steep walls of the ravine. A
group of travellers had spread themselves across the narrow
road. They plodded along at a snail's pace; there was no room

to pass, and they showed not the slightest inclination to move aside.

Guiding the cart-horses as close as he dared, Vespa hailed the individual bringing up the rear of the train. The face that was turned to him looked familiar. The man screamed something, and the people ahead halted and glanced back. There were children, and riding the lead mule was a lady with an infant in her arms. It was the same family whose baby had almost fallen from the mule two days ago.

Vespa called urgently, "Sir, your pardon, but we are in great haste. Could you be so kind as to let us pass?"

The man stared at him expressionlessly.

Pierre stuck his head through the small door behind the driver's seat and shouted, "The soldiers! They are catching up—"

Vespa snapped, "I am aware."

The eyes of the man standing in the rain became very round. He craned his neck, looking back. Then he looked up at Vespa. He ran to the front of his straggling little column and called orders in a Breton dialect so broad it would have been better understood by a Scot than by a Frenchman. In a trice the mules were all at the farthest edge of the road. Vespa drove the team on carefully and as they passed, called his grateful thanks. Nobody said a word in reply, but the lady nodded and waved the infant's tiny hand at him, the little girl smiled shyly, and briefly, on the face of the head of the house was a broad grin.

Looking back a few minutes later, Vespa saw that the family and their mules were all over the road again, and scarcely moving at all. 'God bless 'em,' he thought fervently. 'They've repaid the favour!' Now, the troop of soldiers would be so delayed that he might, after all, have a chance to collect his father and find a hiding place somewhere along the coast road. A slim chance, but at least a chance.

The cart-horses were going along well. The short wintry afternoon was fading, but a distant thread of smoke wound upward. It was lighter than the darkening clouds, and soon dispersed by the wind, but his hopes lifted because it meant they were within sight of the Lannions' tavern.

Consuela opened the small door behind the seat and tugged at his coat.

"Almost there, m'dear," he said with a triumphant grin.

"We must stop," she cried in distress. "Look! Look!"

He looked back. Manderville was huddled over the pommel and appeared to be in imminent danger of tumbling from the saddle.

"Toby!" howled Vespa, pulling up the horses.

Broderick turned and waved and Vespa gestured urgently. Reining back, Broderick called, "Now what's to do?"

"Paige is done! We'll have to get him in the waggon. Give me a hand."

Manderville was quite unconscious and breathing in an alarmingly rasping fashion. Between them, they carried him to the waggon and Consuela's care.

"Silly chawbacon," muttered Broderick. "Why didn't he say something?"

But they both knew why Manderville had held out for as long as he could, and that they would have done the same.

As they closed the back doors Vespa slanted a glance up the road. It was impossible to see very far in the fading light, but for as far as he could determine there was no sign of any *cuirassiers*. Climbing up to the driver's seat, he could only pray they would not reach the tavern and find Monteil waiting for them. At least the road from here was fairly level and there were few travellers on this cold afternoon. He urged the cart-horses to greater speed and promised them they would very soon be in a warm barn. The waggon rumbled along and the minutes slid past, and at last they were turning into the Lannions' yard.

The host ran out, waving his arms excitedly. The ostler hurried to the heads of the lathered horses.

Climbing down from the seat, Vespa was stiff and tired. He'd had little in the way of sleep these past two nights, but there was no time for rest now, nor time for them to summon the skill of Monsieur Aunay, the farrier-apothecary. Before he reached the waggon doors Manderville swung them open and disdaining assistance proclaimed himself a blockhead but well-rested. It was a courageous attempt but he stumbled over the front steps, and Consuela, looking weary herself as Vespa lifted her down, whispered that she was afraid that Paige might have the pneumonia.

"And you, my brave girl, are exhausted," he said, tightening his arms about her.

"No, no," she lied. "I am very hardy, you know. But Pierre is fast asleep. I suppose we had as well leave him in the waggon. We shall have to press on at once—no?"

Vespa had already made up his mind that the boy must stay at the tavern, however, and that word should be sent to de Coligny. Broderick volunteered to carry the sleeping child, and Vespa and Consuela followed Manderville inside.

Lord Kincraig, fully dressed, lay on the parlour sofa. He started up eagerly as they came into the room. He looked pale and haggard but insisted he was 'doing very much better,' and was delighted to learn that not only had Consuela and Pierre been rescued, but the waggon was safely in the barn.

"Bravo!" he said, watching Vespa proudly. "You've done splendidly, my boy!"

Madame Lannion hurried in and, after a shocked look at Consuela, said a chamber was ready and that the young lady would want to wash and rest after her ordeal. Longing to offer such luxuries to his beloved, Vespa dared not, and said reluctantly that they must leave at once. "Are you able to travel, sir?"

"But no, he is not!" interjected Madame, outraged. "No more is that one!" She stabbed a finger at Manderville who had sat down on the first chair he encountered and fallen asleep. "Only hear how he breathes—as if someone in his lungs was sifting wheat! More journeying, and you will be burying them both! Nor are you yourself but a step from the grave," she added, taking in Vespa's drawn face and the dark shadows under his eyes. "Come, Mademoiselle, you at least shall wash your poor self and have a hot cup of coffee, if only in my kitchen!"

"I'll be very quick," promised Consuela.

Vespa nodded and smiled at her, then pulled a chair close to the sofa and sank into it gratefully.

Kincraig asked, low-voiced, "You are pursued?"

"Yes, sir. A troop of *cuirassiers*. At most, a mile or so behind. We've some friends along the road who will, I think, do their best to delay them but—"

"Jupiter!" Dismayed, his lordship exclaimed, "We must not

fail at this stage of the game! Lend me your arm, Jack, and we'll be on our way."

Vespa helped him to sit up, watching his face anxiously. Kincraig was obviously in pain and momentarily bereft of breath, but he declared staunchly that with a little help he would go on nicely.

Vespa left him to rest for a minute and went out to check on the horses. Toby had not yet brought Pierre inside and he was quite prepared to find his friend snoring beside the boy in the back of the waggon.

He stretched wearily as he walked across the yard. It was dark now, and raining again, but the wind had dropped and it was very still. There was no sign of Broderick or the ostler.

The sense of danger was sudden and strong. His hand reached down to the pistol in his belt.

Pain seared across his forearm and the pistol fell from his numbed grasp.

Amused and triumphant, Duncan Keith said, "My, but you're fast, brother dear!"

A strong hand shoved Vespa between the shoulder blades, sending him into violent collision with the side of the waggon. The horses snorted and stamped nervously. The shutter on a lantern was opened, releasing a bright beam of light.

Supporting himself against the waggon, Vespa blinked at a squat individual with a pouty mouth and sparse red hair under a sodden hat. The man glared at him and demanded, "What did you do with my crossbow, curse you?"

"Threw it . . . in the lake," lied Vespa.

The squat man swore and started forward.

"Not yet, Rand!" Duncan Keith flourished a crimson-stained sabre. "First, we talk."

Horrified, Vespa cried, "My God! What have you done to the boy?"

"Nothing as yet," said Keith. "This is all yours."

Vespa glanced down, shocked; his sleeve was wet with blood.

From his temporary shelter under the waggon Pierre called fiercely, "You didn't have to cut him!"

"No." Keith grinned. "But you must not deny me life's simple pleasures, child. And before you ask, Captain, sir, your comrade in arms is in the waggon. We got him when he tried to carry off the boy."

The muscles under Vespa's ribs cramped. He endeavoured to keep his voice calm. "Dead?"

"He will be. Unless you cooperate. I met up with my man Rand, you see. And Rand found out that Monsieur Monteil has been following my father. Now Imre Monteil is a greedy man but he is also very shrewd. He would follow this stupid cart only if it contained something of great value. I have come to relieve you of it. And"—he stepped closer to the open waggon doors—"and I do not propose to wait."

Vespa said curtly, "I take it you've already searched the waggon?"

"And found only some moth-eaten rugs. Don't attempt a delaying war of words, Vespa. You know what the old man is carrying. Tell me—and fast. My patience is short at the best of times." He grinned broadly. "No one will miss Broderick very much, and there is always the boy—if all else fails."

"All right, all right! You heard about the Belgian Mint robbery?"

Keith stared at him.

"I have." Rand grunted, "A fine haul they made. Lovely fat sacks of gold!"

Incredulous, Keith said, "Do you say my so-high-and-noble father was involved in that piece of lawlessness?"

"Yes. And not for the first time, I'm afraid."

Rand laughed, and Keith exclaimed, "Why—the old fraud! So *that's* why he's wandered about Europe all these years pretending to search for valuable carpets!"

"They're valuable when gold *louis* are sewn into the backings," said Vespa.

"Aha!" cried Rand and darted for the waggon doors.

Broderick's limp figure was pushed out and dumped on the ground. Vespa gritted his teeth with rage and started towards him, but Keith shouted a furious, "Stay back!" flailing the sabre about so menacingly that Vespa had no choice but to obey.

From inside the waggon Rand shouted, "There's nothing in this one but moths and dust. . . . I can't feel anything solid, here, either. . . . I think. . . . your bastard brother was lying in his— Wait! Yes, by God! Here it is, Mr. Keith! And—in this other also!"

Keith gave a yell of triumph. "How much?"

"Lord knows. There's just these two, so far as I can tell. We'll have to tear them apart to find out!"

"Not here! We'll take them in my coach! Get over there and help him, *mon Capitaine.*"

The gold-filled rugs were heavy and the cut in Vespa's arm made the transfer of them a painful business. It was all he could do to lift the second heavy rug. As it was loaded inside his half-brother's coach he heard hoofbeats.

Rand cried shrilly, "Horses! Coming fast. It's those damned dragoons, like as not!"

Keith made a sudden dart and snatched for the boy.

Whipping the pistol from his pocket, Vespa shouted, "Let him be, or I'll fire, Keith!"

Rand sprang onto the box of the coach.

Under no illusions as to the loyalty of his hireling, Keith howled, "Wait, you cur!"

Broderick, who had crawled nearer, shoved a rake at Keith's feet. Keith tripped, cursing furiously and swung the sabre high. Broderick ducked lower and flung up an arm to shield his head.

Aiming carefully, Vespa fired.

Keith staggered, and grabbed at his arm.

"Damn you, Vespa!" He dropped the sabre, ran to his coach and clambered to the box, snatching the reins from Rand. "You lose, even so," he shouted. "The *cuirassiers* know you're English spies! I hope you all go to Madame Guillotine!"

Vespa sprang from the box, but he was slow. Keith whipped up the team and with a shrill vindictive laugh turned his coach onto the road and disappeared into the night with a rumble of high, fast wheels.

"Never—saw you miss—such an easy shot," said Broderick faintly.

Crawling from under the waggon, Pierre wailed, "Oh, sir! He got away!"

"And . . . with all the . . . blasted loot," said Broderick.

Vespa's smile was mirthless. "Enough, at all events, to hang him," he said, and blew out the lantern.

Scant seconds later there came the pounding of many hooves, the jingle of spurs and harness and a French voice upraised in command. "There they go! After them!"

At a thundering gallop the troop shot past in pursuit of Duncan Keith's coach.

Vespa knelt beside Broderick. "My poor fellow, are you badly hurt?"

"Bent . . . brainbox, I think. Jove, but . . . you're a real sly-boots, Jack! You *meant* that . . . that wart to take the carpets!"

Actually, Vespa's initial plan had been to foist the two gold-laden rugs off onto Imre Monteil. Fate had decreed differently, but his plan had not gone to waste. It had, in fact, come in very handy.

Broderick was staring at him.

He said with a smile, "What a thing to say!"

Seventeen

"Are they all going to die, Capitaine Jacques?"

Somewhat bewildered, Vespa looked down at the boy who sat so close beside him on the seat of the waggon. He recalled the Lannions' adamant refusal to keep the boy with them, but he couldn't seem to remember Pierre waking up and climbing out to him. Nor did he recall the coming of the streaks of light that were now painting the eastern sky to announce the arrival of dawn.

When they'd left the hedge-tavern it had been necessary to go along with caution, for it was so dark. Gradually, however, as if relenting, the rain had eased to a drizzle and then stopped, the clouds had begun to unravel and a full moon had sailed into view to light the heavens with its glory and to show him the road ahead. He had driven all night, torn by the conflicting needs to race on and attempt a rendezvous with the ship and to stop and seek out an apothecary for his father and his friends.

The constant jolting had wrought havoc with Lord Kincraig, who had insisted, even as he stifled a groan of pain, that they keep on, no matter what happened. Manderville was no better: burning with fever and coughing rackingly but whispering that he was starting to feel 'more the thing.' Broderick was deathly pale, tight-lipped and silent, his clenched fists a mute testimony to his suffering, yet able somehow to muster a grin when, it having been necessary to stop and rest the horses, Vespa had twice looked in on what Consuela called her 'field hospital.'

Distraught, he knew that he had no choice. As a British officer, his first duty was to his country. Through that long night, it sometimes seemed to him that he could see Wellington's fierce dark eyes fixed on him. He knew quite well what his Chief would expect of him. To fail that expectation was unthinkable.

So here he was, driving with three very sick men being bounced and jostled about in the waggon, who should have been in bed and under a doctor's care.

"Are they?" the boy repeated now.

"Eh? Oh—no, of course they're not going to die. They're just—just a little bit out of curl, but they'll be better when they've rested and had something to eat."

"So will I." Pierre watched his face anxiously. "Are you out of curl too, sir? If your arm is very bad I can take the ribbons, you know."

The cut in his arm was a continuing nuisance, but only one of several. His various bruises ached and his leg nagged at him ceaselessly, but the worst thing was the very odd feeling that his head was no longer in its proper place, but drifting along beside him. The temperature had plunged after the rain stopped, the cold helping him to stay awake, but he dreaded that he might fall asleep and the waggon would go off the road and get stuck in the mud, or tumble from one of the bridges spanning the rivers and streams that abounded in this region. To hand the reins over to someone else, even for half an hour, would be bliss, but a small boy, however willing, could not tool a four-in-hand. "Thank you, Pierre," he said with a smile. "I shall keep it in mind. Meanwhile, you can help by making sure I stay awake." He peered at the road ahead. "I wonder if we are anywhere near the coast yet."

"I don't know, but I am cold, and this is not a good place, Capitaine."

Vespa looked at him sharply. "Why do you say that?"

"They're all around us." Pierre lowered his voice. "I think they have gathered here, to catch us!"

Startled, Vespa scanned the surrounding countryside, and in the brightening light he saw menhirs, which indeed seemed everywhere and were of all shapes and sizes, some towering towards the heavens, some balanced horizontally one above the other, but all mighty.

They were on a broad heath and ahead was a village looking very ancient and peaceful in the early morning. They must stop

now. The horses were ready to drop and must be baited, and
everyone was hungry.

He said something to Pierre about the menhirs; he wasn't
sure what. The boy seemed reassured, however, and a moment
later was pointing out the sign on a tiny inn at the edge of the
village.

Vespa turned the team into the yard and climbed from the
seat. He had to cling to a wheel for a moment, as the inn ebbed
and flowed before his eyes, but the dizziness passed and he
went to open the back doors of the waggon. Consuela had fallen
asleep holding Manderville's hand. She woke when Vespa called
to her, and came at once to him. Shocked by his haggard appearance, she exclaimed, "Oh, my dear! How terribly tired you
are."

He kissed the cool soft fingers that caressed his cheek and,
looking in at the casualties, asked, "How do they go on?"

"Your father has slept much of the night. Toby, I think, must
have a concussion, and has been in considerable pain. He has
only now dropped off to sleep. Paige has been delirious at
times. He is full of fever, poor soul. I'm afraid . . ." The words
trailed off, then she said a touch too brightly, "Dare we go in
and command some breakfast? Just a cup of coffee would be
heaven!"

He agreed and sent her off with Pierre to see what they could
buy.

A wizened little ostler came out of the stables pulling on
a coat and yawning, his breath hanging like a small white
cloud on the frosty air. In later years the one thing about the
inn that stood out in Vespa's memory was the scorn on the
face of that solitary ostler. "Monsieur," he said acidly, "is
doubtless aware he is killing his horses. Monsieur is no doubt
on a mission of supreme urgency that he would so ill treat
these fine beasts."

At this point Manderville began to mutter wildly. The ostler
viewed the waggon suspiciously.

"Mon Père," said Vespa, tapping his temple. "Poor old fellow."

The ostler led the team towards the barn, the curl of his lip
conveying his belief that monsieur's papa was not the only one
in the family with a brain-box full of maggots. "Poor beasts,"
he grumbled. "I shall take off your harness and walk you until
you have cooled a trifle, then—"

"No!" Feeling the ultimate villain, Vespa said, "Rub them

down and water them, if you please. But keep them poled up, and they can have no feed. I must press on as soon as possible."

With a dark scowl the ostler observed that monsieur's accent was not that of a Breton. Vespa repeated the tale of his Italian birth.

Staring, the ostler said, "Monsieur have the bad injury."

Vespa glanced down. There was a dark stain on his gauntlet; the bandage around the cut on his arm had been a very make-shift affair and must have slipped. "I was—er, chopping wood," he said.

The ostler met his eyes steadily, then began to lead the team up and down and around the yard.

Very sure that the man had not believed a word of his story and that the moment their backs were turned they would be reported to the authorities as suspicious foreigners, Vespa stamped up and down trying to get warm while he kept watch.

A very young and sleepy fire-boy was the only person yet stirring in the kitchens and the most Consuela was able to bring away was a bowl of chicken broth and some stale baguettes. When she carried these provisions outside, Vespa marvelled be-cause, in the miraculous fashion of creatures feminine, she had brushed out her lustrous curls and washed her face, and looked as bright and pretty as though she was a happy young girl set-ting forth on some carefree excursion. Pierre trailed after her, carrying a pan of water, and the ostler's curiosity reawakened when they both disappeared into the waggon.

It was growing lighter with each passing minute, and as soon as he dared Vespa guided the team out onto the road once more, followed by the incensed ostler who stood shaking his fist after them. For the next few hours they travelled through increasingly populated areas, skirting little towns and pictur-esque villages, halting occasionally at some secluded spot for a brief rest, and coming at length into a richly forested area, and then a succession of green gentle valleys.

They had not once been challenged nor had there been any sign of Monteil or soldiers, and Vespa was half asleep when Consuela asked, "Where are we going, Jack?"

She was sitting beside him. He looked at her blankly. It seemed a very foolish question. Where were they going? He replied, "I've no idea. Except . . ." he racked his brain ,"except that we're heading to the west. I hope."

"Yes, dear." She reached up and pushed the damp hair back

from his forehead. "But do you know where we are to meet the ship?"

Of course he didn't know where they were to meet the ship. He said severely, "You know we don't know. They know we don't know. *They* must find *us*, you see, but they can't sail on French soil." That didn't sound quite right, and he paused, frowning.

Somewhere, somebody shouted. Consuela slid to the side and looked back. "We are being followed! Oh, Jack, they're coming very fast!"

"Is it those blasted *cuirassiers* again?"

"No. I think it must be Monsieur Monteil!"

"Devil take him," moaned Vespa, whipping up the team. "Does he never give up?"

They raced at a thundering gallop along the road. The reins must be soaking wet because they were so heavy it was all Vespa could do to hold them up. Now, something was blinding him. Blinking, he realized it was sunlight. Pale winter sunlight on water. There was a beach—a long beautiful beach. The sand was white, and glittering.

Pierre screamed, "Look! Look! A great ship!"

Vespa muttered, "I see a sort of lagoon—are those all ships?"

Consuela looked at him worriedly. "They are islands, dear. The ship is far out and at least five miles to the south. It will never find us."

Peering from the small window behind the seat. Broderick called weakly, "Someone has! See there!"

"Soldiers!" cried Pierre. "And they're coming right for us, Captain Jack!"

Vespa was concentrating on trying to lift the whip. It was incredibly heavy and he was so very tired. He'd just close his eyes for a minute. . . . His head nodded and he jerked himself awake. This wouldn't do! He must keep on—he *must not* fail his General and his country. But why couldn't he hold onto the reins? What on earth . . . was the matter with him?

And then came another pair of hands; strong little hands that took the reins from his failing grasp, and a beloved voice that said, "Let me help, my love. Can you see the soldiers now?"

He shook his head hard. Yes, he could see them now. Coming from the south. Straight for them. At the gallop. A troop of—of what? The uniforms seemed to be red, but he couldn't distinguish the brass plate with the imperial N and the crown that would brand them Lancers. And now they were clad in dazzling white—like Carabiniers but minus the easily identifiable tall helmets. Why on earth had they changed their uniforms?

Consuela wailed, "Oh, my heavens!"

She was staring to the east. He turned his head slowly, and saw a coach and four and two outriders on dapple greys bearing down on them. Monteil! Pox on the wretch! But if that was Monteil, then who was behind? More *cuirassiers,* perhaps? At all events, he thought wearily, there was nowhere to turn now, but into the water. Could the cart-horses swim? That thought struck him as hilarious and he chuckled foolishly.

Consuela was pulling up the team.

He said feebly, "No, love. No—we mustn't give up yet."

Pierre shrieked, "Papa! Papa!"

Clinging to the side, Vespa managed to look back again. The coach and the escorting riders approaching from the north looked murderous. Small wonder, if it was de Coligny. And he had given the poor fellow his word of honour that in seeking Lord Kincraig he did nothing against France. Nothing against France . . . Except to provide Lord Wellington with part of the means to continue the war! His word of honour . . . "Oh, Gad!" he muttered.

"What did you say, my dear?" asked Consuela.

"Nothing that—makes sense. Pierre, get down, lad. Hurry to your father. And—God speed!"

The boy looked at him, suddenly tearful. To Vespa's astonishment, his hand was seized and kissed. Then Pierre was in the road and running back to the slowing coach of the chevalier.

The military troop was less than a mile to the south.

Monteil's carriage was bearing down from the east.

De Coligny was behind them.

'A touch ticklish,' thought Vespa.

Consuela had managed to whip up the team and they were charging straight towards the soldiers. Bless her brave heart. He tried, not successfully, to encourage her. Monteil's coach became a blur that seemed to swerve suddenly. Consuela was crying out. She needed him! He pulled himself together and took back the leathers and in a burst of strength, cracked the whip over the horses' heads. The waggon seemed to fly. Those

French troopers had best get out of the way, by God, for he was going right through their centre!

There was a lot of shouting and noise.

The troopers were scattering in all directions.

Consuela was screaming.

Lord Kincraig was cheering.

Someone howled, "He's done it!"

If he had done it, he could go to sleep.

Grateful, he sighed and his head sank onto Consuela's shoulder. He wondered vaguely if they had crossed into Spain.

It seemed to him that he heard shots.

The man who stood at the window was young, and a colonel. The window was round, and the floor was moving up and down. So this must be a ship. How he came to be aboard ship, and why he was in bed at what appeared to be late afternoon, Vespa could not imagine, but he had a vague sense of having made a horrible bumblebroth of something. After two attempts that were inaudible, he managed to ask, "Am I under arrest, sir?"

The man at the porthole turned and approached the bed.

"Oh," said Vespa. "It's you."

"It's me." Colonel the Honourable Hastings Adair sat on the end of the bunk, his handsome face grave. "How do you feel?"

"Puzzled. How long have I been here?"

"Two days. We had a rendezvous to keep before we turned for home."

Vespa knit his brows, trying to sort it all out.

The young colonel asked, "What's the last thing you remember before you dozed off?"

Dozed off . . . ? Was that what he'd done? Not during an action, surely? Lord! He said slowly, "I seem to recollect a road, and— Great heavens!" He started up and found it such an effort that he lay back again, panting. "My father! Broderick and Manderville! And—Consuela! What—what . . . ?"

Adair sighed. "I was afraid you'd remember Consuela."

"Hasty, you villain! You're teasing the poor fellow!" Broderick came in, clean and shaved and with a neat bandage around his head.

"I'll point out," said Adair, "that I am a colonel, and despite that romantical bandage, you, Broderick, are a lowly lieutenant!"

"An alive lieutenant!" exclaimed Vespa, greatly relieved as Broderick came to grip his hand. "Toby, is my father—"

"He's not quite as alive as this impertinent cloth-head," said Adair. "But he's going on very well and should be up and about within a week, so the ship's apothecary tells us."

Broderick said mournfully, "Poor old Manderville is in a bad way."

"Oh, blast the luck! It was the pneumonia, then?"

"Yes. He's through the worst of it, apparently. But"— Broderick winked—"poor sailor, you know."

Vespa grinned, then said apprehensively, "Does Wellington know what happened?"

"He does." Adair said with a sober look. "He's going to demand an explanation, Captain, of why you disobeyed orders, and—"

"What orders? I never received any orders!"

"—and why you blithely gave away one hundred *louis!*"

"That ain't fair," exclaimed Broderick. "Against all odds he got the rest of the loot through!"

"I—did?" said Vespa hopefully. "But—how on earth—"

Someone was knocking at the door. Adair sprang up and opened it, then bowed, and Consuela hurried in.

"Oh!" she cried in delight. "He's awake! And you didn't call me!"

Broderick pulled a chair beside the bunk and she flashed him a smile as she ran to occupy it and take the hand that Vespa tried, and failed, to reach out. Nursing it to her cheek, she asked, "How are you today, dearest Captain Jack?"

"I feel very well," he answered, smiling at her adoringly. "Except—I cannot understand why I am still so pulled."

"You great clunch," said Broderick. "You drove all night without tightening the bandage around that cut on your arm. It's a wonder you ain't bled white!" He settled onto the side of the bunk and went on: "There are some very interesting studies being undertaken on blood. For instance, did you know that the body of the average male contains about five litres of the stuff? And that although a fellow can lose a considerable amount without turning up his toes, at a certain point he will go into shock—which is likely what happened to you only you were too dense to—"

"Go away," murmured Vespa not taking his eyes from Consuela's radiant face.

"Well, of all the—"

Adair took Broderick by the collar. "This way, Lieutenant," he said firmly, propelling him to the door.

"If that ain't the outside of—"

"The outside of Captain Vespa's cabin," said Adair, and closed the door behind them.

"Alone at last," sighed Vespa. "Now, if I only had the strength . . ."

Consuela pointed out, "I am very strong."

"And I swore an oath not to try and fix my interest—"

"Whereas," she murmured, leaning closer, "I am very interested, and I have sworn no oaths. . . ."

After a delightful interlude he asked dreamily, "Did we really get the gold through?"

"No. *You* got it through, dearest!"

"Never! Paige and Toby helped, my father was superb and you—you were a real heroine, my signorina! How you hung onto the reins with those precious little hands while I was totally useless—"

"How you kept going for as long as you did was a miracle, my poor darling. And when you broke the ranks of that troop . . ." She chuckled. "There was no stopping the team. What an uproar!"

"I can guess. And if I know Frenchmen—"

"They weren't French, Jack."

He stared at her, bewildered.

Tidying her hair, Consuela said, "They were British dragoons."

"British?" he gasped. "A troop—of *our* dragoons—in *Brittany?* You're roasting me!"

"No such thing. The captain of the warship had been told to rendezvous with us between Lorient and Quiberon and that we would signal by lantern—which we did not know, of course. He tacked about offshore, waiting, then sent an intelligence agent in to try and trace us."

"The poor fellow we found killed at that abandoned farm?"

"No. But the intelligence officer had met that gentleman and told him where we could meet the ship. You'll recall that he had managed to draw an arrow in the dirt, pointing to the southwest. When we didn't keep the rendezvous, Hasty Adair, who was aboard the warship, demanded that a troop be landed."

"Good Lord! They'd come to help and I charged—"

"Right through them, dearest."

He groaned. "When am I to be shot? Were any of the poor fellows hurt?"

"Only their pride. But they've forgiven you. In fact, they seem quite proud of their encounter with the Flying Captain!"

He looked at her amused face uneasily. "What a thing to do—after they'd taken such a chance for our sake. I wonder they didn't have to fight every inch of the way!"

"Yes. It was a desperate venture, but Lord Wellington had said nothing was to be left undone that might get the waggon through. I suppose nobody expected a troop of British dragoons to be there. Luckily, we met up with them fairly soon, and the warship changed course and sailed back to us."

"But—I distinctly recall seeing a great lagoon—with ships that you said were islands."

"So they are." She stroked his cheek gently. "And you are talking too much and must rest now. Is your arm very painful?"

"A little stiff merely, I thank you. But how could a warship put into a lagoon?"

"It didn't, my love. The water was shallow when the tide went out. We drove across to one of the islands and two longboats came with a landing party, and all the gold was loaded, and rowed out to the ship. We left the poor waggon and the carthorses behind."

"The French did nothing while all this was going on?"

"Hasty thought that at first they were taken by surprise. Then there seems to have been a panic—the local people thought Wellington had broken through Marshal Soult's lines and was invading."

Vespa laughed. "What—with one troop? But I was sure I heard shots."

"You did. The chevalier restored order and rallied the people, then led an attack on our little island. He really was magnificent, Jack, and I'm very sure he will be given a medal or some sort of honour."

"Still, he didn't prevail."

"No, thank the Lord. And we were safely away before those fierce *cuirassiers* came charging to help him. Now, go to sleep."

He yawned drowsily. "Then Wellington will have his funds.

And my father is a fine brave gentleman . . . Consuela—my beloved one—your Grandmama won't deny me now . . . do you think?"

But before she could answer, he was contentedly asleep.

It had been snowing all day. The village of Gallery-on-Tang looked like an artist's depiction of Christmastime, with smoke curling from the chimneys, thatched roofs buried under a white mantle and people bustling about the slippery street, bundled in their winter cloaks and scarves, exchanging cheery greetings.

Some two miles east of the village the ancient manor house at Alabaster Royal also wore winter white, and lights from many windows painted amber glows on the snowy lawns. The steward, Hezekiah Strickley, and Harper, the groom, were busily at work in the stables; rotund Chef Henri sang uproariously in his kitchen; Mr. Thornhill, the statuesque butler, issued a constant stream of orders; Peg, the stout head housemaid, trotted about happily, picking up the various items she dropped along the way, and encouraging her rather ill-assorted retinue of assistants to make haste because "all the rest of 'em is coming today!"

In the great drawing room Captain John Wansdyke Vespa paced restlessly, glancing often to the front windows, and running a nervous finger around the neckcloth that Thornhill had adjusted with, it would seem, an eye to strangling him. At his heels Corporal trotted patiently, and Manderville, strolling in from the stairs, observed that the little dog must have walked miles this last hour. "By George, but you look impressive, Jack. Regimentals, eh? Jolly good touch."

Vespa turned to face him. "I'd hoped they might help my cause a little. The ladies love a uniform, you know. Is my father coming down?"

"Said he'd be at your side in time to welcome— But I think he won't. Someone's arrived."

"Oh, Lord!" moaned Vespa, paling. "Paige, do you think the duchess still will have none of me?"

Manderville pursed his lips. "Hmm. Well, she might very well, of course." And thinking that the old lady would be short of a sheet to even consider rejecting his gallant friend, he thought also of the scandal that seemed to grow more lurid every day and had so tarnished the name of Vespa. Stifling a sigh, he added: "Best to be prepared, dear boy."

The doors were thrown open. Thornhill announced in his great dramatic voice, "The Duchess of Ottavio. Miss Consuela Jones."

Vespa's eyes flashed to his beloved. She wore a gown of white velvet trimmed with pink embroidered flowers, and a silver fillet was threaded through her dusky curls. He thought she looked virginal and adorable, but there was worry in her blue eyes and his heart sank as he bowed before her grandmother.

The diminutive Lady Francesca, regal in dark red brocade with gold piping around the high-standing collar and down the front openings, and an undergown of gold silk, allowed him her hand to kiss. "It is taking the unfair advantage to wear that uniform munificent," she said, tapping him on the wrist with her fan, and passing on to Manderville. "I see by your so impudent grin that I have said something not right, Lieutenant Paige. But I will forgive you because it is agreeable that you will not die, after all."

Under cover of Manderville's laugh, Vespa whispered, "Has she made up her mind?"

Consuela murmured, "Have you seen the newspapers?"

It was no more than he had expected, but his hopes plummetted. London had been seething with rumour this past week. The Society columns had named no names, but even the most naive of their readers must guess who was the 'late lamented diplomatist' they pilloried.

". . . It has been learned that this once greatly admired gentleman had intended to abandon his wife . . ."

". . . the inamorata who was young enough to be (and almost had become!) his daughter . . ."

". . . the sudden and violent demise of a famous and hitherto much respected gentleman of diplomacy . . ."

". . . One can scarce wonder that the late Sir K—— V——'s faithful wife fled the country, or that his son, Captain J—— V——, a popular young officer of impeccable reputation, has not yet gone into mourning. . . ."

And all this when they knew only a few of the true facts. If the whole should ever be revealed . . . ! Vespa pushed that fearsome prospect away and ushered the duchess to the most com-

fortable fireside chair while Manderville drew up another for
Consuela.

Stroking Corporal, Lady Francesca said, "Thank you for your
welcome, small dog. Although you are not the one I expected
would be here to receive me."

"Lord Kincraig is a little delayed." Vespa darted a pleading
glance at his friend, and Manderville drifted from the room.
"My apologies," Vespa went on, "but he will be here directly.
Had you a—er, very cold ride, ma'am?"

"We will dispense with a discussion of the weather, if you
please."

He bowed and stood before her silently, as if in tribunal.

At her most formidable, the duchess said, "I hope I need
not tell you, Captain Jack, that I have much admire you. It
would have been exceeding easy on this latest escapade of my
naughty granddaughter for you to force my hand. This, you
have not doing, which is the reason I am here today. You
brought her home safe, and nobody is knowing she is running
about Brittany with you, so her reputation is still contact!"

Consuela said, "Yes, but—"

The duchess quelled her with a glance. "Even so," she resumed, "the gossip mongers they gabble and twitter all over
London Town about Sir Kendrick's wickednesses. I know, I
know," she said cutting off his attempt to speak. "For this
you are not to be blamed, and you are not his son. But London *thinks* you are. Your name, every day it drags lower in
the dust, Captain Jack, and my little meadowlark is of a proud
and, er—" She paused, and murmured to Consuela, "*Senza
macchia?*"

"Unblemished," supplied Consuela, looking mutinous.

"*Si.* An unhenriched royal house. It is with real regret, my
dear Jack, that—"

"My deepest apologies for being tardy." Lord Blair Kincraig
came briskly into the room, and paused on the threshold.

It was an entry Thornhill could not have bettered for dramatic effect, and there was a momentary hush.

His lordship was a vision of the sort of sartorial splendour
that might be attempted when attending a great function at
Carlton House, or some other London palace, but was seldom
seen in the country. In formal evening dress, his black coat
hugged his shoulders to perfection; his waistcoat was faultless;
peerlessly tied, his neckcloth gleamed no less brightly than the

snow on the lawns; and knee breeches and silk stockings displayed his shapely legs to advantage. Jewelled Orders flashed on his breast, and a great emerald glowed on one hand.

Awed, Vespa performed the introductions.

Kincraig bowed over the bony little claw the duchess extended, and with exquisite grace occupied the chair nearest her. "I must tell you, ma'am," he said, smiling into her cold eyes, "that I am a great admirer of your granddaughter."

"Under the circumstances which were then, I find that remarkable," she said tartly.

"But—no. She is a very brave girl. Were it not for her, we none of us would be sitting here today."

"I could wish, sir," said the duchess, leaning forward, "that we were not!"

Thornhill relieved this awkward moment by leading a small procession into the room. Two housemaids, one struggling with a uniform that was at least two sizes too large, and the other wearing an eye patch, carried laden trays. Tea was poured and passed around, and little cakes and pastries were offered.

When the servants left, Vespa tried again. "My lady, I may have small cause for pride in the man I believed to be my father. Lord Kincraig, however, is willing to acknowledge me."

"Say 'proud' to acknowledge you, rather," said his lordship warmly. "Forgive if I become vulgar, but I am a rich man, Lady Francesca. I will be happy to have my man of affairs lay my son's expectations before you and discuss the matter of a dowry, if you give your sanction to the match."

"Easy said! But under what name would my granddaughter leave the altar? London is fairly rocked by the scandal Kendrick Vespa has left behind."

"It is my wish and my intention to adopt Jack. Legally. He can be wed under the name John Wansdyke Keith."

"*San Pietro* aid me!" The old lady gave a crow of mirthless laughter. "A fine mare's nest that would stirring up!"

Vespa put in quietly, "No, sir. I thank you, but I cannot change my name without shaming my mother, and that I will never do."

"My dear boy," said his lordship. "People will only have to see us side by side and our tale will be told."

"Just so," agreed Lady Francesca. "And there will be more

of the horrid scandals! No! I will not have my granddaughter tainted by murders and treasonings!"

Consuela looked frightened, and said in desperation, "*Nonna*—I love him! I owe him my life! Have you no gratitude for—"

"Child, child," said the duchess, distressed. "I know what I am owing to our fine Captain Jack. But can you not see that I must be guided by what your sainted mama would wish? Would your fine English father be proud if I permit that you carry the name of a murdering philanderer, who—"

Corporal was barking, voices were in the hall and, belatedly, Vespa realized that Manderville stood in the doorway beckoning him frenziedly. He sprang to his feet, then stood gazing in astonishment at the latest arrival.

Clad in a magnificent robe of black satin with an overskirt of black lace, a black lace cap on her luxuriant light brown hair and stark horror in her big blue eyes, Faith, Lady Vespa, tripped into the room.

"Jack! What on earth—? How can you be *entertaining* at such a time? And—*heavens!*—why are you not in mourning?"

Recovering his wits, Vespa hurried to take her hand and drop a kiss on her cheek. "Mama! How glad I am to see you! When did you come home? Had I known you were on the way— Oh, Gad! Forgive me! I must present you! The Duchess of Ottavio, Miss Consuela Jones and Lord . . . Blair . . ." His words trailed off.

Lady Faith had bobbed a curtsey to the duchess and nodded in obvious perplexity at Consuela, but it was clear that the final introduction was not required. As if mesmerized, she stared at Lord Kincraig, and he, equally affected, gazed at her.

She whispered disbelievingly, "Blair . . . ? Oh, Blair, is it *really* you?"

In a voice ineffably tender, his lordship said, "Yes. It's me, my dear."

A soft blush crept into her pale cheeks. Watching her, Vespa thought that never in his life had he seen her look so radiant.

The Duchess of Ottavio regarded the little tableau thoughtfully. "Bless you, my dear *San Pietro,*" she said with a sudden beaming grin, "I do believe you have sent us the answer!"

Epilogue

The February morning was very bright but bitterly cold, giving Vespa the excuse to keep his lady's hand tucked very tightly in his arm as they walked across the frosty meadow together, a small and happy dog frolicking along more or less with them. When they came to a spreading old oak tree, Vespa pulled Consuela even closer.

"Jack Vespa!" she said primly, when she could say anything at all. "That was naughty, beside which it is the third time you've kissed me this morning!"

"I have to make up for lost time, you see."

"And *outside!* In full view of—of . . ." She glanced around the deserted meadow.

"Of Corporal? He likes it when I kiss my future wife. Sweetheart, you didn't answer me. Shall you mind living down here at Alabaster after we're married?"

"Oh, no. I love the old place. But—I must confess, your house on the river is very beautiful."

His face became closed. "My mother's house."

"Yes, but your mama will be Lady Kincraig next year, and living up at Lambent Grove or in Scotland much of the time. She won't need the Richmond house."

"Then I'll close it."

"And what about that very nice butler who tried so hard to help you when you were searching for clues to your real papa? I suppose he will be cast carelessly into the street to starve?"

He chuckled. "You mean Rennett. I suspect many gentlemen would try to lure him into much more exalted houses than Richmond if he chose to leave me. But, d'you know I think I'll see if he wants to come down here. Thorny really prefers to valet, and I don't think he'll object if Rennett takes over the tasks of butler. There, does that satisfy you, future Mrs. John—" He hesitated.

"Mrs. John Wansdyke Keith," she finished merrily. "Oh, Jack, I do like that name. And I love your kind papa! Only . . . it would be nice if we could spend a *little* time in Town each year. During the Season, you know."

He tilted up her chin and kissed her again, then with his lips brushing hers, murmured, "You would hate the Season."

"But *Nonna* would love it. And she has been so good, Jack, keeping in the country with me all these years. And I *would* like to shop—and shop—and shop! I never have *really* visited all the Town bazaars and warehouses."

"Heaven help me! I'll be ruined!"

"Within a week," she agreed. "Oh, look, here comes Paige, and riding his precious Trouble at the gallop."

Vespa sighed. "Now what?"

"I bring news," called Manderville, flourishing a letter. "The great man has sent you a communiqué!"

"Wellington?" Vespa took the letter and broke the seal apprehensively.

"Likely means to have you shot on a charge of donating one hundred *louis* to the enemy," said Manderville, but also looking concerned. "Jove! Have you read it already?"

Vespa said with a grin, "It's not lengthy," and showed the letter to Consuela.

She laughed and handed it up to Manderville, who read aloud, " 'Well done!' Is that all? I suppose it constitutes rare eloquence, coming from old Nosey!"

Feeling as if he'd been given a medal, Vespa said, "The allied army is advancing again. He must be in high fettle. I wonder he could spare the time even for so short a note."

"He finds time if he is really moved." Manderville said, "Speaking of moving—you've received a gift, old lad. Best come up to the house and see."

Always excited by a present, Consuela exclaimed, "Oh, how lovely! Hurry, Jack!"

"Who sent it?" asked Vespa. "Do you know?"

Manderville said airily, "Oh, yes," and with a grin sent Trouble cantering back to the Manor.

He was outside the barn, and taunted them for being such

a pair of slowtops when they walked up the drive. "Stay there! I'll bring out your gift. It's from poor old de Coligny."

Startled, Vespa exclaimed, "Stay back, my love! It's likely a mine!"

Manderville laughed and, returning, said, "I rather doubt that."

Vespa stared. A soft muzzle pushed against his ear and an affectionate whicker sounded. He reached up to caress the firm neck. "Bruine!" he said, deeply touched. "Oh, how very good of him! Is there a letter—or a message?"

"A message, only. A rascally fellow brought the mare up from Willy Leggett's *Saucy Maid*. He was to tell you that Gaston de Coligny is grateful because you took such good care of his son. And that when the war is over he will come and knock you down!"

Vespa laughed. "Nor would I blame him, poor fellow!"

He patted the mare and told her she was a very welcome enemy agent.

Then, holding his lady's hand tightly, he walked up the steps and into the great house that was his birthright, and that they would share through all the shining years to come.

More Zebra Regency Romances

Celebrate Romance With Two of Today's Hottest Authors

Meagan McKinney

__In the Dark	$6.99US/$8.99CAN	0-8217-6341-5
__The Fortune Hunter	$6.50US/$8.00CAN	0-8217-6037-8
__Gentle from the Night	$5.99US/$7.50CAN	0-8217-5803-9
__A Man to Slay Dragons	$5.99US/$6.99CAN	0-8217-5345-2
__My Wicked Enchantress	$5.99US/$7.50CAN	0-8217-5661-3
__No Choice But Surrender	$5.99US/$7.50CAN	0-8217-5859-4

Meryl Sawyer

__Thunder Island	$6.99US/$8.99CAN	0-8217-6378-4
__Half Moon Bay	$6.50US/$8.00CAN	0-8217-6144-7
__The Hideaway	$5.99US/$7.50CAN	0-8217-5780-6
__Tempting Fate	$6.50US/$8.00CAN	0-8217-5858-6
__Unforgettable	$6.50US/$8.00CAN	0-8217-5564-1

Call toll free **1-888-345-BOOK** to order by phone, use this coupon to order by mail, or order online at **www.kensingtonbooks.com**.

Name _____

Address _____

City _____ State _____ Zip _____

Please send me the books I have checked above.

I am enclosing	$_____
Plus postage and handling*	$_____
Sales tax (in New York and Tennessee only)	$_____
Total amount enclosed	$_____

*Add $2.50 for the first book and $.50 for each additional book.

Send check or money order (no cash or CODs) to:

Kensington Publishing Corp., Dept. C.O., 850 Third Avenue, New York, NY 10022

Prices and numbers subject to change without notice.

All orders subject to availability.

Visit our website at **www.kensingtonbooks.com**.